Praise for *Argonaut*

"*Analog* editor Stanley Schmidt's first book in sixteen years is good solid SF."

—SFRevu.com

"Alien invasion stories are old hat in SF, but sometimes a writer comes along and gives it a new twist. Schmidt's story is one of those . . . [and] you're unlikely to anticipate Schmidt's plot."

—*Science Fiction Chronicle*

"*Analog* editor Schmidt takes to heart Peter Graham's adage that the Golden Age of SF is twelve, in the best possible way, in his instructive tale of first contact. . . .The novel's straightforward expository style recalls classic-era SF. . . . Schmidt may teach his readers a didactic lesson, but it's one well worth learning."

—*Publishers Weekly*

"Schmidt, an experienced editor, knows good SF, and he can write it . . . In a surprisingly enlightened dénouement that acknowledges immaturity and human and alien reactions to difference, both parties learn something from first contact."

—*Booklist*

"I enjoyed it. It's a good traditional story of alien discovery, with imaginative twists and a thoughtful ending. The depiction of alien technology with a biological flavor is well done."

—Joan Slonczewski

"Schmidt has cooked up the oddest alien invasion yet."

—Michael Flynn

BOOKS BY STANLEY SCHMIDT

NONFICTION
Aliens and Alien Societies:
A Writer's Guide to Creating Extraterrestrial Life-Forms

*Which Way to the Future**

FICTION
The Sins of the Fathers
Newton and the Quasi-Apple
Lifeboat Earth
Tweedlioop
*Argonaut**

*Currently available from Tor Books

Argonaut

STANLEY SCHMIDT

A Tom Doherty Associates Book **TOR**® New York

This is a work of fiction. All the characters and events portrayed in this novel are either fictitious or are used fictitiously.

ARGONAUT

Book design by Jane Adele Regina

Edited by David G. Hartwell

A Tor Book
Published by Tom Doherty Associates, LLC
175 Fifth Avenue
New York, NY 10010

www.tor.com

Tor® is a registered trademark of Tom Doherty Associates, LLC.

Library of Congress Cataloging-in-Publication Data

Schmidt, Stanley.
    Argonaut / Stanley Schmidt.
        p. cm.
    "A Tom Doherty Associates book."
    ISBN 0-312-87726-9 (hc)
    ISBN 0-312-87727-7 (pbk)
        1. Human-alien encounters—Fiction. 2. Cognition disorders—Fiction
3. Entomologists—Fiction. 4. Insects—Fiction. I. Title.

    PS3569.C5158 A89 2002
    813'.54—dc21   2001059657

First Edition: July 2002
First Trade Paperback Edition: August 2003

Printed in the United States of America

0 9 8 7 6 5 4 3 2 1

To Jerry and Kathy Oltion,

great friends always
and critics when I needed them

Acknowledgments

I would like to express special gratitude to several people who made important contributions to this book, including Jerry and Kathy Oltion for valuable suggestions and advice on an embryonic form of it; Eleanor Wood, my agent; David G. Hartwell and Moshe Feder, my editors; H. G. Stratmann, Janet Asimov, and Joyce Schmidt for information on medicine and medical technology; and to Joyce (my wife) for a whole lot of other things, too.

Author's Note

This is a work of fiction. All characters and events portrayed in this book are fictional, and any resemblance to real people or incidents is purely coincidental. This applies also to institutions. Even where a present-day place or organization exists with a name similar or identical to one in the story, by the time the story takes place, staffing and policies will be entirely different. Nothing portrayed in the story should be construed as reflecting in any way on contemporary persons or actions.

Argonaut

 **It began with** a bug in a garden. Most folks wouldn't even have noticed, but to Lester Ordway it was quite obvious that it didn't belong—and in that fact he saw a challenge. A modest challenge, or so it seemed at the time, but one that a part of him had been wishing for for a very long time.

The bug caught his eye as he strolled through the garden in late afternoon sunlight, increasingly alone as the Memorial Day crowds began to thin out. Up to then things had been comfortingly familiar: the richly textured green lawn stretching off to the historic yellow clapboard house, late tulips and daffodils glowing as if each blossom contained a tiny electric light, their scent filling the air, the soothing buzz of honeybees and the occasional bumblebee flitting from flower to flower, plying their trade. Except for the visitors' often garish garb and their sheer numbers, it almost recaptured the tranquillity of days before people forgot what Memorial Day was, before Boscobel became a lonely island in a sea of "development."

But then there was this thing that was *not* a honeybee or bumblebee, and flew about in a way not quite like theirs. Lester's first thought was that it was a hummingbird; but when he locked onto it enough to follow it for a while, he soon decided it was too small. There was only one kind of hummingbird in the Hudson Valley, and Lester knew very well what it looked like.

A hawk moth or sphinx moth? It wasn't hard to watch; it moved very fast, in short, straight lines, then stopped and hovered for a while—yet it seldom actually landed on a flower.

Frowning, he scrutinized it, comparing it with the mental images he'd been accumulating over the many decades since boyhood. None of them quite matched, not even closely enough to convince him he had the right family.

Greg and Jill Saunders had mentioned seeing some insects they didn't recognize recently. Might this be one of them?

It didn't take Lester long to decide it was nothing he had ever seen before—and therein lay the exciting possibility that he latched onto and held. Ever since he was a boy, chasing butterflies and garter snakes through summer fields, he'd dreamed of discovering a new species. He didn't care what it was a new species *of,* and the idea of having it named after him was purely secondary. The kick would have been the simple fact of finding something no human had found before him.

He'd always assumed that actually doing that would have required going a long way down a path he hadn't taken—until now. Now, suddenly and incredibly, in a public garden less than two hours north of New York City, on a bluff overlooking the Hudson River, the possibility seemed within his grasp.

Provided, of course, he could get the *thing* in his grasp. He hesitated a little over that. An unknown insect might have a nasty sting. He would have preferred to catch it with a net or a jar or a coffee can.

But none of those things was at hand, and the bug was. Bare hands it would have to be, and he'd just have to take his chances.

Long-conditioned habits kept him motionless as he pondered his strategy. He was quite sure, when he thought about it later, that he hadn't moved a muscle up to that point. At some point he became aware of the odd sensation that the bug was studying him as intently as he was studying it, glowering at him from a foot in front of his face. It hovered on wings blurred to virtual invisibility, whining ominously, its jewel-like eyes burning deep into his own.

But it came as a total shock when, *before* he started his grab, the bug shot toward him with a startling crescendo of its wings, landing right between his eyes.

His time sense must have already slowed down by then. He felt tiny, prickly-tickly feet on the bridge of his nose, a sharp little sensation, and then a tremendous explosion of *Pain*.

Physical pain was the least of it. In retrospect, that probably didn't really amount to much. What hurt beyond all imagining was the sudden upwelling of *everything* from the depths of his mind. In a flash, he felt the wildest extremes of heat and cold, agony and ecstasy, buoyancy and oppression. In such rapid succession that it felt as if it were all happening at once, he was back in those sunlit boyhood fields and in dreary classrooms and drafting at a CAD screen in the nineties, plagued by fears of the Gulf War turning into another Vietnam. In less than a breath he met and married Marella and they had Sylvia and he worried about what kind of world she would have to grow up in, and she rekindled his *joie de vivre* on long walks in the country and then he watched them both die and felt the agony all over again. In microseconds he relived the long, arid years after that, and the time when he briefly hoped Claire would bring the good parts back, and the disappointment of realizing she couldn't, and . . .

And ever so much more. What he experienced in that instant was his *life,* squeezed into so little time that its intensity was unbearable. It left too little mind to control his body and he was dimly aware of himself collapsing—though one small sliver of his fast-dimming consciousness noted curiously that folklore claimed this sort of thing happened to people who were dying.

I'm not ready to die! he objected, but it made no difference. The ground kept rising and the mystery bug was still on his forehead, stinging—or whatever it was doing.

And that cool little part of Lester's mind changed its tack. It couldn't stop him from falling and it couldn't stop the pain and the memories, but it became more determined than ever to know what this thing was. Through all the agony of spilled and roiledup sensation and emotion, it set itself one goal and locked onto it like a pit bull. *Get that thing off, but don't let it get away!*

Far away, through a thickening blackness and a shriek of agony, he watched his own hand rise to his forehead, watched his fingers curl around the bug, felt it pull away from his head, squirming against his confining fingers. . . .

And from an even greater distance, he saw a young couple, dressed more for the beach than for this day or place, loping toward him with great slow strides. "What's wrong?" asked one of them (he couldn't tell which), while the other mouthed, "Can we help?"

He thought he saw them reaching out to catch him, stop his fall. But the last thing he actually remembered before blackness took over was the mental image of turning the key on a great lock that held his fingers around the bug, and hurling the key into the darkness.

Chapter 1

The whole hospital's a madhouse, Pilar Ramirez fumed as she hurried through the corridors to the ER, her half-unbuttoned lab coat flapping and swishing about her like ruffled wings. Dodging pedestrians and gurneys, she thought, *I shouldn't even have to come down here. As if I didn't have enough to do back in the lab!*

A whole raft of alcohol and drug tests, for instance, and the antibody work-up on that old lady on the third floor who was having problems after her transfusion. To say nothing of that baby Pilar was probably going to have to draw herself, with all the extra work and aggravation that entailed, since there was only one phlebotomist on duty and half the time she couldn't even find him. She wasn't sure he was good enough to handle a baby yet, anyway.

They didn't tell you about holidays and midnight shifts in classes and internships. Those you found out about too late, when you were past all that and on the job. Her Aunt Juanita said it was worse in the old days, when everything had to be done in the hospital instead of via the telemetry most regular patients now used. But somebody still always had to be here for the walk-ins and carry-ins, especially on these odd shifts. And they were always like this: too many patients, because too many people had time to go out and get themselves in trouble; and too few staff, because nobody wanted to work those shifts so the bosses put on only as many as they absolutely had to.

Which, typically, meant too few to do it right. Everybody

17

working a holiday grumbled about having too few hands on deck; but whenever they tried to put on more, everybody grumbled about that, too. Pilar used to think it was just Hudson Hospital, but she'd been to meetings and it seemed to be that way everywhere.

So here she was: up to her elbows in jobs that just had to be done right now, and nobody doing them because Pilar was hurrying down to the emergency room to draw blood *stat* because she couldn't find Link. And it was *supposed* to be almost the end of her shift, and she hadn't seen her relief yet, either.

She waded through the check-in area, past moaning and bleeding patients wanting to know when a doctor would see them and why they took somebody first who came in later, and relatives pacing and threatening to sue if they didn't get some action soon. With some relief she hustled through the door past the receptionist into the relative sanity of the treatment room.

Even that was pretty frantic this evening. There were two doctors on duty, the very young Thomson and the very old Schneider, and it was fairly obvious which one wanted her *stat*. The young woman on the left table, in front of Thomson, was clearly an accident victim. She'd obviously lost so much blood, and was still losing more, that she'd be needing a transfusion Real Soon Now. That fit the work order Pilar had ripped off the printer in the lab two minutes earlier: four tubes, CBC, biochem panel, coag, drugs and alcohol, type and screen, crossmatch four units.

Less than three years out of her internship, Pilar had already done it all so often she could do it with part of her mind on autopilot while the rest just as automatically observed what was going on around her. As she pulled on gloves, checked name and ID number, applied a tourniquet (at least they'd already cleaned up one arm fairly well), and whisked out an alcohol prep for Dr. Thomson's patient, she half-listened to the incoherent babbling coming from Dr. Schneider's table.

Schneider's patient was a man, maybe in his mid-sixties but

with a wiry build and hair gone almost white, just starting to grope his way up from unconsciousness. Dressed in the one-piece gray pinstripes fashionable a few years ago, he looked about as distinguished as a guy could be expected to in his situation.

Pilar couldn't see his wrist tag or make much out of what he was saying, though an occasional word suggested it was English. A young couple in skimpy summersuits stood next to him, twentyish, college students maybe, the guy with green-flecked black curls and glasses, the woman's hair in peppermint waves, watching anxiously as the doctor checked vitals.

"You think it's an allergic reaction to the bug bite?" the girl asked as Pilar stuck her patient (*Got her on the first try!* she grinned inwardly). "Or sting, or whatever it is?"

"Too early to say," Schneider said with a frown. Pilar could see him thinking, *I wish this guy'd start making sense on his own so I can send these two back out where they belong.* "That's certainly one of the first things to check for. But anaphylactic shock would be my first concern there, and this doesn't look . . . right." His frown deepened, and Pilar realized with surprise that he looked puzzled. Even as she filled her first tube and switched to a second, she found herself listening more attentively to Schneider.

"Classic symptoms are itching, spasms, swelling, breathing difficulty, and a drastic drop in blood pressure." Still frowning, he watched the puzzlingly normal and unwavering readings on the digital BP monitor. "Usually all that's so obvious I'd give the poor guy an antihistamine and epinephrine before he hit the table. But I don't see any of it. Hell, I don't even see the usual swelling and pinkness a nonallergic person would get from a mosquito or a bee."

Pilar switched to her third tube. Schneider put down his rubber bulb and leaned back, looking at the young couple who had apparently brought the man in. "You're sure it was a bug bite or sting? And he collapsed suddenly?"

"Very," said the woman. "It stung him right between the eyes—though I'll admit I don't see anything there now. But I sure saw him trying to pull it off. The poor guy was obviously in agony." She looked at his right hand, clenched in a fist. "This sounds weird, but I think he's still holding the bug."

"Really? Let's see what it is." As Pilar switched to her last tube, Schneider gently tried to pry the guy's fist open. He seemed to be meeting quite a bit of resistance—not just stiffness, but as if the man were actively fighting the effort to uncurl his fingers. His gibberings became more animated, with more and more recognizable words among them. But he wasn't quite strong enough to keep Schneider from opening his hand.

The doctor stared at the thing in his patient's palm, frowning his deepest frown yet. "Ugly thing," he said, wrinkling his nose. "Either of you recognize it?"

The two shook their heads. Hurrying to finish up—last tube labelled and placed neatly on the tray, needle out, clean gauze and bandage on her patient's arm, blood bank ID on the wrist—Pilar strained to see what all the fuss was about.

She didn't recognize it, either. Admittedly she hadn't lived in this area, or even on the mainland, long enough to recognize everything that might be found here; but this thing looked *wrong*. It was dead and mangled, of course, the main body crushed and tiny pieces of it sprinkled like pepper and oregano over the white-haired gent's palm. But she could tell it was bigger than any bug and smaller than any bird she knew around here. It was much more buglike than birdlike, but even so it jarred at first sight and grew stranger with every detail she noticed: the eyes that were too angular, with too few facets; the prevalence of metallic colors on the body, rather like a greenbottle fly but more varied. . . .

Picking up her tray, she routed herself past that table, trying to get a better look without being too obvious about it. It didn't work. Schneider looked up, right at her, and said, "Pilar, you ever see one of these before?" He picked up the main remnant with his gloved hand and held it out to her.

She stopped and looked, trying to anticipate his next question and also itching to know the answer. "No," she said, "and we don't do bugs here. But I'm on my way back to the lab now. If you'd like me to take it along, we could send it out—"

Suddenly Schneider's patient sat up, looking wildly around. "Where am I?" he demanded clearly. "This looks like a hospital. What am I doing here?"

Schneider blinked, patting the man's hand soothingly. "Easy, there. You're in Hudson Hospital, in Peekskill, and you're doing just fine. You collapsed and these folks here brought you in. Seems to have been something of a false alarm, though I'm a little afraid to dismiss it too casually . . ." He paused, looking his newly alert patient up and down. "I can't find anything wrong, at the moment. Yet you *did* collapse. . . . Why don't we keep you here for observation for a while, just to make sure?"

"I don't *want* to stay for observation," the man stated emphatically. "I just want to get out of here. I was in the middle of something—"

"Excuse me," Pilar interrupted, as politely as possible, "but I've got a terrific backlog in the lab. Do you want me to take it back and send it out?"

Schneider hesitated, deliberating. As he did so, an uncharacteristically frantic voice came from his pager. "Dr. Schneider, how's it coming in there? We just got three burn cases you'll want to see as soon as possible—"

And, simultaneously, dozens of the specks of debris that had remained in his patient's hand suddenly took wing, exploding out in a multitude of directions with a chorus of mosquitolike whines. All at once everybody in the room was slapping at them.

Pilar swatted one on her forehead. A couple of people screamed; at first Pilar didn't understand why, but an instant later she felt an explosion of sensations and images from some point in the middle of her head and she screamed, too. The overload was like a crowd shrieking at the tops of their lungs in a boiler factory, but somewhere in the midst of it she could barely detect, like a child trying to be heard over all that, a small part of her mind telling her she ought to trap the bug that was still on her forehead.

But when she reached up, it was gone—and the dizzying sense of overload, that ultracentrifuge of a kaleidoscope in her head, was fading away. What seemed like an hour, but the clock said was less than a minute after it started, it was already beginning to feel like a bad dream. She still felt dizzy, but not too dazed to remember where she was.

Or to notice that the bug patient was sitting up and looking around, vaguely puzzled but otherwise calm. Apparently he was the only one in the room who had *not* been hit by one of the buglets. Everyone else, including Dr. Schneider, showed some combination of dizziness, disorientation, and anger. Patients were muttering things like, "What happened?" "What kind of place is this?" "Don't they ever get an exterminator in here?"

And a variety of dark imprecations including the words "lawyer" and "sue."

Over it all, Schneider's pager spoke urgently again. "Dr. Schneider, are you ready for these burn patients?"

That seemed to snap him back to reality. Time is everything in treating burns, and it would do neither the patients nor Schneider's reputation any good to delay them any longer. "OK," he snapped loudly. "Sorry about that little incident, but it's over now and everybody seems to be all right. I'm afraid I have to ask you all to clear out." He whipped his gaze around to his white-haired patient. "Except you. I'm going to have to insist that you stay a little longer. And yes, Pilar, take that bug out for analysis, *stat!*"

"Yes, doctor." She picked it up gingerly, noticing that his face was a poor match for his confident words, and dropped it into a vial. She wanted to stay and ask him privately what he really thought about what had just happened. But he was already turning his attention to the gurneys being wheeled into the room, and a nurse was herding everyone else toward the door.

Except Dr. Schneider's distinguished-looking patient, who tugged Pilar's sleeve as she was leaving and looked into her eyes with an odd mixture of pleading, bewilderment, and fear. "Please, miss," he half-whispered. "I want to know what it is, too. But when they're done with it, I have to get it back. OK?"

"I'll see what I can do," said Pilar. Then she turned away and hurried back to the lab.

Chapter 2

**What do you** mean, you can't find it?"

The white-haired man leaned forward from his tilted bed, obviously agitated. Pilar looked at him with sympathy and unspoken apology. She'd gotten to know him a little over the last couple of days; the hospital was understaffed as usual (management was more interested in saving pennies than patients or employees, and *they* didn't have to work in the trenches), so all too often she found herself up on the floors, sticking patients. Including this one. But that same understaffing left little time for conversation. Even though she'd talked to him several times, she still didn't know much about him except that his name was Lester Ordway—and he was understandably distraught that he was being held so long in the hospital. That just wasn't done much anymore, and anybody to whom it *was* done wanted to know what was so frighteningly special about his or her case. Pilar couldn't tell him, of course; she didn't know either.

Every time she saw him, he asked about his bug. So far she'd managed to stall him. But she was beginning to feel guilty about that, and it was becoming pretty clear that he wasn't going to get it back. "I'm afraid it's gone, Mr. Ordway," she admitted finally. "Specimens are normally discarded once the tests are done, and—"

"Didn't you ask them to save it?"

"Yes, I did. I knew it was unusual, and I wanted to find out what it was, too. But the more unusual a request is, the more likely it is to be overlooked or ignored. I'm truly sorry, Mr. Ordway, but I don't know what else I can do. Now if you'll just lean back and relax . . ."

He collapsed against the elevated head of his bed with a defeated sigh, and lay there inert as Pilar did what she had come to do. After a few moments, as his blood trickled into containers, he said, "So what about the tests? Why am I still here? I feel fine."

That was obviously stretching the point, but Pilar didn't say so. "Inconclusive," she said. She looked around furtively before adding in a quiet and hurried voice, "Look, I'm not supposed to talk to patients about their results, but I'll tell you just a little if you'll promise not to tell anyone I did. They haven't found any abnormalities in you, or any pathogens or toxins in your bug. Yet obviously it did something really weird to you, and to the rest of us—"

" 'The rest of us'?"

"You saw what happened in the ER—to everybody who was there, except you. Apparently it wasn't as severe as what happened to you, but it was bad enough, let me tell you. And it was scary."

"Exactly!" Ordway leaned forward again, and winced at the pain from disturbing a needle still in place. "It was scary and way out of the ordinary. That's why it's so important that we find out what it was. Originally I just thought I'd discovered a new species of insect and I wanted the credit for it. But now I think there's more to it than that."

"So do I," said Pilar, "off the record. But I don't see what more we can do about it. The bug's gone."

"But . . ." Ordway chewed nervously on his lower lip, then said, "This is so frustrating! But I'm not convinced there's no more we can do. Look, you said you think it's important and want to know what it is, too. I have some ideas. If the hospital's given up, why don't we see what we can find on our own, you and me?"

She pulled his last tube and looked at him warily for quite a while before answering. "Well, we can talk about it, at least. But I don't think this is the time or place for it, and I have a lot of other work to do. See you later, Mr. Ordway."

HE WAS DISCHARGED THAT AFTERNOON, AND THEY MET AT A picnic table on the Riverfront Green, well away from other tables, but close enough so that someone would hear the tiny air horn Pilar carried in her purse if she had to use it—which didn't seem likely, given Ordway's slight build and mild demeanor. "Sorry to be so standoffish in the hospital," Pilar said as she slid onto a bench facing him, "but they're very touchy about anybody but doctors discussing patients' medical situations with them. Especially in cases where they don't really know what's going on, and patients are making threatening noises."

"Threatening noises?"

"Yes. Some of the people who were in the room when all those little bugs came out of your big one are very unhappy. The hospital is worried about lawsuits and how they'll handle them. I think Dr. Schneider's worried sick that he'll be called to testify. Nobody seems to have suffered any permanent physical damage, but there's always 'mental anguish.' And they don't know how they'll respond if anybody tries it, since they don't know what actually happened." She leaned toward Ordway across the table. "What *did* happen, Mr. Ordway? I gather that what we experienced wasn't as bad as what you did, but I think it might have been similar. So what did bring you into the hospital? Did that big bug sting you?"

"Well, I suppose so—right between the eyes. Except to this day I'm not sure 'sting' is the right word."

"What do you mean?"

"Well, it didn't really *hurt*. At least not physically. It's not easy to explain . . . or to talk about." He shuddered involuntarily and cradled his face in his hands, hiding his eyes for a long moment as if composing himself. "Somehow it triggered an upwelling of memories and feelings. It was like something poked a hole in my mind and sucked out everything that had ever gone in with a huge vacuum, then sprayed it back into me under extreme pressure. Sort of like trying to drink from a mental fire hydrant." He forced a smile. "I guess that sounds pretty silly, doesn't it?"

"Not at all. Scary, yes. Silly, no. What happened to us was something like that, but milder. None of us were knocked out the way you were." Pilar paused. "I've never heard of a bug bite doing anything like that."

"Neither have I. Some kind of neurotoxin or hallucinogen?" He shuddered again. "Except it wasn't hallucinations. Unbearably vivid images, yes. But every one of them was something I'd either actually experienced or imagined earlier in my real life. There wasn't anything there I wasn't equipped to handle. I just wasn't equipped to handle it all at once. And to this day I don't understand why I had to." He buried his face in his hands for another half minute, then looked up with a firm set to his jaw. "But I sure want to find out."

"But what can we do? The bug's gone."

"Maybe we can find another one. I know an entomologist we could take it to. . . ." He frowned into the distance. A mockingbird sang somewhere in the distance and faint floral fragrance tickled Pilar's nose. "Of course," Ordway mused, "I'm not sure she's really the right person to ask. But at least she's a logical place to start."

Now Pilar frowned. "What do you mean by that? An entomologist is the *perfect* person to identify a bug, isn't she?"

"Sure, *if* it's a bug." He waved a hand. "I'd rather not say any more right now. Maybe I shouldn't have said anything. I don't want to get you worrying about things that are probably nonsense. Let's just keep focused on what we can do. Obviously it's a bug. Let's catch another one and take it to my entomologist friend. OK?"

"Sure." Pilar paused and added gently, "You sure you're comfortable with that? You're not afraid—"

"Of course I am!" he interrupted with surprising roughness. "But it has to be done, OK? So let's do it."

"OK. So where? And when?"

"Well, let's start by going back where the first one came from. And if that doesn't pan out . . . well, I hang around with the local Audubonians quite a bit. Some of them say they've seen some other oddities—oddities that just might have a connection with ours. Are you up for hiking a few miles?"

 You know," Lester remarked as they climbed a rock pitch on Mt. Taurus through a laurel thicket on the brink of bloom, "I didn't even know what a medical technologist was until they told me you were one."

"You're not alone," said Pilar, musing on how easily they'd drifted to first-name terms even before hitting the trail. "Anybody who's ever been in a hospital has had their lives depend on us, yet most don't even know that we exist, much less what we do." Something rustled to the right of the trail—a deer, Pilar suspected, though she couldn't see very well. At Lester's insistence, they both wore full mosquito gear including head nets. Pilar couldn't argue with that. She'd had a small taste of what he'd experienced, back in the ER. If they found what they were looking for here on the mountain (they hadn't in the garden), there could be a danger of repeating his ordeal at full strength.

"I'm still not entirely clear on what you do," he confessed. "When I saw you drawing blood, I figured you were a nurse."

"A common misconception," she said. "Actually, most blood is drawn by phlebotomists, who don't do anything else. My real job is back in the lab, analyzing the samples—of blood and other stuff. I just happened to be out there the times you saw me because nobody else was on hand to do it."

The trail leveled out and opened up a bit, into maple-beech woods with its understory overbrowsed by deer. They walked on for a minute or so, silently except for the soft classical music emanating from the small compack on Lester's belt. Normally

31

Pilar hated radios in the backcountry, and she'd been taken a bit aback when he asked whether she minded if he carried one today. She didn't, but she had admitted her surprise. He'd explained that without it he'd be too easily distracted by everything they saw or heard, and today he had a definite goal and wanted to go straight to it. Pilar wanted to get there, too, but was a little apprehensive about the prospect. Lester's music was just soothing enough to keep her from being too nervous—and she suspected that was another reason he wanted it.

"And what do you do?" she asked after a while. "Besides watch birds and bugs and get zapped by psychedelic mothoids?"

"Not a whole lot, anymore," he said—rather wistfully, Pilar thought. "I like to travel, mostly to the wildest places I can find and afford. I used to be an electrical engineer, drifting farther and farther into computers until I was downsized into early retirement a few years ago. No, a *lot* of years ago. I worked at—Oh, God, there it is again."

"What?" Pilar stepped anxiously ahead of him to see his face. He looked haggard and haunted. "What's wrong?"

"I can't remember where I worked," said Lester. "And that's ridiculous, because I know it was one of the biggest and most important companies around here. I have vivid memories of working there. But I can't remember its name." He flopped down onto a rock ledge and stared at his feet instead of the sweeping view south over the river and the subdivisions and strip malls that clogged its shore, the castle-like edifices of West Point almost lost among them. "And I didn't really retire then. I bounced around among a lot of other companies for a while . . . I don't remember their names either, or when I finally did retire." He shook his head. "I'm afraid I'm not as fully recovered as I led them to believe," he confessed. "But I had to get out. I had to come out here and try to find out what was going on."

She patted his hand and wondered whether the psych department had checked him out before his discharge. "Maybe it's not as bad as it seems," she said. "Everybody has trouble remembering things now and then."

"Not like this. I've got holes in my memory, Pilar. Whatever sucked all my memories out didn't put them all back. At least, not in the right places, where I know how to find them." He sat breathing heavily for several seconds, and then added, very quietly, "I'm scared, Pilar."

She shucked off her daypack, sat down on the warm granite, and pulled out a water bottle. Lester sat down beside her and did the same. They didn't talk for a few minutes, but eventually the mountain worked some of its calming magic. Eventually, after a good deal of hesitation, Pilar said quietly, "Maybe you should ask for help."

Lester frowned. "What kind of help? With what?"

"The holes in your memory. The fear. There are doctors who can help with that sort of thing. We have some at the hospital. Maybe you should have talked to one instead of being in such a hurry to get out."

"Maybe," he said flatly. "But so far I find the prospect of opening that can of worms even scarier. It's not as if I can't function, and there are things I need to do out here. Besides, it's gotten somewhat better already. Maybe it will come back on its own."

"Maybe," she said, letting her voice show how unconvinced she was. "But I'm concerned about you, Lester. Please think about it, at least."

"I'll think about it," he said. "And if it doesn't keep getting better . . . maybe later. Now, I've got to see what's up there." He gestured toward the summit.

Pilar looked over her shoulder and saw how much of the mountain still loomed above them. The Hudson Highlands are small, as mountains go, but not as small as they sound. Their summits are all under two thousand feet, but they get there right from sea level—and whatever Lester was looking for was supposed to be at the top. "Well," she sighed, "I guess we should get moving again."

ALMOST AN HOUR LATER, AS THE TRAIL LEVELED OUT ON THE broad summit, a strange buzzing gradually emerged from the background sounds of breezes and Lester's radio, growing first obvious and then insistent. Pilar felt a prickling at the back of her neck, and gradually became aware that there were an awful lot of flies up here today.

Then the trail, winding through a low thicket of blueberry bushes, emerged into a tiny clearing and squeezed past a big tree stump that looked vaguely wrong.

She stopped abruptly, trying to put a mental finger on what bothered her. Lester stopped too, but didn't say anything, though a burst of static from his compack almost fooled her into thinking he had.

It was too big, she decided finally. These woods were second growth, not first, and trees didn't grow that fast or well up here on the exposed summit. So what was this one doing here?

Well, maybe it wasn't really so strange, she told herself. Why shouldn't one tree have been left over from the first growth? Even if somebody eventually cut it down and hauled most of it away, its stump could still be here, one last relic of an earlier time.

Not quite convinced, she shrugged it off and made herself look at the stump's surroundings. Insects swarmed around it, constantly coming and going, sometimes disappearing into holes in the rotted top, sometimes emerging from them and flying off. Pilar couldn't tell what kind—or kinds—they were, but they weren't any bee or winged ant she knew.

"Is this what your friend described?" she asked finally.

"I think so," said Lester. "Come on, let's collect some samples." He put his pack down on a flat rock, well away from the vaguely wrong stump, and took out some gloves and collecting bottles.

For several minutes he and Pilar gathered insects from around the stump, scooping them into bottles and slapping the caps on before they could get back out. It was surprisingly easy. The swarms seemed to pay no heed to the humans, making no attempt either to flee or to defend what Pilar assumed to be their nest.

That, too, seemed wrong.

Through it all Lester's radio provided a soothing counterpoint to the insectile buzz, though sometimes when he leaned over the stump to cut off a "skin" sample, the music broke up into static and squeals. That struck Pilar as odd since she knew a mountaintop like this should be one of the best places for reception. But then, she'd never actually brought a radio up here before, and they were pretty far from the station.

It was a bit disappointing not to find anything clearly related to what had attacked Lester in the first place, but eventually they decided they'd collected enough to get started. *Maybe* something here would prove useful.

As they turned to step away from the stump, Pilar found the music overwhelmed by a buzzing very close at hand. She looked down and saw one small fly that had somehow gotten inside her head net. For a moment she almost panicked, but then it squeezed past the elastic edge of the net without doing anything patently offensive, flew straight to the stump, and disappeared into the rotted wood. At the same time, another emerged from Lester's net and did the same thing. Pilar frowned. "That's odd. How did those get inside there?"

Lester shrugged. "It's not a perfect seal. Bug nets depend on bugs being stupid. If most lines of access are blocked, not many bugs will get through. One each doesn't seem too bad."

"I guess not. But two at once, acting the same way? And I

didn't notice when mine came inside. . . ." She stopped abruptly, her attention riveted by a new kind of whine, getting louder. "Lester!" she cried out reflexively. "Look at this one."

Her ears had led her eyes to it, and now it paused in midflight, hovering a foot in front of her face on almost invisible whirring wings. It was much bigger than the others they'd seen here, gleaming in metallic colors, and it seemed to be studying her intently with big, jewel-like eyes. Remembering Lester's story of his first encounter, she shuddered involuntarily and for the first time felt unequivocally glad she'd worn the mosquito netting—even if it wasn't perfect. "Is this like the one that stung you?" she asked, her voice a tense whisper.

"Yes." His voice sounded uncharacteristically grim. "I guess this is what we came for. Hold still, Pilar." He began inching toward her, his last specimen bottle in one hand and its cap in the other. He had gloves on this time, and with the bottle he might not even have to touch the thing with his hands. Even so, his hands were shaking visibly, as if he didn't really want to do this but felt that he must. The bottle was barely big enough to hold the creature undamaged, if that, and Lester's hands were shaking so hard it wasn't at all clear that he'd succeed.

The flying thing had been hovering in place for an unnaturally long time, showing no sign of noticing Lester until he had the two jaws of his trap mere inches from it on either side. Then, just as he clapped them together, hoping to catch the bug neatly, it swooped suddenly downward, then back up, landing on Pilar's neck and squeezing up under the loose elastic of her head net in a single smooth motion. Then it was flying around *inside* the net, so close that its buzz sounded like an aerospace plane on takeoff and she could feel the wind from its wings.

And then it landed low on her forehead, so she could see its wings but not focus on them, and she felt something tiny and very sharp pierce her skin—and another explosion of sights and sounds and feelings burst forth from the very core of her being.

It was not the same as the one in the hospital. That had re-minded her of a kaleidoscope or a surrealistic animation shown much too fast; this one had images that were more powerful, more vivid and concrete, and delivered even faster. These were memories: a recurring bad dream she'd had when she was two; lying on her back on a warm rock in the haystack hills near Arecibo, looking up at the stars; a grade school field trip to the giant radiotelescope; Grandpa Rodolfo being hit by a beer truck in town; the childish taunts that crushed her dream of becoming an astronaut . . .

Everything else was there, too, far too much of it, far too fast. Like Lester before her, she found herself sinking to the ground, feeling utterly overwhelmed by a flood she was not equipped to handle. Unlike him, she did not lose consciousness, though her consciousness was so overwhelmed that everything seemed both too close and too far. One small part of it managed to notice that Lester reached out to tear her bug net off her face and clamp down with his collecting jar.

And this time he succeeded. The bug was evidently too ab-sorbed in whatever it was doing to see the jar coming, and sud-denly it was inside.

And the torrent stopped, as abruptly as a fire hydrant suddenly shut off, with just a few stray drops falling here and there. For a little while the world seemed to be spinning, and then it slowed and stopped. Pilar found herself stretched out on dry grass, pant-ing, with a white-haired man bending over her with obvious con-cern. It seemed to take her forever to remember that his name was Lester, and she found that vaguely scary.

"Are you all right?" he asked.

"I . . . think so. Is that what happened to you?"

"It looked like it, though I don't think it was quite as bad for you."

"It was bad enough."

"I'm sure it was, but at least you never blacked out. Maybe

that's because you already had some idea of what to expect, or because you're younger. Maybe you're just stronger than me, or less sensitive to whatever these things do." He looked darkly at his newly filled jar, still abuzz with wings beating futilely against the walls, and shuddered. "Or maybe they're just getting better at it. Of course, I'm not sure that's a comforting thought."

Pilar frowned. "What do you mean by that?"

He shook his head and forced a smile. "Nothing. Just babbling." She wondered briefly whether that babbling was another manifestation of the mental beating he'd taken, and what kind of damage *she'd* sustained. But he cut that thought off with, "All I really know is that we need to get this thing to an entomologist ASAP."

She couldn't argue with that. But before she pulled her net back together and got up to leave, she made herself take a close look at the thing in the bottle, which now seemed to be running out of steam. "It's actually quite pretty, isn't it?" she remarked.

"Yes," he agreed. "So's a coral snake. Now let's get out of here."

 **Pilar's first impression** was that Maybelle Terwilliger *belonged* in a natural history museum. Pilar had been to the American Museum many times, but never before "backstage," which seemed an entirely different world. Half-hidden behind mounds of electronics and disks and a surprising amount of paper and books on a scuffed old wooden desk, her wrinkled face wreathed by snowy white curls and topped off with rimless glasses, Dr. Terwilliger could almost qualify as a fossil herself. She must be at least eighty. But a second glance showed her looking out of that face through clear eyes as young as Pilar's own (but blue), and at least as impish. It made it hard to decide how to address her. *Abuelita* was the first word that popped into Pilar's mind, but what came out of her mouth was, "Thanks so much for agreeing to see us, Dr. Terwilliger. I was a little afraid nobody would."

"Oh, piffle!" said the grandmotherly old lady with a wave of her hand. Her voice was a bit cracked, but strong, and her words carried a twang that even to Pilar suggested she came from far beyond the Hudson. "What kind of scientists are we if we can't take time to look at things? And please, call me Maybelle. 'Dr. Terwilliger' makes me feel so old, and I'm only a hundred and six." She gestured at two visitors' chairs. "You young'uns make yourselves comfy. Now, what'd you bring me?"

She leaned forward across her desk with almost childlike eagerness. As Lester pulled out his special specimen bottle, he said, "I have to thank you, too, Dr. . . . er, Maybelle. I wasn't sure you'd even remember me. After all, we only talked briefly that one time when you spoke to our Audubon group. Anyway, it started with this—or one very much like it."

He put their prize catch down in the biggest open spot he could find. Maybelle stared at it, leaning closer and closer, her pixyish expression metamorphosing over several seconds into an intent frown. Pilar stared, too, fascinated and feeling a little safer with some glass between her and it and a building full of scientists all around. Finally Maybelle, with her face a mere six inches from the critter, looked up over the tops of her glasses, first at Lester and then at Pilar. "Where'd you get this?"

"This one came from the top of Mount Taurus, up in the Hudson Highlands. The first one stung me in the Boscobel garden, a few miles from there, and I had a bad reaction to it. Pilar worked on my blood while I was in the hospital, which is how we met. Unfortunately, the lab they sent the bug out to lost it, so we had to go out and get another."

Maybelle held up a hand. "Now hold your horses, young man. I can only take in so much at a time. If it stung you in a garden and sent you to the hospital, how did the lab get hold of the bug at all?"

"I held onto it. I thought having it might help them treat me— and I thought it might be a new species." He paused, then added, "Those are the only things I can remember thinking. It . . . did weird things to my mind."

Maybelle frowned. "To your mind? Hm-m-m. . . ."

When she said nothing else, Lester prompted, "*Is* it a new species? Do you know what it is?"

Maybelle was silent for a long time, still staring at the bug. It was motionless now, and after tapping the glass a few times to convince herself it wouldn't fly away, she dumped it out on the desktop. Pilar flinched, hoping Maybelle wasn't making a dangerous mistake.

Maybelle produced a magnifying glass from her top middle desk drawer and scrutinized the bug more closely. Then she laid the glass down and leaned back. "Nope," she said. "And that's an understatement." She grinned. "I sure do thank you for brightening my day. I haven't been this puzzled in a coon's age." She looked back at the bug, then at Lester. "You say it stung you and did weird things to your mind. What kind of weird things?"

Lester described the way it had hovered in front of his face right before it attacked, and then—with obvious reluctance—the way he had felt as he collapsed.

"That was the one that put you in the hospital," said Maybelle. "How about this one? Did it do anything like that?"

"This one got me," said Pilar. "It was pretty much like he said." She tried not to remember too well.

"Hm-m-m. How'd you come by another one, anyway? I've never seen one before, but you've got two of them. Don't tell me these critters are common up in your neck of the woods."

"Well, not common, exactly," said Lester, "at least as far as I know. But some of the other Audubon folks had mentioned seeing a place with a lot of unusual insect swarm activity, and they didn't know what kinds of insects they were. So I guessed there might be a connection—"

Maybelle interrupted with a nod toward the bug on the desk. "So you went out and caught this, and/or vice versa. Are you saying there were *swarms* of these things?"

"Oh, no," said Lester. "This was the only one we saw like this. But there were lots of little ones, and I didn't recognize them, either. We brought you some of those, too. And some pieces of the stump they were hanging around." He pulled out several more specimen bottles and lined them up on Maybelle's desk.

"And there were more at the hospital, too," Pilar added, suppressing a shudder at the memory. "I think they . . . came from the first big one."

Maybelle looked up sharply. "How's that, young lady . . . er, Pilar?"

"When I first saw Lester, he was unconscious in the ER, but holding something really tight in his hand. When the doctor pried it open, the other thing like this big one was in his palm, but surrounded by little dark specks of stuff. I thought they were just pieces that broke off it, but then all of a sudden they took off flying, like gnats. Do you suppose they could be its . . . babies?"

"It's a tempting notion," said Maybelle. "Except I don't know of any insects that have ready-made babies like this. I'd expect eggs that have to hatch, and larvae or nymphs that have to metamorphose. That takes time. I never heard of larval forms that flew, either. I don't suppose you brought me any of *those*, did you?"

"I'm afraid not. I tried to save one that I swatted on my forehead, but then I couldn't find it. Because it was so small, I guess."

"On your forehead," Maybelle repeated. "Trying to do the same thing as the big one?"

"Well, maybe. One instant they were just lying there; the next, they were flying all over the room."

"They took off all at once?"

"Yes. It was like an explosion, though it happened too fast for me to think that in words." Pilar searched her memory to see what else she had stored for future reference. It was almost like replaying a videotape in her mind. "And they didn't fly every which way, like you might expect," she said with growing excitement. "I don't know if anybody else noticed—they were too busy swatting and dodging—but they all flew very fast, in very straight lines. And every one went straight to a different person's forehead. I thought that was very odd."

"It is mighty peculiar," Maybelle agreed. "Did you feel anything? Bite? Sting? Pain, itching, odd sensations?"

"Yes. Sort of like the big one, but on a smaller scale. So what is it, Maybelle? Do you think it *is* a totally new kind of insect?"

Instead of answering, Maybelle picked the big bug up in a surgical-gloved hand and shoved off in her wheeled swivel chair, careening over to a lab bench along one side wall that Pilar hadn't even noticed before. Half hidden behind the papers and debris was a state-of-the-art dissecting microscope, and next to that a rather nice 8 × 10 photo of a mountain landscape in a standup frame. Maybelle dumped the specimen into a small dish, put it on the illuminated stage of the microscope, and studied it for a full minute, occasionally probing at it with a needle. Then she rolled over to the picture, touched a corner of its frame, and it turned into a very respectable flatscreen computer. She did a quick flit through several regions of cyberspace unfamiliar to Pilar, and finally rolled swiftly back to the desk to address her visitors again.

"I think you realize you've got something unusual here," she said finally, "but I suspect that you've just begun to realize *how* unusual. For starters, I don't think it's an insect at all. I don't think it's even an animal."

Pilar sat silent, feeling a prickle at the back of her neck. "Not an animal? Then what it is it?"

"Technology. Think about it. It looks more like an insect than anything else natural, but I've been an entomologist for mumble-mumph years and everything about it looks wrong. You haven't been an entomologist at all—at least the card-carrying kind—and you could still tell at a glance that it didn't fit into your past experience. Well, the closer you look, the more right you are. Obviously I haven't tried looking for DNA or anything like that yet—though I want to—but I can tell you that some of those little flecks that look like metal *are* metal. All that points to its being made, not 'jist growed.' "

"But what . . . who . . ."

Maybelle held up a hand, interrupting with a patient smile. "All in good time, my dear. There's more. The mere fact of its flying in a controlled and apparently purposeful way suggests that, if it *is* technology, it's mighty sophisticated technology, to pack all that ability into this small and neat a package. Then there's the matter of the gnatoids. At first glance they'd seem to be more of the same, only more so. But even beyond that, the way they came out of the same hand that held the big one suggests that it's some sort of *replicating* technology. That is, the big machine (and I use the term loosely) makes little ones at least vaguely like itself.

"But the capper was the way Pilar said they acted in the hospital. If they really all came out and made beelines, so to speak, for people's foreheads, no two to the same one . . . well, that sounds like intelligent behavior, or at least volitional. What's intelligent? The big one? Each of the little ones? The whole group collectively, like a honeybee hive? Either way, it is, in the immortal words of Pogo, a mighty soberin' thought. It looks to me an awful lot like a combination of miniaturization and artificial intelligence that's way beyond what human scientists I know of can do so far—and we've been doing quite a bit lately."

"Are you saying," Pilar asked slowly, not quite believing her ears, "you think these things were made by . . . nonhumans?"

"Maybe. Or maybe just humans who aren't working out in the open and know more than the rest of us. I grew up with science fiction in the last century. There were good, stimulating ideas there; they had a lot to do with why I went into science. But there was also silliness, or so it seemed to me then. One thing in particular always bothered me." She leaned forward with her hands folded on the desktop.

"In story after story," she said, "it seemed to me that exploring teams were learning far more about planets they visited than they reasonably could in the time they'd have available. They'd cruise into a new solar system, spend a few days parked in orbit around a planet no human had ever seen, and learn as much about it as all the humans in history had learned in thousands of years about the planet they grew up on. Figure out the whole geological history and how the atmosphere worked, catalog half the life forms

and which ones are dangerous and how the explorers could protect themselves, and then they'd go down and do it. Usually
they'd get themselves into trouble, of course, because they'd overlooked some little detail and the author had to thicken the plot.
But the amount they *didn't* overlook was just mind-boggling. I've
spent my life plodding along doing my own bit to understand
one small slice of this planet, so I know what it takes. So how
in whatever world could these characters learn so much so fast?

"Well, as you were talking, I thought of those stories and a
way it *might* be done. If somebody's doing it to Earth, it could
explain all this stuff we've been seeing."

Both Lester and Pilar stared at her for quite a while before
either said anything. Then Pilar said, without bothering to hide
her incredulity, "You're serious, aren't you?"

"You betcha," said Maybelle. "*Our* scientists couldn't do
what the people in those stories did. We don't have the tools—
at least, none that are public knowledge. But suppose a few of
our descendants—or clandestine colleagues—came to a planet
with highly developed computers, telepresence, and nanotechnology. Put them all together, they could spell something damn
near instant omniscience—or at least a local approximation."

Lester frowned. "You mean something like this? They seed the
planet with little bitty things that can grow and multiply into
vast numbers of little mobile information gatherers—"

Maybelle nodded vigorously. "Yes! Like Argus, the mytholog-
ical watchman with a hundred eyes. Only these can be a lot more
than a hundred, and they don't have to just be eyes. Your critters
have eyes, for instance, but they also seem to be able to rummage
around in folks' nervous systems. And our Argus's 'eyes' don't
have to all be where he is. They can go pretty much everywhere
and collect all kinds of information about everything."

"And since they're all doing it at once," Pilar joined in, momentarily forgetting this was a serious problem and not just a

game, "they can collect it much faster than a handful of humans. But . . . it's still going to take a lot of time to analyze all that information and decide what it means."

"Yes," said Lester. "But if whoever made them can build this kind of computing power into bug-sized things"—he gestured at Maybelle's collection—"they could build *really* powerful central computers to sort out the results. And they could devote whole teams to doing the final interpretations—"

"My idea exactly." Maybelle nodded approvingly. "If the whole planet really *is* bugged—sorry 'bout that—those must be *big* computers and big teams. But who are they and where are they? And if the information is being gathered by all these zillions of teensy little spies, how are they getting it back to wherever it's analyzed?"

Pilar could see Lester's boyish enthusiasm collapse like a punctured balloon. "They can't," he said flatly, shaking his head. "So your whole scheme falls apart. I can imagine a pseudo-gnat with nanocomputers being able to gather quite a bit of information, but I don't see how it can transmit it to a distant station. These things are just too small, except maybe the biggest ones."

"Like that one?" Maybelle gestured at the one that had zapped Pilar.

"Maybe, but even that's stretching it. Power is one problem, to say nothing of getting a suitable antenna size."

Maybelle waved a hand toward the computer on her desk. "Not many years ago, not even the science fiction writers imagined that we'd ever have that much computing power in a box that size. Yet there it is, and practically everybody has something like it at home and a compack or two in their pockets."

"True," Lester admitted, looking vaguely uncomfortable. "Even so, there are fundamental physical limits. The kind of antenna you need depends on the wavelengths you're using, and even the shortest radio waves are too long for most of these bugs to be sending. So what's the point of collecting a lot of information, if that's really what they're doing, if they can't send it anywhere?"

"Maybe," Maybelle said gently, "somebody has thought of something you haven't."

"I know physical law," Lester insisted—a little too positively, Pilar thought. "And I have a pretty good idea how far nanotechnology has progressed. It's nowhere near this."

"As far as you know," said Maybelle. She shrugged. "On the other hand, what I'm describing is just an extreme-case scenario of what *might* be possible. What we're seeing might be considerably more modest—say, just a few isolated spy bugs. Except we have already seen quite a few, and we know they replicate. . . ."

"I don't know which is scarier," said Pilar, finding both possibilities more than amply disquieting. "Humans who are that far ahead of the rest of us, or those nonhumans Maybelle mentioned. But if it really was that, wouldn't we have seen some other sign of them?"

"Maybe we have," said Maybelle. "Were you listening to the radio on the way into the city?"

"No," said Lester. "We took a railcar, and we just talked."

"You missed an interesting item," said Maybelle. "Seems an asp blew up while you were on the way."

Pilar frowned deeply. "An aerospace plane? I didn't even know there were any up now."

"Neither did anyone else," Maybelle said darkly. "At least, in the general public. Interesting, ain't it? No shuttle missions were scheduled, yet suddenly one is blown up. Lots of people saw it, so the government can't pretend it didn't happen. They're falling all over themselves trying to come up with plausible explanations for why it was up there unannounced and what happened to it. So far they haven't come up with anything convincing. I think it's pretty obvious that they're stalling, embarrassed, and maybe scared. Think there might be a connection?"

Pilar felt herself breaking out in a sweat. Her first reaction had been to the mere incongruity of a news story about a shuttle being up when none was scheduled. Now the enormity of the tragedy of a spacecraft's *destruction* was beginning to penetrate. Nothing like it had happened in her lifetime, but her parents had so vividly described the consternation that had followed the *Challenger* explosion, and how long it had taken those wounds to heal, that the memories seemed almost her own.

And the circumstances of what Maybelle was describing sounded even more sinister than those of *Challenger*—especially if you knew about the bugs that had brought Pilar and Lester here.

"Has the government," Pilar asked quietly, "said anything about aliens? Or bugs? Or a connection?"

"I don't know if the government even knows about the bugs," said Maybelle. "I haven't heard a thing about them from anybody but you two."

"Isn't that odd?" Pilar asked, clutching at a straw. "I mean, if they're really all over like you said, shouldn't there be *lots* of reports of them?"

"Maybe, maybe not. First, I suspect it's not a kind of thing that people would talk about a lot. Second, Lester *did* get at least one other report, and you deliberately looked for a place with mystery bugs. And wherever they're coming from, somebody has to be the first to see them." She shrugged. "At this point there's a lot more that we don't know than that we do. I think we'd better try to find out just what these things are, how common they are, and what they're up to."

"So where do we start?" asked Lester. "None of us is a nanotechnologist."

"Ah, but I know lots of them." For a moment, a hint of Maybelle's impish grin reilluminated her face, and the contrast merely emphasized to Pilar how conspicuously absent it had been for the last few minutes. "I wasn't kidding about being a hundred and six, you know. My grandson's a nanotech researcher, and he arranged for me to be one of the first guinea pigs for nanotech antisenescence treatments, back when I was eighty-seven. They're still not far into rejuve, of course, though my doctors tell me that physiologically I've gone back about five years instead of aging nineteen.

"Dan's still working on it. I also have lots of contacts in all kinds of fields, quite a few of them my own children and grandchildren and nieces and nephews. I'm going to send out some feelers and see if I can find anybody else who's had experiences like yours. I'll also see if I can find anybody who knows anything about the shuttle incident. That'll be harder, though; I have a lot more contacts in the sciences than in government or the military." For a moment she stared out the window, and then turned back to Lester and Pilar. "I assume you two will keep me posted on anything new you find out. But please, be careful."

"Careful?" Pilar echoed, not liking the way Maybelle said it.

"Careful. If these things really are supposed to be watching us surreptitiously, whoever's behind them might not appreciate being watched back."

Chapter 5

**Pilar found it** comforting and reassuring to sit in her apartment composing an e-mail letter to her sister, despite that letter's subject matter. In here, surrounded by cheap but familiar furniture and pictures of her family and homeland on the walls, her recent experiences and Maybelle's speculations seemed wildly remote. Those stretched her mind till it hurt, but e-mail was so easy it was almost mindless.

This was the room to which she had so often retreated when the outside world seemed inhospitable, and to the extent that she kept her mind within its walls, it looked and felt the same as ever. Sitting at her computer, conjuring characters on the screen that linked her even more to familiar things, she gradually relaxed.

But not completely. Normally she would have just talked to the computer as if Rosa were in the room, letting it transcribe what she said. Tonight she felt vaguely uncomfortable with that, and instead dusted off her seldom-used keyboard and her modest skills in using it.

Still, it helped. But there came the inevitable time when she had to confront her real reason for writing. Rosa was one of the few people she could mention this to, but even with her it wasn't easy. She typed, in Spanish:

> *I have to ask you something that may sound a bit strange. Have you seen any sort of bugs or flies you don't recognize around there? Or anything else that you don't recognize, or*

that seems out of place? If so, I'd like you to tell me any-
thing you can about it.

She stopped and frowned, unsatisfied with the wording. After
a moment she resumed:

I had a conversation recently with an entomologist who has
seen some things that may be new species of insects. She's
trying to find out if anybody else has seen anything like
them. If so, she'd like to find out how common and wide-
spread they are. I told her I'd ask around, and since you're
pretty knowledgeable about the kinds of things that live
around there

She stopped again. It was true enough, as far as it went, but
withheld enough to be misleading. She didn't like doing that to
Rosa, ever. Should she throw caution to the winds and spill it all
out, crazy as it sounded?
Before she could decide, there was a sharp knock on the door.

SHE ALMOST JUMPED OUT OF HER CHAIR, THEN CAUGHT HER-
self. *Stop that!* she scolded herself. *It's probably just Karen or*
Bob, or maybe old Mrs. Frederick has locked herself out
again. . . .
Reflexively, she saved her letter to disk and started to get up.
Her visitor knocked again, and again she jumped. "Who is it?"
she called out.
"I need to talk to you," said an unfamiliar voice, probably
male but oddly indefinite, with an unfamiliar accent. "*Un mo-*
mentito." The voice's Spanish sounded a little off, too.
"Just a minute," Pilar called back. "I'm in the middle of something." Maybe she was paranoid, but she suddenly felt impelled
to take a precaution she'd never taken before. Fingers zipping

over the keys, occasionally stumbling and having to redo, she hurriedly closed her letter, opened a new document and typed a terse message in, and saved it. Anyone touching the onspot once would see the last words she'd typed—a phrase she hoped would prove irrelevant and unnecessary.

Then she scooped the air horn and Mace from her purse, cradling one in each cupped hand, and went to the door.

The figure beyond the peephole, even allowing for its fisheye distortion, was nobody she knew. It was a man, superficially handsome yet oddly nondescript. "Who are you?" she demanded. "What do you want?"

"I need to talk to you," he repeated. "Privately. May I come in?"

"I don't let strangers into my apartment." She paused. "What's this about?"

"I told you. It's private. I must come in."

"You can't come in." She remembered how she'd handled Lester's call and thought maybe something similar could work here. "Look, if you really need to talk to me about something, maybe we can meet in a public place. But you have to give me an idea what it is first."

"Too private for public place," the stranger insisted. "We must talk here, now." He was silent for a few seconds, then said, "Open your door a bit. Leave it on the chain if you want."

Pilar hesitated. Even that could be risky, but she had a hunch she had to learn who this creep was before she sent him away. Otherwise she'd keep wondering—and he might return.

She made sure the chain was secure and opened the door just a crack, keeping her weight firmly against it, poised to slam it hard if she needed to—and could. She looked just far enough around the edge to get a direct, undistorted view—and almost gasped aloud.

Her first impression was that he didn't look real. "Handsome" could still apply, but in a way that reminded her vaguely of a department store mannequin—except this one walked and talked. "Who are you?" she managed to get out.

"Just a visitor," he said, too carefully. "One who has a small bit of necessary business with you."

"I don't even know you," she said. With more hope than confidence, she added, "And you don't know me."

"But I do," he said. "I know much about you."

"Prove it," her voice grated.

"Your sister in Puerto Rico will be concerned if you do not finish your letter to her. It's been longer than usual since you wrote—but you will have to change some of what you say. You have a small tattoo of a flower in a place almost no one else has seen. And you and some of your friends have been snooping in matters which they should not. This must stop."

Breathing hard and thinking fast, Pilar weighed her options. This could be far worse than she'd feared—yet she had to know who he was and what he wanted. She'd rather not let him in, of course; but even if he was willing, did she want to talk to him where other people could hear? *I should have taken more time,* she thought wildly. *Set up an e-mail that I could send to a bunch of people with one click.*

But what would I have said?

He made the decision easier. "I must insist on coming in," he said quietly. "If you refuse, Rosa will find a very special bug in her bed tonight."

That did it. "Get in here," she half-growled. "But don't get any funny ideas. I'm well equipped to take care of myself."

"I KNOW ALL ABOUT YOUR EQUIPMENT," HE SAID AS HE CAME in, "including the Mace, the air horn, and the message you left on your monitor in case anything happens to you. But you needn't worry about that, at least tonight. I have no wish to harm you or anyone. I would have preferred to avoid direct contact with you. But what you and your friends are doing threatens to undermine everything *we* are trying to do. That cannot be allowed."

You feel threatened? Pilar thought. *That's wonderful—if it's true.* "Who are 'we'?" she demanded aloud. "What are we doing that you don't like? How dare you threaten my sister? How do you even know about her?" The stranger started to put his hands in the pockets of his loose jacket that didn't belong to any style Pilar knew. "Don't do that!" she snapped. "Keep your hands out where I can see them. Like this. And answer my questions."

He obeyed. "Where do I begin?" he asked rhetorically. "I suppose your sister concerns you most. We know about her the same way we know of so many other things. We—"

"How many?" Pilar demanded. "Just how much do you know?"

"A great deal," he said, "yet there is still more to learn. Do you wish to test me? Ask what you will, about matters great or small. I may or may not answer. If I do not, that may or may not mean I do not know."

"What kind of pet does Rosa have?"

He seemed to ponder for a moment, his curiously expressionless eyes meanwhile wandering with no apparent aim around the room. Then he said, "A green iguana, about this long." He held his hands a little farther apart than Pilar remembered; but then, the lizard had had time to do some growing since she last saw it. "And," the stranger added, "a small black and white and yellow bird that she found injured last summer."

Pilar's throat felt very dry. She'd even loaded the question to mislead him, and he got it right anyway. "Who is this country's Secretary of the Interior?"

"Mildred Piaget," he said immediately.

"How many species of hummingbird live wild in this state?"

"Only one," said the stranger. "An interesting selection of questions."

"I think so. Now the biggy: How do you know all this stuff?"

"It would be counterproductive for you to know too much about that," said the odd man, "which is why I'm here. But I sense it will be difficult to get you to mind your own business unless I tell you *something*. I can tell you that the old lady is closer to the truth than even she suspects."

Pilar chewed on that for awhile. "You mean the bugs really are gathering information? And they're really all over?"

"Not *all* over. There are none in your neighbor Elmer Glantz's refrigerator at this moment, for instance. But there *are* quite many of them, and they are quite widespread."

"I see," said Pilar, as flatly as she could. "And where is all this information going? Who are the 'we' you spoke of, and what *are* you trying to do?"

"Telling you that would have the same effect as letting you continue what you're doing. The answers needn't concern you. All I ask is that you and your friends drop this matter."

Pilar looked at him for a long time, trying to pin down the many details of his behavior that seemed vaguely wrong. "If you expect us to accept that," she said finally, "you don't know much about people."

"I don't understand," he said. "Why are you so obsessed with these little anomalies? I have already assured you that they do not concern you. It's such a simple matter for you just to ignore them—"

"It's not simple at all! Do you seriously expect any human being to sit here and listen to you hint that you're spying on all of us—"

"You're accustomed to being spied on," he interrupted. "Your public areas are full of surveillance cameras."

"That's different. We put them there ourselves, for a good reason. We don't even know who you are or what you want. Do you really expect us to accept *your* spying and not feel threatened and want to defend ourselves? And you did threaten my sister. How can you expect me to accept that?"

He didn't answer right away. "Perhaps it was a mistake to mention your sister. I did not mean that any real harm would come to her, of course—"

"It's too late for that now." She asked in a low voice, "Are you human? Are you from this planet?"

He hesitated even longer before saying, "I will not dignify that with an answer. But I must repeat that the snooping you and your friends are doing can do neither of us any good. You would be well advised to regard it as dangerous. In a word, stop it."

"And you," she hissed, "would be well advised that there are important things *you* don't know about *us*. Trying to stifle us may endanger *you* in ways you can't even imagine."

He stared at her for a few seconds. "Perhaps you're right," he said finally. "Or perhaps you're not. I strongly advise you to give serious thought to my request. You have nothing to gain by continuing, and nothing to lose by stopping. Nothing we are doing endangers you or anyone else—as long as you do not try to interfere."

"How can you say that after what happened to poor Lester—and me? Do you have any idea what you put him through?"

The stranger looked down. "We're truly sorry about that. We were inexperienced then, but we learn fast. In any case, as I understand it, no lasting harm was done, except for starting you and him on this misguided quest." His gaze rose to meet hers again. "We will be watching to make sure you decide wisely."

"Get out!" she snapped.

He nodded calmly. "I was on my way."

He turned and was almost to the door when Pilar had one last thought. "Wait!"

He paused, hand on the knob, and turned back to face her. "Yes?"

"How can I contact you if I need to?"

"I told you we'll be watching," he said. "We'll know if you need to—though it would be best if we had *no* further contact."

"But suppose I *need* to," she persisted. "Suppose I've found a way to prevent your knowing every move I make. And suppose . . . suppose I know that *you're* in danger, and I can tell you how to get out of it." Not that she could imagine wanting to do that, but she could imagine wanting to trick him, if she ever saw a way. And she would not give him an advantage without at least trying to gain one of her own.

For the first time, he laughed, a single harsh, amorphous syllable. "I find that hard to imagine. I appreciate the offer, but your premise is absurd." He stared at her for a long time, as if sizing her up and pondering a difficult decision. "Perhaps my attempt to reason with you was absurd, too. Sometimes subtlety and accommodation are more trouble than they are worth. I had hoped to deal with this little dilemma without anything like this, but sometimes the only real way to deal with a problem is to cut it off right at the source. Cleanly and swiftly, before it gets out of hand."

As he spoke, one hand had moved slowly into a pocket. Now it reappeared, with a very small, very sharp-looking blade held at waist level. He pointed its tip toward Pilar and took a fast, surprisingly long step toward her, his other hand reaching out toward her mouth.

She reacted reflexively, hitting the air horn and Mace simultaneously even before her mind had time to form the incredulous words, *He's trying to kill me!*

She held the button down for what seemed a long time, astounded at how loud the horn sounded in the tight quarters. Some of the Mace diffused in the close air, swirling back toward Pilar, stinging her eyes and nose and making her feel woozy.

To her astonishment, it seemed to have no effect on the stranger, despite her having given him a full blast right in the face. He lunged forward and stabbed her in the neck. Agonizing pain exploded from the wound through her whole being, almost making her black out, and for a horrifying instant she was sure she was dead.

But then, incongruously, her attacker stopped in midstride, hesitating, staring at her with wide-open, unflinching eyes. In slow motion, as slamming doors, footsteps, and shouts sounded in the hall and fists banged on the door, he withdrew the blade and stuck it back in his jacket. He wheeled suddenly and dove through the window, shattering the glass with his passage.

For a long moment, as her time sense returned to normal, Pilar just stood there, shaking violently and staring after him, afraid to look away. Then, when nothing else happened at the window and she finally became fully aware of the pounding and shouts at her door, she went to open it.

Karen and Bob and Mrs. Frederick were all there, all clamoring to know what was wrong. Mrs. Frederick threw her arms around Pilar to comfort her and Pilar let the tears flow as she kept saying, "He tried to kill me!" over and over. Bob said he'd called 911, and soon Pilar got control of herself enough to say that her attacker had jumped out the window.

But when they all looked out, there was no sign of anyone there, and no blood or skin or hair on the broken glass. When the police came, a few minutes later, they couldn't find anything either. The crime-eyes out on the street showed nothing.

Pilar's wound wasn't as bad as it first seemed. It bled a bit, which was scary, but not all that much, and the policeman who bandaged it said she was lucky: it had narrowly missed a lethal spot. "If he'd hit the carotid artery," he said, shaking his head, "you might have bled to death before we could stop you."

"I'm not sure that blade could have even reached it," she said, but she wondered. Was that really what he was aiming for, or did he just want her to think so? "Maybe he was just trying to scare me to death."

"Maybe," said the officer, but he didn't sound convinced. His partner was still looking around outside, but Pilar had the feeling his heart wasn't in it. "Look," said the one in front of her, "why don't you just let me run you down to the hospital and see if there's any hidden damage?"

She shook her head. "It's not that big a wound. You said so yourself."

"But if the knife was contaminated—"

"I *work* at the hospital," she said, more brusquely than she intended. "My tetanus and hepatitis shots are up to date, and if I think of any reason to worry about anything else, I can analyze it my—It'll keep till tomorrow. Maybe I'll go then."

He didn't put much more effort into persuading her. Everyone was very sympathetic, but as they dispersed, she could imagine them shaking their heads just beyond the door and saying, *Poor girl's finally cracked. Breaks her own windows, makes up wild stories, tries to kill herself but botches the job . . . Maybe she's just desperate for attention. . . .*

Pilar walked slowly back into the room, shaking, reprogramming the main door lock and latching all the old mechanical backups that she seldom bothered with anymore. There was no longer any doubt that she was in danger, and that Maybelle was at least vaguely on the right track. But Pilar had no proof—why *hadn't* the police found anything outside?—and after tonight, who would even listen to her, much less believe her?

Drained, she collapsed in front of her computer and reopened her letter to Rosa. Typing as fast as she could, she instructed the system to send copies to a dozen friends and well-placed acquaintances when she was finished. Then she returned to the text of the letter itself.

She'd been interrupted in midsentence. Now she filled the line out with capital Xs, skipped a couple of lines, and started over. This time she *would* spill it all, desperately sure that the most urgent thing in her world right now was to get word of what little they knew out as fast and far and wide as possible. And there might be very little time to do that.

She read the letter over once more, quickly, to make sure she had it all right. Then she clicked SEND NOW.

And her system—her system that had never failed her before—crashed.

And nothing she could do would bring it back up.

 **Pilar did not** sleep well that night. Even in the dark, with every chain and lock in her apartment fastened and triple-checked, and a board nailed across the broken window, she felt like a child again, in all the worst senses of the phrase. Only in her earliest years had she ever experienced such a feeling of being menaced by things whose existence she could barely perceive, and of being watched in everything she did. The difference was that in those days she really *was* continually watched, by more powerful beings who, no matter how exasperating they could be at times, were always and unshakably on her side. Now, she suspected, the beings watching her were far more powerful, and most definitely *not* on her side.

And she had nowhere to turn for help, and even if she tried, *that* would be watched, too.

For long hours in the middle of the night she lay trembling, feeling trapped and with nowhere to hide. Sometimes her thoughts turned back to the policeman last night, trying to talk her into going to the ER. She knew that wasn't necessary; she had nothing to show but a trivial cut, and she knew how the ER staff would handle that. The burst of pain she'd thought she felt must have been psychological, from the sheer shock of realizing that anyone would stab her, even with a tiny knife. And her shots *were* up to date.

For things they knew how to inoculate against. But what if that tiny blade was never intended to do serious physical damage, but to *inject* something they *didn't* know about? Something like

Maybelle's nanobugs, designed to do who-knew-what inside her body?

She broke out in a cold sweat, suddenly so desperate to know what was inside her that she almost jumped out of bed to go to the lab and find out. But that would mean traveling from here to there in the dark, with who-knew-what out there. . . .

She shuddered to think how paranoid she'd become in a couple of days. But things tend to look darkest at 3 AM, and it was not in her nature to accept defeat. Toward morning she began to realize that maybe there *were* things she could do and places she could turn for help. Not many, but a few. . . .

SHE GREETED DAWN WITH RELIEF AND DETERMINATION. SHE couldn't know whether "they" would even let her talk to Lester and Maybelle, but she had to try. She still felt an urgent determination to look at her own blood, but that could wait—mostly. She usually had a few professional supplies around her apartment, and it was a simple matter to draw a tube from her own arm and pop it into the fridge for future examination. Then she could tackle what could be even more urgent: finding out what the others' nights had been like.

She called in sick, then started with e-mail, without success. Her computer gave her a startup screen, but ignored any attempt to go beyond that. She tried to call Lester and then Maybelle, and got only a dead line when she should be getting a ring signal. The weather number worked fine; so did another call to the lab. She waited for an answer, just to see if she could get one, then explained that she was having a problem with her comcenter and just wanted to test it. A couple more calls to people having nothing to do with Lester's bugs went through without difficulty.

But calls to Lester and Maybelle went nowhere.

So she would have to go to them—if *they* would let her.

SHE WAS RELIEVED, AND A LITTLE SURPRISED, TO BE ABLE TO drive uneventfully to Lester's house, a cozy brick Cape on a wooded cul-de-sac. She didn't even have to steer; despite her fears of having to fight for control of the car, the onboard worked fine.

Her relief didn't last long; he didn't answer the doorbell, and when she crept around the house looking in windows, she found him in the kitchen, sprawled backwards over a chair with his mouth open and his expression blank.

Her throat went dry but she didn't panic. She tapped on the window, hard enough to rattle the pane, but he showed no sign of hearing.

The kitchen door was unlocked, but she hesitated briefly before opening it. Whoever had done whatever to him might still be in there. But what choice did she have?

The kitchen smelled of curry—good curry. A small part of Pilar's mind noted that apparently he still took the trouble to cook for himself, but most of her attention was on more pressing matters. In very few seconds she checked for blood and saw none, and for a pulse—faint, but there and regular. "Lester?" she said. "Are you OK? Can you hear me?" A part of her reflected on how inane that had sounded when her first CPR instructor taught the class to say it to a person who was obviously *not* OK. "Lester? It's Pilar. What happened?"

An incoherent sound, barely audible, began somewhere deep in his throat, gradually taking shape and emerging from his mouth as a barely recognizable, "Pilar? Do I know you?" His head turned slightly so he could see her, but his gaze was alarmingly blank.

"I hope so," she said. "Oh, how I hope so." She looked around, got him a glass of water, and helped him drink it.

Strength and awareness seemed to flow back into him with the clear liquid. "Who are you?" he asked, more clearly. "What happened?"

"That's what we're trying to find out," she said, squeezing his hand and offering him another drink. "What do you remember?"

He frowned at the word. "Remember," he murmured as if trying the word on for size. His frown deepened. "Holes . . . holes . . ."

"Holes," Pilar repeated. "More holes in your memory? Things you can't remember?"

He nodded, very slowly. "Like before?" she prompted. "Like the bug in the garden?"

He twitched, closed his eyes, opened them again. "Worse," he said. "More pain . . ." He closed his eyes again, and kept them shut.

So much for being sorry and careful, Pilar thought. "What was it?" she asked. "Did another bug get in here and do something to you? Or . . . a person?"

His eyes opened suddenly and he looked straight at her, much more focused now. "Can't remember," he said. "That's the worst hole. I know *something* came here and did something to me. But I can't remember anything about who or what it was or what they looked like."

"Well, we're going to find out. We have to go—"

"No!" He looked alarmed. "I'm not supposed to ask questions. That's when they hurt me. And they'll do it again. That much I remember."

Pilar hesitated. That could be a real danger. If Maybelle's hunch was right, this time they could have left something inside him that would hurt him if he did things they didn't like. She didn't want to put him in more danger. . . .

But they had to find out. What was happening to them might well be the very small tip of a very large iceberg.

"OK," she said. "We'll be very careful. But you can't just hide from it. If you're in danger, we have to find out so we can make it go away. That's what we were trying to do before . . . before. Let's just go see Maybelle, OK?" He stared uncertainly. "We'll stay out in public as much as possible. We'll take the rail into the city. And I'll call first. Can I use your com?"

He nodded slowly. She tried, but his center was just as selective as her own. It would call anyone else, but not Maybelle.

Fifteen minutes later she had Lester degrogged enough to lead him out to her car. She stopped at a paycom two blocks away, and from that she had no trouble calling the museum, but Maybelle's extension was dead. "We have somebody checking on it," the museum operator said. "I know she's here, though. Would you like me to page her for you?"

"No, thanks." Just knowing she was there was enough for Pilar, but she added, "Tell her Pilar and Lester are coming to see her."

She turned back to Lester. "One more thing. I think they may have been sneaking Maybelle's nanocritters into us. Would you mind if I took a blood sample?"

He frowned, then nodded slowly. She took a wipe and collection tube from her pocket, and was proud that he felt no pain.

She would wait until later to broach once more the suggestion of a psych exam.

LESTER PERKED UP CONSIDERABLY ON THE RIDE IN, AS THE HUDson and Palisades whizzed blurrily past their bullet car, and again Pilar wondered at the fact that they were allowed to take it. If whoever was behind all this could do what they'd done so far, and really didn't want Pilar and her friends snooping, why were they still alive? Were they playing some bizarre game of cat and mouse? Were there alien rules?

Even though she and Lester were alone in the bullet-shaped car, she kept looking nervously around as if they were being watched even here. She had never thought about it before, but the paranoia made her think how much more secure she might have felt if the Hudson Line still used old-fashioned trains. Back then, when so many people actually commuted that dozens of them rode in every car and several cars were strung together and ran on a fixed schedule, they would have been surrounded by lots of other people. All those eyes, she imagined, would have made foul play far less likely, and provided ample witnesses if it happened anyway.

Maybelle was looking fine when they finally reached her office, but she was not a happy camper. She was scurrying about the room, sweeping papers aside as if looking for something, frowning and hardly noticing her visitors. "My whole hard disk!" she muttered when Pilar tried to ask her what was wrong. "Wiped clean. Likewise all the backups. My computer doctored, or something, so I can't reformat beyond the most basic level. I can load simple software, but it won't accept any new passwords from me—and yes, I have gone back to the masters for security." She shoved off in her swivel chair, screeched to a halt, and spun to face Lester and Pilar, her expression oddly distracted. "So what's new with you two?"

Pilar gave her a quick rundown on her sinister visitor last night and how she found Lester this morning. "So we each had a guest, it seems," she concluded, "though Lester's erased any memory of what he—or it—looked like. How about you, Maybelle? Did somebody come in and ransack your computer, or did you just find it that way after you'd been out?"

"Oh, I had a visitor," said Maybelle, "if you want to call it that. Not a person or a bug, though—a cartoon character. An animated face that popped up on my screen in the middle of a work session, told me I'd been naughty, and proceeded to wipe out several copies of several years' work. No indication of how it got there or who sent it, but I think it's pretty clear that we're onto something. Yesterday this all seemed like a fascinating puzzle, a game. I don't think it's a game anymore. I think we've antagonized somebody who has eyes and fingers in way too many places. I think it's time to get scared."

"Consider me scared," Pilar said grimly. "So who is it and what have they got against us?"

"Don't know," said Maybelle. "The most encouraging thing I can think of is that we've scared them—which may mean there's hope. The discouraging thing is that they seem to know a lot more about us than we know about them, and they have an awful lot of tricks up their sleeves."

Remembering her stabbing last night and finding Lester this morning, Pilar shuddered. "How could *we* have scared *them*?"

"I think they've answered that for us," said Maybelle. "Even though we feel like we understand very little, I think we're getting too close to understanding something they don't want us to."

"The asp that blew up," Lester said suddenly. "Any news on that? We'd thought there might be a connection. . . ."

Maybelle shook her head. "Maybe there is, maybe there isn't. I haven't been able to get more than vague inklings of what's going on there. I still think the government has had a big 'oops' and is trying to cover it up—big news, huh?—but I don't know what it is this time." She frowned. "My *hunch*, though, is that there is a connection and this goes way beyond the three of us."

None of them said anything for a while. Finally Pilar said, "Should we go to the police or something?" Then she remembered last night and laughed bitterly. "I've already *been* to the police. I said someone attacked me; they found no evidence of anyone else. They didn't laugh in my face, but I'm sure they did as soon as they were out of earshot."

Maybelle nodded. "That's the problem. No doubt we *should* tell somebody everything that's happened to us and everything we've guessed. I'd especially like to compare notes with somebody who knows what's going on behind the scenes at NASA. But if we do it with no more concrete evidence than we have so far, who would take us seriously?" *Isn't one bug enough?* Pilar thought, wondering whether Maybelle had forgotten it or for some reason was dismissing it as unimportant—or it hadn't panned out. But she decided not to interrupt now; she'd hear Maybelle out first. "And if they laugh us out once, it'll be that much harder to get them to listen if we go back with more later."

"So we have to wait and see what else they do to us?" Lester asked. Pilar was pleased to hear him taking a more active part in the conversation, and seemingly getting some of his orientation back. But she could feel the pain behind his expression as he thought about subjecting himself to still more of what he'd already been through.

Of course, there was the alternative Pilar's visitor had offered. Back off, stop snooping, and he and his people—or whatever they were—would leave them alone.

If he could be trusted. But what were the chances of that? And what else would they be doing in the meantime?

No, that was no alternative at all.

"That may be all we can do," Pilar said quietly, "at least for a while. Though I may have some ideas for a bit later."

She turned back to Maybelle. "How about Lester's bug? Any word on that?"

"Yes, indeedy. Dan—my grandson—dissected it and looked at the pieces with quite a variety of tools. No DNA. Lots of nanotech—stuff he can barely recognize as such but neither he nor anybody he knows could begin to build." Maybelle paused. "Which suggests an intriguing possibility about your visitor, Pilar. Obviously it had some connection with whoever's behind the bugs, and it *could* be an actual alien, or a human trying to make you think that. Or maybe it was a construct like Lester's bug, but bigger and more complex."

Pilar frowned. "If it was an imitation human, it wasn't a very good one. Hm-m-m . . . might that mean that whoever's behind these things isn't as formidable as we thought?"

"I wouldn't count on it," said Maybelle. "Simulating a human, even badly, is no small job. If this was their first attempt, they might get better with practice."

"Hmph," Lester snorted. "Did Dan figure out what the bug does?"

"Not exactly. It does have eyes, and *very* microprocessors—"

"And did he have an answer to my antenna question?"

"He didn't mention one. Of course, I'm not an electronicker myself, so I'm not sure I passed the question on as well as I might—"

"But whether he has an answer to that or not," Pilar said suddenly, "he has what we need! I assume he was careful to save the pieces—and the smaller specimens. Can't we get them back from him and take *those* to somebody?"

"Not a bad idea," said Maybelle, "though I'm not very confident it will be enough. I kept a couple of the little ones myself, but they disappeared along with all my data. The big one should be a better talking point, anyway." She looked at her phone and frowned. "I suppose this is a waste of time, but let's give it a whirl. . . ." She dialed, waited, frowned with distaste, and hung up. "I didn't think that would work—and I'm certainly not going to try my personal. Let's step outside."

THEY FOLLOWED HER OUT INTO A NARROW, UNCROWDED HALL-way, through a door whose outside read AUTHORIZED PERSON-NEL ONLY, down a flight of stairs, out another door labeled FIRE EXIT, and emerged onto one of the exhibit floors—that iceberg tip that the public tends to equate with the museum itself. They passed couples and families and grade school classes peering into the oldest dioramas of Asian habitat groups, soon to be phased out, and the newest holohalls, narrow corridors lined with panels that acted like windows into far larger and more exotic spaces than they actually occupied. Pilar took a curious comfort in the presence of so many other people who paid them no heed at all.

At the far end of the holorama hall was a door into a public corridor with several paycoms on the wall. Maybelle went to one of them and dialed a number while carefully shielding the keypad with her hand. "Dan Felder, please," she said a few seconds later. Pilar had to lean quite close to hear her. A pause, then, "Dan, it's me. About those specimens I sent you . . . I'd like them back for a while. I need to show them to somebody."

A much longer pause, during which Maybelle's face grew slack and its color, which wasn't much to begin with, drained from it. "I see," she said finally. "Well, we'll do what we can. You be careful, now. I mean *really* careful."

She hung up and turned back to Lester and Pilar. "They've vanished," she said. "So we have no proof to make ourselves credible, we're all in personal danger, and now they're onto Dan, too. I don't know just how pervasive their eyes and ears are, but we can't keep talking by a phone that's just been talking to Dan." She chewed her lower lip for a while, then said, "But we have to keep talking. If what's happening is anything like I've guessed, *everybody* may be in danger, and we may be the only ones who suspect—or at least an important piece of the puzzle." She pondered a while longer, then said, "Follow me."

She led them quickly back out of the public areas and into the labyrinth of labs and offices behind the scenes. They wound up in another cluttered little office in the geology department. "I hate to ask the favor, Milt," she said to the bearded young man peering intently at his screen, "but I'm having some trouble with my com connections and I have some things I really need to check. Could I use yours for a few minutes?"

"No problem." Milt stood up and started toward the door. "Just give me a holler when you're through. Do you want the door closed?"

"That would be grand."

With an unconvincing approximation of privacy briefly in

hand, Maybelle sat down. Like Pilar in her apartment, she opted for the keyboard, but her wiry fingers danced more deftly over the keys. A home page materialized on the monitor with the cryptic title "ConCatenation Π." Pilar frowned and started to ask a question, but Maybelle held a finger up to her lips in a "Shh!" signal, then pointed at the screen.

She scrolled as if searching the display for something, then highlighted a group of words that seemed to indicate, if Pilar was reading it rightly, that ConCatenation Π was some sort of science fiction convention. Pilar had never heard of such a thing. Maybelle glanced up at Pilar's and Lester's faces as if to confirm that they had got the message, then went back to the screen. She highlighted the website address, then typed over it: "Let's meet there." One more check, then she highlighted the time and place—this weekend, in a hotel here in Manhattan. "10 AM tomorrow," she typed in the address box. "OK?"

She looked up. Pilar and Lester nodded, but Pilar was full of questions she didn't dare ask. Should she try to go home tonight, or was that too dangerous? Would it be safer to spend the night in the city? Could she find a place to stay that she could afford?

And should they stick together, or separate until their planned meeting?

In the end she *had* to ask, and they had to plan. They did it all using Maybelle's trick of writing messages in the address block on the website screen and deleting them when they'd been read. There was no assurance that the trick would work; they knew so little about how thoroughly or by what means they were being monitored.

The upshot was that they would all go to the convention hotel now and meet tonight, but they would go separately and take separate rooms. The website indicated that rooms were still available, so they shouldn't have to risk trying to reserve from here.

*　　　*　　　*

PILAR AGAIN FELT VERY ALONE AND VULNERABLE AS SHE MADE her way across town and down, taking buses because they seemed somehow more public and therefore perhaps a bit safer than the subway. As she traveled, without the distraction of conversation, she had time to worry about something else, and to chide herself for not having worried about it long before.

What, if anything, had happened to Rosa?

She tried to call, from a lobby paycom, as soon as she'd settled into the hotel. The call went through to Puerto Rico, all right, but the only answer came from Rosa's machine. Pilar talked fast to it, fearing she might be interrupted at any time. "Just tell me you're all right," she said. "Call me at this number . . ." She gave the hotel number, but not the room, and added, "I'll explain later. Try e-mail, too; I don't know what will be the best way to reach me. Oh . . . and . . ." She hesitated almost too long, then added, on a hunch, "How's El Gran Lagartijo?"

 I thought this would be one of the best places we could talk," said Maybelle that night. She was startlingly dressed in a flamboyant old-time pirate getup with an antique slide rule stuck through her scarlet sash like a dagger. "Here, we'll fit right in. Anybody spying will have trouble picking out our conversation from a dozen like it."

Two hours earlier Pilar would have doubted that there could be such a place, but she was beginning to believe. The strangest things, it seemed, came out after dark at a science fiction convention, and most of them seemed to view it all as quite ordinary. She still had to make an effort not to stare at the throngs milling around them: men and women of all shapes and ages, but with a heavy emphasis on . . . well, geezers. These things used to be much commoner, according to Maybelle, but the line between what used to be far-out science fiction and what had become everyday life had faded so much that few still saw SF as a separate entity. Most of those who did, and kept these "cons" alive, were folks who had been doing it for a long time. Their garb ranged from business suits to chain-mail bikinis and utterly natural-looking horns, their talk from proposals for radical political systems to speculations on what was behind the asp explosion to how to rescue somebody from an unbreachable prison with a chlorine atmosphere. Yes, maybe here her group *could* talk about what they needed to talk about and not attract undue attention.

Making no visible attempt to conceal her words, Maybelle

said, "After all, even though our most urgent goal is to protect ourselves against the aliens—"

"If they *are* aliens," Pilar cautioned.

"—anybody hearing us talk about that here will assume we're brainstorming a story or playing a game. We may even find somebody who can help us without suspecting they're doing any more than that. So let's get right down to it.

"As I see it, there are three things we have to try to do, all of which sound pretty hopeless at first glance. Protecting ourselves comes first. We also need to find some more bugs, both to try to figure out what they're doing and how they do it, and so we'll have something to show the authorities. Finally, we need to learn more about what happened with that shuttle. Now, anybody have any bright ideas about any of those?"

All three of them were silent for quite a while. Then Pilar said carefully, "Well, the one hope I see is that I don't believe they're really omniscient. They know enough about humans in general and me in particular to give me quite a scare, but not enough to realize that threats are no way to make us give up the search. That if anything, that will make us more determined than ever to find out what they're doing."

"Is that the idea you mentioned before?" Maybelle asked.

"Well, no. I don't want to say any more about that until I check a couple of things. For now, can we do anything with the idea that they can't *really* be omniscient?"

Maybelle nodded. "It's flimsy, but it's a start. I agree with you, Pilar. Even though I was shooting my mouth off about how quickly they could learn everything about a planet, it stands to reason that any *real* system will have limitations. One of the most useful things we can do will be to learn what they are. I think you've hit on at least an approximation of one."

"And I think," said Lester, "I've suggested another. Even if they're gathering as much information as you think, Maybelle, I still think they're going to hit bottlenecks when they try to get it all back where they can work on it." He frowned. "But I'll have to admit they seem so *close* to omniscient that they scare the pants off me."

"Me, too," said Maybelle. "Unfortunately, I think the only ways we might learn about their limits are to learn exactly how they work, or to push those limits. And we could get into really serious trouble doing that. If anything happens to any of us— and it could—I hope the other two will keep doing whatever they can. Including you, Lester, trying to figure out just what they're doing. Meanwhile, how do we protect ourselves? One thing is what we're doing, I think, though it's just a guided guess. Avoid getting into situations where they can do things to us without other people noticing—which means staying out in the open, out in public, whenever we can."

Pilar nodded, for once feeling actively grateful for Big Brother's eyes, the widely distributed crime-eyes. She felt a little uncomfortable about the passersby who occasionally paused on the periphery of their group, listened awhile, and then moved on; but she tried to follow Maybelle's lead in acting as if it didn't matter. "I think you've got that right. That creep who came to my apartment said the group he represented was doing things that they wanted to do without our knowledge, and that's why he wanted us to stop snooping. I think it's also why he fled when I blew my horn and got the neighbors and police in—though I'd sure love to know how he managed to make the evidence disappear as soon as he was gone. If he was telling the truth about even that much, I think they'll keep looking for ways to get rid of us as long as they can do it secretly, but they'll avoid anything that's likely to attract attention."

She paused and pursed her lips. "Of course, he also said whatever they were doing was no threat to us or anybody else as long as we didn't try to interfere. And we know we don't dare believe that. Don't we?"

"We sure do," Maybelle and Lester said as one. Maybelle

added, "Suppose they *are* aliens learning all they can about Earth and us. Even if they're not interested in conquest or something equally unpleasant, who might they sell the information to? And what might *they* do with it? No, we don't want that sort of thing going on, any more than you want a peeping Tom at your window every night."

Things kept spilling out of Pilar's memory, things that she'd been too preoccupied to fully grasp at the time. "He also said," she told Maybelle, "that you were closer to the truth than even you thought. He said in so many words that there *are* a lot of bugs, and they are gathering information. Have you managed to establish anything more about that?"

"Yes and no." Maybelle drew her slide rule with a flourish, clasped it between her teeth, and stared thoughtfully into space for several seconds as Pilar marvelled yet again that people of Maybelle's generation had actually calculated with such things. Then she stuck it back into her sash and spoke again. "I did manage to get some feelers out before my saboteurs struck. I even had a couple of responses, but not the concrete kinds I'd hoped for. There were a couple of reports of bug experiences something like yours, from widely scattered parts of the world. But nobody sent me any specimens, which was what I really wanted. There are still people out there who know I want them—or at least I *hope* there are—and a couple have even promised to send me some. But with the surveillance we're now under, I don't know how likely it is that any of them will actually reach me."

"How are they supposed to come?" Lester asked.

"I suggested different channels to different people, but I think it's best I not talk about the details, even here. And getting them here is only half the battle. Our first specimens lasted long enough for some study, then disappeared. We haven't *watched* any disappear, so we don't know how it happens. But the traces Pilar's visitor must have left disappeared almost immediately. I'd guess that the disappearing act is nanotechnological, too, and that bugs sent out before they knew any humans were onto them didn't have the self-destruct preprogrammed in, but more recent ones do.

"Let's hope somebody can send us an early one. Because if they do, if we can get even one sample that will hold together long enough to show anybody, that's exactly what we're going to do with it."

"But do we dare wait for that?" Pilar asked, feeling frustrated. "What if the shuttle incident *did* involve aliens, and the bugs are a huge network of spies for them? Don't we need to get everybody possible thinking about whether there's a connection?"

"She's right," Lester said. "If that's how it is, they may be able to do a lot of damage before anybody puts two and two together and starts to do anything about it. Way I see it, we know a little bit—admittedly a *very* little bit—about the bugs, and next to nothing about whatever happened in space. NASA or the Air Force or whoever's in charge may know more than they're telling us about that, and nothing at all about the bugs. So it's like we have two, and they have two, and we're never going to get four until we bring all that *anybody* knows together."

"In principle," said Maybelle, "I couldn't agree more. But we have *so* little to show . . . we're going to sound like a bunch of saucer nuts if we go to anybody with the story we have so far."

"I agree," said Lester, "but I think we have to do it anyway."

"So do I," said Pilar, though she dreaded the prospect. "And we do have a *little* to back us up. The hospital will have records from Lester's ER visit, and your grandson can give a report on what he found—"

"Before it disappeared." Maybelle sighed. "Yes, dear friends, I suppose you're right. We do have to do our part to make sure that the folks who know something about the space incident also know about the bugs, even though they're not likely to believe it and may not appreciate our getting too inquisitive about the shuttle. But who, precisely, do we go to?"

"You mentioned having a lot of contacts," Lester reminded her.

"True," said Maybelle, "but mainly in the sciences. Politicians and soldiers aren't my long suit—and neither is space science, despite my longstanding casual interest in the stuff. To put it bluntly, I don't really know anybody in a suitable position who I can comfortably go to about this."

"So we'll have to go to somebody none of us knows," said Pilar. "There's a National Guard base up near where I live, and I know they do some aerial operations. Maybe somebody there will know something about it, or be able to put us in touch with somebody who does."

"For lack of something better," Maybelle said with a frown, "I guess that's as good a place to start as any. I suppose we should all go—" She broke off abruptly, her frown changing to a scowl directed at a tall, almost spidery young man in some sort of alien costume who had been standing next to Lester for at least a full minute, listening intently. "Can I help you, young man?"

"I didn't mean to intrude," he said in a surprisingly deep voice, but without stepping away. "I just couldn't help overhearing your references to bugs."

PILAR SHUDDERED INVOLUNTARILY, SUDDENLY WARY. WAS THIS somebody who had had a bug encounter himself, and might therefore be exactly what they'd been hoping for? Or was he one of *them*, the people or beings behind the bugs, and therefore a clear and present danger?

"Oh," Maybelle said after several seconds of silence. "Are you an entomologist, too?"

"No," the young man said. "But I'm fascinated by the idea of tiny information-gathering devices."

"Really," said Maybelle. "Have you had . . . ah . . . personal experience with them?"

He grinned. "You're really into this, aren't you? OK, sure I have."

"Which side were you on? User or usee?"

"Why, user, of course. My spies are everywhere." He winked. "I can't wait to read your story when it's finished."

"So," Lester asked carefully, "what are you trying to learn?"

"Anything and everything, my man." He clapped Lester jovially on the shoulder and Pilar had to suppress an urge to step away from him. "Aren't you?" His voice turned conspiratorial. "Just *be careful*."

"Look," Maybelle interrupted, with surprising sternness, "if you're really using these things, then why are you talking to us? And if you're not, but have had experiences with them, like us, can you prove it? Do you have, say, a specimen in your pocket?"

For the first time the young man's façade cracked and he backed away, almost imperceptibly. "Say, don't you think you people are a little *too much* into this game? I'm sorry I intruded; no need to get huffy. I'll go quietly." Just as quickly, his playacting bravado returned. "Just remember," he repeated as he sidled away, "*be careful*."

"WHAT JUST HAPPENED HERE?" PILAR ASKED WHEN SHE JUDGED he was out of earshot. "Was he or wasn't he?"

"At one of these things," said Maybelle, "it can be hard to tell. Let's just say that I no longer feel as safe here as I did a few minutes ago. I think I've had enough of this party. I'm going to my room, and suggest you do the same. Let's meet for breakfast"—she flashed seven fingers and hoped they caught the signal—"and head on out to do what Pilar said. Together."

They dispersed to their rooms soon after that. Pilar found the message light blinking on her comcenter, and dialed voicemail to see what it was. "I'm fine," her sister Rosa's voice said, sounding worried. "Are you? But the iguana . . . he's gone, Pilar. Something happened, something so strange I can barely talk about it. I found him lying in his cage, decapitated. But there was no blood. His head was just gone, and his neck had regular skin all the way over it, like the way an amputee's stump heals over." A long pause, and a hint of snuffling. "How could that happen, Pilar? And what made you ask about him? Is something going on that you—"

Her voice cut off abruptly, replaced by static that went on until Pilar hung up.

Chapter 8

 The trip up the river the next morning was as easy as the night's sleep had been difficult. Their destination was off the rail line, but Maybelle had a car; and though the thought of getting into it reminded Pilar of dozens of movie scenes of booby-trapped cars blowing up, it gave them no trouble at all. Once underway, in fact, and with a little effort not to think about the possibility that it too was bugged, it gave a comforting sense of being isolated and armored against the rest of the world. Pilar sat in the back seat and watched the broad Hudson go by at her left, the ruddy sunlight gleaming on the sculpted cliffs of the Palisades on the far side, and almost managed to forget why they were doing this.

Until they got to Camp Smith, nestled among suddenly rugged hills at the north end of the Tappan Zee. Then things got more difficult, for a while, though for more mundane reasons.

At the gate of the Guard base was a checkpoint manned by a trim, close-cropped youth with an MP armband. "Good morning," he said. "Visiting?"

"Yes," said Maybelle. "We—"

The MP, brandishing an electronic clipboard and stylus, didn't wait for her to finish. "Name of party expecting you?"

"No one's expecting us," said Maybelle.

The MP looked taken aback. "You don't have an appointment?"

"No. Look, what we need to talk about is a little hard to describe, so I didn't try to make one. But we need to talk to whoever's in charge about some odd things that have been happening. They just might be a threat to national security."

The MP rolled his eyes, just enough to notice. "I see. I'm afraid, ma'am, I'll need something a bit more specific."

"They *may* have something to do with the shuttle explosion," Lester said from across the front seat. "And we're all scientifically trained observers. All we ask is five minutes—"

The MP frowned. "Just a moment." He stepped into his glass and metal booth and they saw, but couldn't hear, him talking and poking a touchscreen. Then he hung up and handed Maybelle a small chip. "Stick this in your onboard. When you get where it takes you, ask for Staff Sergeant Calvin."

SERGEANT CALVIN WAS A CHOCOLATE-BROWN GENTLEMAN OF thirty-five or so, with a shiny bald pate and gold-rimmed glasses, who wore his uniform and stripes with obvious pride. Seated behind a gray steel desk when they arrived, he stood up and walked across the room to meet them, introducing himself and shaking each of their hands. Simultaneously he looked them up and down, and Pilar had the feeling that the only reason he had stood up to greet them was to get the best possible look at these curious intruders.

Introductions completed, he gestured them to three straight-backed visitors' chairs and resumed his own comfortable seat behind his desk. "So," he said with a genial smile, "you think you know something about the asp explosion?"

"Not exactly," said Maybelle. "The fact is, as you well know, we know next to nothing about the asp explosion. But, like everybody else, we're mighty curious. And we've been seeing some puzzling phenomena of our own. We wondered if there might be a connection. But since we only know about what *we've* experienced, we thought we should talk to somebody who might know more about . . . the other thing."

"I see. Well, ma'am, I'm pretty low on the totem pole, so I don't know nearly as much as you might think. But if you have something important to say, I'll be happy to pass it up the chain. I should warn you, though, my schedule's quite full today."

"We'll try to be brief," Maybelle assured him. "And I should warn you that what we're going to tell you is likely to sound pretty odd. So maybe I should start by telling you a little about us, so you don't think we're just a bunch of kooks. Lester, here, is an electrical engineer who's been with several prominent firms, including IBM. Pilar is an ASCP-certified medical technologist at Hudson Hospital. I've been an entomologist with major museums for longer than I care to admit, and at the American Museum in New York for the last twenty years. We're all scientifically trained and have good reputations in our fields. We know how to observe critically and analyze data."

Were Calvin's eyes starting to glaze over? "So just what have you observed?" he asked, meticulously polite.

"At first we thought they were new kinds of insects," said Maybelle. "Lester had the first experience with one; it stung him and produced some weird psychedelic effects. He wound up in Pilar's hospital, but brought the bug with him. It released some others, and several other people had similar experiences, including Pilar. They brought a couple of the bugs in to me, to see if I could identify them, and I knew right away that whatever they were, they weren't bugs. I suspected they were nanotechnological information-gathering devices—spy robots, if you will.

"So I showed them to my grandson, who's a nanotechnologist. He confirmed their essential nature and said they appeared to be way beyond state of the art."

"I see. Could you . . . ah . . . *show* me one of these devices?"

Pilar winced. She kept fighting the urge to put in her own two cents worth, not because she found Calvin intimidating but because she thought he might be more inclined to listen to someone who looked older and wiser, and Maybelle seemed to be doing fine. But now she just said, "I'm afraid not, at least right now. The ones we had . . . disappeared."

A raised eyebrow. "Disappeared?"

"Yes. We don't know how, but that may well be part of the advanced nanotechnology. Anyway, I'm hoping to get more specimens, but I can't be sure when, or even if."

"What about Mount Taurus?" Pilar asked suddenly. "There were lots of them up there. Maybe we could go back and catch more—"

"No!" Lester blurted out in an alarmed tone. "It hurt too much the other times, and I think they know me by now. They might kill me if I go back."

"Or maybe that's disappeared, too," Calvin said reasonably.

"Maybe," Maybelle conceded. "Or maybe not. It's worth a try, but I do think we would be in inordinate danger if we went again. Maybe you could send a couple of men up there with proper equipment. . . ."

"Ms. Terwilliger—" Calvin began with exaggerated patience.

"*Dr.* Terwilliger," she corrected.

"*Dr.* Terwilliger," Calvin continued smoothly, "you have to understand that everyone here is very busy. I can't go sending men and material out to chase will-o'-the-wisps on mountaintops without a very good reason. A better reason than you've given me so far, I'm afraid. Now, tell me, please . . . assuming that these critters exist, just why should the National Guard be interested in them?"

"Because they may be a threat to national security, of course," said Maybelle. "Did I mention that these things make copies of themselves? Every copy is a new spy. Whoever is using them has the potential to gather huge amounts of information and use it against us. That may mean the whole country, maybe even the whole world. We can't afford to let that happen."

"No, I suppose we can't." Calvin drummed his fingers on his desktop for a few seconds. Then he said, "And just what connection do you think this may have with the shuttle accident?"

"Was it really an accident?" Maybelle asked. "Maybe it was, but the news media have raised far more questions than they've answered. As I said, we know next to nothing about the asp accident . . . or whatever it was. But I do know that my nano-technologist grandson tells me that these things are way beyond any human technology he's seen. So when we heard about the explosion, we wondered if the spy bugs might be *non*-human technology—made by the same beings who blew up the shuttle."

"What could be more logical?" Calvin asked. "Tell me, Dr. Terwilliger, what is your grandson's name?"

"Daniel Felder."

Calvin's fingers played over his comp and he frowned slightly. "Can you tell me something about him?"

"Sure. Born 1976, Ph.D. Stanford 2002, associate professor . . ." She rattled off a little more till Calvin waved her off.

"OK," Calvin said. "Do you mind if I give him a call?"

"Not at all."

He did. Fortuitously, he got Dan right away, identified himself, and told Dan that his grandmother and two friends were in his office with a rather odd story. He gave him a quick summary, listened awhile, then said, "I see. Well, thanks anyway. Please do give me a call if anything turns up."

He hung up and turned back to his visitors. "Well, for what it's worth, he agrees with you—but he doesn't have any proof, either. And in the absence of that, Dr. Terwilliger and Mr. Ordway and Ms. Ramirez, I'm afraid there's nothing I can do." He stood up, walked to the door, and opened it for them. "Thank you very much for coming, and I assure you I'll keep my ears open for anything else on this. I'll certainly pass your report on to my superiors. And if you can bring me a nanobug, then we can talk some more."

Pilar could hold back no longer. "We can't bring you a bug right now," she said urgently, "but Dr. Terwilliger and I can both show you computers that have been seriously messed with. We won't even ask you to send anybody to look at them; we can bring them—"

Calvin interrupted with an audible sigh. "Lots of people have computer problems, Ms. Ramirez," he said, and she bristled at his patronizing tone because it simply wasn't true anymore. She'd heard stories about how things were in the old days, but that was a long time ago. Now computers were reliable, and when they acted as weird as these did, there had to be a weird reason for it. But before she could compose a suitable retort, Calvin went on smoothly, "I'll tell you what. I can let each of you fill out an affidavit describing what you think you've observed, and I'll see that it gets all the attention it deserves." *Which*, Pilar thought, *probably means none at all.* "Fair enough?"

She hesitated, partly because it seemed likely to be a waste of time but partly because of the small chance it wouldn't be. Did she really want to go on written record with a story that sounded this crazy?

But it really wasn't a hard choice. "I'll do it," she said after only a moment's hesitation, and Maybelle and Lester promptly followed her lead.

Chapter 9

He was patronizing us," Pilar sniffed as they got back into Maybelle's car. Being back in familiar surroundings, with no one but friends, was a comfort of sorts, but she knew it was a hollow one.

"Of course," said Maybelle. "We expected no less." She started the engine and pulled out into the long driveway. "Actually, it may not have been as bad as I expected. He did call Dan. He could easily have had us turned away at the gate." She frowned as she turned onto the hilly, winding road back toward Peekskill. "I wonder why he didn't."

"Could it be," Lester mused, "that somebody actually told him to listen for stories like ours?"

"He didn't seem *that* interested," said Maybelle. "I don't expect him to actually do anything unless we come back with the hard evidence he wants. Or claims to want."

"We do have some evidence," Pilar said as they drove down the last hill, Peekskill looming, in its modest way, across the bay. "Even if he doesn't look at the computers, and even if we don't get any more bug specimens. The best things we have are the ones we least want to talk about, or even think about. But I think we're going to have to face them."

Maybelle didn't say anything until she had negotiated the Annsville Circle, a kind of challenge she seldom had to deal with in the big city. Then she said, "And what are those, Pilar?"

"Well, we've already talked about what you and Dan have seen. Even if you can't produce the physical evidence anymore, sworn statements from people with your credentials ought to count for something, with somebody."

"Well, maybe."

"We've also talked about trying to get statements from the other people who were in the ER when Lester was. Again, hearsay—though some of those folks may be carrying physical evidence, too—and probably not easy to get. But all three of us may be carrying physical evidence, too. And we *know* we can get hold of us. The question is, are we willing to do what it takes?"

"I'm not sure I follow you," Lester said as Pilar directed Maybelle through the streets with silent hand gestures.

"I think you do," said Pilar, "but don't want to face it. I don't blame you; I don't either. But I'll go first. In fact, I've already started." She closed her eyes for several seconds as the car, now back on the grid, paused to wait its turn at an intersection. "I drew a sample of my own blood yesterday morning and stuck it in my refrigerator. I hope it's still there and hasn't changed too much. At least you and I, Lester, quite likely have things in us that don't belong there, injected by our visitors. I think it's high time we started finding out what they are.

"Furthermore, by your own admission, your mind has been tampered with. If you'll let a psychiatrist take a look at *how*, he might find patterns that would give a hint of what happened." Lester looked a little pale but said nothing. Pilar went on, "And even if Calvin isn't interested, Maybelle, you have a whole room full of computer equipment that's been raided. Maybe we can get somebody else to take a look at what's happened to it. Somebody who knows your hardware and software might be able to get some idea of how it was done."

"Well, maybe," Maybelle said again. "But there's so much in there, and so many hackers with so many tricks up their sleeves—"

"Of course," said Pilar. "But it can't hurt to look, can it?"

Maybelle was silent quite a while before she said, "I wish I knew."

"This isn't going to be easy for me, either," said Pilar. "But we've got to do what we can. I suggest you start by swinging by my house just long enough for me to pick up that blood sample, then drop me and Lester off at the hospital—Er, no. You go on home and work on your thread and I'll take us to the hospital in my car—me for the lab, and Lester for the psych clinic."

"If I must," said Lester, staring stiffly straight ahead. "Uh . . . they got you, too, Pilar. Are you going to the clinic too?"

"If I must. But I have other things to do first."

NOT *QUITE* FIRST, ACTUALLY. PILAR UNDERSTOOD HOW DIFFI-cult this must be for Lester, and she wanted to make it as easy for him as possible. Maybelle dropped them both off together in front of the grandiose Greek Deco entry to the hospital, and Pilar personally took Lester up to the psych clinic on the third floor. She introduced him to Jenny, her favorite receptionist, watched her make a good start on putting him at ease, and headed down to the lab.

As a matter of form, she first sought out Eddie, the weekend supervisor. She said she was feeling better and asked if they could use her for the rest of the day shift.

Eddie assured her they could, and she settled down to acting as normal as possible. As she'd guessed and hoped, he put her in hematology, the easiest place to do what she'd actually come for. The workload was pretty frenetic for much of the morning, but slowed down a bit before lunch. With the weekend staff reduced even below the usual minimal levels, it wasn't too hard to find a chance to surreptitiously transfer some of her own sample to a slide and slip it under an optical microscope.

The view was hardly as dramatic as she'd feared. At first

glance, the red and white cells and their environment looked perfectly ordinary. But as she kept looking . . .

She remembered a time back home when she'd strolled the beach at Luquillo at sunset, ever so slowly, watching the gentle surf and the sand it stirred up washing over her feet. At first it seemed blank and featureless: just sand and salty foam. But as her mind relaxed and slipped into a meditative state, she began seeing details that hadn't registered at all at first glance. Tiny shells, for instance—multitudes of tiny shells, of several different shapes . . .

Now she had the same feeling as she gazed through the lab microscope—except that on the beach it had been soothing, and here it was anything but. It was nice to know that her red and white cells and platelets looked normal; but after a while, as she moved the slide around on the stage, she thought she saw something else. Not many somethings; just an isolated dot here and there, as much smaller than platelets as platelets were smaller than red cells. That put them at this scope's limit of detection, though she did have the feeling they looked more sharp-edged and angular than any cells she knew. She was pretty sure they were real and didn't belong there, but this equipment offered no hope of showing any structure they might have.

Or shedding any light on the most important questions: what were they, how did they get there, and what would they do?

Which just might be matters of life and death—or worse.

Pilar felt sweat break out on her forehead. She had to know more about those dots, but the only equipment here with any hope of resolving any detail in them was the electron microscope over in virology. And virology was one area Pilar *never* worked in. She had no idea how to use that scope, and had no plausible excuse to go near it.

Her pulse had sped up; she could feel it throbbing in her temple. She'd have to figure out a way to get a sample to somebody who *could* look at it the way it needed to be looked at, and without drawing unwanted attention to herself.

Part of her mind started thinking about how she might approach somebody in virology. Pam, maybe, or Eldred . . .

Or if not here, maybe Maybelle's grandson Dan. Or Sergeant Calvin. Or both. Probably she should try to get samples into several *different* sets of hands.

And hope that whatever she was seeing was still there when they looked.

That was one thing she could check, at least qualitatively, right now. At the first chance she got, she drew a fresh sample of her blood and took it straight to the microscope. She found herself holding her breath as she approached the eyepiece to see how the numbers and sizes of mystery dots in a fresh sample compared with the one refrigerated hours earlier.

PILAR MET LESTER WHEN THE SHIFT ENDED AT FOUR AND THEY sat in her car in the parking lot behind the lab. "So," she asked, "how did it go?"

"Well, the doctor wasn't as scary as I'd feared, but she wasn't very helpful, either. I told her my main symptom was spotty memory loss, since I thought that was a less crazy-sounding place to start than the Big Bug of Boscobel. But it wasn't long before she asked if the onset was gradual or sudden, and whether I could remember any unusual recent events that might have upset me. So then I had to tell her about the bug, and my visit to the ER. She frowned and made some notes about that, and then told me that the bug attack was probably a hallucination or delusion. She gave me some mumbo-jumbo about possible physiological causes, and gave me a prescription to try." Now Lester frowned and looked with an oddly pleading expression at Pilar. "Pilar, you know that what happened in the ER was no hallucination, don't you?"

"Of course. But then, the doctor wasn't there."

"But she could check the records. I don't know enough about psychiatry to tell whether what she said made sense or not. But remembering what you said, I couldn't help the feeling she was more interested in getting rid of me than in figuring out what really happened. That would be unethical, wouldn't it?"

Pilar pondered awhile before answering, while redwings and a yellowthroat chattered in the little remnant wetland beyond the edge of the parking lot. "I think so," she said finally. "But you'd have to be careful with such accusations—and I'd have to be even more so. If she *is* trying to tar you with a preselected brush, she could easily claim they were symptoms of paranoia. And she could probably convince plenty of other people, including her colleagues."

"I told her I had witnesses," he said sullenly. "She said she'd be glad to consider their testimony if I brought them in, but she didn't seem the least bit interested in having me actually do it."

"We may do it anyway," said Pilar. "But except for Maybelle and me, it won't be easy, and it's not a step I can take lightly. I have to work here, you know." She stared at the marshlet a little longer, then said, "I can't think of anything we can do about it till Monday morning, in any case. So until then, I guess we just have to hang on."

"I was hoping for a CAT scan or something," Lester muttered. "Something to look for any structural damage in my wetware. I know modern psychiatry's philosophy is to pop a pill whenever possible, and I know it often works. But this isn't one of those cases. I know what she should be looking for. Why is she wasting time?" He shook his head. "How about you, Pilar? Did you have any better luck with your blood sample?"

"Well, yes and no. I do think I saw some unusual things, but they were too tiny to see any details—"

"Which fits right in with Maybelle's theory."

"Yes, and that scares me silly. I need to figure out a way to get somebody to look at them with an electron microscope, which may not be quite as forlorn a hope as it sounds like. I took a fresh sample several hours after the first and couldn't see any change. So whatever's in there may still be there when I take samples to other people. I think I'll hold off on Calvin, though, until I'm sure I'm seeing something real.

"But if I am, it makes me wonder. If they haven't changed, am I seeing the remains of something that's dead and disintegrated? Or something dormant and waiting to wake up?"

PILAR PASSED SUNDAY AT HOME IN A STATE OF QUIET SUSPENSE. Nothing really happened to her—with one possible exception—but at the back of her mind lurked the constant feeling that it might at any time.

The one maybe-exception wasn't entirely a surprise. She spent much of the day mulling over what she knew she had to do Monday morning, and trying to think of something to do today. It would have been nice to have somebody in virology look at her blood right away. But such an unusual request would surely arouse suspicion. And if whoever did it found something unusual, could they be trusted to keep it to themselves?

So she didn't do that. But how about taking a sample to Maybelle, to pass on to Dan? The only problem there was that Maybelle was not likely to be at the museum today, and Pilar didn't know where she lived.

That, she realized now, would have to change. If the three of them were all in this together, as deeply as they thought, they needed to know how to contact each other whenever necessary.

Pilar might have time to visit Maybelle today, if she could locate her. Expecting nothing, she tried calling Maybelle's office at the museum. To her surprise, she got through—but only to a voicemail recording that said Maybelle was not available.

Did "they" let Pilar call Maybelle's numbers if and only if Maybelle was not at them?

After some deliberation, she called up the com directory and found Maybelle's home address—on the Upper West Side, not far from the museum—and phone number. She thought about just going, but she had no reason to assume Maybelle would be at home just because she wasn't at work. Dared she hope that she could call to ask?

She could hope, but she couldn't call. When she tried, not only did she get no answer, but she got a definite, painful shock from the handset—something that had never happened before. She sat glaring at the phone for a while, and then, with some apprehension, tried calling the local movie theater for schedule information.

No problem.

But when she went down the hall to try Mrs. Frederick's phone, that drew a blank—no shock, but no ring or busy signal, either. Just silence.

So Pilar went back to her apartment, picturing Mrs. Frederick shaking her head behind her as she left, and spent the rest of the day and night waiting and feeling frustrated.

DAYLIGHT ONCE AGAIN BROUGHT HOPE, THOUGH MEAGER. SHE was scheduled to work, so it wouldn't seem too odd if she slipped off to the records office for a few minutes. She wasn't eager to do that under any circumstances, and Monday morning was probably the worst possible time to bug bureaucrats. But she didn't think she could wait.

Lester, on the other hand, had to. They wanted to go to the office together, but Pilar couldn't predict exactly when she'd have a lull, and she got another shock when she tried to call Lester. So she'd slipped a note under the front door of his house and hoped it would stay readable long enough for him to find it.

That much, at least, worked. When she found a chance for a "coffee break," she found Lester reading old magazines in the lobby. And without further ado they were off to the office.

"YOU WANT *WHAT*?"

Madeleine, the chief dragon guarding Hospital Records, was both personally and professionally proper and prim. Pilar was used to that; normally she found the diminutive redhead's tight lips and face that seemed constantly on the brink of a frown harmlessly amusing. Today they seemed more threatening, her expression teetering more seriously on the brink of that metaphorical precipice and her eyes boring into Pilar's as if she couldn't believe what she'd just heard.

"I said," Pilar repeated very patiently, "that we're trying to understand exactly what happened when Mr. Ordway here was in the ER last Monday evening. We all know that some . . . ah, *unusual* things happened that night and it's very important to us to find out exactly what they were. So we'd like to talk to as many as possible of the other patients who were there—"

Madeleine's frown fell very decisively over the edge. "Patients?" A carefully timed pause, and then her face lit up with a very professional Smile of Sudden Enlightenment. "Oh, you mean *customers*. Well, I suppose I can understand, sort of, how you might find that interesting—though I *really* don't know what you mean by 'unusual events.' But I'm afraid I must remind you that our customers' relationship to the hospital is entirely confidential, and we simply can't give out any personal information about them."

"Of course not," said Pilar. "Patient . . . er, *customer* confidentiality is sacred. But we're not asking you to give us their names, addresses, or phone numbers. You already have all that information, and I wouldn't dream of asking you to share it. All we're asking is that you pass a brief message from us on to them. Do it as e-mail and it might take you as much as twenty seconds. Whether and how they reply is entirely up to them, and they can send the replies through the hospital net, so we still won't know where they're coming from unless they choose to include that in text. If nobody answers, nobody's any worse off than they already are. But if even one does, it just might help save lives— maybe even a lot of lives."

"Oh, puh-leeze!" Madeleine sniffed. "Don't go getting all melodramatic on me, *Ms*. Ramirez. I wasn't born yesterday. I don't know what you've got into your head about what happened in the ER that night, but as far as the hospital is concerned, it was business as usual. And business as usual says very plainly, the hospital does not get involved in games like this. We do not give out confidential information about pa— . . . er, customers . . . and we do not act as messenger boys to pass secret messages back and forth between anyone. Now, if that's all, I think we both have other work to do."

Pilar counted silently to ten, first in English, then in Spanish, then once more in English. "Look," she said, *ever* so reasonably, "I know the hospital is concerned about possible lawsuits. What I want to do might—"

"*Ms*. Ramirez," Madeleine interrupted haughtily. "May I speak to you privately for a moment?" She gestured toward an alcove and Pilar followed her there. "Does your Employee Pledge mean nothing to you?" Madeleine demanded in a raspy whisper. "Let me remind you—"

"You mean the loyalty oath?" Pilar interrupted. "Yes, that means a lot to me, but we won't go into that. I'm actually trying to help the hosp—"

"By blabbing about internal affairs in front of customers? We just don't do that, Ms. Ramirez. Period. Now let's go put an end to this, as professionally and courteously as possible." Without waiting for a reply she spun on her heel and strode briskly back out front, greeting Lester with a positively radiant (but professional) smile. "I'm really sorry we can't help you, Mr. Ordway, but you understand that procedures must be followed. Please let us know if there's anything else we can do for you."

"Oh, I will," said Lester, who had said hardly a word up to this point. "I won't bother you any more today, but let me leave you with one thought. In case you've forgotten, I'm one of those 'customers,' though if you don't mind I'd rather be thought of as a patient. Either way, I'm not one of the ones who's threatened to sue you—yet. But you've just made me reconsider that. Whether you're supposed to admit it or not, something strange did happen in your ER. I was held too long against my wishes, and came out with nothing to show for it. Personal property I had specifically asked to have returned was instead destroyed. Your so-called mental health clinic gives me pills to pop instead of listening to what I say and checking what I need to have checked. And you give me a pompous brush-off when I make a perfectly reasonable request for help in trying to get to the bottom of this. Oh, I think my lawyers will have fun with this. And when they show up at your boss's door, just remember that it was *you*, Madeleine, not Ms. Ramirez, who brought them there."

Chapter 10

Lester went home, and Pilar spent the rest of the day doing her job on autopilot, avoiding the records office, and stewing over the one more thing she could try at the hospital. It was a drastic step, one she couldn't take lightly. Techs do *not* question doctors. But Schneider was one of the good ones, she thought; he actually called her by name and spoke an unnecessary friendly word to her on occasion. Sometimes he even asked her opinion about something when he didn't have to, like when Lester had brought that first bug into the ER. Maybe he would understand.

In any case, what else could she do?

She checked a schedule and found he was working the ER again tonight. Once more chance worked in her favor—something that wasn't happening much lately—and the lab got quiet enough that she was able to slip out a little before the nominal end of her shift. She found him in the little cubbyhole that served as his office a few minutes before his shift began, struggling to catch up on paperless "paperwork."

She hesitated a moment outside his glass door, partly from concern about the personal risk she was taking, and partly because he looked so haggard and harried she hated to bother him. But she hesitated only a moment, because it had to be done. She rapped lightly, twice, and as soon as he looked up she opened the door just a crack. "Dr. Schneider? May I see you privately for a moment?"

He frowned. Probably this wasn't a good time—but would there ever be a good time? "I suppose," he said. "But just a moment. I'm swamped."

No first name, she noted as she slipped in and closed the door behind her. "It's about that patient a week ago," she said. "Mr. Ordway. The one with the bug."

Was it her imagination, or did his face turn pale? Certainly his lips pressed tightly together. "What about him?" he asked.

"We need to know what really happened that night. And we're not getting any cooperation from hospital records."

He shrugged. "What kind of cooperation would you expect? They're bound by patient confidentiality." He stared into space for a moment and added, more pointedly than she would have expected, "So am I. And so are you."

"But we can't ignore the fact that something strange and possibly dangerous happened. I know Mr. Ordway. There are . . . lingering effects. If he has them, others may too. If we all talk to each other—or at least some of us—maybe we can figure out what happened and what we can do about it."

"*I* haven't seen any lingering effects." Schneider put down his palmpad. "Look, Pilar. I'll grant you something strange happened in there. I have no idea what it was. But I haven't seen that it had any significant impact on the world, and I haven't seen it happen again. My professional opinion is that it was an isolated, inconsequential incident, and the sooner we put it behind us and move on, the better for everybody."

Would that be your professional opinion if you weren't hoping to retire quietly and soon? Pilar wondered. But all she asked aloud was, "Will we be able to do that? I've heard the rumors of lawsuits. Le—Mr. Ordway is even threatening us. He has—"

Schneider cut her off with the air of a cornered animal. "And you think putting all these people in touch with each other will help anybody? God help us if they put their *lawyers* together!"

"Dr. Schneider," Pilar said quietly, "this hasn't been easy for any of us. But I *know* there are aftereffects. I've seen things in my own blood that don't belong there, but they're too small to analyze optically. Somebody needs to look at them with an EM, and I was hoping you would—"

"I don't do lab work," he said curtly. "That's *your* job, remember?" She hadn't been going to ask him to do it, of course, but she didn't correct him. "Mine," he went on, "is to make medical decisions, and I've done that. I count on you to do your part in helping to implement them." He paused and she noticed a slight tremor in his face. "Look, Pilar," he said, his tone softer, "I've always liked working with you, and you know I've never been one to pull rank on you."

"That's true," she said. "And I've appreciated that, Dr. Schneider."

"But this time I'm going to have to ask you as emphatically as possible to stop rocking the boat. Without more evidence than we have—"

"But I *have* more evidence! I'm just asking you to look at it!"

"Without more evidence than we have," he pressed on as if he hadn't heard her, "it sounds . . . well, crazy. It can't help you, me, or the hospital." He paused for a long time, not meeting her eyes. Then, abruptly, he skewered her with his and said, "If you insist on pushing this, and I think you're endangering me, patients, or the hospital, I could easily make a case that your behavior and accusations are too irresponsible to trust you to continue in your job. And who do you think they would listen to: you or me?" He again averted his eyes, looking drained. "I wouldn't want to do that, but I will if I feel it's necessary. Do I make myself clear?"

Pilar stared unbelievingly at him. She'd never seen him like this, and even though she'd intellectually considered the possibility, she found the reality hard to grasp. "Perfectly," she said finally. "Thank you for your time, Dr. Schneider."

She turned to go, but she paused and looked back at him

before she opened the door. "I just hope you'll consider this. I remember that you were stung, too. You might want to take a look at your own blood."

Then she left.

Chapter 11

He *threatened* me!" Pilar half-wailed, still hardly able to believe it. "He said it was an isolated incident and we should forget about it and move on. And he said, almost in so many words, that he'd get me fired if I kept asking questions about it!" She sniffed. "And this is a doctor I *respect*!"

"Well," Lester said mildly as the bullet whizzed between the forbidding walls of the Sing Sing Historic Museum, "there are worse things than being fired. At least it would give you more time to work on this thing."

"While cutting me off from my best means to do it. I also have to eat."

"Sorry," said Lester, gently patting her hand. "I didn't mean to sound cold. I do sympathize, and I hope it doesn't come to that. But if it should, don't worry about starving. I won't let that happen." She looked at him, startled at the implied offer. She wasn't sure at first whether the startlement was pleasant or un, but on a moment's reflection leaned toward the former.

By now the railcar had emerged onto another open stretch of riverbank, with the cliffs of High Tor and Hook Mountain glistening in the sun across two miles of river. "I'm sorry Doc Schneider wasn't more sympathetic," Lester went on, "but at the same time I can sympathize with his position, at least a little. He's on borrowed time, isn't he? Well past normal retirement age?" Pilar nodded. "Well, I can't identify with *that* part from experience. I never made it that far. But if I had, I think I would have wanted my last years on the job to be nice and quiet. I'll bet he was counting on that. Now he's caught up in a whirl of things he doesn't understand, and potential legal problems. . . . It doesn't bode well for his tranquil future, and it could easily drag on and on."

"I suppose you're right." She studied Lester's face for several seconds and added, "I marvel at how you can look at his viewpoint even while *we're* caught up in all this."

"A trick I learned from some of the few managers I've really admired," said Lester. "But anybody can benefit from it." They were both silent a while longer, staring blankly out at the passing river. Then Lester changed the subject completely. "I did some thinking after we left the records office. All those records are stored electronically, with plenty of safeguards. Time was when I would have had no trouble hacking past those barriers, and I must confess I thought seriously about trying. Then I found I couldn't remember how."

"More holes?" Pilar asked gently. He nodded. Now she patted the back of his hand and said, "Maybe it doesn't matter anyway. I haven't even been able to get online lately. Have you?"

"No."

"I don't suppose your prescription has helped any? Not with getting online, but . . . you know."

"Of course not. I didn't have any delusions that it would— any more than I had the kind of delusions she thinks she's treating me for."

Another long silence, except for the whir of the car along the rail. Then, as the car plunged into the blackness of the Park Avenue tunnel, Pilar said, "Lester, do you suppose all this could actually be an isolated incident, like Dr. Schneider thinks?"

"Highly unlikely," he said. "If somebody were doing all this to just a handful of people, why us? We're just not that important."

"True. And there is the fact that they know about Rosa and

do nasty things to her. . . . But if it's not an isolated cluster of incidents, where are all the others?"

"We already talked about that," Lester reminded her. "In Maybelle's office."

"Yes, but that was . . . days ago." *It seems like weeks*, she thought. She watched the news scrolling across the display on the bulkhead in front of them, including a passing mention of STILL NO NEWS ON ASP EXPLOSION. "Even if we were the first, if things like this have been happening to other people, shouldn't some of them have surfaced by now?"

"Maybe some of them are trying, and meeting the same kinds of obstacles we are. And if the bugs are still spreading, maybe the newer models are less alien-looking. Which reminds me: I thought of one other slim lead we might try. The couple who brought me in to the ER could be useful as corroborating witnesses, if nothing else."

"Yes, but how would we contact them? A personal on the internet's the obvious way to try, but we've already established that we have no luck using that to reach anybody of interest."

"True," Lester granted, "but how about the old-fashioned way—a personal in the newspaper?"

"Might be worth a try. But how likely is it that they'll read the personals—or even the papers? These are *young* people."

"You're right, but for lack of something better to try . . . Hey, maybe we could also try that for the ER pa—"

He was cut off with a startled grunt, his body thrown against Pilar's, as the car swerved suddenly off onto a platform siding and stopped, with an abruptness she hadn't known it was capable of. In the ensuing hush, she said, "What happened?"

"I think it thinks we've arrived. But I know this isn't the stop we ordered, and it doesn't even look functional. Look, it's still black as the ace of spades out there."

Pilar felt a chill. There were lots of platsides along the rail line, especially in the city—little loops where passengers could wait for a pickup or be dropped off at a destination, the central Control computer coordinating all the cars on the line so that they could cruise fast and enter and leave the flow smoothly. But part of Control's job was making sure that they stopped at the *right* destination, and that all accelerations were kept to comfortable levels—and destination platforms were well lit and car doors opened when they arrived.

None of that had happened just now. Something was very wrong here.

For a long moment they sat in their tiny island of light and silence, letting the realization sink in. "Lester," Pilar barely whispered, "do you think *they've* hacked into Transit Control?"

"Looks likely," he said. "But let's not panic. Let's think this through. All systems have failures; we've just got used to having them so seldom that even a small one is scary." He looked thoughtfully at an inconspicuous panel below the news display, then reached out and opened it, exposing a big red button labeled HELP.

He pressed it.

Nothing happened.

Next to that was a small black grill with the touchword EMERGENCY PHONE under it. He touched that and said, "Can anybody hear me?"

If anybody could, nobody admitted it.

After a couple more tries, he said, "I think we're going to have to get out—if we can. Maybe the platform exit will work." He tried the DOOR OPEN button, normally disabled while the car was in motion but available for emergency exit when it wasn't. Nothing happened the first two times, and Pilar felt her throat going dry.

The third time, though, with no apparent change in technique, the door slid smoothly and quietly open. Lester started to get out and Pilar asked, "Should I come, too, or wait in case it tries to start again?" There was an EMERGENCY STOP lever, too, behind glass.

"Better come," Lester grunted. "I don't know what's happening, but I don't think we want to get separated."

She followed. The platform was atypically narrow, and there were no working lamps on the grimy, almost black walls. The air felt dank, and somewhere liquid was dripping slowly. Just enough light spilled through the bullet's window to show the door, narrow, plain, and without the usual passenger-oriented placards. It did, however, have a familiar-looking pushbar for opening it.

Except it didn't work.

Lester tried again, pushing harder. "I don't think this is even a passenger station," he muttered. "Maybe just a maintenance access—and maybe not in use any more." He threw his whole weight against it. There was a faint crackling sound somewhere in the mechanism, but the door didn't budge. "Let me see if I can see anything about the latch or hinges. . . ." He shifted slightly and his shadow obligingly stepped aside, letting light fall where one side of the door met the jamb.

But when Lester stopped moving, his shadow didn't. "Hey!" he yelped, and both he and Pilar whirled around just in time to see their bullet take off in a jackrabbit start, shooting off with a shriek to rejoin the main line and vanish into the dark tunnel.

Leaving Lester and Pilar in pitch darkness, and once again silence—except that Pilar could swear she heard her own heart hammering. "I'm not into screaming," she said tightly, "I'm really not. But if this goes on one more—"

"Help me push," Lester said quickly. "Maybe if we *both* throw ourselves against it . . . On three. One . . . two . . . three!"

They hit simultaneously all right, and heard something crack. Pilar hoped it wasn't bones, though it felt as if it could be.

"One more time," Lester urged.

Three more times did it. On their last impact the door gave

enough so they fell against it, though its hinges were evidently too rusted to let it swing open very far. But to Pilar's immense relief (and, she was sure, Lester's) they were able to push it open wide enough to squeeze through—and two small, faint shafts of light came from somewhere above.

It didn't take long to determine that they were at the foot of a narrow stairway. They couldn't see details, but they were able to pick their way up without impaling themselves on any tetanus-bearing artifacts. "I think what saved us," Lester mused as they approached the top of the light shafts, "was that it *has* been so long since anybody used this. The door latch was too corroded to—"

"If it did save us," Pilar interrupted in spite of herself. "We're not out yet."

"But I think this is just an ordinary manhole," said Lester, already banging its underside experimentally with his knuckles. "Help me push it up, Pilar."

She tried. At first it wouldn't yield at all and panic tried to reassert itself. What if it had been welded shut? But then it gave a little, just for an instant, and then again. She and Lester realized at the same time what was happening and started banging on the underside of the metal disk. "Stand clear!" she yelled. "We're coming out!"

And then, with people no longer walking over the top, they managed to push the lid aside enough to squeeze past, though it was so heavy that as soon as she'd done it Pilar realized they would both be sore for days to come. It made a considerable clang; but as they poked their heads out into blinding sunshine and looked around at a forest of feet, they saw most of the passersby simply swerving around the new obstacle with barely a glance, many of them talking on invisible cell phones or otherwise absorbed in their own affairs. "New York never changes," Lester muttered. "Come on, let's get out of here."

They pushed the heavy lid just enough to the side to squeeze by and stand up, then made a perfunctory attempt to re-cover the hole enough to protect self-absorbed passersby from catastrophe. Then they looked around to get their bearings. It was a sunny day, so the sun made it easy to find south, the direction in which blocks were short. A minute's walk that way brought them to a street sign—81st and Park—and a right turn and two long blocks got them into Central Park. The museum, they both knew, was more or less straight across the park, but of course there were no direct paths to take them there. They had to wiggle through fields and thickets and past beds of spring flowers, choosing paths at junctions to try to keep their average vector aimed westward.

It should have been a pleasant stroll, and for a few moments at the beginning it almost seemed as if it might be today. But gradually Pilar became aware of a persistent faint buzz near her head, and noticed a fly buzzing around Lester's. When he swatted at it, she asked him, "Do I have one of those following me, too?"

He stopped and turned to look; his fly kept patiently buzzing around his head. "Yes," he said. He swung a hand at his follower to try to shoo it away. It didn't shoo; it dodged adroitly and stayed in its holding pattern. So did Pilar's.

She asked, "Do you think it's . . . you know."

He considered. "It looks like an ordinary housefly," he said finally. "That could mean it is."

"Or it could mean that whoever's making the funny ones is getting better at making them look normal. And showing off. Come on, let's try to shake them." They both started walking again, faster this time, but instead of getting rid of their pursuers, they attracted more. All of the newcomers looked like perfectly ordinary local species—houseflies, dragonflies, mosquitos—but their numbers and behavior, tenaciously pursuing two people in a mixed flock of multiple species, were disquietingly odd. Pilar and Lester found themselves walking faster and faster, and attracting more and more followers.

By the time they emerged from the park at 82nd Street and turned south, they were practically running, and surrounded by a veritable cloud of weirdly mixed insects. The critters never landed or bit, but they stayed close to their humans, as if hounding them, all the way up the big front steps of the museum. They paused just outside the door, both humans trying frantically to shake their pursuers while scattered onlookers stared and giggled.

Finally, feeling frustrated, scared, and exasperated, Pilar said, "I'm going in. If they follow, maybe somebody inside will know what to do about them. In fact, maybe they're just what Maybelle needs." With that she clapped cupped hands together, hoping to catch one to take to Maybelle.

But the nearest ones dodged too quickly, and the whole cloud suddenly shot off in all directions, quickly disappearing from sight.

"Well, it was worth a try," Pilar said with a shrug. Then she grabbed the big brass handle and pulled the door open, and they went inside.

"WHAT HAPPENED TO YOU TWO?" MAYBELLE ASKED, LOOKING them up and down as Pilar tried to dust herself off and catch her breath when they reached her office. Escaping from an abandoned subway exit and running across Central Park on a warm day had not been kind to their clothes or complexions. "Or don't I want to know?"

"It was a . . . peculiar trip in," said Lester. He started filling her in on the details, Pilar joining in from time to time. In just a few minutes they recapped the frustrations of the last few days, from psychiatric runarounds and bureaucratic hassles at the hospital to the joys of their trip in today. "So in essence," Lester summarized, "we have no specimens, no statements from anybody, no contact with other patients, and Dr. Schneider not only won't cooperate but has threatened to get Pilar fired."

"Well, actually," said Pilar, "we do have some samples—that blood from the two of us. I was going to try to bring them to you Sunday, but I wasn't sure where you'd be and I couldn't call you. My phone shocked me when I tried, and the neighbor's just wouldn't let me. Neither of them seemed to care if I called anybody else. Just you."

"Hm-m-m." Maybelle frowned pensively. "I wonder if they've really doctored that many phones to that degree, or if most of the tampering is in *you*. That shock, for instance. Was it real, or just the *sensation* of a shock, produced from within?"

"I suppose that's possible," said Pilar. "We do have strange things in our blood, and we don't know what they do." She reached into a well-concealed pocket and pulled out three sample tubes, two labeled with her name and one with Lester's. "Can you get these to Dan? Does he have an electron microscope?"

"He did the last I heard, and I can try. I've stopped making promises." Maybelle took the tubes and tucked them away. "Except that I'll try, ASAP."

"Thanks," said Pilar. "Say, where is Dan, anyway? We all need to be able to contact each other as many ways as possible."

"Jersey," said Maybelle, "and I quite agree." She scribbled something on each of two pieces of paper from a pad and handed one to each of her visitors. Each contained several kinds of contact information for Maybelle—address, phone, e-mail, etc. She shoved the pad across the desk, along with two pens. "I'd like the same from each of you—and I suggest we all memorize them as quickly as possible, and then destroy them. Just in case."

"Agreed." Everyone was silent for half a minute or so, writing and then studying the slips of paper. Then Pilar said, "So have you accomplished any more than we have, Maybelle?"

"Not really." Maybelle shrugged. "At least I was able to contact Dan and ask him for a statement about what he's seen so far. Well, no . . . actually I just sent him an e-mail and didn't get any notice that it wasn't delivered. But I haven't had any confirmation that it was, either. Maybe I should be worried." For a few seconds she *looked* worried, her brow heavily furrowed, lips pressed tightly together, and those blue eyes seeming to bore into the desktop. "I also had the museum's head computer guy take a look at my machine. He agreed that the damage to it is strange and erratic; once in a while it even seems to work, in a limited sort of way. The most interesting thing he said is that it wasn't just a matter of erasing the hard disk. Something is messed up at a deep hardware level, even though there's no macroscopically obvious damage."

"That could fit," said Lester. "I think you should send some of your circuit boards for Dan to look at, too."

"Good idea," said Maybelle. "I'm not sure I should *send* them, though. Maybe I should take them myself, to be sure they get there—though after hearing about your trip here today, I'm not sure I'm up to it. I'm not ninety any more, you know."

"Think about it," Lester suggested. "I trust whatever you decide. Just don't wait too long. How about more bug specimens? Anything come back from any of your feelers?"

Maybelle shrugged again, wearily. "Like throwing salt into the ocean, for all the results they've had." Another lengthy silence, and then she suddenly unslumped. "Well, at least we do have a few ideas to try. They may not be good, but they're what we've got. I think we should get on them."

"I suppose." Lester stood up, then said, "You mentioned that sometimes your computer still does something. Maybe you should give it one more try before we leave."

"Why not?" Maybelle touched a corner of the landscape photo—today it was a seascape—and for a moment it dissolved into colorful chaos. Then that resolved itself into clear 36-point type spelling out a simple, unsigned message:

MAYBELLE, LESTER, AND PILAR:
DON'T BOTHER US, AND WE WON'T BOTHER YOU.

 **Maybelle felt uncharacteristically** dejected as she watched them go, and silently wished them a safe trip home. Meanwhile a part of her mind was mulling the question of how to get the blood and computer board samples to Dan. Not letting them out of her sight seemed highly desirable, but Dan lived quite some distance out and she wasn't even sure he'd be there when she arrived.

As she mulled, she shut down her computer and pulled out a couple of chips. She wasn't even sure what they did, but maybe a microscopic look at them would give Dan some ideas about what had happened to them.

A soft knock at her door made her start more than it should have. She whirled around to see Fred, a gnarled old man who was actually a good deal younger than she was, putting a small sheaf of envelopes down. "Morning, Dr. Terwilliger," he said. "Didn't mean to startle you. It's just the mail."

She smiled. "Thanks, Fred. I didn't mean to startle you, either."

He left and she stared vacantly at the pile before actually looking at it. Even today, with almost everything electronic, snail mail survived and had a few uses. After the events of the last week, she wondered if maybe it deserved more. It was a lot harder to wipe out its infrastructure with a single well-placed zap than that of e-mail. Well, maybe it would come back. The current fad for "When you care enough to send real paper" just might be a first step in that direction.

With a sigh she picked up the top envelope and read it. She'd been selected to participate in a highly important survey . . . that is, she'd been mass-mailed a questionnaire attached to a fund-raising solicitation. She didn't bother to open it.

Next was a sample issue of a new journal, then two flashy ads, and . . .

The one that made her gasp at first got no response at all. It was a small, plain card from the post office, informing her that she had a registered parcel to pick up, from an address that initially drew a blank. Yet there was something about it that seemed vaguely familiar, that tickled the back of her mind. And when it succeeded in waking something up back there, *then* she gasped—loudly.

Shaking palpably, she wheeled her chair over to the dusty corner where she still kept her ancient Rolodex. She didn't bother putting the chips back in the computer to check its files; it probably wouldn't have worked anyway. At last she felt vindicated in her quaint old-timer's habit, oft gently ridiculed by her colleagues, of keeping a lot of things in hard copy, too.

And there it was—one of the addresses to which she'd sent "feelers."

Had somebody actually come through?

The mere possibility, however slight, was enough to galvanize her into action. Uncertainty vanished in a puff; it was now clear that the post office was her next stop, and the sooner the better. She could decide when she got there what to do about Dan and the samples. For now, she just scooped them into a handbag and headed for the door.

The world looked bright, cheery, and harmless from the top of the front stairs, looking out over the brightly colored Brownian motion of pedestrians and the green treetops of Central Park beyond. Maybelle couldn't descend them as fast or nonchalantly as in decades past, but she felt a little more in control with each step down. By the time she hit the sidewalk and turned south, there was almost a spring in her step.

Until the big, sleek, silver-gray car with tinted windows pulled up alongside her, slowed to her speed, and a rear window rolled down just enough to show a shadowed hint of a man's face. "Dr. Terwilliger," said a quiet but firm baritone voice, with no suggestion of uncertainty about whom it was addressing, "may we have a word with you?"

She shivered inwardly, but didn't let it show. She stopped. So did the car. She stepped back two good strides, putting herself beyond arm's reach from within. "Who are you?" she demanded.

"United States Aerospace Force," said the voice, and a hand appeared at the open window, displaying a letter case with what looked like thoroughly real credentials—and Maybelle took her time looking for anything that didn't ring true. "Staff Sergeant Riccardo Kovich."

Maybelle didn't move. This could be all kinds of things. It could be a trap, set by whoever had sent all the other traps. Or it could be the sign she'd been hoping for, that Sergeant Calvin actually had bumped their report upstairs and somebody had listened to it. "What's the word you want with me?" she asked.

"We'd like you to come with us. My superiors urgently want to discuss something with you."

"And if I refuse?"

"They will be very disappointed."

"But you won't try to force me?"

"Not without further orders, ma'am. But I can't say whether those orders would be forthcoming. National security is at stake."

"Hm-m-m," she said by way of stalling. She wished she'd paid more attention to cloak-and-dagger novels. There must be some way to decide which side these people were on—if "sides" was even an appropriate concept. "And what makes anybody think I have anything to contribute to national security?"

"That I can't tell you, ma'am. I'm only a messenger. But my orders are to encourage you as urgently and emphatically as possible to come with us."

"I see." She pondered a few seconds longer, her heart pounding. If they wanted to take her by force, there was little she could do to stop them. What bothered her most was that if she went who-knows-where with these people, Lester and Pilar would have no way of knowing what happened to her. Unless she could leave a message. . . . "Hang on a sec," she said, turning away. She tongued on her personal, hoping she could reach either Pilar's or Lester's phone and subvocalize a message. But it was not to be.

With a resigned sigh, she turned back to Sergeant Kovich. "I'll go with you on one condition," she said as firmly as she could. "Can you stop by the post office on the way there? It's right down the street."

The sergeant smiled quite convincingly. "No problem, ma'am. Thanks for your cooperation."

He got out—at least he was wearing an apparently genuine USAF uniform—and held the door for her as she climbed in, wondering what she was getting into now. Then he got back in, sitting next to her but not too close, and the car pulled out with a low purr.

The one potentially encouraging sign was that they did stop at the post office.

Maybelle clutched her package tightly against her as they drove down the avenue. It was a plain brown foampack, about four centimeters thick and eight square, and light for its size. She was dying to know what was inside, but there was no way she was going to open it now, in the presence of these people. She tried instead to act nonchalant, going along with their sporadic attempts at small talk while being careful not to say anything significant, and all the while trying to notice where they were going.

They made no attempt to hide that information, which could be either a good sign or a very bad one. Crossing the George Washington Bridge and continuing west, then south, made it clear that they were somewhere in New Jersey. But Maybelle didn't know this area well. It was hilly enough to break the road system into a chaotic jumble, and in half an hour or so they'd entered an area so rural and wooded that for a surprisingly long time there were no place signs or obvious landmarks.

So she had only the most general sort of idea where they were when the car turned up a long, winding lane with trees pressing tightly in upon it. At one point they stopped for a guardhouse, of sorts, but with no obvious human inhabitants. The driver dropped a window and did something with a smart card and a reader mounted on the building. A gate opened, and they continued on another half mile or so.

Finally the car pulled into an old-fashioned porte-cochere on the front of a yellow stucco house set against the base of a modest cliff. The driver shut off the engine, got out, and opened a door. "This is it, ma'am," he said. "Welcome."

"To what?" she mumbled, but he pretended not to hear. She didn't press the point, but let Sergeant Kovich lead her into the building.

Inside, it looked like a perfectly ordinary office building, perhaps belonging to a small company of modest means and meticulous habits. Kovich greeted the lone receptionist informally and whisked her right past him to a double door at the far side of the rather plain vestibule. The corridor beyond extended so far back that the house was clearly just a front for something much larger dug deep into the hillside. Maybelle anticipated a long, labyrinthine walk, and was pleasantly surprised when Kovich said, "Right here, ma'am," and opened the third door they came to.

Reflexively, Maybelle scanned the interior. At first glance, it was a modest-sized conference room, dominated by the perennially popular oval table of polished ebony or a decent imitation. Several heavily padded black armchairs on casters surrounded that and pitchers of ice water stood on the table. What drew her attention more forcefully was the far end of the room, which looked notably unlike any conference room she could remember.

It wasn't big; maybe a quarter of the room, but clearly a space unto itself. Half a dozen fixed chairs formed an arc, all facing a central spot a couple of feet in front of the wall. That wall was featureless and painted dead, flat black, as were the adjacent portions of floor, ceiling, and side walls. Each of the chairs sported a veritable forest of what appeared to be electronics and assorted protuberances of unobvious function.

It's a theater, Maybelle decided with intuitive certainty. *I wonder what the show is?*

Well, she'd find out soon enough, if that equipment was used in the meeting, and probably no sooner. She turned her attention to the people in the room, still unsure whether she should view them as captors. All, unless you counted Kovich, were strangers: an Aerospace major and two colonels, all in uniform, and two iron-haired individuals in expensive civilian business suits. One of the latter was a stern-faced woman; neither of them wore any obvious personal identification. The Aerospace officers had name tags, but their names rang no bells.

That much looking, for all the good it did, took very little time. Before Maybelle could give the situation much thought, Kovich sprang to attention and snapped off a salute toward the Aerospace officers. "Staff Sergeant Kovich reporting as ordered, sirs," he announced crisply. "With Dr. Terwilliger."

They returned his salute—the two colonels snappily, the major rather perfunctorily, it seemed to Maybelle. One of the colonels— Edwards, by his name tag—smiled and said, "At ease, Sergeant. Thank you." He turned to Maybelle with a professionally ingratiating smile. "And thank you, Dr. Terwilliger, for coming. The others should be here shortly. Why don't you just take a seat"— he gestured toward one on a long side of the oval table—"and make yourself comfortable? Then we can do all the introductions at once."

Maybelle took the chair, but couldn't get comfortable. The wait, filled with nervous silence punctuated only by an occasional guarded whisper among the unknowns already waiting, only increased her uneasiness. But it only lasted a few minutes, and she felt a surge of relief—quickly followed by heightened concern— when another sergeant entered the room and reported as Kovich had done.

But this one was accompanied by Pilar and Lester, both looking apprehensive.

 **Colonel Edwards showed** them to chairs next to Maybelle's, dismissed the sergeants, and turned to one of the suits—the elderly gent with the fractal necktie and bushy sideburns. "Thank you all very much for coming," Necktie-and-Sideburns rumbled. "I'm sorry if we've inconvenienced you—and I know we have— but I hope you'll agree in a few minutes that it was worthwhile.

"I know a roomful of strangers can be uncomfortable, so let's make sure you know everybody first. I'm Linley Delacorte of NASA. This"—he nodded toward the stern-faced and impeccably suited woman—"is Iona Branford of the State Department. Colonel Edwards is from the combat arm of USAF, Colonel Weston heads the research division, and Major Simonetti . . . well, the major is, in at least one way, the most important person here."

Maybelle frowned privately. She had the names now, but no real information. Why were any of these people here? In particular, why the high-ranking people from the military and State? That didn't sound good. . . .

"Last Saturday," Delacorte from NASA went on, "you folks told Sergeant Calvin you'd had some disconcerting experiences and suspected that they might be . . . uh . . . somehow related to the recent aerospace plane explosion. Well, we've studied your statements and we've gradually been forced to consider the possibility that you're right. Since we've imposed on you, we think we should start by telling you what we know—get us onto more or less equal footing, as it were. Since each group of us may know more than the other about one half of a puzzle, we need to establish some common ground. You've made your initial presentation; it's time for us to make ours. Afterward, no doubt, we'll both want to ask some questions." He harrumphed. "I must emphasize, though I'm sure you already realize, that we tell you these things in strictest confidence—confidence that could, if necessary, be enforced by whatever means necessary."

He seemed to be studying his shoes, too uncomfortable to face his audience. Finally, though, he forced his eyes back up to meet theirs and went on, "The explosion did not come completely from the blue—uh, no pun intended. It was the climactic event of a series, but we fear it wasn't the end. Since Major Simonetti made the initial discovery, we'll let him explain. Major?"

Delacorte sat down with visible relief, and Major Simonetti stood at the end of the table near the closed door. "Thank you, Linley—and thank all of you for coming." He had the fit physique and confident bearing of a military man, Maybelle thought, but something about him didn't quite fit that mold. In his mid-thirties, with close-cropped brown hair, he seemed in some intangible way a little too much his own man, and he spoke too softly, almost apologetically. "This all goes back," he said, "to the middle of last month. I wear a uniform, but most of the time I think of myself primarily as an astrophysicist. I joined the Aerospace Force because that's where I found the best research opportunity I could: searching the sky for things that don't belong there.

"That's not pure science, of course, not just idle curiosity. As you know, things have been pretty quiet lately on the defensive front. Some folks think we should have folded up our tents and gone home a long time ago, but we don't agree. As the Terror War taught us, enemies don't have to be big to do a lot of damage, so it's still a good idea to keep an eye out for missiles from enemies we might not even realize we have, from obscure nations down to lone terrorists. And meteoroids—things that could wipe us out like the dinosaurs, that *probably* won't hit us this week or this century, but surely will hit *sometime*, and *could* hit any time.

"That's what I was doing on May fifteenth when I stumbled onto something odd and puzzling. At first I didn't even notice it; the image was too faint, no matter what wavelengths we tried. It didn't seem to be either of the kinds of threatening objects we were watching for. A missile would have been close in, astronomically speaking, and coming closer fast. A meteorite or asteroid would have been slower, but in an orbit around the Sun. I had trouble even keeping a usable signal from this thing, and I wasn't sure I could justify spending much time on it. But it tickled my curiosity so much I kept sneaking another look at it and plotting its position and velocity.

"When it became clear that it was drifting slowly westward in our sky, in a way consistent with a circular orbit centered on *Earth*, slightly higher than geosynchronous, and slightly inclined, I began to feel a prickly sensation that something was really not right here. I mulled it over and decided to go out on a limb. I asked Colonel Weston for permission to put the routine stuff on hold and get some detailed observations of the new thing. Someday we may all be grateful that he agreed, even though I frankly couldn't give him a very good reason."

"Don't be so modest, Marv," Weston said quietly. "Your hunches *are* a good reason."

"Thank you, sir. Anyway, with authorization to spend more time and get help from other groups, we began to build up a picture of this thing. And the more detailed it got, the more puzzling it got. We tried laser and radar bounces quite early, and even though the returns we got were painfully faint—almost buried in noise—they pretty definitely confirmed the idea of an Earth-centered orbit not too far out.

"How long had it been there? We don't know. An object that hard to detect could have been there a long time without our noticing it—millions, even billions of years. Or it could have been put there the day before, though it was hard to see how somebody could have launched a new satellite without anybody's noticing.

"Something about that thought kept niggling at my subconscious. Eventually it drifted up close enough to the surface to become a conscious question: how can you stealth a satellite launch? Then one thing led to another. Why was I thinking about 'stealth'? You all know about stealth planes, I'm sure—military aircraft first developed before the turn of the century, designed to be difficult or impossible to detect by sight, radar, or sound. But whoever heard of applying that technology to anything as hard to hide as a ground-to-orbit rocket launch? And why bother?

"By then we were into the weekend, when I normally would have been unwinding and relaxing like a normal person. But I sure didn't feel like I was unwinding or relaxing. My mind was chugging away, sometimes consciously and sometimes just below the surface, playing with that elusive idea that 'stealth' might have something to do with what I was just barely seeing. Regardless of how long it had been there, the object itself almost seemed stealthed. When we started looking at the size and mass this thing seemed to have, it just didn't make sense that it should be so hard to see. And when I tried to come up with a natural explanation for that, I couldn't. I felt forced to the suspicion that it was hard to see because somebody had made it that way. Nature doesn't stealth things, as far as we know, but people do. But . . . *only* people?"

"Aliens!" Pilar whispered.

"I wasn't quite ready to say that out loud," Simonetti said with a nod in Pilar's direction, "but I was thinking it. It was getting harder and harder to avoid the idea that this thing was deliberately and artificially stealthed, and I still didn't believe that anybody on Earth had the technology to do it. The more I thought about that, the more it suggested that somebody *else* had done it—maybe by coasting the thing into orbit from somewhere much farther away. Or maybe driving it, with a technology we haven't even begun to develop—and yes, by 'we' I mean 'humans.'

"This was tremendously exciting to me, and more than a little scary. As a scientist interested in space, growing up around the turn of the century with video games and science fiction movies, I'd long been interested in SETI, the search for extraterrestrial intelligence. But until that weekend it had been purely academic. ETI was something I'd like to believe existed, and I thought I'd like to meet some, but I didn't really expect to.

"Now it seemed that maybe I'd discovered some, or at least the most direct evidence of it ever seen. If somebody else had put that thing there, was anybody aboard it, or at least in the neighborhood? And if so, what should we do about it?

"This posed a real dilemma. I was familiar with the Statements of Principle that many nations agreed to, back when I was a kid, about how any contact with extraterrestrials should be handled. You probably haven't heard much about them lately, so I'll remind you that they prescribed a cautious approach, with a strong emphasis on diplomacy. I would have loved to be the one to start the ball rolling in that direction, reporting our findings simultaneously to all the appropriate civilian and military agencies I could think of, so that if there *was* somebody out there, we could start working toward a nice, civilized relationship.

"But the fact remained that I am a career officer in the Aerospace Force, and even if that mainly means doing science, I take this uniform seriously and I can never forget what it stands for. My position required me to consider the danger that anybody behind this thing could pose to us, and there was only one place I *could* take my report. That was to my commanding officer, with the hope and confidence that he would do the best thing."

"Major," Maybelle asked warily, "are you softening us up to tell us we're at war with somebody we know nothing about?"

"Not at all," he said, "and I hope it doesn't come to that. But I had to consider the possibility. At the crack of dawn on Monday, four days after the anomaly was first spotted, I called Colonel Weston and told him I thought this needed to be considered a possible threat and investigated by all possible means. Especially since by then we'd been able to discern, though more vaguely than we'd like, some structure in the object—suggesting that it was really a *lot* of objects."

"And a good move that was," said Weston. "I agreed with the major's analysis and made two phone calls right away: one to Colonel Edwards and one to Ms. Branford. Would each of you like to say a few words about your response? Ms. Branford?"

The stern-faced woman from State nodded. "Certainly, Colonel." Her voice was surprisingly soft and smooth. "The first thing we had to do, from the civilian and diplomatic standpoint, was to try to make sure nothing developed into a military confrontation. That meant making sure that nothing we were seeing constituted hostile action or espionage by other nations—and that they couldn't misinterpret anything they were seeing as such action by us. So we sent out messages to all our diplomatic contacts—both our own people and their opposite numbers in many other countries—to ask about any indication of unknown satellites or military space activity that we might not have been told about by other countries. Nobody would admit to having done any or knowing of any, but the mere act of asking was a delicate business. It tipped our hand: Now other governments would be wondering why we would ask such a thing, and starting their own investigations."

"Good," Lester muttered, not quite to himself.

"Finally, in case anybody we talked to through diplomatic channels was less than candid or forthcoming, we also asked our own intelligence agencies to poke around for anything that was being done but not admitted to. So far they, too, have come up dry.

"All of which leaves open the question of whether this thing is Earth-based or extraterrestrial. Either way, we had to be prepared for the possibility that what's up there is potentially hostile and can't be defused by diplomatic means. Colonel Edwards?"

Edwards, tall and ramrod-straight with a steel-gray crewcut, took the floor. "Our job was simple, in principle. We alerted every defensive observer we could think of to watch for anything potentially threatening. That included Moonbase and the Space Station, which we hoped might have a better perspective than us on something in orbit. So far, they've been able to add very little. They have trouble seeing it, too." He cleared his throat. "Our alert at this point did not include the directive which eventually led to your presence here. Maybe things would have been better if it had—or maybe they wouldn't.

"Anyway, we got all the *official* observers we could into the act, and sent notice to the very highest levels that initiated the process of putting all combat units in all branches of the service on standby alert. None of the observers found anything to act on, so things haven't proceeded any further on that front—but neither have they retreated one step." He sat down.

"So there we were," Weston resumed. "Everybody chasing a shadow, a little scared, ready to act, but still with only the vaguest idea of what we were scared *of* or what we might have to do. Not a position any military man likes—or any human, I guess. So my research groups kept observing, by every means we could think of.

"Including radio. I didn't tell anybody we were looking for aliens; officially, we were just being thorough. But I'll bet everybody was thinking it by then. We had no idea *how* such beings would use radio, if they used it all. So we listened for anything, in a wide range of frequencies. All we got was noise—what most folks would call 'static.'

"Or was it sporadic microbursts of high-frequency radio traffic from the objects, so compressed in time and space that we couldn't make anything of them? Static could be described the same way, but the right kind of analysis could show the difference. We weren't able to.

"However, we knew of no natural explanation for what we were seeing. We debated long and hard—or as long and hard as one can with one's back to the wall—and decided to try sending our own signal *to* the object. At this point, it seemed silly not to. If anybody was up there who could detect us by radio signals, they'd long since done it. They were *here*, for God's sake! So we started beaming very basic signals that we hoped couldn't be seen as hostile, using lots of frequencies and languages and modulation types.

"Nothing came back, but we kept trying for a couple of days. Either there was nobody there, or they were ignoring us. Finally, a little more than a week after our first observations, we decided to try a closer look. And I might emphasize to you that getting anything like that to happen that fast, in anything but an overt combat situation, shows that some very highly placed people were taking this very, very seriously."

"Are you saying," Maybelle asked, "that the asp that exploded was trying to get a close-up look at this thing?"

"Not yet," said Simonetti, "but that's a good guess. Since we weren't in an overt combat situation, we were still being at least a little bit cautious. What we sent up first was an unmanned probe with an assortment of instruments. It got fairly close, and gave us some interesting additions to the puzzle. But before it got as close as we'd hoped, its readings started going haywire.

"All of them, and we couldn't tell why. We'd put it together so hastily, and stuffed it so full of instruments to try to learn about its quarry, that it didn't occur to anybody to give it a full set of monitors for its own internal conditions. So we don't know what happened to it, but its telemetry broke up into chaos and within five minutes died altogether. For all we know it's still out there, mortally crippled, but it can't tell us a thing. That thorough a breakdown, in just that way, strongly suggests malicious intervention. In a phrase, it looked like somebody fried its whole instrument package, and we couldn't tell why or how.

"Which was scary, but we still needed to know. Those things aren't cheap, so we did some more thinking before we put up another one. When we did decide to send another, we decided it *had* to have the best, most versatile, most flexible internal monitors we could provide—which meant a couple of highly trained pilot-scientists."

"We didn't like that," the NASA official broke in. "The negative publicity from a mishap involving a manned mission can do tremendous damage—and of course we'd feel terrible about having sent anyone into it. But it wasn't hard to find a pair who were more than willing to go. And they did come back—but without much more information than the lost probe. When they got close, they started complaining that it was getting uncomfortably hot in their cabin. They couldn't find an obvious cause for it, but the temperature was rising faster and faster and by now some of the instruments were starting to malf. When the crew were down to their skivvies and sweating buckets and hadn't found a way to stop the heating, they decided they'd better turn tail and see if things improved with some r-squared between themselves and the target. A dead astronaut does nobody any good.

"It worked, at least in a minimal way. As soon as they turned around, the temperature stopped climbing so fast, and as they sped away from the 'Stealth Satellite,' pretty soon it was back to pretty much normal."

"Like a cow bumping an electric fence," Maybelle muttered. "Or a dog getting too close to one of those 'invisible fences.' "

Delacorte nodded. "All too exactly, I'm afraid. We couldn't escape the feeling that somebody had viewed us as pests and put something up to make it uncomfortable for us to get too close. We're still not sure what, but our best guess is that somebody aboard the satellite was somehow using our own ship as a microwave oven, though not a terribly efficient one."

"Efficient enough," Lester observed. "And that doesn't necessarily require anybody up there. It could all be automated."

"Possibly," granted Delacorte. "But the crew was mad as hell—even more so than the rest of us—and determined to go back and get that close look. The captain—"

"Who was the captain?" Pilar asked suddenly.

"We prefer not to divulge names just now. The important thing is that he had an idea. Heating processes are generally relatively slow, so he thought if they went back with an overpowered, minimally loaded plane, they might be able to get in and out of the satellite's intimate neighborhood fast enough to collect some real data before the heat buildup reached a critical level. It was risky, but we couldn't think of anything better. So after some decidedly heated discussion—no pun intended—we let them try it. I think the best way to tell you about that is to let you experience it from the crew's point of view. Colonel Weston?"

"You've all heard of police sketchbooks," said Weston. "The idea was that if a victim or a witness saw a crime but had no opportunity to get a photograph, the next best thing was to have an artist construct a sketch of the perpetrator from the victim or witness's memories. It wasn't as good as a photo, of course— though these days it might almost seem better since photos are so easily doctored. In the old days the artist would interview victims about what they remembered of the perp's appearance and draw a preliminary sketch of somebody with those characteristics. If the victim said, 'No, the chin was pointier and the hair curlier,' the artist could make a new draft, progressively fine-tuning it until the victim said, 'That's him!'. Then the sketch could be compared to mug shots of known criminals.

"These days, of course, the process is a lot faster, easier, and better because digital image processing lets sketches be refined faster and easier, and pattern-recognition software based on the face-specific methods of the human brain make it easy to look for a match. But the principle remains the same.

"What you are about to experience is an extension of that method. Our brave crew, for obvious reasons, were not able to give us a full eyewitness account of what they saw as they approached the intruder. But they did say a little before . . . it was too late . . . and you'll recall that this time we were getting a lot of telemetry, both internal and external, from their vehicle. Putting all that together, we've constructed a virtual reality simulation of what we think they experienced in their last few minutes. We're offering you the chance to experience a playback, and we hope you'll accept it because we hope one of you might see something in it that we didn't.

"We realize none of you have actual space experience, but naturally you've all seen enough news footage and simulations to have a pretty good idea what a lot of things are like on a routine space mission. Some of what you're about to see is far from routine, and we're playing the long shot that you might see some connection between this unusual experience and yours. I should also warn you that you've never seen a simulation this realistic, and you don't *have* to watch it. It is, to put it mildly, disconcerting. Do any of you have heart problems?"

The three of them shook their heads no.

"Very good," said Weston. "Anybody not willing to go through it?"

Nobody said anything.

"OK, let's go for it. If you'll each take one of the chairs at the end of the room . . ." They got up and proceeded to do so, as Weston's voice continued, "The dark end of the room is a large holographic projection volume that will show you what the crew saw outside their ship as they approached. Speakers will give you what they heard. Small projectors built into your viewing chairs will show each of you the pilot's immediate surroundings as if you were in his seat. Other senses we'll simulate to the best of our ability by tactile stimulators built into the chairs. Admittedly that's the weakest part of the simulation, but you'll probably be glad it isn't perfectly realistic. You'll find a headrest into which your head will fit fairly naturally, and it will fine-tune the fit once you're there. The same for your hands. Simply rest your fingers and palms in the corresponding indentations on the ends of your chair arms. . . ."

They followed his instructions. The smooth, soft plastic under the hands and behind the neck felt odd, almost alive, as it adjusted itself to their exact contours. Straps wrapped themselves around various parts of them to hold them gently but firmly in place.

". . . and try to relax," Weston finished. "Here we go."

With no further warning, the room lights faded rapidly to nothing, an almost subliminal throbbing sound rose from nowhere, and faint new lights emerged from the darkness, brightening swiftly.

And everything changed.

Chapter 14

Pilar had never been aboard a spacecraft before, but she was now, with a feeling of reality far beyond any simulation she'd experienced before. All her senses told her her chair was now part of something flying through black space dotted with bright stars, vibrating slightly with the operations of hidden machinery. All around her, mere inches away, were glowing readouts that told her nothing because she didn't know how to read them. Directly in front of her, though, was an unobstructed area through which she was looking straight ahead. She felt oddly certain that that meant in the direction the ship was moving, though at first she couldn't tell where the sense of motion was coming from. The stars, after all, were much too far away to show any relative motion. . . .

Gradually, though, as her eyes grew accustomed to the darkness, a faint shape—or shapes—emerged from the darkness ahead, growing slowly. That, she realized, was the motion she sensed. Yet the shape itself was maddeningly indistinct. At first she could barely be sure it was there; then she couldn't tell whether it was one or several. She found herself leaning more and more toward the latter, but she still vacillated. Even when she felt sure there were multiple shapes, she couldn't agree with herself on how many there were, or exactly what they looked like. It was as if her eyes couldn't quite focus on them.

As she wrestled with her perceptions, a quiet baritone voice spoke as if from inside her. "OK, it's time. This is almost as close as we got before, and the temperature's starting to rise. Just on

137

the readouts, so far, but we want to get this over with before we start feeling it ourselves. So here goes. . . ."

Suddenly the sound grew much louder and Pilar felt the seat pushing hard against her back, just as if they were accelerating rapidly forward. The rockets were firing, she realized with a sudden thrill, catapulting her and the ship toward the shadowy shapes ahead. They remained maddeningly indistinct, yet palpably present; despite their indistinct edges, they blocked stars beyond so thoroughly as to leave no doubt of their reality. And they grew, not only visibly, but faster and faster, as Pilar felt herself pressed harder and harder into her seat back. It reminded her of some of the best amusement park rides she'd experienced, except this was real. Real people had gone through this and—

She was sweating and felt uncomfortably hot. Was that just the induced excitement as the illusion of impending impact grew exponentially?

Did she hear a fan somewhere, smooth-running but big and powerful?

No. Forget fans; she *was* aboard that shuttle, barreling down on something big and dark and mysterious. They would collide in mere seconds, unless somebody did something soon.

And it was getting *awfully* hot in here. She began to feel a hint of queasiness, partly from the heat and partly from the dark forms now looming not only ahead but off to the sides. Her muscles tensed involuntarily against the impact—

And the ship swerved, its acceleration both seen and felt, as somebody unseen threw the helm to miss the object most nearly dead ahead. That danger passed, but now another shape was bearing down on them.

And the heat grew suddenly worse, shooting up terrifyingly. The chair shook violently as the walls and instruments around her shattered into uncountable fragments and flew in all directions. Light flared up so brilliantly that she could see nothing except a flood of dazzling white that drowned out everything else.

Everything except the silhouette of a shard of instrument panel flying straight toward her face, so fast that only the adrenaline-induced slowdown of subjective time let her see it at all.

Maybelle screamed.

Chapter 15

Pilar didn't scream, but she was shaking all over and she could feel her heart pounding as the illusion dissolved and the room lights came on, the theater end of the conference room returning to its soothing flat black. Maybelle's outcry riveted her attention and when reality returned she found herself staring at the older woman, concerned for her health and safety. She seemed to be OK, though shaken. She and her clothes were visibly sweaty, but then so was Pilar—and, she saw, Lester (who seemed in turn to be staring with equal concern at the two women).

She definitely heard a fan now, and felt a strong, cooling breeze, as if whoever had staged that show now had the machinery working overtime to undo it. For a long moment there was no other sound.

Then Major Simonetti's soft voice asked, "Everybody OK?" He stood at the end of the table, surveying his guests as they mopped their brows and exchanged nervous glances. They murmured weak affirmations and he went on, "It wasn't completely realistic, of course, but it's probably just as well. We couldn't do weightlessness, for instance, but probably none of you could have handled it without training anyway. And we didn't really heat you as much as they did, or do it the way it happened to them. Nevertheless, I suspect you get the idea—or as much of it as you'd care to.

"As I suggested before, we think that whoever or whatever is out there was trying to disable our unmanned probe—successfully—and discourage our manned ones from getting too close by heating them internally with microwaves. If so, it worked once. When we went back and got too close anyway, they carried the strategy to its logical conclusion. We haven't confirmed that directly, and our analysis teams are still arguing over just how, if at all, that would work. It seems likely that most of the heating effect would be on the hull, which is largely metallic, but there could have been some leakage inside, too. If the interior really was acting like a microwave oven, you can imagine what happened to the crew—if you really want to. But we suspect that before that happened, the hull ruptured and/or the fuel tanks exploded, leaving nothing for us to analyze."

"So," Lester ventured, "did you actually learn anything—except how to make a really scary multimovie?"

"Yes," Simonetti said dryly. "We learned that whatever is out there is really dangerous. But we still don't know *how* dangerous, or how it does what it does, or why. And we're completely baffled and frustrated by the fact that although it acts like it's controlled by something intelligent and possibly malicious, it shows no perceptible response to our attempts to communicate with it. So we still don't know whether what happened was a natural phenomenon of a kind we don't recognize, or an accident, or an act of aggression. We need to know, because our appropriate response would be quite different in those three cases. Not knowing makes it all seem . . . spooky. Like hearing footsteps and heavy breathing behind you, but getting no answer when you speak and not seeing anybody when you turn around."

Pilar shivered at the analogy, but also frowned. She felt a little nervous about speaking up in this assemblage, but the point seemed so obvious that somebody had to say it. "If there's somebody there," she said, "it doesn't seem to me that they're really ignoring your efforts to contact them. I think they're making it pretty clear that they don't want us getting too close."

"Well, it does seem that way—if what happened was done deliberately. But we seem to be up against a wall in our efforts to find that out. That's where you folks come in. Mr. Delacorte?"

The NASA man nodded and stood up. "Thank you, Major. I think you've made it pretty clear that by the time of the . . . incident . . . we were thinking, however reluctantly, about a very wide range of possible explanations, up to and including hostile extraterrestrials. After that shock, with no further progress worth mentioning from our own efforts to study the orbiter in isolation, we decided it was time to start looking for anything else that might have some connection with what we were seeing. Yet we still felt an obligation to make every effort to avoid alarming the public. Within hours, a memo went out electronically to military bases all over asking people to pass along any reports of unusual phenomena, regardless of whether they seemed to make sense or have any relevance.

"We weren't surprised to get several. Nor were we surprised that most of them were of the clichéd UFO-tale variety, with nothing to back them up." He made a half sour, half wistful face. "I've often marveled that if those UFOs are real, one of their main characteristics seems to be producing a field that incapacitates cameras or fogs film.

"Anyway, we were hoping for somebody with hard evidence, and we didn't get that. But we did notice the report of your visit to Camp Smith, which at least had the virtue of being three people with respectable credentials and willing to go on record with a story that many people would be afraid to have their names associated with. You also have in some ways the most interesting story of anybody we've heard from, if it holds up—especially Ms. Ramirez, with the alleged attempt on her life. We will want to look long and hard at that, of course. I assume since you've come this far you're all willing to submit to things like verbal cross-examination, thorough physical and psychiatric exams, and lie-detector tests. Unless, of course, you've managed to come up with some hard physical evidence since you filed your statements with Sergeant Calvin. Uh . . . I don't suppose you have?"

"As a matter of fact," Maybelle said with a gleeful grin that looked to Pilar more like her accustomed self, "we have. But before we tell you what it is, I reckon you want to hear more about what's happened to us, so you can see what it has to do with anything. Right?"

Both Delacorte and Simonetti nodded agreement. "It's a matter of checking the data for consistency," Simonetti said. "We'd like to start by having you orally retell what happened to you, so we can watch for any apparent discrepancies. And we'll probably have some questions along the way."

"Makes sense to me," said Maybelle, "and for the record, all those tests you hope we'll submit to are just what we hoped somebody would do. Y'all make yourselves comfy, because this will take a while. You want to kick things off, Lester?"

"I suppose I should," he said. "I guess our side of things sort of started with me. . . ."

THEY RECAPPED EVERYTHING THEY COULD REMEMBER, BEGIN-ning with the first "insect" that attacked Lester in the garden. Weston listened intently while fiddling with a small control panel, presumably recording the entire proceedings. Pilar, initially feel-ing that simply repeating what they'd already written was a waste of time, took up the narration when Lester got to the ER, and Maybelle when they both got to the museum for the first time.

It wasn't long before Pilar's feeling of wasting time gave way to a more serious concern. When all three of them were involved and things were happening in several places and often made little sense in terms of everyday expectations, they didn't always tell things the same way on the first try—which raised a few eye-brows and some pointed questions from their interrogators. That scared Pilar a little; these people's help, dubious as its quality might be, was the straw they'd all been reaching for, and she hated to think of that slim hope being snatched away. After all, this *was* serious business; her life had been threatened, and two astronauts had been killed. Surely these people would understand how the events of the last few days could get a bit blurred in memory. Couldn't they?

At least they kept listening, and sometimes questioning. Eventually Pilar and her companions had most of it on record, and were in substantial agreement on at least the main points. "And now the evidence," she said, to make sure it *got* said. "Dr. Terwilliger's carrying most of it. You do have it, don't you, Maybelle?"

"You bet." Maybelle had been sitting with her hands folded stiffly on top of her handbag on the table in front of her. Now she opened it and began taking out the goodies. "Chips from my crazy computer," she said as she drew them out. "Blood samples Pilar drew from herself and Lester—"

"And I think," Pilar interrupted, "you should take fresh ones from all three of us. I know I saw oddities, but I have no idea how stable they are. It might even be good if you could have your own techs draw them with equipment I haven't handled, and examine them as quickly as possible. But the important thing is that you need to use an electron microscope. The things I saw were too small to show structure with an optical—"

"I understand," said Weston with a patient smile. "That can certainly be arranged. And I assure you we'll do everything we can. We're at least as interested in getting to the bottom of this as you are."

"And the computer chips," Maybelle reminded. "They look OK, but the guy who checked my computer said they were corrupted at the hardware level, but at a scale too small—"

"Yes, I got that," said Weston.

"I was taking these to my grandson," said Maybelle. "Dan—"

"Felder," Weston finished. "Yes, the nanotechnologist."

"Can you get him here, too?" Maybelle asked suddenly. "I know his specimens disappeared, but that's significant in its—"

"We'll see what we can do. I'm sure we'd like to hear what he saw . . . before. In fact, we were hoping to have him here for this meeting, but weren't able to contact him."

"Neither was I," said Maybelle with a worried frown. "I do hope you'll try again. Meanwhile, I may have the *pièce de résistance* here." With dramatic flair, she put her handbag aside and began, with her wrinkled fingers shaking visibly, to unwrap the package she'd picked up at the post office. It went slowly and she babbled as she worked, while Pilar strained to see every detail of what she did and what it revealed. "I sent out a call for some people I know to send me anything odd they'd encountered, and had about given up hope on ever getting anything back. When your boys picked me up I was just on my way out to pick up a parcel the post office was holding—from one of *those* addresses."

She had a lot of trouble with the last couple of fastenings on the box, but solved them with a battle-scarred old pocket knife she fished out of her handbag. "Well, here goes . . ."

Pilar held her breath as Maybelle slowly folded the flaps back, with an expression compounded of hope and fear about what she might see—or not see. But that gave way to a big grin as she grasped the box by its flaps, holding it up by them to show what lay nestled in the foam cushioning within.

A flying bug, very much like the one that had first stung Lester. "There you are, ladies and gentlemen. Now get that into a lab, *stat*!"

Pilar's voice joined Maybelle's on the last word. "And," she added, "us with it!"

THERE WASN'T MUCH MORE TO DO JUST THEN. FOR THE TIME being, at least, Weston seemed to be in charge, with Simonetti a close second. Everybody's first order of business, after all, was to learn all they could, as quickly as possible, from the specimens at hand. Pilar, Maybelle, and Lester all wanted to be in on that, but Weston warned them that regulations would make it hard to get civilians access to government labs; he would do what he could, but couldn't promise anything. Pilar found that disappointing and frustrating; she'd been one of the first people in on this investigation, had a strong personal stake in it, and resented the possibility of being cut out of it. On the other hand, she suspected these people had a lot better chance than she did of getting somewhere with it, so she decided not to rock the boat—yet, anyway.

"In any case," Weston was saying, "we would like you to stay nearby. It will be more convenient if we *can* get you involved in the investigation, and I think you might appreciate the protection. At this point I can't order you to stay, but I must emphasize that secrecy is essential in this whole business, and if you leave we will have to insist that you say nothing about what's going on, and I can't deny that we'll be keeping an eye on you. But I think we can do that better, while at the same time providing you more privacy, if you accept our offer of quarters right here in this complex."

There was a certain appeal to that, Pilar thought, though she wondered whether Weston was being completely honest with them. Part of her suspected that he had no intention of getting them involved in the actual research, that he was vaguely embarrassed to need them here at all, and that he wouldn't really let them leave if anybody wanted to. But, of course, he wouldn't say any of that, even if it was true.

Somewhat to her surprise, she realized that she had no intention of calling his bluff. She certainly hadn't felt very secure lately, and she didn't expect to if she went home. She wasn't even sure she could *get* home. Yes, they might well be safer here. But . . . "How about my job?" she asked. "I've been using sick days and personal days, but there's a limit to how far I can go with that."

"Not a problem," Weston assured her. "We'll make excuses

to your employers, and anyone else you feel needs them." He smiled. "A judicious reference to serving your country should ensure that you don't wipe out the time off you have coming. Now, anybody want to leave?"

Nobody did, and a short time later they were all being shown to private rooms deeper in the hillside, and given directions on when and where they could get meals. Pilar's room was decent enough, with such basics as a bed and a comcenter and a couple of generic landscapes on the walls, but lacked any of the personal touches that made her apartment a home. She did feel a little safer there, at least provisionally, but she also felt a startling, sudden sense of loneliness, almost as if she'd been jailed, when the door closed behind her escort.

THAT DIDN'T LAST TOO LONG. IT SOON OCCURRED TO HER TO ask the comcenter what kinds of facilities were available to them and what kinds of restrictions governed where they could go and what they could do. The best thing she learned was that the complex actually extended *through* the hill and on the other side opened into a secluded "bowl" surrounded by wooded hills and threaded by paths that they were welcome to walk. She suspected there'd be fences, maybe hidden, to make sure they didn't wander too far. But she felt an overpowering need to wander as she could, and she was outside within minutes.

It was the wrong kind of vegetation, but it glowed in the late afternoon sunshine and the bowl-like topography reminded her faintly of home. After a few minutes on winding paths paved with soft pine-bark chips, she felt more relaxed than she had in more than a week, even though she knew intellectually that her problems were far from solved.

"Mind if I join you?"

Well, maybe not *that* relaxed. She jumped half a foot before she realized the voice from behind her was Lester's. Her first reaction, other than startlement, was a frown at having her tranquility interrupted. But by the time she turned to answer him, it had become a smile. "Not at all. I just thought I'd try to unwind a little before dinner."

"Me, too." He fell in beside her. "I was watching you when that show ended in there. Pretty intense, wasn't it?"

"Yes. Scary."

"Can't argue with that. Yet I thought I saw something else in your face then. Something besides fear."

"Was it that obvious?" She grinned. "I guess you've found me out. Yes, it was terrifying, and felt so real. But before it got to the terrifying part, it reawakened something else in me—something I'd almost forgotten. And *that* felt very real, too."

"What was that?" Lester asked quietly.

Pilar sighed. "When I was little, I wanted to be an astronaut when I grew up. But the other kids always teased me about it, to the point where I gradually stopped talking about it in front of them. And my family kept telling me how hard it was to become an astronaut, especially for a girl, and trying to steer me toward something more 'realistic.' What it finally boiled down to was the fact that I needed to help them out soon, and I needed financial help for college, so I looked for something that was available, paid reasonably well, and I could do soon without a lot of uncertainty. So here I am, a med tech. I'm not complaining; it *is* important work, and has its satisfactions. But it's not where I originally had my sights set. The first part of that colonel's 'show' reminded me very vividly of why."

"So what is the 'why,' Pilar? What was it that originally attracted you to astronautery?"

She smiled at his made-up word. "Part of it was the sheer fun that I imagined it would be, and that's what the simulation brought back in full force. Before it got scary, I felt like I really *was* out there, accelerating through space and surrounded by all the stars of the universe, and it was so exhilarating I got tears in my eyes imagining what it would be like to be doing that for real.

"The other part was that I've always loved finding out. To many people the stars are just pinpoints of light in the sky, but for as long as I can remember they've been more than that to me. I used to lie out on the rocks near my village at night, and look up at the stars and dream. I grew up near Arecibo, Puerto Rico, but out in the hills where the skies were clear and deep. I used to lie out on the rocks near my village at night, and look up at the stars and dream. I don't remember when I found out that other stars were as big and powerful as the Sun; I just always knew that they were, and might have their own worlds as big and rich and wonderful as this one.

"One time my grade school class took a field trip to the radio observatory and it took me weeks to stop thinking about it. In a way, I guess I never did." She grinned shyly and added, "I thought of it as a giant mouth that the Earth could use to take great bites of the Universe, to savor and draw nourishment from. And I thought it was a shame that nobody was doing much with it anymore."

"That's a lovely image, Pilar. I wish I'd thought of it."

"Thank you. Well, anyway, that's why I thought I might like to be a planetologist or an astronaut. Astronaut would have been best, because it was so much more direct—the very idea that someday I might fly my own ship right onto a new world and see firsthand what was there . . ."

"Well, if you'd been *my* daughter," Lester said, "I would have encouraged you to pursue that dream. I think you would have been good at it. In fact, maybe you still should. You're still quite young—"

"And still living on a shoestring, and suddenly, painfully unsure whether I even *have* a future. Whether any of us—" She bit it off and changed the subject. "Lester, do you have any kids?"

Now he sighed. "I did. One daughter. All this that we've been going through has got me thinking about might-have-beens, too. You remind me a little of Sylvia, or what she might have been if she'd ever grown up. She and her mother—Marella—were killed in an auto accident on the way into the city when she was seven."

"I'm sorry," Pilar said softly. "And I'm sorry if I've reawakened painful memories."

"Don't be. It's true that I've been thinking more about them lately than I had in a long time, but not so much about the loss as the good times we had before that. We did all kinds of things together, the three of us, much of it in the Highlands. And while I worried about the kind of future Sylvia would have, she could have handled it. I had high hopes for that girl. She would have been a few years older than you now, but I would have been proud as punch if she'd been either an astronaut or a medical technologist." He paused quite a while. "Now I find myself wondering, as you started to say, what kind of future any of us have. If any."

"Let's not get too pessimistic before we're sure we have to," Pilar cautioned. "We've still seen only a few scattered bits of evidence that anything big is going on."

"Yet those bits are very suggestive of a potential enemy with fearsome powers."

"Which may or may not mean we actually have one, or that we can't do anything about it. What if our scattered bits are all there are?"

"They're still pretty scary."

"Yes." Pilar walked silently for several seconds, not quite chewing on her lip, but steadying it with her teeth to keep it from trembling. "I'm scared, too, Lester. But the key fact is that what kind of future we have will depend on what comes out of the research they're doing here. At least somebody's *doing* it now. Let's give it a chance. In the meantime, let's go get some dinner."

Chapter 16

 There was a new person present when the group next assembled in the conference room, two mornings later. Pilar had found the intervening day frustrating; she would almost have preferred being back at work. Weston had not been able, or so he said, to get her and her civilian colleagues in where the action was, where the samples were being examined. It wasn't *fair,* she kept telling herself and anyone who would listen—which meant Lester and Maybelle, and they all soon tired of telling each other that and listening to the others saying the same thing. So they all spent a fair amount of the day alone, fidgeting and wondering what, if anything, other people were accomplishing. But at least the tests on them had begun, and Weston had called them back for another meeting "to compare notes," though he emphasized—unnecessarily, Pilar thought—that they should not think of that as any more than a courtesy briefing or perhaps an informal brainstorming session.

A new face at least meant the prospect of *something* new, especially a face that seemed as out of place in this gathering as this one. He was there when Lester arrived, a tall, skinny man, perhaps in his mid-fifties, with long, unruly red hair and a matching beard going gray in irregular streaks. Clad in jeans and a pullover shirt, not tucked in, in some Amerindian pattern, he reminded Pilar of pictures she'd seen in old history books showing "hippies" from the time of Korea or Vietnam or one of those old wars. Which, even to her, made him an incongruous contrast to the only other people in the room, the three Aerospace officers.

The four of them were standing near the end of the table in the "theater" end of the room, talking what sounded like physics. Colonel Edwards looked out of his element: trim in his uniform, he kept looking at the newcomer with ill-concealed distaste and saying very little—probably, Pilar suspected, because for him the conversation was in a foreign language. Major Simonetti, on the other hand, seemed quite engrossed in what the "aging hippie" was saying, and indifferent to his appearance. Even Weston looked interested, though not quite as comfortable with the company, and occasionally even contributed something.

None of them showed any sign of noticing Pilar's entrance.

Then Maybelle came in and her face lit up. "Dan!" she exclaimed, rushing over to interrupt the newcomer with a hug. "I was worried about you. It's so good to see you here." She beckoned Pilar over. "Pilar, I want you to meet my grandson, Dan Felder. He's the one I told you about. Leading light in nanotech research—"

"Hi, Pilar," he said, grinning and extending his hand. "I've heard about you, too. Don't pay too much attention to Grandma. It's part of her job description to say things like that. My son, who's something like your age and a *real* leading light in nanotech, considers me an old fogey."

"I'm pleased to meet you," said Pilar with a smile. "I know about grandmas, but I'll bet you're as glad as I am to have one. I have to tell you, yours is already one of my heroes." A momentary worry about how her own was doing flickered across Pilar's mind and she changed the subject. "I can't wait to hear what you've learned."

"Don't get your hopes too high," Dan cautioned.

To the Aerospace guys Maybelle said, "I can see you've all met already, so I don't need—" But by then Lester and Linley Delacorte and Iona Branford were coming in, and introductions were completed all around. The process was pretty obviously more informal than Weston had planned, but eventually he some-how got everybody settled around the table and quieted down.

"This meeting," he said, "is by way of a progress report, though I'll tell everybody right up front I wish we had more progress to report. I'd like to offer the floor first to our new guest. Dr. Felder?"

"Thanks," said Dan. He spoke softly and didn't stand up, but he nonetheless riveted all their attention. "First of all, I'd like to thank everybody involved in getting that new specimen to me. By the way, Grandma, if you didn't get a note with that thing, you should definitely try to contact whoever sent it and find out anything they can tell you about how they found it and what it was doing.

"Anyway, you're all wondering: what did we find out about it? First of all, I'm pleased to be able to tell you that this one did not vanish mysteriously and we were able to run some tests on it. As far as I know, the bug itself is still intact, or as intact as it can be after our testing, and safely stored in our labs, with some extra security provided by Aerospace. We were able to make records of our test results and store multiple copies of them. The last I heard, all those copies were still intact and accessible.

"Now, if only we knew what they meant . . .

"OK, we did learn a *little* from them. They definitely incor-porate nanotechnology. If any of you are not too familiar with nanotech and are frowning and thinking, 'That thing is obviously much bigger than nanoscale,' let me assure you that I'm not using the terminology sloppily. Obviously Grandma's bug is macro-scopic, but its constituent parts are nanoscopic. That implies that there are a *lot* of constituent parts in there, and we've only begun to understand what they do. The eyes really are eyes—that is, optical signal processors. On the few occasions when we man-aged to get any output from them, though, it wasn't related to the input in any way we've seen before. And after a while we were unable to get any output. This may mean that we damaged it, or it may mean that it's programmed to 'play possum' if certain things happen to it.

"When we tried tracing internal connections beyond the eyes, we ran into several problems. There are an awful lot of them, and many of the structures are even more compact than we'd imagined possible. We're pretty sure we've recognized some of them as information-processing circuitry, but it doesn't seem to work in any familiar way. There obviously has to *be* a lot of info-processing capability, because from Grandma's description of the behavior of the first one she sent me and the others she'd heard about, it's mobile and responds to stimuli in complex ways. The mobility, by the way, implies that there are also complex motor mechanisms and feedback loops.

"However, we've built things like that, so we know what kind of circuitry is required to make them work. What's in these things seems to be *way* more than enough, even if it doesn't include quantum computers—and we have reason to suspect that it does."

"So what's all the extra?" Lester asked. "Do you think they *are* espionage devices, like Maybelle speculated?"

Dan shrugged. "I can't rule it out. There's plenty of storage medium there."

"But . . ." Lester frowned. "I've thought about this before, and I keep stumbling against the same wall. If they're gathering a lot of information, what do they do with it? On their own, I don't think they could take much action on it. Assuming there are great swarms of these things collecting data, I'd think it would have to go to some central place for processing. And I just don't see how that little thing can carry a suitable antenna to transmit it."

"Nor did we find any," Dan granted. "And I'll have to admit, that's the biggest bugaboo—sorry—bothering us, too. We basically agree with your objection, and we haven't thought of a good way around it." He grinned nervously. "We have thought of some that we suspect are pretty bad. For example, maybe they don't have to send it all to a central clearing house, but are somehow linked so that a swarm of them *is* the clearing house and big computer that it must take to analyze the data and act on it."

"But that would still take antennas," Lester pointed out.

"True. So we're not really happy with that idea. Another we considered is that they don't need an antenna because they simply *go* to the clearing house, physically carrying what they've collected."

"Too clunky," Lester grumbled. "They fly many orders of magnitude slower than an electromagnetic signal. And if they have to go far, there's a good chance they'll meet some mishap and never make it."

"Quite true. So we're pretty much driven back to saying they must be sending their findings somewhere, and we're baffled as to how." He chewed his lip. "Of course, this area isn't really my specialty. Maybe we need to find somebody in a different field to take a look at the problem. Frankly, I've had very little occasion to think about antennas. My work has mostly been with nanoprocessors and medical nanobots."

"Which leads us to the other samples," said Pilar. "How about the things in our blood?"

"And my computer?" Maybelle added.

Dan nodded as if relieved to have attention diverted away from an area where he wasn't much at home. Even so, he said, "More puzzles. The blood structures appear to include a good deal of memory storage and processing power, but we don't know what they're storing or what they might eventually do with it. They have a vague resemblance to some specialized assemblers, but we don't know what they would assemble. The one thing we can be grateful for is that at the moment they don't seem to be doing anything."

But there's no assurance that that will last, Pilar thought grimly. "Is there any way you can get them out?"

"That's one of the many things we have people looking into," said Dan. "I wish I could tell you something more positive, but you've got to understand that there's an *awful* lot of work to be done to try to understand these things, and very few points of familiarity to use as toeholds to get started on it. And we'll have to be very careful about any countermeasures we might try. The only avenue that looks at all promising is sending in our own nanomechs to disable the ones in your blood. But they may have defense mechanisms that would be far more dangerous than leaving them alone. And we're not even sure our skills are up to building counterbugs. We're pretty new at this; whoever made these apparently isn't."

"Meaning aliens," said Pilar, her throat dry.

"Looks likelier than the alternative," said Dan. "As for Grandma's computer boards, they have indeed been rewired way down at the intrachip level—almost certainly by dedicated and programmed disassemblers and assemblers." He chuckled nervously. "This may give a whole new meaning to the term 'computer virus.'"

Nobody else chuckled. After a long, awkward silence, Edwards—the colonel from combat, Pilar recalled—said, "So what's the bottom line? If they were sent by aliens in that orbiting fleet, what do they want? How dangerous are they? What can we do about them?"

Dan shook his head. "They're good questions, I agree, but we'll have no good answers until we learn more about them, and they're not making that easy. However, if you're interested in my wild speculations and personal opinions about what the key variables are, I can give you those." He paused as if awaiting permission.

"Please do," said Edwards, his impatience barely concealed.

"Well, sir, they're potentially very, *very* dangerous—if there are enough of them and if their operators have hostile intentions or careless habits. On the other hand, if they don't, these things may be perfectly harmless, no matter how many of them there are. But I personally consider that highly unlikely. I realize the risks of trying to imagine how aliens would think, but it seems to me that anybody who goes to the expense and trouble of developing these things and sending them to somebody else's planet is going to want to get a return on the investment—a *big* return on investment. And I don't see how that can be good for us."

"I can imagine possible ways," said Maybelle. "Maybe they're sizing us up before they approach us about trade, economic or cultural—"

"Nice try, Grandma, and I'll grant you that it's *conceivable*. But I still don't believe it's likely. They haven't offered to let us size *them* up—"

"Maybe they have. Maybe giving us these tantalizing glimpses and seeing how we respond is their way of doing that, and at the same time a test."

"Maybe, but if so, I don't like their way of doing it, and that makes me doubt that I'm going to like them. As you well know, I've never been a fan of Big Brother's eyes. I'd rather accept responsibility for my own life and security than have Someone to Watch Over Me. And I sure don't want somebody *else's* government watching over me, especially with the efficiency these things seem likely to have."

Edwards broke in with a sigh pointedly lacking in subtlety. "The bottom line, Dr. Felder. If we have to, can we fight them?"

Dan looked the colonel right in the eyes. "I certainly hope we can avoid that. As a wise man once wrote, 'Violence is the last refuge of the incompetent.' Of course, I realize that he was too optimistic and sometimes it's the *first* refuge, so we could get forced into it. And I sure hope that doesn't happen in this case, because no, Colonel, I *don't* think we can fight them. Their nanotech, and especially the way they seem to integrate it with remote sensing and massive data-crunching, is just too far beyond ours. Of course, we can't assume that. It may well be that we *will* have to fight them, and we'd better prepare by learning everything we can that might at least help us defend ourselves." He allowed himself a wistful look. "What I'd much prefer, of course, would be to talk to them. If we could take a few lessons, we might be able to give our own development a real boost."

Edwards did not look pleased with the answer. "So in your opinion, and bearing in mind that they may be here for a very different purpose than giving lessons, what should we be doing now?"

"Two main things, besides continuing to have everybody possible look at our few specimens of handiwork from as many angles as possible. First, try even harder to establish communication. I realize lessons are probably too much to hope for, but talking to them may be our only hope of making sure it doesn't come to fighting."

"So far," the colonel observed dryly, "we seem a lot more interested in talking than they do."

"Which is all the more reason to keep trying—and perhaps we'd better keep in mind that, for whatever reason, their only known attempts at communicating so far have involved these three people. And those attempts have been intended to close off communication, not open it up. Their general lack of apparent interest in talking is also a reason for the second thing we must do: try to find out just how widespread the spy-bugs are—if that's what they are."

"We really don't have many reports of them," Edwards mused, and it seemed to Pilar that he was clutching at straws. "Basically, just from the handful of people in this room. It's true that you've described a good deal of strange activity, but might we hope that this is a purely local anomaly?"

"No," Pilar said flatly. "I know they're in Puerto Rico, too. Didn't I tell you what happened to my sister?" As she said it, she wondered what else might have happened to Rosa since then, and cringed.

"I suppose," said Dan, "we could allow ourselves the luxury of *hoping* that it's limited to a few spots in the Hudson Valley and an island more than a thousand miles away. It would be more prudent to assume that they may be everywhere and try to find out. Think of how much trouble the people here had getting anybody to pay any attention to them, and how few others have heard what they have to say. There may be thousands of others in the same boat, and less persistent.

"There may also be lots of others who don't even realize they're seeing anything unusual. To recognize an odd bug, you have to have some familiarity with the normal ones. And there's evidence that the operators are learning from experience. We already knew that they apparently added self-destruct mechanisms to later models that the first ones didn't have. There are hints that they're getting better at camouflage, too. That weird swarm of apparently normal insects that followed Pilar and Lester across Central Park, for—"

"Excuse me, sirs," a new voice broke in. Dan stopped in mid-sentence and frowned as an Aerospace corporal opened the door, strode across the room, and saluted the officers. He held an envelope out to Simonetti. "I was told to deliver this to you right away, sir."

"Thank you, Corporal." Simonetti flipped him an indifferent salute and added, when the corporal didn't move, "Dismissed."

The corporal left and everyone else, including Dan, waited patiently as Simonetti read the contents, his expression growing more rigid with each line. "Ladies and gentlemen," he said as he finished, "I fear things have just gotten more complicated. My group has been searching for any evidence of more suspicious objects out there, and I've just been informed that after a diligent check for other explanations, they've confirmed finding two stealthed fleets, very much like the first, equally spaced around the same orbit."

 **Simonetti was right:** the discovery of two more fleets of stealthed orbiters did complicate things, to put it mildly. In addition to substantially raising the prevailing fear level, it inspired a renewed emphasis on trying to communicate with any occupants of any of the satellites—so all messages were now beamed to all three stealthed fleets.

"Unfortunately," Edwards said when the group reconvened two days later, "it seems that three can ignore us as cheaply as one. We've repeated everything we'd already tried on the first orbiter we spotted, this time to all three, and added several new approaches as well. The results were exactly the same as before: absolutely nothing." It seemed to Pilar that he looked harried, as if the strain were wearing him down. She suspected he wasn't getting much sleep.

"Do the new groups appear to be sending anything?" Lester asked.

"Maybe. The same kinds of sporadic, staticky bursts we saw from the first—stuff that could be random noise, or communications among entities scarily better at data compression than we are."

"Moonbase and the Space Station looked too?"

"Yes. They saw about the same. None of us saw much. All of us are haunted by the possibility that there's more to what we're seeing than meets the eye."

"Have any probes been launched toward the newcomers? Manned or unmanned?"

"No. At this point we're treating that as a last resort. It seems prudent not to kick these sleeping dogs, at least until we're sure they *are* sleeping dogs and not wide-awake wolves. Of course, if we can't find out . . ." Edwards's voice trailed off as if he were too worried by the implied thought to finish speaking it aloud—and that worried Pilar.

Maybelle filled the lull. "Last time we met I gave you contact information for some of the people I'd asked for bug samples or unusual phenomenon reports. You were going to try to follow them up. Has anything come of that?"

Simonetti answered, but he didn't meet her eyes. "I'm afraid so. Luther Miltons, who sent you the sample Dr. Felder is analyzing, can't tell us anything. He's hospitalized and in a coma following a car accident."

"Oh, God," Maybelle breathed, but then her analytical side kicked right back in. "Single car or multiple? Auto or manual?"

"We don't have the official report from the police yet, but the preliminary word is that he was alone and on autopilot."

"Impound the car," Lester blurted. "Check all its processors for the kind of tampering Maybelle's computer showed."

"And check *him*," Pilar added. "Run a full blood profile and EM scan, right away. And get a neurologist checking for any damage there."

"And keep me posted on his condition and any new developments there," said Maybelle. "How about the others?"

"Two we can't find," said Simonetti. "They seem to have disappeared, and nobody knows where they are. Another is dead and buried, and it may be too late to learn anything from an autopsy."

"None was done?" Maybelle asked incredulously.

"HMOs," Pilar muttered through clenched teeth, and nobody needed any further explanation.

"Two were on vacation," Simonetti went on. "They didn't

leave itineraries with anyone and they haven't turned up online. That could mean the worst—"

"Or it may just mean that they're stubborn old geezers like me who still value privacy when they're on their own time," said Maybelle. "I know them; they are. But just this once, I wish they had caved in to modern ways."

"So there's still hope," Simonetti finished. "We haven't found those two, but we haven't given up, either. If they went away early enough, they may never have got your messages. Which means they may have nothing to tell us, but at least maybe they haven't suffered the consequences of knowing too much." He sighed. "I don't know if you were counting, Dr. Terwilliger, but that pretty much exhausts the list, except for a couple you indicated were particularly close to you. I'm glad to tell you we *were* able to find them, but they had nothing to tell us. I gather you didn't ask people to reply if they had nothing of interest."

"No," Maybelle admitted. "Though I suppose I should have thought of it. So what now?"

Edwards resumed the floor, so visibly distraught that Pilar guessed that even he hadn't heard what Simonetti had just reported until now. "We have to try harder," he said grimly. "I know I said just minutes ago that we considered more probes a last resort, and anything of that nature will certainly require approval from higher up. But I think the time has come to seriously consider it. I'd suggest more probes, this time to all three known orbiting clusters. Unmanned first, of course, but this time equipped with better internal monitors so we can watch very carefully what happens to them, inside and out. And if those don't work, maybe we should try launching a weapon at them— a *big* weapon."

Simonetti looked aghast. "Colonel, are you talking about a nuke?"

"Quite possibly, Major."

"Do you really think that's wise? Whoever they are, we still know very little about either their intentions or their capabilities. Deliberately starting a fight with somebody you know so little about could be extremely dangerous."

"So could waiting while they strengthen their position." Edwards smiled thinly. "Don't worry, Major, I'm not proposing that we plunge rashly into anything. Any decision like this would be discussed thoroughly at the very highest levels—which, I hardly need remind you, does not mean here. But if there's anybody out there, and they can do what we've seen so far, I for one don't believe they can't understand us. Ms. Ramirez's mysterious visitor alone seems more than ample proof of that. I'm quite sure they've understood a great deal of what we've said among ourselves, but for whatever reason have been ignoring everything we've addressed directly to them. If we give them a direct warning that we're going to destroy them if they don't respond, and they ignore—"

"You've got that right," an unfamiliar bass voice boomed from no identifiable direction, as the room plunged into darkness and a shiver shot like lightning along Pilar's spine.

The darkness was not quite complete, she realized as the initial shock passed and her eyes—along with everyone else's—were drawn to the "theater" end of the room. There greenish mists swirled in a vaguely defined globe in midair, not quite hiding a huge, disembodied face: a bald man with craggy eyebrows and a sardonic expression. It reminded her of something, but at first she couldn't think of what it was. Then she remembered the time when she was little when her Grandmother had taken her to see the umpteenth digital remake of *The Wizard of Oz*, and the phrase "Pay no attention to the man behind the curtain" popped into her mind.

But the man—or whoever, or whatever—behind *this* apparition had everybody's fully riveted attention.

"The part about ignoring you, I mean," it went on. "And the part about understanding a great deal of what you say to each other.

"I see, by the way, that you're devoting too much of your attention to our audiovisual effects. Please don't; try to concentrate on what we say. It was very kind of you, by the way, to provide this nifty equipment for communication. Not bad, for such primitive creatures. But let's not forget that it *is* just equipment for communication. The message is more important than the medium." The face morphed momentarily into that of an old gypsy woman leading a cartoonesque seance, then back. "We did give some thought to what form we should appear to you in. We toyed, for example, with being an angelic host—" For a moment it *became* an angelic host, with a few shiny, winged beings here in the room and untold numbers of others stretching off into infinity. "—or the Devil." Suddenly the face became Satan, red and horned, laughing evilly, his surrounding mists now hellishly red and swirling as if blown by fierce winds.

Then the "Wizard" was back, with his cooler, calmer green mists and his almost avuncular visage. "But then we thought, those are too loaded with connotations for you folks. You'd *never* see the message through the medium if we used those. We'd better stick to something a little more neutral. So here we are."

"Who *are* you?" Maybelle demanded.

"We are scientists," the Wizardly image boomed, "attempting to study your planet. The old lady made a lucky guess: what we are doing is very much as she surmised. But it seems necessary to remind you that we are also, as some of you have guessed, a huge and powerful fleet currently deployed in several groups around your world. I personally am Xipharatangzap, the Exalted High Commander of that great fleet. If you find my name too difficult to pronounce, even though that form of it has been customized to fit your tongues, you may address me as Xiphar— provided you do so with fitting respect."

"Why should we respect you?" Iona Branford demanded, presumably on behalf of State.

"Must I repeat myself?" Xiphar asked with a creditable sigh. "Because I am Xipharatangzap, Exalted High Commander of a great and powerful fleet which has your world surrounded. Because we are, as some of you have guessed, nearly omniscient— though not yet quite as nearly as we plan to be. The obvious inference is that you cannot hope to prevent us from doing what we want, should you be so unwise as to try. Yet you have already done things that interfere seriously with our mission, things that have gone on more than long enough. You are not alone in this, though you were among the first. But all of you must stop." Again that sigh. Xiphar, or whoever or whatever was speaking for him, must be pleased with that effect. "We have several hundred of these dialogs going on as we speak. We frankly have better uses for our resources."

"What must stop?" Branford demanded. "Why must it stop? What *is* your mission?"

"Our mission," Xiphar explained with exaggerated patience (and Pilar mused that this simulation was a lot smoother than the one in her apartment), "is to learn everything about your world. It's just a small part of our larger mission to learn everything about the universe, just as your little planet is a very small part of the universe. But even your scientists know that to learn how a system really functions, the observer must disturb it as little as possible. That is what we had hoped to do here: to observe everyone here without attracting anyone's attention to ourselves. That is why we ignored your efforts to contact us. We hoped you'd give up, decide we weren't here, and start ignoring us, too. But we underestimated your stubbornness and snoopiness.

"Then you started throwing things at us. That was rude, but we couldn't ignore it. Still, we hoped that after a few frustrating and frightening experiences, you'd give it up and go back to your own business."

"You may have collected a lot of data," Maybelle snorted, "but you have a lot to learn about human nature. I wonder if you're up to it." She paused. "So why are you showing yourselves now, and so flamboyantly at that?"

"Because showing ourselves to a few of you is our best hope of avoiding having to deal with a lot of you later, and still salvage some of our original goal. 'Damage control,' I believe you call it. Our hope, as we've already told you repeatedly, is to learn about your world and its normal operations, not what happens when it's disturbed by something unfamiliar and confusing." Oddly, Pilar understood exactly what he was saying. She remembered the time when she'd tried to videotape a baby nephew, hoping to capture his natural expressions and antics, but every time she started the camera, the baby stopped what he was doing to stare at the whirring black box.

Yes, she understood. But she was not ready to think of humanity as a baby, or these aliens as their collective aunt.

"Why this particular moment?" Xiphar went on. "Because one of you has just broached an idea so unacceptable that it needs to be nipped in the bud. And we prefer to do that with as little contact as possible."

"So your idea," Pilar said, "is that if you can talk those of us who've noticed you into pretending we haven't, then you can go back to watching all of us as if nobody knows about you?"

"Something like that," said Xiphar. "Of course, we are not so stupid or gullible as to believe things can ever be *exactly* as they were. The cat is out of the bag, so to speak. You forced our hand, regrettably, with your probes. Our response was unavoidable, but highly visible. Even after we persuade all of you to do the right thing, we cannot go back to a state where those unfortunate incidents never happened. What you *can* do is to explain to your fellow beings that we mean them no harm and they should forget about us and go on as if we weren't here."

"How can you claim to be nearly omniscient," Edwards demanded, "and ask something as asinine as that? You obviously haven't learned the first thing about—"

"If I may, Colonel?" Branford interrupted gently. Edwards was so taken aback that he shut up, and Ms. Branford addressed Xiphar. "Certainly we're willing to listen to whatever you have to say, Xiphar, but I must agree with my esteemed colleague that what you propose seems a bit less than realistic. Simply from a practical standpoint, what makes you think the world *could* forget about you even if we told them they should? We noticed your spy bugs, and by your own admission many others have done so, too. If you continue to use them, your subjects will continue to notice them. Your only hope of not being caught observing us is to *stop* observing us."

"Not so," Xiphar snapped.

"Oh?" Branford asked mildly. "Perhaps you could enlighten us on the way out of that dilemma."

"A magician does not explain his tricks," Xiphar declared. "But I believe one of you has already answered that question. If you failed to recognize that you were doing so, I'm certainly not going to help you." He paused. "But you can make all of our lives much easier if you will help me."

"That's another thing I don't quite grasp," said Branford. "You seem quite comfortable demanding help and information from us, but completely unwilling to share any about yourself. From our point of view, that isn't a reasonable expectation. We might be very interested in some sort of *exchange*, but this one-sided giving—or taking, if we want to be completely honest about it—simply won't do. If those are the only terms you're willing to consider, we have very little—"

Edwards lost patience. "Oh, let's stop pussyfooting, Iona." He glared at the "Wizard." "What you're demanding is simply out of the question. Humans will not be intimidated like this, or let ourselves be spied upon for who knows what purpose, because that's not how we're built. It's as simple as this. Either you show yourselves and discuss things face-to-face, leave, or we will destroy you or drive you off. Is that clear enough?"

The Wizard responded with a startling, chilling burst of Mephistophelean laughter. When the peals finally faded away, he said, "Quite clear, Colonel, and quite amusing. I appreciate your speaking plainly, so I will do the same. Surely you can't imagine that you could have any real hope of destroying or repelling us, given our relative levels of technology."

"There are a whole planetful of us," Edwards said, "against—how many of you?"

"More than enough. And when was the last time your whole planetful managed to do anything in a concerted way?" He paused for effect, and Pilar had to admit that it worked, at least for her. "No, ladies and gentlemen, your only hope is to forget about us and go on about your business. We have no desire to harm or interfere with you, but we are determined to carry out our mission. If you are unable to grasp the true nature of our relationship and persist in trying to interfere with us, we shall reluctantly adopt an alternate approach—which both you and we will find far less satisfactory."

Pilar felt herself go pale, despite the dark room and her swarthy complexion. "And what," Edwards asked defiantly, "do you mean by that?"

"I mean," said Xiphar, "if we can no longer observe like astronomers, we shall experiment like physicists." And with a dramatic roar and swirling of green mists that gradually faded to black, he vanished.

*   *   *

For a moment they all sat in stunned silence and pitch darkness. Then, smoothly but not quite reassuringly, the room lights came back up. "Nobody say anything," Edwards barked, and then he muttered something Pilar couldn't quite make out to his lapel. Nobody disobeyed his order, and the silence remained, give or take an occasional stifled cough or throat-clearing, for several minutes until a corporal came in with several candles and flashlights. Wordlessly, he distributed them around the table, lit the candles, and left the room.

Then all the lights went out, including the tiny indicators on the wall sockets. Even the faint hum of the air conditioners, normally beneath conscious notice, stopped, leaving a deafening silence against which Pilar could hear her own blood pumping.

Only then did Edwards speak again, his face eerily lit from beneath by the candles. "Obviously," he said, his voice tightly controlled, "we can no longer assume this room is safe for discussing these matters, though I hope turning off the electricity will buy us a little time. Not only were they able to gain control of our own equipment, but they knew what was being said here and were able to respond to it in real time. This is not a comfortable situation we're in."

"Will *any* place be safe?" Pilar barely breathed.

"I don't know," said Edwards. "I hope my more scientifically minded colleagues"—he gestured vaguely toward Weston, Simonetti, and Dan—"will be able to help us find a good answer. But yes, I do have some ideas of my own. They require the best our country can provide; but then, it's abundantly clear that we're going to have to take this to the very top anyway."

"Abundantly clear," agreed Branford, who had been staring incredulously at him ever since the lights came back on. "Colonel, do you realize what you've just done?"

"All too well," he said grimly. "But, by God, I don't see that I had any choice in the matter! Nobody could have anticipated being put on this spot. I'm prepared to defend what I did, and to do everything in my power to make sure we *can* make good on it, if that becomes necessary."

"I hope," Iona Branson said very quietly, "that we can, if it comes to that. I hope even more that it will *not* come to that."

Pilar sat numbly, trying without much success to grasp the potential enormity of what had just happened here. The threat of Earth being overrun by hostile and powerful aliens, though, seemed oddly distant and unreal. She instead found herself staring into the blank theater area at the end of the room, concentrating harder and harder on the blank wall as if determined to see what was there, even though she knew there was no longer anything.

But then, in a sense, nothing ever had been. Had it?

She frowned and chewed her lip, trying to grasp the unformed thought that was gnawing at her subconscious.

 The room where next they met was very different. First of all, it was far away—much closer to Washington, D.C., though Pilar couldn't say exactly where, since the last part of the trip involved an astoundingly long underground train ride. The whole trip was tense; nobody talked much, for fear that whatever they said would be overheard by the seemingly ubiquitous peeping aliens. But she had no trouble sensing the unspoken but general apprehension that the trip would be a good opportunity for Xiphar's hordes, who had already demonstrated that they were not limited to passive observing, to get all these pesky humans out of their way.

Yet no mishaps occurred. Pilar tried to think about why that would be, which meant trying to see the situation from the aliens' point of view, despite her profound ignorance about who they were and what made them tick. But their actions had to make *some* sort of sense, and she was trying hard to recognize patterns in them.

Oddly, the best explanation she could come up with involved the assumption that Xiphar was telling the truth, at least about the aliens trying to observe Earth without calling attention to themselves. *Why* they were observing Earth remained a vexing and profoundly troubling question. But if that single fact was true, and the aliens (*We need a better name for them*, she thought) had already learned *something* about humans, then they might realize that doing away with the human "snoops" would attract even more unwanted attention.

175

Which left open the question of what more devious plans they might be hatching for later.

Her thinking got no further than that when the train came to a stop and the second big difference in their new meeting facilities made itself evident. As she and Lester and Maybelle and Dan disembarked, they were led by still more military underlings into a long tunnel, and from that through a series of decontamination chambers full of warning lights and scanners and things that flashed and buzzed and hissed, some of which Pilar recognized and some she didn't.

She was hardly surprised, somehow, that the last barrier was a long counter behind which sat several bureaucrats who grilled the newcomers with inane questions to establish that they were who they said they were, no one else had handled their luggage, etc., even though they had never been out of their escorts' sight during the whole trip. Pilar bore it patiently, but meanwhile strained to hear the conversation drifting through the half-open door on the far side of that room.

"—made a threat that clearly exceeded your authority," said a gruff male voice that sounded vaguely familiar. "Now we may be forced to make good on it, and I'm not at all sure we can. It was, to put it as politely as I can, pure irresponsible bravado, Colonel, and when—*if*—all this blows over, you'll be held fully accountable. I thought you people could be trusted to do a rational investigation to find out how serious this was before you let things escalate to this level. You know as well as I that I should have been called in well before any action like this."

"Of course, sir," said a voice that Pilar, walking down the hall toward the last door, recognized at once as Edwards. "But it all happened so suddenly—"

"Thanks largely to your impulsiveness. I'm not interested in excuses, Colonel. Yes, they caught you by surprise, but for all you know they were bluffing."

"I'd like to believe that, sir. But maybe they weren't."

"Which is all the more reason for you to stall instead of countering with a foolish bluff that you—we—can't afford to have called. Now we're going to have to—" By then Pilar was at the semi-open door. The speaker saw her and cut off in midsentence, and Pilar was startled to recognize him from his media pictures. "We'll finish this later, Colonel," President Herman Hwang said curtly. Then he got up and walked to the door with his patented public smile and outstretched hand. "Come in, ladies and gentlemen. I'm so glad you could join us."

After personal greetings all around, the whole New York–New Jersey contingent was shown to seats around a table much like the one they had left, except that this one looked like mahogany. Pilar was vaguely relieved to see that there was no obvious holotheater in the room.

The table had a clearly defined head, and Hwang sat there. He looked more "real" than in the media; at this distance she could see worry lines that were never transmitted by wires or waves. But he still exuded the personal charisma that kept getting him elected, even though, at least for Pilar, it inspired little real confidence. Puerto Rico and the U.S. had been trying for decades to figure out what their relationship should be, and Hwang had always seemed to her to have made singularly little progress toward that goal.

But he did look like the very epitome of "American," as defined by current fashion. After all the oscillations she'd read about in school, the "melting pot" concept was fashionable once more, and Hwang looked like a one-man melting pot. His features, like his name, were archetypically Chinese, but he bore them atop a tall, rangy frame topped off with startlingly blonde hair more suggestive of Scandinavia than Szechwan.

When everyone else was seated, Hwang nodded toward a noncom standing near the door, who stepped outside and closed it so tightly that Pilar felt the pressure change in her ears. "I think we all realize," the president said quietly as he settled into his own seat, "that we're in what may be a very large-scale emergency situation and still know far too little about either the threat or our options. Obviously we have to figure some out—a necessity which has become rather more pressing rather sooner than I had hoped—and we also know that it may be very difficult to have a secure conversation. But I want to begin by reassuring you that our chances of achieving that are at least as good in this room as anywhere on the planet.

"I apologize, *pro forma*, for what you may have perceived as the indignity of the search and decontamination procedures you were subjected to on the way in; but I trust you will agree that they were necessary. After the obviously disturbing encounter—if that's the word—at your last meeting, we want to be as sure as humanly possible that nobody uses you to slip any kind of espionage or communication device into this one.

"I realize, of course, that our efforts weren't *quite* as complete as we might like. I'm aware of the unusual structures some of you are carrying in your blood, but I agree with Dr. Felder that trying to remove or deactivate them at this point would carry an unacceptable personal risk to you. Fortunately they don't seem very active so far, anyway. So we'll pass on that, at least for now.

"To compensate for that gap in our procedures, and guard against any other invasive actions that we might not have anticipated, this room is completely shielded against all forms of electromagnetic radiation, incoming or outgoing. In addition, in case anything *tries* to come in, this area is surrounded by detectors to pick up any unauthorized signals and trace them to their source. I hope you'll understand that, for the duration of this investigation, we'll have to ask you to remain as our guests, in similarly shielded quarters. Naturally, all comings and goings will be through the same inspection and decontamination system you used coming in. I regret the inconvenience, but I see no alternative."

"What if there's a fire?" Maybelle asked. "Or a bomb threat?"

Hwang smiled thinly. "I trust you all hope as devoutly as I do that nothing like that happens. Any such emergency would make us extra vulnerable, at least temporarily. Yes, we have anticipated the possibility, and none of us has any intention of being trapped in here, or trapping anyone else, in the unlikely event that it happens. You will notice quite ordinary fire alarm triggers liberally scattered throughout the complex. If you're ever *sure* such a danger exists, naturally you will use the nearest trigger. That will activate heat sensors coupled to automatic fire extinguishers, among other things. It will also temporarily deactivate all the usual security barriers so everyone can get out without delay, and floor lights will direct you to the nearest exit.

"But if you are ever tempted to use one of those triggers, I can't emphasize too strongly that you must be *very* sure the danger is real and imminent—because during the time security is down, just about anything can get in or out. Need I elaborate?"

He scowled at the notepad in front of him, then looked back up at his literally captive audience as if daring anyone to challenge him. "Good," he said after a carefully timed pause. "Just one more thing before we get down to our main item of business. Some of you are probably wondering why you're here—and why I'm here. For reasons of their own—and they may or may not be as simple as a desire to communicate directly with as few humans as possible—on the rare occasions when the aliens have communicated with humans, one or more of you three"—he nodded—"have always been present. That shouldn't matter, with shielding in place; but if at some point we want to deactivate shields and try again to initiate a dialog, our experience so far suggests that it may be necessary for you to be present and somewhat knowledgeable about what's going on on our side. We may even use some of your suggestions, if you have really good ones. But you won't be *completely* informed and you won't be setting policy. These sessions are purely advisory. I won't have time to be at many of them, but I will look in from time to time because I'm a hands-on kind of guy and I'm not comfortable getting all my information through bureaucratic filters.

"Any questions?" Again he surveyed the assemblage. "Good. Now we get down to business. What are our alternatives? Our main problem has unfortunately been brought rather suddenly into much sharper focus. Colonel Edwards has, in effect, made a threat on our behalf on which we may at any time be forced to follow through. The key question is: what, if anything, can we do if that happens?" He smiled ironically at Edwards. "I assume, Colonel, you have some ideas?"

Edwards drew himself up with at least an outward semblance of pride. "Yes, Mr. President, I do. Our first priority, of course, is to continue trying to learn as much as possible about the threat. But at the same time we must be prepared to defend ourselves if necessary."

"I see. And how goes our progress on learning what's going on?"

"Frustratingly slow, sir. I assume Colonel Weston and Dr. Felder have already briefed you on their labs' attempts to analyze the few specimens we have, and to determine exactly what's in orbit."

"I'm afraid so," said the president. "I'd hoped for more."

"So had we, sir. We know the specimens are nanotech, but so far beyond our own that we haven't been able to understand much about what they do or how they do it. We assume they're connected with the stealthed orbiters, and our . . . uh . . . visitors seem to confirm that. But you already know what's happened to our few efforts to examine the orbiters."

"All too well, Colonel. So what are you doing to learn more about them?"

Edwards swallowed visibly. "Very little, at the moment, sir. That's because what I think we should do next requires your approval. I think we should launch more probes, to all three orbiters."

"Indeed. And if their occupants interpret them as aggression, as they apparently did with your previous attempts?"

"Then we'll have to be prepared to defend ourselves against whatever they do."

"An indisputable suggestion, in principle, but probably unacceptable in practice. *How* will we defend ourselves, either if they attack us in response to our probes or if we decide that honor demands that we actually try to repel them if they ignore your little ultimatum?"

Pilar could have sworn she saw Edwards getting progressively paler. "That's a tough one," he admitted. "But we do have to try. Even if they're doing exactly what they say, just gathering information about us, we can't afford to have anyone learning that much about us without revealing anything about themselves in return."

"On that," said the president, with a thin smile, "I agree with you, Colonel. And yet there remains the practical problem of what we can do against them. I assume you do have some answers to that?"

"Well, sir, their capabilities can hardly be unlimited. If we launched enough rocket-propelled nukes against them, maybe they couldn't defend themselves against all of them."

"Or maybe they could. Rockets take a good deal of time to get where they're going. What if we needed to do something really fast?"

Marv Simonetti, who had been sitting so quietly Pilar had almost forgotten about him, was squirming like a schoolchild who knew the answer. "Permission to speak, sir?"

"Granted," Edwards and Hwang said together.

Simonetti directed his response to the president. "In more normal times, sir, a major part of my work consists of watching for

Earth-crossing asteroids, meteoroids, and comets that might pose a threat to Earth. The vast majority of that consists of watching, watching, and more watching. But the whole idea is that once in a great while we might find something that requires action, and there may not be much time for it. The public doesn't hear much about it, but we have an arsenal of tools intended for deflecting or destroying objects of various sorts. They include a variety of missiles—and some very potent lasers. This might be a good alternate use for some of those tools—if it comes to that."

"I'll certainly keep that in mind," said the president. "Obviously the lasers would be the tool of choice in a case of extreme urgency, but not nearly as useful for information-gathering. So at present I'm leaning, rather cautiously, toward approving some more probes."

"The probes themselves could be armed," Edwards said in a sudden burst of inspiration. "So that any attempt to tamper with them would result in fire directed at the tamperer. We could make sure that they knew that in advance—"

"From what you've told me," Hwang said dryly, "we may not need to tell them. And we don't want to expend either probes, weapons, or laser power reserves too hastily. If we start using them and turn out to need them more later, there may be no time to make new ones."

"I would hope," Iona Branford said quietly, "that that is not our *only* reason for proceeding cautiously. I must say that the saber-rattling has gotten alarmingly loud in here. Let's try to remember that if we can just get these beings to talk to us, we may have a great deal to learn from them."

"Or," Edwards muttered before he could stop himself, "if we can capture some of their orbiters and artifacts reasonably intact."

"Yet another argument," Branford said with a smile, "against using either missiles or lasers except in desperation—and I don't believe we've reached that point yet. No, Mr. President, we should *not* be rushing to decide whether to kick the sleeping dog—to use Colonel Edwards' own apt turn of phrase—or throw rocks at him. We should be trying to learn everything we can about him *before* he wakes up. We're all agreed that that's a dauntingly difficult task, but I know of none more important."

"I agree," said Hwang, "though I also agree with Colonel Edwards that we need to be sure our feet are well shod and a good pile of rocks is at hand." His face underwent a subtle but dramatic shift, as if he had reached a major decision. "Ladies and gentlemen, it's clear that our most urgent priority is to step up our learning curve, both to get whatever general knowledge we can and to know what we're up against. We'll start with a stepped-up investigation of the specimens at hand. You research people will get whatever you need; just tell us what it is and I'll cut through any necessary red tape. You folks in Aerospace, give me a briefing on what kinds of probes we can put together, with and without weapons. Secretary Branford, round up any ideas you can on how we can strike up a conversation with beings who want us to ignore them while they're doing anything but ignoring us. You might also explore—quickly—possibilities for international cooperation, to put up a united front if we need one. All of you, I want any ideas you can come up with for how we can communicate and coordinate plans in the face of the surveillance we seem to be under. And let's meet back here tomorrow."

He started to get up, but a lone voice halted him. "One question, Mr. President?"

It was Maybelle.

"Yes?" Hwang settled back into his seat with a slight frown.

"It seems to me," said Maybelle, deliberately emphasizing her Kansas drawl, "that one of the most urgent questions we're up against is just how much surveillance *are* we under? We're hoping that the security measures you've taken in this room will enable us to talk without being overheard, but we need to know how many places—if any—are like that. One of the things my friends and I were trying to do before y'all shanghaied us was to find out just how widespread these bugs, or things like Lester and Pilar saw on their mountaintop, really are. We didn't have much luck, but you folks have better ways. I think it's important that you use them, right away."

"Hm-m-m." The president stroked his chin. "I'll agree that the question is important, and we can certainly try to put out feelers. But we'll have to do it discreetly. We don't want to panic the people or tip our hand, such as it is, so secrecy is essential—"

"I don't think so," Pilar heard herself blurting out. "I think secrecy is exactly the wrong way to go."

And suddenly the president's eyes were fixed on her, a situation she had not even remotely anticipated—but which did not bother her nearly as much as it might have some people. Pilar had decided at quite an early age that fame and power were highly overrated; folks were just folks, no matter how much of either they had. And the worth of an idea was not determined by who expressed it.

"Oh?" said President Hwang. "An interesting view. Please tell us more."

Pilar swallowed once and did so. "I appreciate your concerns about not panicking people, sir, but it seems to me that if you try to get this kind of information with a bunch of secret inquiries, you're not going to get much farther than we got. Your feelers might not even be directed to the right places, and if the aliens notice you doing it, they may not even get where they're aimed. I think you'd do better to ask *everybody*, all at once."

"But would they allow that?" Hwang asked.

"It's one of the few things they might *have* to allow. One of the things we've agreed on is that no matter how big their computers and study teams are, the amount of information they're getting is probably so huge that it would take time to notice which pieces or patterns are important. If we flood them by sending the same question out to everybody at once, they probably can't stop everybody from answering at once. It may even take them a while to notice that they'd want to. In the meantime, maybe we get enough answers to tell us something useful."

"Hm-m-m." Hwang stroked his chin. "There might be something in that. There's already so much garbage on the internet that even we have trouble picking out the worthwhile parts. If we zap this all over it, and hit radio and television at the same time with the emergency override system we have for hurricanes and such . . . It just might work. I'm not looking forward to the side effects, but I guess every good treatment has those . . . I won't say we'll do it, but I will ask the inner circle to consider it. Thank you, Ms. Ramirez."

As if suddenly oblivious to the people around him, he pulled out his PDA and started working intently on it.

Chapter 19

 It did work, up to a point—and it did have side effects.

It took two days before the president and his security staff, with a good deal of input from Dan and the Aerospace guys, got things coordinated for the simultaneous release of a single, succinct burst of information through virtually every electronic information channel on the planet. That was an unprecedented accomplishment in itself, but it was accompanied by another almost as large: the content of that burst was a closely guarded secret right up to the moment of release.

The content was also a very simple thing, sent forth in roughly a hundred languages, breaking into whatever else might be in progress at the time. It was quite close to what Pilar had sent to her sister Rosa, and Maybelle to her friends and colleagues, but under official auspices and, inevitably, in somewhat official language. In essence: "Have you recently seen or otherwise had contact or experience with any unfamiliar plants, animals, or other objects? If so, please send details and, if possible, specimens to . . ."

The first result was, as they'd hoped, a veritable landslide of stories and quite a few specimens—some of them clearly examples of the alien technology they'd already sampled, plus a lot of perfectly ordinary Earthly arthropods.

Or were they? If the aliens were getting better at disguising their creations, as several experiences had already suggested, it might be harder and harder to tell the invaders' artifacts from things that belonged here. . . .

In any case, there were suddenly enough things to look at to keep lots of scientists and technologists busy. Hwang's minions set about spreading them around and pressing labs into emergency service, and hoped to have important new insights soon.

Meanwhile, there was the main side effect to deal with. Ask that many people that kind of a question, especially when they're already wondering what you're hiding about something like an unexplained shuttle explosion, and you'll get lots of questions back. Most of them boil down to: "Okay, this happened to me, and here's part of a weird bug to prove it. Now, what prompted you to ask? What the hell is going on, and what are you doing about it?" It became a firestorm of question, opinion, and speculation, on the streets and the internet, with the flames fanned to roaring life by the tabloids and their even more potent internet counterparts.

None of which Pilar, Lester, or Maybelle saw firsthand. Those first days after Pilar's suggestion was implemented brought them a little third-hand news and a heavy load of industrial-strength frustration. They were still subjected to occasional testing and cross-examination, but mostly that had reached the stage where unseen and nameless workers were analyzing data already collected. If they learned anything useful, they weren't telling the subjects; and nobody even talked about getting them in on the work anymore. And Hwang's security people were, probably rightly, very serious about keeping this hidey-hole as isolated from the rest of the world as possible. That meant no internet, no telephone, no television, and no radio.

A few newspapers were brought in, through the usual exhaustive decontamination procedures plus some special scans for alien nanotech hitchhikers. Iona Branford told them that special one-shot arrangements for an emergency phone call might be made, should genuine need arise. But basically they were left to stew in their own speculative juices. While that provided plenty of chance for them to get to know each other better, there were also moments when cabin fever threatened to take over. The few newspapers that found their way in raised more questions than they answered about what was going on in the labs and in the outside world, and Pilar and her friends depended heavily on occasional briefings "from the front."

Pacifying the public would keep Hwang too busy to appear personally at most of those, and the first didn't happen until three days after the call for data and specimens went out. Once more the same group—minus Hwang—gathered in the original shielded conference room, this time opening with Marv Simonetti presiding and Dan Felder at his right.

"The bad news," Simonetti opened, "or at least part of it, is that we still haven't been able to learn much about the details of either the orbiters or the spy-bugs. But we do have some gross data that gives us a little more definite idea of the scope of the problem. My group—in collaboration with observers on the Moon and in space—has continued observing the three orbiting groups, and the more we see—or the less we see, depending on how you look at it—the more impressed we are by their stealth technology. Which is a fancy way of saying we don't know much else about them except where they are and that they appear to be big—probably fleets of spacecraft."

"As you've suspected all along," said Lester. "Can't you even put some limits on the total mass of each group?"

Simonetti shook his head. "Not easily or reliably. Assuming they're actually in free orbit, the period-radius relationship is essentially independent of their mass, as long as it's much less than the Earth's—and we're reasonably sure we can assume that, at least. We're less sure that we can assume that they *are* in free orbit. With an advanced alien technology, they could be under continuous thrust from some driver we can't detect, so that even the period-radius relationship is misleading."

"Well, conceivably," said Lester, with a not-quite-concealed scowl. "But if you think that way, they could conceivably be doing *anything* with science we haven't learned yet. If they are, we can't deduce anything about the possibilities. I think we should keep that possibility in mind, somewhere way at the back, and concentrate on what's suggested by what we do know."

"I quite agree," said Simonetti with a smile, "provisionally. For now, let's just say, then, that there appear to be a lot of them, in the positions we've already described, and we've already seen impressive demonstrations of what they can do—which are probably just teasers. And let's note that those possibilities include being in contact with essentially the whole Earth essentially all the time. So it's going to be very hard to get into a position where we're really hidden from them, though I hope this room does the trick. How much they're learning about any place on the globe will depend partly on their direct observation, which we know from our own experience can be very good, especially in middle latitudes. And it will depend partly on how extensive the spy-bug network is, and how it works.

"Which leads me to Part Two. Dr. Felder has been playing a key role in that, since his work provided the starting point for ours, so I thought you might prefer to get the progress report on that end of things from him. Dan?"

"Sure, Marv." Simonetti sat down; Dan didn't bother to stand. "Progress report is a pretty charitable description of what I can offer, but we have learned a few things. I won't repeat what I've already told you about what we've learned and guessed about the structure and functioning of individual bugs. There's not much new to report there; the walls we were up against are holding just fine. What we do have, which is valuable if not encouraging, is a lot more information about extent and distribution.

"We have reports similar to yours, and recognizable specimens, from so many parts of the world that we can conclude that coverage is pretty much global. How dense is it? We're not sure; bear in mind that what we've got our hands on is just a lower limit for what's out there. Our several thousand data points average out to an average separation of several hundred miles, but Grandma and Pilar and Lester's experiences suggest a much higher density in some areas, which may or may not be typical all over. We strongly suspect that even if it isn't as high everywhere as you've observed here, there are probably a lot going undetected for every one captured or described."

"There can't be *too* many, though," Lester pointed out. "If they were sent down directly, the fleets couldn't carry a very large total mass of them. If the fleets just sent down microscopic seeds that grew the bugs using local materials and energy, they could make a whole lot more—but if the numbers got too big, they'd start having an obvious effect on their environment."

Dan nodded. "True. The vast majority of the ones that we've examined fall into a handful of basic models, including the ones you've already shown us. The ones we're seeing are, we suspect, old ones that don't have the self-destruct mechanisms that were apparently added to later models to keep them from being analyzed if we got hold of them. The really scary ones are the very few that are nearly impossible to distinguish macroscopically from ordinary individuals of standard terrestrial species of insects. We suspect these are recent models that will be very hard to recognize, and we were only able to dissect them because these few specimens had defective security mechanisms."

"Or maybe," suggested Weston, "the security mechanisms were left off a few intentionally, just to make sure we'd get the message that they can make them this good."

"I can't rule that out," said Dan. "In any case, our best guess is that there are at least a few for every square mile, and perhaps many more—and growing. We haven't yet managed to make any of our specimens replicate—it may be that the only reason we have them in our possession is that they've lost that ability, among others—but we're pretty sure they can, under appropriate conditions. One of our fondest goals is to learn what those conditions are, so we can make sure they don't have them. On the other hand, if we accidentally manage to turn those conditions on, things could get hairy while we figure out how to turn them back off.

"Still, it's information we need. Work on that front has to go on, as well as continued efforts to figure out how the equipment inside the bugs works—though the difficulties there are large. Partly because the circuitry, if that's the right word, is so tiny; and partly because it seems to use architectures conceptually different from any of ours. For example, we suspect that where we think in terms of circuits that can be diagrammed clearly in two dimensions, theirs require three—"

"The bottom line, Dr. Felder," Edwards interrupted. "How much of a threat are they?"

"I thought I'd made that clear enough," Dan answered, not quite concealing his impatience. "They have the *potential* to be a *very* large threat."

"But we don't *know*," said Pilar, "that they're any threat at all—because we don't know what they're for. So far most of them haven't actually done anything to anybody or anything—"

"You're one of the last people I'd expect to say that," Edwards said with a sneer. "I've heard some of the things that have happened to you. And how about our shuttle, and the brave men who flew it to their deaths?"

"They look bad, all right," Pilar granted. "But these are aliens, after all. Their reasons for doing things may be completely different from what they look like to us. You or I might swat a fly because we want to enjoy a picnic in peace. The fly, if it could think about it, might see us as a huge monster whose main goal in life was the fly's destruction."

"Are you saying we're no more significant than a fly? Young lady, I think you'd better leave this to people more qualified—"

"Do we have any way to know who *is* qualified, Colonel? Sorry if I sound like some upstart kid stepping on your toes, but we know so little about these beings that we need all the ideas we can get, wherever they come from. So no, Colonel, with all due respect, I will *not* shut up and wait for somebody 'better' to get us out of this. If I have an idea that I think needs to be thrown out, I will throw it out; you can shoot it down if you see how. And I'll do the same for you.

"So right now I ask you: how do you *know* that they're not doing exactly what they said, trying to study the Earth just for the sake of knowledge? And that the Aerospace Force and my friends and I don't look to them like just a few pests that threaten to mess up their experiment?"

Edwards glared at her for several seconds before he answered. "I suppose that's conceivable," he said finally, grudgingly. "But even if it is, how do *you* know they're not just doing it so they can later use the knowledge against us?"

"I don't," Pilar answered at once and with a disarming smile. "So we need *both* our ideas, Colonel, and all the others we can get. But tell me, do you have any *new* evidence of anything they've done that looks hostile?"

Now Colonel Edwards smiled. "As a matter of fact," he said slyly, "I just may. I have a clearinghouse back at my office geared to collect any such reports. Maybe now would be a good time to check in with them." Pilar saw a little flicker of motion under the skin of his left cheek that she recognized as his tongue switching on his personal, the late-model cellular phone that wrapped around the base of his left ear, so tiny and so skillfully matched to his skin color and texture that it normally went unnoticed. "I'm using a scrambled signal, of course," he said aloud, and then, looking a little like a not-quite-professional ventriloquist, he subvocalized a call.

Or tried to. A hint of a frown appeared on his forehead and grew. In a few seconds, it was beginning to look like panic. She found herself wondering how Edwards had managed to advance to such a powerful position. Of course, she told herself, we all must have our breaking points. Maybe he's been through a lot even before this all started, and he's just now reaching his. . . .

But he did show signs of just that. "This isn't going through!" he said, sounding as if he were gagging on the words. "They're getting to us even—" He stopped abruptly, looking a bit embarrassed. "Oh. It's the shielding, isn't it? My signal isn't going anywhere." He frowned. "But President Hwang was using his PDA to talk outside—"

"Through wires," Lester said suddenly, with a smile that seemed inappropriate to the circumstances. "But it's a natural mistake; we're all so used to those things working that it's easy to forget we're in an artificial environment where they can't. And I'm glad you tried. I think you've just unwittingly shown me a possible answer to a question that's been bugging me for quite a while. Eureka, one might say—and thank you, Colonel."

Edwards glared at Lester. "What are you babbling about?" he demanded.

"The president's PDA," Lester said quietly, "was connected into a shielded cable network to get a signal out. Major Simonetti tells me that even those cables are now disconnected most of the time, to avoid having *any* breaks in our EM shielding. But if the shielding weren't there . . . Do you know how a cell phone works, Colonel?"

"Well . . . not in great detail, of course. That's not my department. We have specialists for that sort of thing."

"I hope you have some generalists, too. Anyway, watching you try to use that thing just woke up something in my memory. I think my last employer had something to do with phone systems, among other things . . . but that's not the important thing. The important thing is I've been thinking all along that even if all these bugs were gathering vast quantities of information, I couldn't see how they were getting it back to where it could be analyzed. Now I think I do, thanks to you."

"Then will you please come to the point?"

"Of course, Colonel. What bothered me was that at least most of the bugs seemed much too small to transmit appropriate wavelengths as far as they'd have to to reach any of the orbiters. But a cell phone has much the same limitation, though not as severely. A cell phone is a little radio transceiver. You can talk on yours to somebody else on his halfway around the globe, but neither of them has a powerful enough transmitter or a sensitive enough receiver to reach anything like that distance. It doesn't have to. It's called a cellular system because the whole coverage area is divided into lots of 'cells,' each with a relay station that can receive those weak signals and pass them along via the landline network, or receive a signal from the landlines and send it out as a weak radio signal that nearby cell phones can receive, but which won't interfere with distant ones. An individual phone just needs to put out enough signal to reach the nearest cell site.

"Well, suppose the aliens' bugs work something like that. They're too puny to transmit anything to the orbiters, but they don't have to. They just transmit them to the nearest relay station. Or maybe they don't even transmit them. They do fly, after all. Maybe they just take what they've gathered to a transmitting station, dump it, and *that* passes it on to the orbiter."

Dan was nodding. "I like it."

Edwards frowned. "Are you suggesting that the aliens have built transmitting stations all over the planet?"

"Yep," said Lester. "Well, not built, exactly. Grown. But the effect is the same."

"Then why haven't we seen them? Surely we'd notice the transmissions—"

"Not necessarily," said Lester. "They wouldn't be broadcast; that's too inefficient. They'd be using very tight beams, likely tighter than we know how to produce. And maybe not very intense, either, especially if they have sensitive receivers and good noise filters."

"But the antennas themselves!" Edwards objected. "You said those would have to be big—"

"Big*ger*," Lester corrected. "Not necessarily big in an absolute sense."

"But *conspicuous*," Edwards insisted. "Something that doesn't belong."

Pilar felt a tingling at the back of her mind, as if all this was trying to remind her of something not quite remembered.

"Maybe," Lester was saying. "Maybe not. Considering how they seem to have been improving at camouflage, any antennas they've added recently might be very hard to recognize. Earlier ones might be easier, more odd-looking. We should sift through the anecdotal evidence our broadcast brought in to see if anything sounds like what we're looking for."

"Which is?" Edwards prodded.

"Didn't I already say? My idea is that their information-gatherers take what they've collected back to a central location, like bees going back to a hive. So we're looking for—"

The connection broke through into Pilar's consciousness so suddenly she almost leaped out of her chair. "Mount Taurus!" she shouted.

Lester beamed at her. "Yes. Mount Taurus. The place where we saw swarms of these things around a stump that didn't look quite right and interfered with my radio when I got too close to it. I think it's time for another look at what's up there—and anything else that sounds similar."

Chapter 20

 **The trip back** to Mt. Taurus provided their first chance in several days to see some of the outside world firsthand, but Pilar viewed the opportunity with mixed feelings. She kept thinking, as she had throughout that last meeting, that while they had heard from a great many people in response to the broadcast appeal she suggested, there was one message they had *not* received that was conspicuous by its absence.

Why had there been no response from Xiphar and his fleets to such flagrant defiance of their ultimatum?

Pilar couldn't help wondering what sort of other shoe was preparing to drop, and when. That colored her whole view of leaving their shelter to go somewhere else—especially somewhere like Mt. Taurus, which they already had strong reason to view as a nexus of alien activity. And especially when most of the trip would be by air.

Pilar had always liked flying, but she felt oddly naked, in the least pleasant sense of the word, when their small party stepped out of its underground fortress into the bright but hazy sun of a Mid-Atlantic June day. The rim of hills surrounding the tarmac, their forest cover unbroken by human construction, gave some slight feeling of continued shelter, as did the knowledge that this was a well-patrolled government airfield. But the bright sun and open sky overhead, after the days underground, gave a surprisingly sharp feeling of exposure and vulnerability, as if her every move were open to scrutiny and retaliation by—whoever was out there.

The flight crew, two uniformed Aerospace officers who hadn't been introduced, led the way out to the waiting corporate-style jet, painted blue-gray on the belly, camouflage-mottled on top, and otherwise unmarked except for a long number beginning with "N" on the tail. A small knot of noncoms in fatigues, coming along as laborers and gofers, followed them, keeping to themselves. The research party—Marv, Dan, Lester, Maybelle, and Pilar—brought up the rear.

They only had to walk out in the open for fifteen yards or so, but Pilar felt relieved to reach the top of the short stairway and disappear once more into the shelter of the plane—until new questions occurred to her. Had the plane been infiltrated, possibly sabotaged? She was well aware that takeoffs and landings were the most dangerous parts of any flight—normally only minimally so, but might this flight be special? Suppose the watchers really did want to get these particular humans out of the way, but didn't want to attract more attention in the process? This might be the perfect time to do it; a crash on takeoff or landing wouldn't be *too* surprising, and might be tied up in investigation for months or years. . . .

She squelched the thought hard as she looked around for a seat. As she hesitated, Lester gestured into one of the rows. "Would you like the window?" he asked.

She smiled at his thoughtfulness. "Sure. Thanks." She scooted in and he sat down next to her, with Maybelle across the aisle and Dan next to her.

There was no cautionary spiel by a flight attendant, though there was a laminated emergency procedure card and an airsickness bag in the seat back pocket. Neither was there the usual long wait for taxiing out and lining up for a takeoff slot. A tractor was already hooked up to the nose, and as soon as everybody was aboard, it pushed them out. The pilot revved up the engines, did a quick preflight, then taxied straight out to the end of the runway and roared into a takeoff roll without even pausing.

For the first time in her life, Pilar caught her hands gripping the chair arms tensely as acceleration pressed her into the seat-back. A small part of her mind mused that a housefly that had sneaked aboard, appearing near her face right now, could probably send her right off the deep end. But none materialized, and within seconds the trees were whizzing by in a blur, the nose rotated upward, the landing gear lifted with a "clunk" not much different from those she'd heard on the small planes she rode between San Juan and Arecibo on visits home, and the world was falling away beneath them, all in a way quite reassuringly familiar.

It was a pretty good day for flying, the haze seen from here just a faint blanket of blue-gray that hugged the ground and slightly softened its features. Pilar always enjoyed watching the quiltwork of farms and forests and cities, and today, as the flight progressed without mishap, she gradually fell—almost—into the pleasant quasi-hypnosis of watching the landscape unroll beneath them. She didn't know this part of the country well enough to recognize landmarks and tell exactly where they were, but she could tell from the angle of the sunlight that they were going more or less northeast.

After a while her musings drifted into a sort of envy for what the aliens could apparently do. She had always enjoyed the feeling of being up high and seeing normally big things like houses and rivers and cities become mere details in a much bigger picture. That went all the way back to her first flights, on family visits to relatives who had already moved to the mainland when she was quite small. It was one of the things that had led to her childhood dream of being an astronaut: if it was this exhilarating to see whole farms and lakes as details in a huge canvas, how much more exhilarating could it be to see whole *planets*, perhaps even whole solar systems, that way?

Now, for the first time in her life, she could extend the dream one more step, even though she couldn't live it. How much more exhilarating than even that could it be to see the biggest picture over the entire range of scale and detail? To see the Earth or the Solar System in all its grandeur, and then to have the luxury of zooming in to fill her view with the Grand Canyon, and then with a single cactus, and then with the private life of a wren family nesting in that cactus?

Or an inoffensive med tech heating a microwave dinner in her apartment in a small city in the Hudson Valley . . .

That turn of thought brought her abruptly back to reality, and the fundamental dilemma in all this. Yes, it would be nice—it would be *great*—to have that power to explore the universe she lived in. But it wasn't at all great to be on the other end of it.

If she had that power, could she be trusted to use it responsibly?

Could anybody?

Could Xiphar's aliens?

The dream shattered, her knuckles again gripping the armrest tightly, she was yanked back to present reality. They had come far enough north now that she could recognize landmarks. The Hudson peeked through the hills here and there off to the right, and across the widest section she could make out the graceful S-curve of the Old Tappan Zee Bridge and the utilitarian straight lines of the new. She wondered if anyone else aboard, except the crew, noticed, and became aware that nobody was talking. She decided not to break the spell, such as it was.

It wouldn't be long now, and she tried not to dwell on the fact that landings were the other critical time in flying. They got closer to the river as they got closer to the ground. The hills grew higher and rougher, the river narrowing to squeeze between them. She recognized the Bear Mountain Bridge, the quasi-fortress of West Point, and just a glimpse of Storm King before the pilot swung the plane east over the river as the first stage of a landing approach. They were almost directly over Mt. Taurus, as if the pilot were deliberately thumbing his nose at the aliens who seemed to be using it, before he turned onto final for Stewart Airport.

Pilar grew tenser all the way down, but the landing at Stewart International went smooth as silk.

"I HAD THE COPILOT SHOOT SOME VIDEOS OF THE SUMMIT AS we flew over," Marv Simonetti told her as they entered the terminal. This time there was no walk across the tarmac. As a major commercial airport, Stewart had serpentine jetways that could mate smoothly with even the smallest jets, even in this secluded portion of the terminal reserved for corporate and government flights. "No, it wasn't just coincidence that we flew that close. But we've already taken a preliminary look and didn't see anything remarkable."

Pilar didn't see anything *too* surprising on the drive to the trailhead, either—but neither were things entirely normal. Even with computer guidance, which still seemed to be working normally, traffic crawled up the heavily commercialized access road from the airport to the interstate. Once onto that, and across the bridge, things moved faster and more smoothly. Then it was slow again as they headed south through the continuous string of commercial and residential developments along the east side of the river.

Along the slow stretches on both sides, she saw scattered knots of protestors carrying signs demanding governmental explanations and accountability. A few bypassed all that and cut right to the chase, warning of the end of the world and/or well-earned punishment for human sins. No matter the message, some of the signs were the old-fashioned, hand-misspelled kind, while others were snazzy portable animated light shows. Some of the biggest and most emphatic were right on the main signs in front of large malls.

Pilar sometimes felt, as she passed a knot of protestors, that they were staring right at her, even though she knew intellectually that they couldn't see her through the minibus's heavily tinted windows. She was glad that it, like their plane, had no external markings to indicate who was in it or what it was for.

What would I say, she asked herself, *if somebody I knew saw me here and asked what was going on?*

I have no idea.

PILAR HAD TALKED TO OLD-TIMERS WHO CLAIMED TO REMEMBER when the Mt. Taurus trailhead was just a slight break in a wall of green forest, so inconspicuous that no one could even find it unless they knew where to look for the three white blazes on a tree trunk that marked its beginning. The trailhead hadn't moved, but now it was at the end of an alley lined with dumpsters behind an e-mall warehouse complex.

Pilar was relieved to find no protestors here; that seemed to prove that word of this mountain's possible importance had not yet become public. Still, the driver left the bus out nearer the highway, with two of the noncoms patrolling as inconspicuously as they could, while the others—except Maybelle, who feared she couldn't keep up but wanted to be near the action and hear about any findings right away—started the climb.

It was a perfect day for it, weatherwise, with moderate temperature and humidity and a gentle northwesterly breeze, and the laurel was in full bloom now. It should have been an exhilarating outing, but today it felt sullied, almost obscene. Eight people were, in Pilar's opinion, too many for a hiking party; that many traveling together could *not* travel lightly on the land, no matter how hard they tried. And though these were dressed pretty normally for hikers (except for the headnets, which would normally have been quite unnecessary), knowing what equipment filled their packs and why they were here cast a pall over the whole proceeding.

And when they got to the top, they found nothing to justify any of it. Everything looked perfectly normal, which under other circumstances would have been comforting but today was frustrating. What they'd hoped to find was not comforting normality, but concrete, analyzable evidence of what was wrong.

"You're sure this is the spot?" Marv asked a frowning Lester.

"Yes," said Lester, but he looked worried, as if he didn't trust his own memory or judgment. "I recognize this whole configuration of rock formations and shrubbery. Except . . . the stump should be right here, and it isn't. Just this flat rock . . ." He shook his head.

Marv turned to Pilar and spoke very quietly, as if trying not to embarrass Lester. "And you . . . ?"

"Yes," she said. "That's the way it was. And it's obviously gone."

"And have you seen any of your unusual bugs?"

Pilar and Lester both shook their heads.

Marv mulled, his face carefully blank. Then he shrugged, ever so slightly, and told the noncoms, "We're here. Might as well look around and take some readings anyway."

The three men and a woman in camouflage suits put down their packs and pulled out a variety of electronic devices and cameras—and laser sidearms. They scattered over an acre or so, reading instruments and gradually working their way back to the alleged stump site.

"This is really embarrassing," Lester murmured, looking at the ground.

"Not necessarily," said Marv. "We knew we might not find anything, even if every word you told us was exactly accurate—which I have no reason to doubt. We'd already thought of some of the reasons that might happen. Even if the stump was exactly what you guessed it was, maybe they cleared it out because our security wasn't as good as we thought and they knew we were coming up to look at it."

"Or maybe," Pilar suggested, "it's still here, but better camouflaged now."

"Maybe," said Lester. "But if it's still being used, there ought to be some detectable signs of that. Remember how it was interfering with my compack." He turned to Dan. "I don't remember your ever saying what you found out about the stump samples we sent you with that first batch of bugs. Anything interesting there?"

Dan shook his head. "Not that I could recognize. Just looked like old wood to me. Of course, I'm not a botanist. With hindsight, maybe I should have shown it to one. On the other hand, maybe it *was* just wood, but only on the surface, for camouflage. Who knows what was deep in the innards?"

"I don't guess we ever will," Lester said wistfully. "Ah, hindsight! But how are you supposed to know what's important to look at in a case like this?"

"Too bad we can't look at *everything*," Pilar began, "like—" She cut off abruptly, vaguely embarrassed.

By then the first of the electronic surveyors was almost back to them. "Not a thing," he called out to Marv. "No bugs, no unusual structures, not even radio static."

Pilar was sorry to hear that, and could see that Lester was, too. One by one all the noncoms drifted back with the same report and put their equipment back in their packs. Soon afterward they all started back down, not saying much on the way. Questions were forming in Pilar's mind, but she waited until they were back on the plane and safely airborne (by then she was too tired of the whole business to be tense on takeoff) before she asked them—and then she prefaced them with another.

"Lester?" she asked quietly over the hum of the engines, as the sky darkened in the west.

"Hm-m-m?"

"I've been thinking. Do you think it's safe to talk about our plans on this plane?"

He shrugged. "I don't trust anything any more, but this is probably as good a place as any. I doubt that anything can get in or out, at least while we're in flight, and the hull should be a pretty good shield against anything electromagnetic that isn't connected to an antenna on the outside."

"Antennas, again. I hope you're right." She sat silent for half a minute, then said, "A couple of things have been bothering me. All the descriptions we've heard of the orbiters are very vague——"

Lester smiled. "That's bothered me, too."

"Well, I've been wondering. They keep talking about them being 'stealthed.' Does that just mean that they're hard to see? Or might it mean that even if you try very hard to see them, they'd look like something other than what they are?"

"Like a fuzzed-up image?" he said. "Yes, I suppose that's possible. They could generate interference for the express purpose of keeping us from learning too much . . . Yes, I believe I've even heard of the military doing something like that with planes. 'Active stealth,' I believe they call it." Now he paused thoughtfully, seeming to ponder, then changed the subject. "What's the other thing bothering you?"

"The obvious one. Mount Taurus. You and I know what was up there before, but I'll bet everybody else thinks we just led them on a wild goose chase. I'm not willing to give it up that easily. Even if our evidence has been pulled out from under us, there must be others. Think we could use the same trick we used for our insect collection?"

He frowned for several seconds before he realized what she meant. Then, slowly and guardedly, he smiled. "It's worth a try."

Chapter 21

Herman Hwang, looking harried and haggard, was at their next meeting in the shielded hideout, three days later. Pilar wasn't at all sure that was a good sign.

"It wasn't easy," he began, "but the Ramirez Method paid off again." His voice sounded grudging. She suspected he only continued to invite her and her friends to these meetings, and to attend them himself, because they had provided useful input that he wasn't getting elsewhere—and he resented depending on such unorthodox sources. "I say it wasn't easy," he went on, "for at least two reasons. One is that our shy friends apparently caught on at least a little to how we managed to get the same request out to so many at the same time before, and decided not to let it happen again. When we first tried it this time, our old emergency override on the major nets didn't work—much less the impromptu hacks we'd cobbled together for extending it into secondary channels. But we have some really good hackers, some behind bars and some outside, and it didn't take them too long to find a new way to do it again.

"Of course, we only got away with it by an extension of the same technique: we did so much other stuff at the same time that our unseen watchers would have trouble telling which parts, if any, were worth paying attention to. After the fact, of course, they'll know, and we won't be able to use the same way again. But we're hoping that we've generalized the technique to the point where we can generate new versions on short notice, and without getting caught beforehand. Of course, the oftener we try it, the more likely it is that they'll catch onto that, too—so we're not going to make a habit of doing it casually."

"I'd say," Edwards said, "that the fact that we got away with it even this time is a hopeful sign. You *did* imply that it worked?"

"Well, yes," the president said, "we did get the message out. But we didn't get as much useful response as before. We've thought of several possible reasons for that, all of which may be contributing factors. The big one—what I called the second reason it wasn't easy—was public resistance. A lot of people are miffed that we still haven't given them a satisfactory explanation of either the shuttle incident or our first broadcast request for help. That made them less eager to cooperate with a second, so more people ignored us." He chewed his lip. "Too bad we're not in a position to explain that we don't dare explain even what little we know.

"Anyway, there are a couple of other factors that probably kept response smaller than we'd hoped. One is simply that, if Mr. Ordway's general theory is right, there'll be a lot more bugs than relay stations. Another is that the relay stations will tend to be sited in remote locations to make them less likely to be noticed. And, for the same reason, they'll be trying to look like something else."

"But the bottom line," said Edwards. "We did get some response?"

"Oh, yes," said Hwang, his face impassive, "we did get responses. Less than a hundred, compared to several thousand for the bug request. Most of them are just stories, but those are more or less consistent with Mr. Ordway's idea. And a half dozen were verifiable: real structures that were still there when our investigators got to them."

"And . . . ?" Lester asked eagerly.

"They seem to be much as you guessed, and they're scattered all over the planet. Mind you, we don't understand everything about them, but we do know that they contain a lot of nanocircuitry and mechanisms, most of which people like Dr. Felder tell me we can't begin to understand. And we know they sporadically transmit very low-power, very tight beams—tighter than our engineers thought possible at the wavelengths they're using, often aimed right at one or more of the orbiters. Sometimes such beams seem to be coming *from* the orbiters, again so tight that we'd never notice them if we didn't happen to be looking at exactly the right times and places."

"Have any been recorded and analyzed?" Lester asked.

"Recorded, yes. We intercepted a few before the aliens apparently caught us in the act and shut up. Analyzed, no. If they really do carry messages, they're *extremely* compressed, like the microbursts that first caught Major Simonetti's attention. Some of the labs are still trying to get something out of them."

"So what did the other relay stations look like?" Pilar asked. "Ours was a stump that didn't look quite right for where it was. Were they all like that?"

"They varied a lot," said Hwang, his nose wrinkling involuntarily. "Some of them looked *exactly* like something that belonged where they were. One was incorporated right into a pre-existing and long-occupied horse barn in Kentucky, with the works below the packed-dirt floor under a manure pile.

"Another was an outhouse, but they made one mistake. They built the whole thing from scratch, in the backyard of a family who took great pride in having the most advanced plumbing money could buy. Dignified old gent looked out the window one morning and saw the thing out in the middle of his prize petunia bed. Called the police to complain and ranted that his granddad used to tell about juvenile pranksters tipping privies over, back when they were common, but he never heard of anybody taking the trouble to set one up in a yard that hadn't had one in a hundred years. He wanted to know what the world was coming to." Hwang was chuckling in spite of himself by the time he reached that point, but he sobered abruptly. "I guess we'd all like to know that, wouldn't we?"

A murmur of assent ran round the table. Then Hwang became grimly businesslike again. "Meanwhile, we have a situation to deal with. We've pretty well established that we *are* being spied on in a way much as some of you have speculated, utterly unprecedented in both scope and depth of detail. And it's taken another turn for the worse. You may recall that Dr. Felder spoke of trying to get some of the spy-bug specimens to replicate in a lab. Well, that's happened—twice. Once, apparently, when our guys did something the specimens liked, and they started proliferating, sending out tiny ones. Our researchers thought they knew what precipitated it, but when they reversed the change, it made no difference. So they're not sure, and in the meantime they have this private plague on their hands. So far it hasn't done any obvious damage, but they feel like the sorcerer's apprentice trying to stop a herd of broomsticks."

"What do these things use for energy?" Lester asked.

The president said nothing, but just glanced at Dan, who picked up the cue. "We're not completely sure. Part of it's probably solar. Another part, in the outside world, must come from eating their surroundings, just like real bugs, though their efficiency seems surprisingly high. The ones in the 'broomstick' lab aren't giving us many clues. The little ones don't seem to be growing or taking anything in, so far, but just running on energy their progenitors had already stored." He scowled. "Or maybe they do something *really* exotic, like tapping into zero-point energy."

"Sure would be nice to get some of those goodies," Lester mused.

"Sure would," Dan agreed. "We don't really know what they have. Depending on where they come from, for all we know they could have some kind of faster-than-light—"

"But we mustn't get our hearts set on it," President Hwang broke in. "Getting any of their technology would require either capturing it and analyzing it, which is probably way beyond our abilities; or getting them to talk to us and share it voluntarily, which they've shown absolutely no interest in doing."

"But they *have* talked to us," Pilar objected. "We all saw what happened in the other conference room. And I'll never forget the one who came to my apartment—"

"And tried to kill you," Hwang interrupted with palpable impatience. "You call those conversations? I repeat, they've shown no interest in talking to us—"

"I certainly won't claim we got off to a smooth start," Pilar granted, unmindful of protocol, "but we *have* talked. Maybe that's not so bad for the first contact between two kinds of beings who grew out of totally different worlds. Haven't there been plenty of disputes in human history that were just as bad, but eventually got resolved? That's what skilled diplomats specialize in, isn't it? Maybe we need to get some—"

"Young lady," said the president, dangerously close to losing his cool, "it seems to me that you're getting out of your—"

"What President Hwang means, I think," Iona Branford interposed smoothly, "is that diplomacy is a very delicate business. You may well be right that we'll ultimately achieve a breakthrough that way. But we're not ready yet; we know too little about what we're up against. Certainly we have some of our best diplomatic personnel analyzing those few interactions we've had so far, but it would be premature to jump into new ones until we've learned all we can from those."

Pilar could think of a reply or two to that, but perhaps it was just as well that Hwang jumped back in before she could deliver them. She reminded herself that she, too, needed to try to exercise some diplomacy, and she was not highly skilled at it.

"Meanwhile," Hwang was saying, "there is the other incident of replication in a lab, which is much more alarming than the first. In this one the things that replicated were things the researchers didn't even know they had there, and they destroyed enough equipment to ruin any hope of getting meaningful information from the specimens they had. Also, that lab didn't have as tight security as this room, and we suspect some of the introduced bugs got away with information about the work being done there. As we speak, they're seriously considering burning the building down to try to stop the damage from spreading."

He paused to let that sink in, and Pilar shivered involuntarily. A nice peaceful conversation would be a wish come true, but perhaps not a realistic goal if humans were under active threat from powerful beings who even Pilar had to admit showed, at best, very *limited* interest in chitchat.

"I agree," the president was saying, in a very soft, reasonable tone, "that it would be wonderful if we could learn things from the visitors—and I would like to believe that we might be able to teach them a few things, too. But unless we see far more evidence than we have so far that that has any chance of happening, what has to be uppermost in my mind is the potential danger they pose. So unless they show, and soon, a willingness to engage in a true dialog, a mutual *exchange* of information, our most urgent need is to get them out of our sky."

There was a shocked hush as everyone around the table tried to digest his words. Finally Simonetti said, "Are you suggesting that we *attack* them?"

"That is, of course, an extreme last resort," said Hwang. "But it is an option that we have to consider. Naturally we would make at least one more attempt at discussing things with them first, but we would make it clear that we will not tolerate their continued unilateral snooping, and if necessary will do anything in our power to stop it—up to and including destroying their fleet."

"In other words," Pilar said softly, "pretty much what Colonel Edwards told the Wizard and you later chewed him out for."

The president looked flustered, and Pilar wondered if she was making a very powerful enemy. But what he was proposing seemed so dangerous that she *couldn't* let it pass unchallenged—and he'd already indicated he wanted to hear any potentially relevant opinions, no matter how distasteful. She could only hope he meant it. "The essence is similar," Hwang admitted in very controlled tones. "The difference—and it's a huge difference—is that if we reiterate it, it will be after careful deliberation and with full official backing."

"That does make all the difference," Pilar said neutrally. "Even so, I can't help thinking that you, Mr. President, had a very good point when you expressed concern about whether we could make good on the colonel's threat. Can we? If not, can we afford to risk it?"

"Can we afford *not* to risk it?" Hwang countered. "Even if this fleet personally means us no harm—which I question, in view of their uncooperative attitude and the hostile nature of their few documented encounters so far—we simply cannot afford to let them keep gathering so much information that *anybody* could use against us."

"And yet," said Pilar, "if they really want to smash us, why haven't they already done it? And suppose they *are* for some reason planning to do it later but not yet. If they have spies and agents in as many places as we think they do, how could we possibly plot an attack without their knowing every detail and planning defenses before we tried to carry it out?"

Surprisingly, it was Lester who came to the president's defense. "You know, it might not be quite as impossible as it sounds, though it's certainly daunting. Suppose these things are practically everywhere and every one of them carries not only eyes and ears, but pressure and temperature and magnetic and who knows what other kinds of sensors. And a computer that can record the readings of all of those sensors as a function of time and position. Dan tells me all of this seems quite likely. Well, that lets them build up an astonishingly detailed map of a whole lot of places, maybe the whole planet and everything living on it. But that *doesn't* mean they're omnipotent, or even omniscient. They're powerful and scary as hell, but they still have limitations. If we have to fight them—and I'd be the last person to suggest we should if there's any possible alternative—we'd have to identify those limitations and figure out how to use them."

"I sure could use a few good f'rinstances," Maybelle drawled, and Branford nodded emphatically.

"Well, I think I have some," said Lester, more animatedly than Pilar had ever seen him before. "The simplest one is that they may be as overwhelmed by all that data as many of us are by the internet. Sure, they may have the biggest, most comprehensive database ever assembled about this planet. But no matter how many of them there are, or how big their computers, they can't possibly be paying attention to all of it all the time. It's like the difference between having access to the Library of Congress, and knowing everything in it and understanding all the relationships among all that data. Anything you want to look up is there, but you won't be conscious of most of it at any particular time. Something has to call your attention to one part of it, whether it's a literal kick in the pants or a report from an infobot that flags an item over here as related to something you're already interested in over there."

Pilar saw just a hint of a smile appear on the faces of both Edwards and Branford, and didn't know whether to be cheered or chilled. What Lester said made sense, though how helpful it was depended very much on just how sophisticated a system of infobots and flags the aliens had. "So," Branford said, "the idea is that if you can get enough of their attention focused on things that don't matter, you can sneak around and do something that does without their noticing."

"In my business," Edwards grumbled impatiently, "we call that a diversionary tactic."

"Of course you do, Colonel," Branford said blandly. "I'm still hoping to keep this more my business than yours, but it is nice to know that there may be something like this to fall back on, if necessary. Of course, I daresay what we'd have to divert in this case is a lot more challenging than anything you've had to deal with in the past."

"But again," said Lester, "maybe not as much as you'd think. There are a couple of other things that could work in our favor, too. Their map, as you call it, isn't complete and up-to-date. If they depend on roving sensors, they'll have readings for this point now and that point a little later and so on. As my old physics professors would have said, they can't know all the partial derivatives." He looked around and seemed suddenly abashed by the abrupt epidemic of blank stares. "Er, that is, they don't have a complete map of everything at any time, or a complete history of what's happening at any one spot."

"But they have an awful lot," said Maybelle.

"Yes, but they're not updating a lot of it in real time. Even before attracting conscious attention becomes an issue, they have to wait for the spy-bugs to take their little bundles of information back to a relay station and upload them. So if we can move fast enough at key times, we should be able to do things that have important consequences before they know they need to react."

Lester, Pilar thought with alarm, *whose side are you on?* Aloud, she said, "Lester, aren't you afraid you're making this sound too easy? I can imagine certain people getting tempted to try this sort of thing—a preemptive strike, I guess you'd call it— before they've tried very hard to come up with something better."

Hwang allowed himself a barely visible chuckle at her expense. "Oh, don't blame him, little lady," he said, and she bristled. "I assure you we're quite conscious of how un-easy this would be, and very interested in finding a way to avoid it. But we also know we need to be as prepared as we can be, as soon as we can be. I've already been deep in consultation with Colonel Edwards and his superiors, right up to the Joint Chiefs of Staff, and we already have a plan. That's why I came here today—but I am heartened to know that Mr. Ordway agrees with much of our thinking."

Pilar froze, and then could barely get the words out. "What sort of a plan?"

"A contingency plan," said Hwang, "dedicated to the proposition that this situation cannot be allowed to drag on much longer. We have to get these things out of our sky soon, by whatever method it takes. We will make one last attempt at a diplomatic solution, but if that fails, I think we are all agreed that slow, complicated stratagems run too much risk of being intercepted and unraveled. We've decided, however reluctantly, that the one thing we can try that might have a chance is brute force."

Pilar stared. Finally she said, "What?"

"Blow the things out of the sky," the president said, "if they refuse to cooperate after a clear statement of our intentions."

"Do you know that you can, given how little you've been able to determine about the actual nature of those fleets?"

"We think there's a pretty good chance. The nations of the world have quite a bit of firepower stockpiled from all the way back in the Cold War. To say nothing of what we've added for the meteor watch."

"But what," asked Maybelle, "is to stop them from knowing exactly what we have and how well they can stand up to it? And cutting off whatever we send long before it gets there?"

"Diversionary tactic," the president said smugly. "Remember? They won't know that it's meant for them because it will be stealthed, too. And because there's always a lot going on in aerospace and on the airwaves. And because the only planning for a strike that *sounds* like planning for a strike is happening in this room and a very few similarly shielded others.

"If it becomes necessary to deliver it, it will not be launched by a command that sounds like a command. Instead, there'll be a chain of innocuous-looking actions that seem like they have nothing to do with an attack. Those will be buried in a lot of irrelevant smoke screen, including things that look like threatening commands but aren't, as will the information telling those who need to know how to recognize the things that are serious.

"For example—and I emphasize that this is hypothetical, because we're not going to say any more about the *real* plan than we have to—I might send my brother a note chatting about this and that. In the middle of it I might casually mention that if a certain third party ever calls him and asks him to do something, no matter how strange, and mentions a certain phrase that refers to a childhood memory that only he and I know about, then he is to do that thing without question or delay—but only if he hears that phrase from the right person. Activating a launch will involve a series of such actions, for which the groundwork has been laid in advance, with nobody involved knowing the whole sequence. And it will all start, if it has to start, with me doing something seemingly irrelevant like dialing a certain number and ordering a pizza. On a line that's been *very* thoroughly vandal-proofed, of course."

He paused as if waiting for expressions of approval. Pilar could give him only a scowl. It sounded like a cloak-and-dagger game; and yet, under the circumstances, it might be one of the few ways that a strike could actually be launched.

That, she decided, was what worried her. It just might work—up to the point of doing irreparable damage and triggering consequences that Earth was not prepared to deal with.

You're crazy, she found herself thinking, *Mr. President.* But she couldn't think of anything she could say out loud, or any way to stop him.

Or anything better to suggest.

His eyes met hers once, briefly and with a hint of a frown, and then moved on around the table.

"So," he said at the end, no longer meeting anyone's eyes, "it's settled. It will take a little time to set things up, both for the backup plan and for delivering our ultimatum. But when it's ready, you'll be among the first to know."

Chapter 22

Does anybody else here feel like a prisoner?" Pilar asked.

She and Lester and Maybelle and Dan were gathered in Maybelle's room, variously seated and sprawled on all the surfaces intended for that purpose: armchairs, bed, small couch. "What do you mean?" Lester asked cautiously, with a faint gesture hinting that the walls might have ears.

"Well," said Pilar, "President Hwang hinted that we would at least have the chance to watch and listen when he transmits his ultimatum. Why?"

Everybody else started to say something, then trailed off as their faces became puzzled frowns.

"I mean," Pilar went on, "what's so special about us?"

"Well," said Lester, "we *were* the ones who first brought the spy-bugs to their attention. And their possible connection with the asp explosion, and the possible alien connection—"

"Actually," Maybelle pointed out, "some of them did think of a possible alien connection to the asp."

"But not the bugs," Lester insisted. "They didn't even know about the bugs until we told them. And we were the ones who suggested using broadcasts instead of secret commands, and the relay-station system of alien communication. And we were the only ones who could tell what had changed on Mount Taurus—"

"True," said Pilar, "but now that we've done that, and not much else for a few days, and they have more specimens to examine and people to talk to—"

"Thanks to us," said Maybelle.

"—I don't think they believe we have much else to contribute. Except for Dan, they're certainly not letting us participate in any of the investigation, much as I think all of us would like to."

"They do draw a new sample of our blood every couple of days," Lester pointed out wryly.

"Yes, and they never find anything interesting there. The new samples look just like the old ones. Whatever those structures we've picked up are, I think they're inert. Maybe permanently."

"But maybe not," Dan said quietly.

"Maybe," Pilar granted. "But how long is that 'maybe' going to keep us cooped up here? We spend practically all our time sitting around with singularly little to do, and I think you're getting as tired of it as I am. I think letting us watch Hwang's broadcast is just a little concession to keep us from getting too restless here. I certainly don't believe he's going to let us take any active part in it. Maybe he figures if he keeps us interested, we won't get itchy to be somewhere else. And I have the uncomfortable feeling that if we *wanted* to leave, we wouldn't be allowed to. That bothers me."

"Would you *want* to leave?" Maybelle asked. "Knowing what you do about what's out there—and no more?"

Pilar smiled faintly. "Probably not. Certainly I'd rather be home, if home was still home—but of course it isn't. I do feel safer here, at least a little. But it's the principle of the thing. Being under prolonged house arrest in the Land of the Free makes me very uncomfortable. And I think that's what we are. I think Hwang is making excuses to keep us out of circulation because we know too much and may not support his plan. He wants to make sure we don't ask to leave, because then he'd have to say no and public knowledge of that could be politically embarrassing later." She paused. "Do *you* all think he's doing the right thing?"

A long silence. Then Dan said, "I think he's doing a very dangerous thing. But the alternative may be even worse."

A general murmur of discontented assent. "That's where I am, too," Pilar said finally. "So I guess we're all going to have to console ourselves, at least for now, with the thought that we're less in the dark than the general public."

"There is that," said Maybelle. "So I guess our next move is just to sit back and wait for the show."

THE SHIELDED ROOM HAD CHANGED DRAMATICALLY WHEN THEY next assembled, a surprisingly short two days later. The conference table was gone now; the whole place seemed to have been converted to a holotheater like the one in New Jersey, with big, electronics-laden armchairs in one half, arranged in a loose arc around a single chair in the other half.

And a heavy glass barrier between the two halves.

Hwang was already in place in the single chair on one side, looking grim, as the others who had been attending these meetings filed in and took the "theater" chairs. There were a few extra chairs now, and a few extra people, all in expensive suits or military uniforms with insignia of high rank. No introductions were made, and the newcomers, whom Pilar suspected of being some of the actual high-level officials whose existence had been only vaguely mentioned before, took the outside chairs, giving her an uncomfortable feeling of being surrounded.

"Good morning," Hwang's voice said via concealed speakers when everyone was seated. "Can everyone hear me OK?" He scanned faces through the glass. "Good. This is, for better or worse, a crucial and historic occasion. Some of you know why you are here; others may be wondering."

Has he been spying? Pilar wondered, and then she remembered Lester's unspoken expression of that suspicion two nights earlier.

"You have made an invaluable contribution to our awareness of this problem," Hwang went on, "and we have inconvenienced you by bringing you here and keeping you here. You have continued to contribute, though I know some of you have felt frustrated that you weren't able to play a more active role. In appreciation for your service and compensation for your inconvenience, I feel that the least we can do is be completely open with you when we take this decisive action based on what we have learned together." He chuckled nervously. "Besides, I'd like to have you as witnesses, in case there is ever any question about what I do here today. But the responsibility for that action rests entirely on me."

Smooth, Pilar thought, *very smooth. Almost believable, even. But the* consequences *of your actions, Mr. President, will fall on all of us.*

"You are being accorded a special privilege," the president continued, "and taken into a special confidence." *Thereby making it even less likely that we'd be allowed to leave,* Pilar thought with a shudder at the thought of how far he might go to prevent it. "What we are about to attempt is by its nature so delicate, and the outcome so unpredictable, that it *cannot* be done in full public view. The shields around this room are still in place, except for a cable connection to transceivers outside. What we'll be sending is not a broadcast, but a private message intended solely for the ears—or whatever—of our 'guests.' What I say—and *only* what I say—will be transmitted directly to all three orbiters by the tightest beams our technicians can produce, which means lasers. It's unlikely that any humans will notice them, much less be able to read them. But our uninvited observers can hardly help noticing the beams directed at them; in fact, they're already flashing to make sure we have their attention.

"As for getting the message, we've already established beyond a doubt that they understand many of our languages, including English. And we have reason to believe they've had plenty of experience at decoding the modulated laser beams used in some of our routine communications. So they'll get the message. Then the ball will be in their court. And now, if you'll excuse me, it's time to open the gates."

His expression changed subtly. "Tech staff," he said. "Are we ready?" A green light glowed in the right arm of his chair, and Pilar thought she saw sweat on his forehead. "Let's begin," he said, and he flicked a switch next to the green light.

"I'm not sure who I'm talking to," he said stiffly, "since you've told us so little about yourselves while helping yourselves to so much about us. So I'll simply direct my comments to anyone who can hear me in the craft orbiting Earth. I shall be brief and to the point. This room is now equipped with holographic virtual reality equipment like that which you commandeered once before. It is at your disposal, in case you wish to make any reply.

"You have claimed, despite our explanation that we find the claim unbelievable, that all you want to do is to study us and our world. You have asked us to ignore you, so you can study us in our natural, undisturbed state.

"I am here to tell you unequivocally that any chance you may have had to do that is forever gone. Partly for the obvious reason that you have already disturbed things here so much that what you are seeing is not at all what you allegedly hoped to study. And partly for the simple reason that we will not let you continue your activities. We have offered you an exchange of information, which you rebuffed with the crudest sort of threat. We will tolerate your presence and disruptions no longer. You have only one option left: leave—voluntarily, or we will force you. And we won't wait long for clear signs of your compliance. Two days maximum—and if we see a need to strike sooner, we won't hesitate to do so."

He stopped, beads of sweat now quite obvious on his brow. But he did not switch off the green light.

Pilar felt moisture on her forehead, too, and none in her mouth. She caught herself holding her breath, and had to make a conscious effort to start breathing again. She had the impression of much the same happening all around her. But nobody said anything, on either side of the glass.

A minute went by, then another. Humans fidgeted, fearful of what Hwang might have unleashed. Clocks and watches counted seconds and minutes relentlessly, till seventeen minutes had gone by.

Then the "Wizard" face materialized directly above Hwang, dwarfing him. No swirling mists or dramatic lighting this time, and it was smaller than before—yet it still dwarfed the president. If anything, its matter-of-fact appearance made it even more chilling this time.

Especially when it said, in a correspondingly matter-of-fact voice, "Not likely. You wouldn't dare, because you know how greatly our retaliation could exceed your little tap. Furthermore, I am very annoyed that you have further spoiled things by broadcasting those requests for information. Now—" The voice caught and hesitated, as if briefly trying to go two directions at once, then finished in the same carefully controlled manner, "We warned you earlier. Now we must resort to experiment."

And with that the face vanished, simply fading away into invisibility.

 **What do you** suppose he means by 'experiment'?" Iona Branford asked finally.

"I'm afraid," said Hwang, flicking the switch that turned off the green light on his chair arm and wiping his brow, "we'll find out all too soon." He looked thoughtful. "Or maybe not. Maybe it will take them longer to start any 'experiments' than we've given them to leave. Maybe they'll be too busy getting ready to do that."

"Do you really believe that, Mr. President?" Branford asked quietly.

"I'd like to," he said. Then, more animatedly, "But they really may need time to do whatever it is that they're talking about. And we really will strike if they haven't started leaving by my deadline. And, by God, we *will* make them go!"

"I certainly hope so," said Branford, "if it comes to that. I, for one, don't really care to find out what they mean by 'experiments,' with Earth and its people as guinea pigs. But I suppose we do have to give them some time, just in case they *do* accede to your terms. The bright side is that it gives us a little time to delay kicking the dog—and hope we won't have to."

But it wasn't nearly as much time as any of them hoped. The experiments began almost immediately. Some of them were reported to President Hwang, either through his own intelligence network or via other heads of state. Many others were not.

* * *

THE VILLAGE OF COMTE ANTOINE PERCHED IN A HANGING VALley in the green lower slopes of the French Alps. It wasn't big, but the villagers prided themselves on its nearly invisible integration of the latest technology into an accurate reconstruction of a traditional village, and on the stunning vistas it commanded in all directions. A railed promenade along the lip of its site looked out over the lush pastures and farms of the valley, dotted here and there with similar but less distinctively blessed villages. Just past one end of the promenade mists swirled above the waterfall that plunged two hundred meters toward that valley, unseen until one reached the very end of the promenade, but awesomely heard from along its entire length—and incidentally providing hydroelectric power to the whole valley and points beyond. Behind the village towered peaks, a verdant patchwork of field and forest in the foreground, sloping up to crags and spires of rock, bare but for lingering patches of snow, beyond.

It had been a good winter for snow and a good spring for rain, and fire was the furthest thing from anybody's mind. No signs warned hikers on the network of paths that threaded the meadows and woods. Foliage aloft and underfoot were lush and green; the rivulets that fed brooks and ultimately the waterfall still tripped exuberantly over their rocky beds; the ground itself, even well away from the streams, felt just moist enough to the touch.

So it was a total surprise to everyone when the first people out to stroll the promenade and sip coffee at overlooks that morning found themselves surrounded by leaves that had overnight turned brown and brittle. It was an even bigger surprise when by nightfall the situation had deteriorated markedly. A village meeting formed spontaneously and resolved to call in ecological experts the next morning to find out what was happening.

But by then it was too late. The village woke at 4 AM to the crackle of flames and the acrid smell of smoke. The sky, which should have been black and starry, glowed orange, and a few people could see tongues of flame licking at it.

Rising and falling sirens soon drowned out the crackle, but not long after that the crackle, not to be outdone, had swelled to a roar that drowned even the sirens, and the tongues had grown into towers of flame that dwarfed the feeble sprays of water and foam turned upon them.

And everyone in Comte Antoine realized with dismay that their beloved village was in its last hour, which made no sense at all.

MTO WA MBU TENDED TO LIVE UP TO ITS NAME, WHICH MEANT "Mosquito Creek" in Swahili. So hardly anybody noticed when there were a few more mosquitoes around than usual, especially in the wet season. But little Ronny Makuru, whose eyes were both closer to the ground and more observant than many of his elders', most certainly noticed the dense cloud of them hanging around the statue of Abdullah Smith-Muhindi in the village square—especially when he saw what they were doing.

He ran as fast as his little legs could carry him to the shack where his family lived, clambered over six or seven assorted siblings, and breathlessly told his parents, "They're eating Bwana Smith-Muhindi!"

It took them a few minutes to get that translated into something coherent, and it still wasn't believable. But it was intriguing enough to entice them out to see for themselves. After all, not every village could boast a hero of Smith-Muhindi's stature, and his monument was new enough that everybody remembered—and cared—why it was there. A decade earlier this village, like so many of its neighbors, had been spiraling down into oblivion from a paradoxical combination of AIDS and overcrowding, leading to too many kids, many of them sick, and not enough healthy adults to raise them. Thanks to Smith-Muhindi's tireless efforts, both problems had begun to turn around. But only Mto

Wa Mbu could boast, "Abdullah grew up here. We knew him when . . ."

So it was a matter of both offended civic pride and shared sheer horror when half the eyes in the village gathered around the statue and saw it half-covered with what looked like ordinary mosquitos but paid no attention to the milling crowd of tender, juicy citizens around them. Instead, they did indeed seem to be eating the statue, or at least chewing it into dust. Already its shape was wrong, even allowing for the seething cloak of insects all over it. And where its once solid rock showed through, it was roughened and discolored, and a layer of dust was slowly growing at its base.

Meanwhile, more mosquitos kept coming. . . .

EVERYBODY IN BOOROOLOOLOO REMEMBERED GRANDPAP ANdrew fondly. Some of them remembered him as a bartender, back in the days when this was a tiny prospector's camp in the Outback instead of just another suburb in the vast sprawl of metropolitan Alice Springs. Others, both Aboriginal and Anglo, knew him only far more recently, as an informal teacher of this and that and everything else. The younger ones often had the vague impression that he was as old as Uluru itself.

All agreed that he had been a treasure to both groups, even though they couldn't agree on which he "really" belonged to, and that it was going to be a terrible tragedy to lose him, especially this way. To have known and understood so much, and then to have it all seep gradually away, till he recognized none of his old friends or surroundings and had to have everything done for him . . . He'd been to several doctors, and all said there was nothing they could do.

Now, the handful of faithful gathered around him agreed, the end was surely at hand. The old man lay on his sheets, a frail husk, eyes closed with parchment lids, the rise and fall of his chest barely perceptible as his beloved antique digital clock counted silent seconds. It had been days since he'd opened his eyes, weeks since he'd spoken, months since he'd said anything coherent. Those in attendance had no higher hopes than to minimize the discomfort of his final hours, so it was hardly surprising that no one was looking or listening when he said calmly, "Would somebody please do something about that thermostat? It's much too warm in here. What's the point of having modern conveniences like air conditioning if you don't take advantage of them?"

At first they looked around at each other to see who had spoken. The voice was none that they expected to hear in this room; not only was it that of Grandpap Andrew, it was that of a much *younger* Grandpap Andrew, a voice most of those present had never heard except on recordings.

When his one real granddaughter, Irene, finally chanced to turn her eyes his way, her eyes went wide. "Grandpap!" she shrieked, running to throw her arms around him. Within seconds everyone in the room was gathered in a tight knot about him, marveling at how clear his eyes and voice were (even though his skin was still pale and wrinkled) and babbling about what a miracle this was.

As for Andrew, his only response was a bemused but not unkind, "Aw, what's all the fuss about?"

Until a few hours later, when he was sitting up at the dinner table trying as eagerly as ever to catch up on everything that had happened in the last year. Eventually even he had to agree that his own recovery was one of the more remarkable events of that period—and no, he had no idea how it had happened, but he wasn't complaining, thank you.

As mayor of Regal Heights, one of the most exclusive planned communities in Greater Tiffin, Ralph Lekarski always took great pains not to flaunt his civic pride too blatantly. Yes, he knew that it was an honor and a privilege to live here, and an even greater honor and privilege to serve these fine citizens in an official capacity. He knew the statistics on income, I.Q., education, health, and representation in the various directories of Distinguished Persons. It was obvious to anyone who looked at those statistics that the population here was an elite by any yardstick one chose to apply. And it soon became clear to anyone who aspired to moving here, whether for prestige or to escape the megacities or for whatever reason, that there was a waiting list a mile long, and promotion beyond it was not based simply on how long one had been there.

To get into Regal Heights one had to earn the right and be accepted by a three-fourths majority of those who had already done so. But once there, one could bask in the security of knowing that one's neighbors were fine upstanding folk, that crime was virtually unknown, that the plagues (new and old) that kept ravaging big cities and Less Favored Nations had yet to gain a toehold here—and, Mayor Lekarski was quite confident, would never be allowed to do so. One knew all this, but one did not speak of it in such terms to the general public. There were, after all, such things as discretion and sensitivity toward the less fortunate.

All of which made for a feeling of such general comfort that it was quite a shock for Mayor Lekarski to be awakened at 5 AM by the insistent trilling of several different channels of his comcenter. Throwing on a newsilk bathrobe and dragging himself to the screen, he opened the e-mail at the head of the queue, read the contents, and frowned. He opened another, then another. He opened a dozen of them, with frantically increasing speed. By the time he was finished, his frown had become a shiver and a pounding heart.

How could this have happened to Regal Heights, of all places? A disease, suddenly cropping up overnight in what seemed like half the population, distinguished first and foremost by a symptom that had never, to the best of his knowledge, been recorded in all the annals of medicine?

How had it happened? And what could he possibly do about it?

The first thing you do about it, the professional corner of his mind reminded him sternly, *is the same thing you do about* any *problem that comes up. You let your subconscious, which is much smarter than you, mull it over while you take a nice bracing shower and have a good breakfast and some coffee. Then you take another look at the problem.*

Reassured by that sage advice, he felt at least provisionally better. He even relaxed enough on the way to the bathroom to reflect that the situation was not without its amusing side. After all, none of the messages so far had reported any symptoms that sounded life-threatening or even physically uncomfortable. And, though he would never say this in public either, there was a certain element of drollery in the thought of half the population of Regal Heights with—

The bathroom lights swelled to a comfortable level as he entered, and he turned to look in the mirror.

And screamed.

It might be funny, in a politically incorrect way, to think of half the development's citizens waking up with their noses literally bright blue. It was far less funny when Mayor Lekarski himself was one of them.

Especially when, a few hours later, the fevers began in those afflicted, and rose steadily.

Chapter 24

Herman Hwang's presidential bedroom had a comcenter, too, but his had a lot more messages on it than Mayor Lekarski's. He'd been up all night, poring over the bizarre reports, trying to make any sort of sense of them. If this had ever been a game, it was way beyond that now.

People were *dying* out there, and land and property and history and tradition were being destroyed.

Even if the aliens were serious about considering these things "experiments," to humans generally—and to Hwang in particular—they sure looked like attacks.

But were they parts of a war? If so, what was the war about?

That was the maddening part. Hwang had studied military history—hell, he'd been an Army officer himself, though he'd never seen combat—but what was happening now didn't fit any pattern he knew. In most wars, each side had a clear objective, like taking over somebody else's land or keeping them from taking over yours. Even when the actual fighting consisted of surprise guerrilla raids, if you stood back far enough it should be possible to see that each side was fighting *for* something. Usually there was somebody high up who *said*, at least in the roundabout language of politics and diplomacy, what that something was.

Not this time. The other side was high up, at least literally, but refused to say what it wanted. And there was no apparent pattern in what this Xiphar and his alien hordes were doing. Certainly much of it was destructive, and its scope was more truly worldwide than even the two World Wars. But the closest

Xiphar ever came to expressing a goal was when he told mankind, "Roll over and play dead. Ignore us, and we won't hurt you." And why had they given that message first to that smart-alecky Ramirez woman instead of the people with real power, like him?

And they are *hurting us,* Hwang thought miserably. *In a seemingly random way, as if they're just trying to be annoying.*

Come to think of it, that did sound like some guerrilla wars. Pester them, wear them down until they give you what you want.

But what then of the few odd cases where the alien activity seemed to *help* people? How did those fit into the pattern?

Could it actually be as simple as what Xiphar had said? Hwang just couldn't believe that. And even if he could, how could he make the aliens understand that that simply wasn't something humans could do?

Well, they were aliens, after all. Maybe trying to understand them was not a worthwhile use of Hwang's time and mental energies. Maybe he should cut right to the chase: Whether he understood them or not, their actions of the last couple of days had made it clear that his ultimatum had been the right thing to do. Beings who could do things like this, for whatever reason, were simply not to be tolerated.

They had to go.

The only question was when—and that, too, had become more complicated. Before the "experiments" it had seemed simple: The invaders must leave, or the people of Earth would (they hoped) start destroying their fleets. First one, and then, if necessary, the others in rapid succession, before they could retaliate.

For President Hwang had no delusions that they couldn't or wouldn't retaliate in formidable fashion.

What he hadn't anticipated was the nature of the "experiments," which looked disturbingly like a uniquely effective form of "retaliation in advance." Numerous nanotechnological mini-plagues had been unleashed in various parts of the world. If humans succeeded in destroying the fleets that had unleashed them, how far would they spread? Presumably the crews of the orbiters knew how to neutralize or call them back. Could humans on their own, should the need arise?

Hwang was familiar with the "gray goo" scenario in cautionary tales about the perils of nanotechnology. Precautions against it were written into every grant proposal and every bit of legislation having anything to do with nanotechnology. But there was no reason to expect them in projects being used as weapons against humanity.

Was it more dangerous to wait, hoping that the aliens would leave or, failing that, at least not launch too many more atrocities? Or to strike now, with the hope of destroying the aliens and preventing any future assaults, but also with the risk that some of the spot troubles already in motion would grow out of control?

Hwang shook his head, feeling overwhelmed. He'd had a good career that frequently involved keeping a cool head while dealing with multiple crises. But never before had he been confronted with so many at once.

Well, sometimes the best way to handle a situation like that was to sleep on it and see what his subconscious could come up with. He had doubts about how much sleep he would get, and he hated to leave all these things hanging even for the pitifully few hours remaining till dawn, but it was his best idea at the moment.

He dragged himself to the bathroom for a final pit stop before retiring. But when he got there, he was greeted by an unfamiliar whiny, buzzy sound. At first it was barely audible, but he grew ever more conscious of it. With an uneasy, prickling sensation at the back of his neck, he moved around the room, trying to locate the source of the sound. He turned the lights up all the way, but—

It seemed to be inside the toilet. With a sudden defiant gesture, he flung the lid up. The sound grew abruptly louder and clearer. He saw its source, and gagged.

Swimming madly around in the bowl were dozens of tiny creatures, vaguely resembling peculiarly disgusting tadpoles, but vividly striped in red, white, and blue. Each one had a little vibrating membrane, like a tiny drum, in the top of its head, and they were shrieking at him in a tinny chorus, "Give it up, Mr. President. You know what you have to do."

For a very few seconds, he questioned his own sanity. Then he stood up and said grimly, "You bet I do."

Even though he was shaking all over, he strode resolutely out into the bedroom and picked up the phone. Sometimes all it takes to make a big, terribly difficult decision is to reduce it to a personal level.

One detail in his hypothetical example of how the plan might work was not hypothetical. "Hello," he said when he'd reached the right number. "Al's Pizza? I'd like to place an order."

 It did Pilar's peace of mind no good at all when her normally useless comcenter dragged her out of a fitful sleep to announce that Herman Hwang had called an impromptu meeting of everyone in the complex at 4 AM. And the expression on his face when she got there wasn't the least bit reassuring.

"It will be collecting information as it approaches," he was saying a few minutes later, as Pilar and everyone else were still trying to recover from the shock of his announcement that Operation Flyswatter had been activated and a missile was on its way. "But it won't be transmitting most of the time. We want its very presence to be unsuspected, so it's camouflaged in a variety of ways. It's stealthed as well as we can make it; it's flying as silently as we dare let it. And there are a lot of more obvious things on their way, launched a little earlier and quite conspicuously. We're hoping those will tie up enough of their attention to let the real one get through."

"So," asked Simonetti, "are the decoys armed too? And are they collecting data?"

"Oh, yes," said Hwang, now sitting on the same side of the glass partition as everyone else, "and transmitting it all the while. They're not as *heavily* armed as the real one, because we frankly don't expect them to get through and we don't want to waste too much of our strength. But if any of them *should* get through, we want them to be able to do some damage. We also want to get anything they can learn on the way. So they're transmitting continuously—which is likely to attract attention, but that's part of their job."

"I see," said Iona Branford, sounding less than convinced. "So how, if at all, are we going to get any information from the one that counts? Perhaps even more to the point, how are we going to know whether it's on course, and make any corrections that might be needed?"

The president practically beamed, which Pilar found disturbing. "We may not be as good at compressed data bursts as they are, but we're no beginners, either. Most of the time it's silent, but at irregular intervals known only to our controllers each missile sends back a package of telemetric information. Once they're back here, we can expand those to normal time scale and do several useful things. The first order of business, of course, is to check its progress and plan any necessary course corrections, instructions for which will be sent in the next outgoing burst. We'll also have teams jumping on the new data as soon as it's in hand to see if there's anything we can use either for self-defense or offense. And we can use it to create VR simulations that we can watch here, much as we did for the original asp incident."

Pilar groaned, not sure she wanted to experience any more of that. The first part of that one had been exhilarating, but the last part was the scariest thing she had ever experienced. And there was a lot more riding on this one.

With his characteristic flair for the dramatic, Hwang said, "Like . . . this," and touched a button.

Once more the room faded to black, gradually sprouting pinpoint stars as Pilar's eyes adapted. She felt and heard the faint throbbing of machinery, and a barely detectable sense of motion into the scene. And once again, as her eyes continued to adapt, ghostly almost-shapes tried to separate themselves from the blackness ahead, not quite succeeding. The orbiter, she realized— or at least *an* orbiter. She couldn't tell whether it was the same one she'd seen before, or one of the others. And she still couldn't tell whether it was one shape or many, or exactly what sort of shapes.

The picture held for a couple of minutes, with little change, then dissolved abruptly, leaving a strange feeling of floating in silent space. The room lights stayed off, but after a moment Hwang's voice said, "That's the most recent burst from the real one. We'll look in on it again from time to time." It occurred to Pilar suddenly that this time she'd experienced no sensation of building heat. Was that an encouraging sign?

As if reading her mind, Hwang went on, "We take the lack of heat buildup as a suggestion that our prowler hasn't been noticed yet. While we wait for further developments there, we can also sample telemetry from the decoys." He did something to his chair arm, and the holotheater filled with space again.

The sensations this time were similar, but the shadow-shapes ahead looked subtly different. This must be another of the orbiters.

And here, too, there was no indication of internal heat buildup. Pilar began to wonder whether she dared hope that this might work. It would be a shame to destroy whatever was out there without learning more about it, but she had to admit she would sleep better knowing it wasn't there any more. On the other hand, if they did destroy one orbiter, what would the others do—and how soon?

The next hours passed in a blur of periodic glimpses of telemetry from both the "real" missile and the decoys. Everyone was running on a sleep deficit, so in between samplings they made fitful and largely futile attempts at catnaps. The views didn't change much, though the orbiters did gradually grow larger in the forward view. So the tension in the air, though palpable, was more in anticipation of what might happen than in what actually was happening.

And the views from the various missiles looked so much alike that it was hard to tell which was which. So when Pilar noticed in one sequence that the heat *was* building up, she couldn't remember whether the view she was seeing belonged to the main missile or one of the decoys.

And the heat was growing *fast* this time. Only seconds after she noticed it, it had grown almost unbearable, and with it her feeling of horror. If this was the real missile, its destruction might—

She didn't have time to finish the thought before the explosion. A shower of red-hot fragments flew away all around her, some of them barely missing, and then the room went black again.

But not silent. There was a chorus of everything from shrieks to groans—Pilar couldn't even tell which her own contribution was—fading quickly to a lull with Hwang's voice rising sharply above it. "That was the decoy, folks! That was supposed to happen. Here's the real one. . . ."

But nothing happened. The room remained dark and silent for several very long seconds. Then a female voice that Pilar couldn't place asked plaintively, "Does this mean they killed it between bursts?"

"It could," Hwang said grimly. "But let's wait a little—"

"Yes," Lester agreed. "Electronics have always been prone to intermittent failure. Maybe that's all we have here."

"Or," somebody else said, "it could be a permanent failure."

"Which," Lester countered, "may or may not affect all systems. Even if our telemetry's gone, it may still be able to do its job."

"But will we ever know?" said still another voice.

"Of course!" Lester snapped. "When it's working, this is our best way to see what's happening out there, but it's not our only way."

As it turned out, it *was* an intermittent, but the signal didn't come back for almost twenty minutes. They also lost it briefly three more times, and while all that was going on, they also lost three more decoys in spectacular explosions.

But the Real McCoy, as they had taken to calling it by then, was fully operational when it got in close enough for the kill. The weirdly indistinct shapes filled the viewspace now, with the one that seemed vaguely like the center looming straight ahead. Suddenly Pilar heard the roar and felt the seat-back pressure of acceleration as the distant missile surged toward its prey like a cheetah emerging from a long wait in ambush. The shape ahead grew with easily visible speed, but this time there was no internal heat buildup.

And no swerve. Pilar's muscles tensed and her heart and breathing sped up as the missile she was "riding" surged straight into the heart of the dark thing ahead. In the very last few seconds there finally was a surge of heat, as if whoever was aboard the orbiter had realized too late what was happening and reacted reflexively. But by then it *was* too late. Telemetry lasted long enough for Pilar to see quite clearly that whatever was out there participated fully in this explosion.

Chapter 26

 It was almost *too* easy," a frowning President Hwang said at the postmortem meeting of the advisory group an hour later. He had already met briefly with his top brass, but they wanted distilled analysis of the event before recommending the next move. Now he was back in his single chair—his throne, Pilar thought irreverently—facing everyone else from the far side of the glass. "Telescopic observations from both Earth and space confirm that the explosion happened, and they can't find any fragments big enough to mention."

"Isn't that what you wanted?" asked Pilar, unsure what *she* wanted.

"Yes, but—"

"Maybe it *was* too easy," said Colonel Edwards. "Did we really catch them off guard and destroy a major nerve center? Or did they somehow bait us into wasting defensive strength on something that wasn't really worth it?" He paused, frowning even more deeply than Hwang. "This whole thing may be a trap. We may not be the only ones with the concept of a decoy, you know."

"Just what," Iona Branford asked, "do you think was a decoy?"

"If I knew that," Edwards snapped, "I'd be suggesting our next move. Which I feel like I should be doing anyway—and it's frustrating as hell not to know what to suggest. But how can we know? With aliens, anything is possible."

"No, it isn't," Marv Simonetti and Dan Felder said together.

Dan continued, "Nanotechnology isn't magic, Colonel, any more than the electricity from a wall socket is magic. They're subject to exactly the same physical laws as we are. All we have to do is figure out how they're applying them."

"That's all," Edwards echoed morosely. "I'm told that a modern fighter plane with laser guns and heads-up VR instruments is just applying the same physical laws that applied to World War I biplanes and telegraph stations, too. But could you have explained them to the World War I folks using them? Could they have built one?"

"*Touché,* Colonel," Dan said softly. "I didn't mean to trivialize our predicament. My point was merely that they *are* subject to limits, and we shouldn't assume it's impossible for us to learn anything about those limits and how to make them work for us."

"Actually," said Simonetti, "we may have already done so. What's bothering President Hwang, I think—because it bothers me, too—is that we seem to have succeeded beyond our wildest hopes, and that naturally makes us suspicious. We had hoped to make a serious dent in that orbiter, but we seem to have utterly destroyed it. Frankly, we didn't think that missile had that in it."

"I'm concerned about the 'no fragments worth mentioning,' " said Lester. "If it exploded, there must have been fragments. Some of them must have been headed toward Earth—"

"There were," said Simonetti. "We saw some of them burn up in the atmosphere."

"Did anybody get any measurements of that?" Lester asked. "That might give us an idea of their mass."

"We got some crude numbers," said Simonetti. "We weren't set up to do that really well—"

"But what do the crude numbers say?"

Simonetti sighed. "Our mass estimates, extrapolated over all solid angles, don't give anywhere near as much mass as we would have expected. And yet there doesn't seem to be anything left."

Pilar felt tickled by a vague feeling that everyone around her was looking for too complicated an explanation, but she couldn't quite come up with a simpler one. She half-listened to Maybelle asking, "Might our attack have scared them into activating a still higher level of stealth, so we wouldn't know how much the missile destroyed and how much they had left?"

"Not inconceivable," said Edwards, "but unlikely. If they had better stealthing, why weren't they using it all along?"

"Maybe it was too expensive," Maybelle suggested, "to use unless they really needed it. Or maybe they were keeping it as an ace up their sleeves—something they could pull on us to keep us guessing if it looked like we were learning too much about them. Or to keep us from knowing where we stood in a case like this."

"So why don't we ask them?" Pilar asked.

"What?" The president was staring at her. Pilar was beginning to think he found her annoying, and she reflected casually that it might not be a good idea to make enemies in such high places.

But she was getting annoyed with being kept underground in the dark by people who kept looking right past the obvious and inventing convolutions. So she said calmly, "You're trying to guess just how much damage you did and whether you made any progress toward changing the aliens' minds, right? But you're simply speculating in a vacuum, when you don't even know whether you wiped out a whole orbiter or just sent it deeper into hiding. You don't know whether anybody's still alive out there, or whether they've already launched a fleet of something to retaliate. You've talked to Xiphar before. Why don't you just ring him up and see if he answers?"

Hwang stared at her for a good half minute longer, then broke into a hearty laugh. "Very good, Ms. Ramirez. Of course we planned to do that. Why do you think I'm back over here, on this side of the glass? I just thought it would be good to put all our heads together first and see if any of you could see any angle I might not have considered. But I think we're ready now. Once again, they'll hear only me, but I'd still appreciate your best concert manners. I'm going to need all the concentration I can muster." He closed his eyes and touched a button on his chair arm. "Precheck, please."

He sat that way for at least half a minute, listening to something audible only to him, face immobile. Then he opened his eyes for another half minute, watching a holographic display that was visible from Pilar's position only as a faint flickering haze in front of his face. When that vanished he said conversationally, "Just checking our own spy net for any late developments. No clear evidence of change, I'm afraid." Abruptly his face and voice returned to historic-moment mode. "Pipeline, please!"

Just a brief pause this time. Then, "Xiphar! Are you there? Can you hear me?"

A longer pause, with a dead hush of anticipation in the humans' holotheater. Then a voice with no clear source: "I hear you."

It was the same voice Xiphar had used before, but calm, almost bored. Did that mean it *was* bored, or just that the beings behind it wanted to give that impression?

And it was only a voice this time. No visuals, not even a dramatic darkening of the room. Did that mean their capabilities had been reduced, or just their interest?

No matter. The fact that there was even a voice meant that at least some of them were there, and still capable of things frightening to contemplate.

After those three words, the silence stretched. Finally Hwang said, "I believe we've made our point. We've destroyed one of your orbiters with an ease that should show you the folly of ignoring our warning. We're quite prepared to destroy the others if we see no immediate sign of their departure and the cessation of your 'experiments.' This is your last chance. What are you going to do?"

Several seconds of silence, and then a low chuckle began, at first barely audible, but *poco a poco crescendo*. It might have been (and quite possibly was) stolen directly from some TV cartoon villain. But it was chilling nonetheless. "Last chance, indeed!" Xiphar said finally. "You seem a trifle confused about who is in the disadvantaged position for ignoring the other's ultimata. You've destroyed nothing, little man. Yes, your silly missile knocked off a few chips. But the bulk of our fleet has simply gone into . . . 'subspace.' No doubt your scientists—and soldiers like Colonel Edwards—would like to know how to do that. But that's out of the question.

"As is our retreat. We have already told you what we want and what you must do. There is no need for us to continue annoying one another. You would rather we ceased our experiments; we would like nothing better. We would far rather simply watch you, quietly, from afar, than have any effect on your affairs. What could be simpler?

"We will say it yet again: all you must do is convey that message to your people. Stop your foolish efforts to interfere with us, and we will interfere no more with you."

This is silly, Pilar thought. *Maybe no sillier than a lot of the posturing and jostling human governments have done through the ages, but somehow it seems more blatant, more obvious. More . . . childish.*

The voice had fallen silent. Now President Hwang said, "That, too, is out of the question. We have made our position clear. Either you go voluntarily, or you go involuntarily, the way some of you already have—and surely you don't expect us to fall for that ridiculous bluff about 'subspace.' "

"Suit yourself," said Xiphar, in a tone that carried a shrug. "Then the experiments must continue."

Silence. After a minute Hwang asked, "Just what is it you're trying to learn from these experiments?"

No answer. Hwang let another minute go by, then snapped, "Pipeline off!" He flicked the tiny switch and the green light on his armrest went out.

After one more minute, Iona Branford asked quietly, "Mr. President, do you really think his claim that they're hiding in subspace is a bluff?"

"I really hope so," said Hwang. "Of course I have no way of knowing. But I do know we cannot let ourselves be toyed with and cowed. Our best evidence says we destroyed that orbiter, and Dr. Felder is quite right that we can't let ourselves be paralyzed by the belief that they can do anything. We—and by 'we' I mean the people and governments of Earth, not just this country—have other missiles waiting for launch in various places, and schemes in place for launching them on short notice. It won't happen this minute, but it will be soon. I'm betting we can fool them again—and twice is all we need."

ONCE MORE THE SEQUESTERED HUMANS WERE HERDED OFF TO their quarters for another indefinite period of waiting—beginning with an attempt to catch up on interrupted sleep. There was, finally, one welcome change in their accommodations. A closely guarded "pipeline"—perhaps a variation on the one that had been developed to include or exclude the aliens from the conference room—had been installed to give the occupants a sampling of outside media coverage, almost in real time.

One of the first of those was both sobering and unnerving: a public address in which Hwang came far cleaner with the public than he had yet done. That, Pilar granted, must have taken courage, considering how long he had put it off and how slippery his message still was.

"My fellow Americans," said Hwang's image on the meter-square wall screen around which Pilar and Lester and Maybelle and Dan were gathered. "My fellow *humans*. In recent days my fellow officials and I have come to you for help with a problem whose very nature and scope were largely hidden. My heart swells with pride at the way you have answered our call, even though we were not in a position to tell you much about the circumstances behind our request.

"We deeply regret the necessity to appear less than forthright with you. The time has come to try to make that up to you, to lay our cards on the table, as it were. I want to implore you at the outset to make every effort to remain calm as we learn more. We have faced and met big challenges before, and we can do it again. We can still hope that this one is not even that big—but we dare not assume that.

"The essential facts we can lay before you are these. On May fifteenth, an unidentified object was detected in orbit about Earth. The aerospace plane which mysteriously exploded on May twenty-ninth was attempting to investigate this object. We have reason to believe that its destruction was a deliberate act of aggression by extraterrestrial beings who placed the orbiter there.

"Again I must emphasize to you: panic is to be avoided at all costs. 'Extraterrestrial' does not mean magical or omnipotent. These are beings at least somewhat like us, and subject to the same laws of nature as all of us. They are obviously intelligent in at least some senses of the word. Indeed, we have been in communication with them—but disappointingly limited communication.

"They have repeatedly refused to give a satisfactory accounting of why they are here and what they want from Earth, or to respect the wishes of us who *live* on Earth. We have established that they have more than one orbiter, and have deployed automated 'spies' all over our planet. Determining the extent and nature of that network was the purpose of our admittedly mysterious calls for information about unusual 'bugs' and structures.

"It is extensive; our scientists are hard at work trying to learn more about them. Our visitors have told us that their sole purpose is to study Earth. Even if that's true, we don't care to be spied on, and I don't think you do either.

"We have offered the 'observers' a choice: they engage in an open *exchange* of information, which we would welcome; they leave Earth; or we will force them to leave—or destroy them.

"Their only response was the series of senseless 'experiments' which have brought misery to thousands around the globe, which they claim are for unspecified scientific purposes. We are forced to regard this whole pattern of behavior as a *de facto* declaration of war. There has been no formal declaration—it is possible that the aliens lack that concept, or the sense of honor to which it is tied—and no clear evidence of their real goals. But it has become clear that these are no visitors, but invaders.

"We are duty-bound to retaliate in the only way left to us: by destroying the offending vessels. This process has already begun auspiciously: with our first attempt, we have destroyed an estimated third of their fleet. We hope for a successful conclusion soon, be it by destruction of the remainder or by the invaders' surrender and departure.

"I ask your calm support in this vital venture . . ."

Enough came in through the feed during the ensuing hours to give a vivid sense that things were indeed happening in the outside world now. There was little sense of coherence or purpose in it; Pilar hoped that that was because the coherently purposeful things were being done through the elaborately concealed secret channels at which Hwang had privately hinted. Much of the news was human reactions to Hwang's speech: demonstrations of every imaginable stripe, from enthusiastic support of his valor and decisiveness, to indignation at his rashness and the fact that he had withheld so much for so long. Sometimes groups with differing views clashed directly, leading to bloodshed and occasional loss of human lives by human hands.

If the aliens had really ever aspired to the simple, aloof observation of a world that they claimed, Pilar thought, that chance was hopelessly gone. The world they were seeing now was so far from normal that it was hard to imagine what they could learn from it.

Or was that whole process one big experiment in itself? Observation was, as Xiphar had said, a preferred method of study for astronomers—in part because they usually had no alternative. Physicists and biologists did; they liked to disturb systems and see how they reacted. Xiphar's fleets probably included both. She could easily imagine that as the possibility of unobserved observation disintegrated into chaos, the experimentally inclined members might decide to go all out and disturb things as thoroughly as possible, just to see how humanity dealt with it.

Meanwhile, the "small" experiments Xiphar had warned about continued, apparently unabated: citywide plagues with unprecedented symptoms, things that looked like natural disasters for which conditions had been completely unsuitable . . .

AT THE END OF THAT LONG, LONG DAY, PILAR AND HER FRIENDS were again sitting around their shared flatscreen watching coverage of the widely scattered incidents. The monitor showed an eerie scene of attempted traffic in Philadelphia, where an epidemic of tires sticking to pavement had slowed traffic to a molasses-like crawl, clotted here and there by pileups where the unaffected few had plowed into the afflicted many. An on-the-spot reporter, straining to be heard over the roar of engines struggling mightily to make negligible headway, was saying, "Tires from some of the 'snailized' vehicles are being taken to nearby laboratories for analysis. Of course, we can't say when they'll get there, since most roads are clogged and most of the vehicles trying to carry them have the same problem. Authorities are considering trying helicopters—"

At that point Maybelle stood up abruptly, looking more irritated than Pilar had ever seen her. "Pshaw!" she exclaimed, somehow making it a very potent oath indeed. "None of this makes any sense! Xiphar claims they're 'experimenting,' but this isn't science. It's more like some dumb sadistic kid playing with an anthill! And why isn't there anything about strikes against the other orbiters? Shouldn't something have happened there by now?"

She stomped out of the room as if fed up with the whole business, as indeed they all were. Pilar stared after her, with a vague but intense tickling at the back of her brain. She'd noticed something like that several times lately, as if her subconscious had been collecting pieces of a puzzle and was trying to put them together, and something Maybelle had said had been the last piece. But *which* thing that she'd said, and how did it fit?

And it *did* seem that there should have been news about more orbiter strikes by now, though she didn't know how long they would take to get there. . . .

She turned her attention back to the screen for a few minutes, but couldn't concentrate. And then the news coverage was interrupted in midsentence by President Hwang's face.

Not his public face, with its carefully cultivated aura of calm strength. This was the private face she'd sometimes seen in their meeting room, the one that showed his human uncertainties and self-doubts and vulnerability. Now those things showed more clearly than she'd ever seen them.

And his voice, raspy from overuse, spoke directly to the people in this room. "This isn't the outside line," he said without preamble. "Would all of you in the conference group meet me in the special room right away? We have to talk."

Chapter 27

They fizzled on the pads," President Hwang said as soon as they were assembled. He looked to Pilar even worse than he had on the screen. "Everything seemed to be working just like the first one, but when it came time to go, they didn't."

"Uh, Mr. President," Iona Branford interrupted gently. "Could you slow down a little, please? Remember, we're coming in in the middle of this. If you could take it from the top . . ."

"Oh, right. Sorry." Hwang took a moment to compose himself, with impressively visible results. Then he said, in something more like his public persona, "You all saw how well our command sequence and the launch itself worked to take out the first orbiter. And I remain convinced that we *did* take it out, no matter what they'd like us to believe. We thought we could do it again, to the other two, when the first one didn't produce the result we'd hoped for. And in fact the coded command chain seemed to work just as well, right up to ignition. Then nothing happened."

"Nothing?" Edwards prompted.

"Nothing worth mentioning," said the president. "Little hisses and puffs of smoke, but nothing remotely resembling the spectacle that a rocket launch should be. I'll tell you, I can't imagine many things depressing than the sight of a majestic rocket sitting there making silly little noises and going absolutely nowhere."

"We've had launch problems before," Simonetti pointed out. "They've always been part of frontier work—"

"This isn't frontier work!" the president snapped. "I'm sorry,

Major, but these are some of the most thoroughly tested, reliable weapons systems we've ever had. We know exactly what they should do, and they simply didn't. And yes, we have had engineers scurrying all over them trying to find the problem. Preliminary indications are that the rocket fuel we loaded them with isn't rocket fuel any more. And to add insult to injury, some of the control circuits seemed to have been sabotaged at a microscopic level, just like Dr. Terwilliger's office computer."

"Which means . . . ?" Maybelle asked.

"I think it's pretty obvious what it means," said Hwang. "Those *things* out there have been busy. While we've been scurrying around setting up secret command chains and trying to make sense of their so-called experiments, they've been using some of their spies and manipulators to figure out where our missiles were coming from and sabotage them so we can't do it again. With hindsight, I think those experiments themselves may be decoys, with no purpose beyond tying up so much of our attention that we wouldn't notice what else they were doing."

"Some of them, anyway," Edwards muttered.

"I suppose it's no surprise that we can both play that game," said Branford. "So how much better are they doing it?"

"Oh, we're not giving up," Hwang said ominously. "But we are very concerned. I tell you, our options are getting frighteningly limited. We'll keep trying, but if any of you have ideas, no matter how screwy they may seem, I want to hear them."

He looked around the room, half hopefully and half pleadingly. When nobody moved or said anything, he sighed. "That offer will remain open, as will my door at any time you need to use it. Until then, I thank you all for coming, and wish you as good a night as you can manage."

Everyone else filed out, with vaguely embarrassed murmurings of, "Good night, Mr. President." Only Pilar remained behind, her throat dry and heart hammering, and only she saw how frightened and dejected Hwang looked when he thought no one would notice. She sympathized, and she'd tried hard to follow everything he said. But it hadn't been easy, because somewhere in the midst of it that last puzzle piece from last night had fallen into place. Now she was bursting with excitement, carefully tempered with professional caution.

She approached Hwang slowly, and only when everyone else was gone did she speak, softly. "Mr. President?"

He looked up, with a fleeting expression that suggested annoyance at seeing who it was. "Yes?"

"Could I speak to you privately for a few minutes, Mr. President?"

"What about?"

"I have an idea."

He closed his eyes for a few seconds, as if either praying that she might have a *good* idea or wondering why he was so afflicted. Then he opened them and said calmly, "By all means, Ms. Ramirez. I can't help wondering, though. Why didn't you say something right away, when I asked, so we could get everybody's input?"

"I didn't want everybody's input," she said simply. "I don't think my idea is screwy, but it would probably sound that way. And by its nature, I can't say much about it now. But I have to ask you a favor."

"What's that?"

"I need to go outside."

He answered as if reflexively, with a frown. "What?"

"I need to go outside. Not for long, but long enough to check my hypothesis and see if there's anything to it. I can't do that from in here."

"Why can't you?"

"The shielding. I need to try to talk to the aliens. I need to ask them something."

He rolled his eyes enough to notice before he caught himself. "You could do that from in here—if we decided to let you. You know we can open our electronic pipeline. Why not let us help you, while staying in the relative safety we have here?"

"I'm sorry, Mr. President, but this is something only I can do. I can't tell you any more about it until I know whether I'm right. That shouldn't take long. And if I *am* right, I may have the beginnings of a way out of this mess. Wouldn't that be worth a tiny bit of risk?"

For several seconds he seemed to be consciously tying down the corners of whatever held his exasperation in check. "If you are right about *what*, Ms. Ramirez? Surely you can't expect me to approve something like this without knowing at least a little about what I'm approving."

"I think I've figured out something important about the aliens," she said. "If you heard it, you'd say it sounded crazy, but it fits better than anything else anyone has suggested. I think I can find out more easily than anybody else could—but only if I approach them alone. And I don't want to betray anybody's trust. Anybody's at all."

The president stared at her for a long time. "What could possibly make you think you're in such a special position that you could do what nobody else can?"

"Because I am," she said simply. "Remember the visitor in my apartment? Has anybody else here had that?" She paused, then continued, "Well, things were said that night that I need to follow up on. And then maybe we'll know, and we can use that knowledge."

Hwang shook his head. "I'm sorry, Ms. Ramirez. I just can't do it, for all kinds of reasons. I obviously can't let you make decisions of national and international policy importance on your own. You know too much about what has been going on in here, which you might inadvertently let slip or the aliens might take from you against your will. And you have those things in your blood. God knows what they might do when they decide the time is right."

"I have an idea about those, too," said Pilar.

"I'll bet you do—and I'll bet you don't want to talk about that, either."

She shook her head. "Not now. But I'll be more than happy to explain everything afterward."

Again he stared at her for quite a while. "I'm sorry, Ms. Ramirez, but I'm afraid there can't be an afterward—not if you insist on these conditions. If you really have an idea that could help us, I wish more than anything in the world that you would share it. We would do everything in our power to help you implement it. But if you persist in these . . . conditions, we have nothing to talk about. I do hope you'll think about the fact that if you really have something and don't share it, you could be letting your country . . . your *species* . . . down. And that if I let you go out there alone, and anything you did turned out to work against our interests, that could be construed as treason. Not by me, but by a court."

She looked straight at him. "I'm willing to take that risk," she said. "And yes, I do understand what a grave risk it is. But treason is the furthest thing from my mind. All I'm asking is a few minutes outside, alone—"

"And all I'm saying is that it's completely out of the question. I'm sorry, Ms. Ramirez, but there's nothing more to say."

"I'm sorry, too." She gazed down at the tabletop, projecting as much dejection as she could. "So I guess it's true."

"What?"

"We *are* prisoners here."

He winced. "I'd rather you would think of it as a quarantine, and try to understand why it has to be that way. Surely that shouldn't be too difficult, for a medical person like yourself." He stood up and started toward the door. "Good night, Ms. Ramirez."

"Good night, Mr. President. And thank you for your time."

Chapter 28

Pilar really did understand President Hwang's position. From his point of view, he could hardly do anything else.

But from her point of view, neither could she. With or without his approval.

But how? Security here was, as they were all reminded several times daily, extremely tight. Even if she could work up the nerve to try to escape (and it still bothered her to have to think of it in those terms), and to run the very real legal risks that would entail, how could she do it? How could she get through all the decontamination chambers and officious bureaucrats to the outside world, far enough away to have some time to do what she needed to do?

For she did need to do it.

She tried to sleep, with little success until quite late in the night. Whenever she got close, her hypnagogic half-dreams were so full of worries and frustrations, of visions of failure or execution, of fears about what kind of enemy she'd made, that they snapped her right back to full wakefulness.

Eventually, though, sheer exhaustion from all the tossing and turning and facing down mental specters magnified by the night made it impossible to toss and turn any more. Then, finally, she did sink into a surprisingly deep slumber . . .

From which she awoke with a start, sitting suddenly bolt upright, less than two hours later. As so often happened, her subconscious had seen something that she hadn't, and it didn't wait till she was wide awake to tell her.

There was a way, though it promised to get her into even more trouble. Hwang himself had told them about it soon after they arrived. It wasn't her first choice—she would have preferred to slip out quietly and unobtrusively—but it was the only thing she could think of that she was pretty sure would do the trick.

So it would have to do.

She waited until almost dawn, partly in the hope that some better idea would suggest itself, and partly because she would need at least a modicum of daylight to see where she was going on unfamiliar ground. But twenty minutes before sunrise, she slipped out of her room, as quietly as she could, and strolled with studied nonchalance back to the check-in station just this side of the last decon chamber through which they had entered.

Then she looked around for the nearest little red box on a wall, the kind that said, IN CASE OF FIRE BREAK GLASS, hesitated just a moment, and then pulled it resolutely down.

The glass rod broke more cleanly than she'd expected, with a satisfying snap that she barely heard because the sirens started up so fast they almost drowned it out. They were painfully loud, their wail rising and falling in a labored, mournful way that seemed right for the end of the world. She didn't know whether their oscillations were really that slow, or it was just the effect of that subjective time slowdown she'd heard about in tense situations. For she was pretty sure she was experiencing that.

Even as she heard the snap and the wail of the sirens, her eyes were already scanning the floor for the flowing pattern of lights that was supposed to lead to the nearest exit. To her relief, those came on just as fast, and by the time the lights had been flashing long enough to mark a direction—which was hardly any time—Pilar was running as fast as she could.

She'd never been a particularly good runner, but she was highly motivated right now and she'd planned for a head start—she'd arranged to be as close as possible to this exit before she threw the alarm. She didn't even notice whether anyone was at the guard station, and a small part of her mind wondered coolly whether that was because nobody had been there before dawn, or because there had been but they had a head start even on her, or simply because she was too busy to notice.

No matter; she had no doubt that there were plenty of hidden security cameras. She had no delusions that she could do this without being found out. All she asked—all she *demanded*—was the chance to do it. The rest they could sort out later.

Her footfalls and breathing echoed in her ears as she dashed through the decon chambers, feeling a peculiar thrill of naughtiness about bypassing them for the first time ever. She ran full tilt toward sealed doors and they slid open with quiet hisses to let her pass.

All the sounds seemed even louder in the long, dimly lit tunnel through which they had come in from the train, and it occurred to her that she hadn't noticed any real exit along here. For a frightening moment she thought that maybe it would lead only to the underground railroad platform, and then where would she be?

If she had to back up and start over, all would be lost. And a second chance would be much harder to arrange. . . .

No, that couldn't happen, she told herself, now hearing the pounding of her heart along with her shoes slapping the pavement. The lights were still leading her this way, and somewhere along here they must surely lead her through another automatic door that would slide open just in time to let her out into . . .

Something.

When it happened, she had almost given up hope and was beginning to ache with the exertion. She almost missed the turn where the lights swung to the right, but the hiss of the door caught her ear and she hooked back and through it before it closed again. Her feet clanged up steel steps . . .

*   *   *

AND SHE FOUND HERSELF ALONE ON A PATCH OF APPARENTLY deserted grass, broken only by the door through which she had emerged: an oblong panel of sod that swung up and out, and already seemed to be swinging shut again.

That seemed so odd that she allowed herself just a couple of seconds to catch her breath, ponder the oddity, and look around. That should be enough, with her time sense slowed down the way it was.

It took a fair fraction of that time for her eyes to adjust enough to see much about her surroundings; it was a *lot* brighter out here, even though the sun was barely up. And hot, and muggy; she could already feel her clothes clinging to her skin as she figured out that it was a summery day of hazy sun and billowy cumulus that might well become thunderheads by afternoon. For now, though, the sun was still low and reddish, and reflected millions of times over in dewdrops on the grass.

She didn't see the runway from which they'd taken off for the Mt. Taurus expedition, and the surrounding woods seemed closer than they had that day. That might be one thing working in her favor, at least. Evidently this exit emerged into a separate, smaller clearing than the one air traffic used, which might mean she could minimize the time she spent out in the open.

And they could be coming after her any second. . . .

All that took mere seconds and then she was running again, on a beeline for what seemed to be the nearest point in the forest wall. From time to time she glanced back, but never saw anyone following, or any sign of the sod-covered door reopening. If she'd wanted to go back in now, she wouldn't have known how. But she suspected they'd be solving that problem for her soon enough—and maybe too soon.

She was surprised to see no pursuit yet. She'd already guessed that the doors opened only when they detected someone approaching, and stayed open only long enough to let them pass, to minimize the time security was breached. But why had no one else followed her out yet? Did she really have *that* much of a head start? Or had automatic sensors already scanned the whole enclosure for a fire, sounded the all-clear, and sealed the place back up before anyone else could get out?

In which case they would soon turn their attention to accounting for everybody, realize she was missing, and . . .

Or did they already have their own spy-eyes following her motions out here, to see what she was up to before they intervened?

Despite the pain in her legs and side, she redoubled her efforts and soon plunged into the woods. At least it was a bit cooler there. Beginning to feel just a shade less vulnerable, she began looking about for a hiding place.

Then she remembered that if they were determined enough, they might use dogs or electrochem sniffers to track her down. Which was unlikely to give her enough time, unless—

The understory was relatively open and she could see something of the topography. Just ahead, it seemed to slant down and to the left, and she followed it.

Moments later she found what she was hoping for, or at least an approximation that would have to do. She would have preferred a clean, babbling mountain stream, but a dingy, sluggish one littered with cans and bottles and tires could serve the same purpose. At least it was deep enough to come up to her knees, and fast enough to tell which way it was flowing.

With no hesitation beyond a perfunctory "*Yukh!*" muttered in midstride, she plunged in, splashed out to the middle, and waded upstream as fast as she could, despite several slips on the slimy rocks of the bottom. At least there *were* rocks; she'd had visions of getting hopelessly stuck in foot-deep mud.

After fifty or sixty yards she began scanning the banks for a place to hide on the opposite shore from where she'd entered. In another forty, she found a dense rhododendron thicket, still with some flowers. It wouldn't be fun to get into, but that would apply just as much to any pursuers. So she dragged herself ashore, clothes clinging and dripping, and wrestled her way through the gnarly branches till she estimated she had at least fifteen feet of them on all sides. Then she wriggled into a sort of quasi-sitting position, supported by an irregular network of junglelike vegetation, and settled down to wait.

"OK, Xiphar," she said between pants as her breathing gradually slowed. "Your puppet said you'd be watching if I ever wanted to talk. Don't let me down!"

AT LEAST TEN MINUTES PASSED. IT FELT GOOD FINALLY TO SIT, despite the mosquitos—which, actually, were not as bad as she'd feared. Far worse was the tension: wondering whether they really would respond, or she'd gotten herself into a heap of trouble for nothing. And even if they did respond, would they do it in time?

At the limits of perception, once or twice, she thought she heard a distant baying. Bloodhounds—or imagination? She hoped the latter, but sooner or later the real thing was almost inevitable. At least maybe the stream trick would buy her a little time. Her scent would disappear where she'd waded in, and even the traces she'd left in the water would have washed downstream by now. Eventually, of course, they'd scan up and down the shore on the side where she was now, but that might take them a while. And then they, too, would have to fight their way into the thicket. It wasn't for nothing that southern Appalachian pioneers had called them "laurel hells."

More time passed. She heard the baying again, and this time she felt sure it was real, though still quite distant.

Then again, noticeably closer. . . .

"Come *on!*" Pilar muttered under her breath.

And a little after that, she heard the fluttering, out near the edge of her thicket. At first she saw nothing, but then her peripheral vision caught a glimpse of motion and her eyes locked in on a bird flapping around in the outer branches. Somewhere between robin-and pigeon-sized, it seemed to be struggling to fly through the three-dimensional maze toward her.

And it was definitely neither robin nor pigeon. It bore, in fact, a startling resemblance to a pair of partridge-shaped pewter earrings her mother had found as a girl in a Golden Skillet parking lot in Arecibo, now made large and given life. She fought fear and the urge to flee. She *was* scared, but also almost sure that this was what she had been waiting for. The resemblance of the bird to the earrings was so strong, even to the silvery-metallic sheen of its feathers, that it might as well have had her name on it.

She watched wide-eyed as it struggled toward her, finally coming to rest on a branch two feet in front of her face, looking straight at her. "You certainly didn't try to make this easy, did you!" it grumbled in parrotlike but easily understandable tones. "You requested contact?"

"Yes," she said. "I'm sorry it was hard for you to get here. I didn't see an alternative." She paused. "The things you put in my blood," she said boldly. "They built a transmitter and antenna inside me to act as a beacon, right? So you could track me?" For all their thoroughness, her human examiners had never checked for anything like that. They just kept looking over and over at the assemblers, never thinking to look for things they might have assembled.

"Of course," said the bird-that-wasn't, with a clear hint of impatience, even though there was a perceptible delay before its answer. "For all the good it did me, when they tucked you away in that damned chamber!"

She had to suppress a chuckle at the thought of this alien puppet cursing in humanlike annoyance. "Well, at least you were able to find me when I got out. I hope I can make it worth both our whiles."

"I hope so, too. What do you want to talk about?"

"I think I know your secret," said Pilar. "Would you like to talk about it?"

The bird didn't answer for several seconds, and she imagined she heard coldness in its voice when it asked, "What secret do you think you know?"

"That there aren't as many of you as you'd like us to believe. And before you get the idea that you can keep the others from learning what I've figured out by killing me, let me warn you that before I came out here, I left a message inside that 'damned chamber,' as you call it, that will tell everybody everything if I don't come back."

"An amusing speculation," the bird said flatly, and Pilar noted that even though this one looked like a bird, it had human idiom and inflection down a lot better than the clunky human in her apartment. "But I don't see that you've figured anything out, as you put it. You've made a wild guess and jumped to a bizarre conclusion. Or do you fancy that you have evidence to support it?"

"I do."

"For instance?"

"Well, sometimes you thwart our plans, sometimes you don't. I think there aren't enough of you—even including your seeded robots—to keep track of us consistently."

"And it never occurred to you," the bird challenged, "that we might simply prefer to keep you guessing by not letting you see a consistent pattern? That we might let you get away with a few things that don't really matter simply because it amuses us?"

"Yes," said Pilar. "It's occurred to me. But I think there's more to it than that."

"And I think you'll have to do better than that. What else have you got?"

"Quite a bit," she said. "I've even guessed a few more things than I've told you—or plan to."

"You've got *chutzpah*," the bird granted. "I repeat, what else have you got? Even to support this one ridiculous claim?"

"Well, when we destroyed your orbiter—"

"You *didn't* destroy our orbiter," the bird interrupted. "I've already told you what really happened."

"And I don't believe you. As I was saying, when we destroyed your orbiter, it seemed to be destroyed too completely. Well, the simplest explanation is that there wasn't that much of it to begin with. I wondered about that way back when you did the 'Wizard' effect. Obviously you're pretty good at illusion, and we were all bothered by how insubstantial the orbiters looked. Maybe they were *all* just illusions."

"How can you say such a thing? Do you think what happened to your probes was illusion? Do you think our experiments happening all over your world are illusions?"

Pilar shuddered at the reminder. "No, I don't. OK, I didn't word it quite accurately. My point was simply that there was a lot more illusion and less reality than we once thought. I still believe that. And the clincher was—"

She broke off at the sound of baying hounds, this time unmistakably real and clearly closer. They might already be working up this bank of the creek, and she had to finish this, even though her confidence had been badly shaken in the last couple of minutes.

"That's not the main thing I wanted to talk to you about," she said abruptly, and almost truthfully. "You brought up your experiments. Just what is it that you hope to learn from them?"

"Everything," said the bird. "How your world works. What makes your kind of beings tick."

"And how do you expect to do that by subjecting us to what seems like senseless cruelty?"

"It's a time-honored, basic method of science. You learn about a system by perturbing it in various ways and watching how it reacts."

There was, Pilar had to admit, more than a grain of truth in that. But modern science, probing deeper and deeper levels of both animate and inanimate nature, had moved more and more toward finding less intrusive methods, ways to see how a system behaved under normal conditions, which meant with as little observer interference as possible. "I think," she said, "my people have begun to learn some things about that that yours have not. How sometimes observing is better than—"

"As we already told you," the bird said, "that was our original intent. You wouldn't let us carry it out."

Pilar closed her eyes and counted to ten in both her primary languages. It had answered the thought she hadn't finished voicing so aptly that she worried about how directly her thoughts were being monitored. *Not too much,* she thought and hoped, at least in real time; their oral conversation suggested that the bird and those to whom it reported were missing a great deal that was in her mind but not in her speech.

The hounds definitely sounded closer now. "We are not just 'systems,' " Pilar said through clenched teeth. "We are intelligent, sentient beings who deserve exactly as much respect as you think you deserve."

For a longer moment than usual the bird sat silent. Then it said, "That's the puzzling part. You do give a remarkable imitation of that—"

"It's not an imitation!" she snarled.

"—and yet everyone knows that the Patingar are the only true intelligence, and the odds of its evolving elsewhere are just too—"

"That's just the kind of claptrap," Pilar interrupted, "that humans have always spouted to justify feeling far more superior to everything else than they were. Look, Xiphar . . . May I call you Xiphar even though we're speaking through this bird-thing?"

"If you wish."

"OK, Xiphar, let me ask you something. That night your man-puppet came to my apartment, were you trying to kill me?"

The longest pause yet before his reply. "Yes. Among other things."

She didn't flinch. "Were you monitoring my thoughts and feelings then? My physiological reactions?"

"Yes," he said. "Though my methods were relatively crude then. . . ."

"I noticed. Do you still have recordings of whatever you measured?"

"Yes."

"Play them," she said. "And this time concentrate on me, not just what I'm seeing and hearing. Try to experience what I felt. And the next time you do your 'experiments,' monitor the thoughts and feelings of your subjects. If you want to understand us, you have to realize that a lot of what's most important about us is inside us." The dogs were almost upon them now; she could hear their yapping barely beyond the thicket. "Try to experience your experiments as we experience them," she urged hurriedly. "I think you'll find it the most interesting part of your project." She saw flashing fur and heard human voices through the branches now. "And if you value this 'bird,' you'll get it out of here right now!"

No answer came. The bird fluttered into awkward flight, bumping branches but ultimately finding enough openings to break through the top of the thicket into more open woods and presumably beyond.

And a harsh male voice from straight ahead, from a face she could barely glimpse, called out, "Why don't you just come out, Ms. Ramirez? We have to take you back. Don't make it any harder than it has to be."

Chapter 29

 **They were actually** quite polite, Pilar thought, considering that they were uniformed, armed, and leading a pack of high-strung dogs. At least they didn't handcuff her, or march her across the field with a rifle muzzle pressed into her back, or even try to make her walk especially fast. Nor did they try to make conversation, which was fine with her since her thoughts were more than amply occupied with concerns about the strange encounter she'd just had.

Was there the slightest chance that it would have anything like the effect she'd hoped, without giving too much away? She was pretty sure the aliens' real-time thought-reading wasn't very good, but she had no real idea how much her newly built-in equipment might have been transmitting and recording for their future analysis. Not much, she hoped; she would like to believe she still had a secret or two from Xiphar. But he had implied that they had at least some capabilities in that direction, and she had no doubt that they would be improving rapidly in response to her suggestion.

She also wondered how much of what he'd said was true. That was the perennial problem in dealing with sentient beings, and the freshly burnished realization almost gave her a new respect for lawyers and politicians.

Her captors led her back to the same concealed exit she'd used to escape. One of them opened it a few seconds before they got there with a tiny handheld clicker, and it was almost amusing to watch the dogs stumbling over each other in their eagerness to get down the steel stairs, their yaps echoing off the hard, close walls.

Beyond that, their entrance was anticlimactically similar to their original arrival here, with the same tedious progression through tunnel and decon chambers. The only significant change was in the row of bureaucrats now on duty at their appointed stations at the last long counter. This time they didn't bother with the silly interrogation about where everybody had been and who'd handled their luggage. One of them just looked up at her, nodded without expression, and said, "Good morning, Ms. Ramirez. The president is waiting for you in the conference room."

She felt like a grade school kid being sent to the principal, and Hwang, seated at the far end of the long table, looked the complementary part. He looked up with a stern face as her escorts led her into the room, and as soon as they left and closed the door behind them, he said, "That was not a smart thing to do, Ms. Ramirez."

"I'm sorry you think so, Mr. President," she said. "I'm still hoping that it was. I'm sorry I had to do it that way, but I saw no alternative." She paused. "So what are you going to do to me?"

"I . . . we . . . reserve the right to do a great many things, pending the outcome of all this. I must remind you up front that at the very least, intentionally making a false fire report is a serious offense everywhere that I know of. You don't even deny that one."

"How could I? But I did try to do it the official way."

"And refused to accept the official ruling. That's another serious offense." Pilar wondered exactly what offense he would classify it as, since they did not have a clearly defined legal relationship, but decided the less talking she did, the better. "Far more serious than either of those," he went on, "is the possibility of a treason charge. I'm not saying there will be one, but I'm not saying there won't, either. You pretty clearly had the intent to have a private conversation with the aliens. Did that in fact happen?"

She nodded.

"Are you prepared to discuss the content of that conversation?"

She shook her head. "Not yet."

"Well, then, Ms. Ramirez, I don't think we have a lot more to talk about right now. Obviously we're not going to send you back outside, if only for the reasons I've already mentioned. And I don't want you to feel any more like a prisoner than you apparently already do—"

"Wouldn't you?" she muttered.

He ignored her. "—because our situation is sufficiently desperate that I have to keep open the possibility that we may yet actually have to depend on whatever you did out there. But we do have to be sure that nothing like this happens again. So we've heightened the security on all exits from this complex, as well as your personal quarters. Except for that, you'll be rejoining your comrades and have the same access to outside news that they have. That will be all, Ms. Ramirez. You may return to your quarters—but please don't get any more ideas about leaving them on your own initiative or trying to save the world by yourself." He rose to leave.

Pilar remained seated. "Don't you even want to hear whether I think I accomplished anything?"

He shrugged and continued toward the door. "Not yet," he said in a fair imitation of her. "If you won't talk about what you did, how could I tell whether I agreed with your judgment of whether it was worthwhile? I'm both annoyed and disappointed with you, Ms. Ramirez. I think we both need time to get over it before this discussion is worth continuing."

*　　　*　　　*

WHEN WORD GOT AROUND THAT SHE WAS BACK, LESTER AND Maybelle wanted to hear all about where she'd been and what she'd done and how Hwang reacted. "I don't want to talk about it," she said at first, and turned away.

"But you can't just leave us hanging," Lester said. "We were worried about you out there."

"I appreciate that," said Pilar. "But I'm embarrassed to have had to do it that way and I don't know if it did any good and the walls have ears. Hwang says he's put me under extra surveillance, you know. I'll bet I don't have a second of privacy any more—if I ever did." She made a distasteful face. "We've been fearing the aliens because they seem to be watching everything we do. I'm beginning to wonder now much better it is if our own leaders do the same thing."

"Shucks, girl," said Maybelle, "I've wondered that for a long time. I was grumbling about the mania for security and safety at all costs back when it was new and you hadn't even been imagined yet. But the fact is that the three of us have been in this together from the start. Don't you think we have a right to be kept in the loop if you think you've done something that might help?"

Pilar turned to look at her, torn and exasperated. "Of course I do, Maybelle, and I wouldn't want either of you to think otherwise. But that's not the problem. What I've done is such a long shot . . . but it just *might* work, if given a chance. I'm afraid it won't get that if Hwang and Edwards find out. That's why I wouldn't tell Hwang. And do you really think he won't find out if I tell you?" She gestured around the TV room much as Lester had once done to hint at unseen surveillance tools.

"Of course not," Maybelle said with something surprisingly close to her usual cheerfulness. "So why waste any effort worrying about trying to keep secrets? That's not good for you, dear."

Who do you two think you are? Pilar thought, annoyed. *My parents?* That made thoughts of her real parents and grandparents, and what was happening to them now, pop unbidden into her mind, and she found herself close to tears.

Maybelle must have noticed, for her tone softened abruptly. "Just out of curiosity, Pilar, what made you think Xiphar and his buddies would talk to you, anyway? Or even listen to you?"

"I thought we'd decided they listened to everybody," Pilar snapped. "Like our Sunday school teachers told us God did. So why not me? If you're right that they can pay attention to lots of people, places, and things at once."

"But not *all*," Lester reminded. "We mustn't lose sight of that."

"Right," said Pilar. "But we already knew they were keeping a special eye on *us*, at least until our fearless leaders put us in this cage. So yes, I thought they might be watching for any attempt one of us made to communicate, and I don't think that's being paranoid. And I thought they might pay attention if I had something to say that might either help or hurt them."

"And did you?" Maybelle asked gently.

"I thought so. Two things, actually. I thought I'd guessed something important about them that might help us against them, if necessary, and I wanted to try to feel them out about whether it was true. I also thought I might see a way to trick them into backing off and leaving us alone."

Maybelle whistled. "That's quite a package, if you were right. Do your friends get at least a hint?"

"Oh, why not?" Pilar sighed and shrugged. "You're probably right about trying to keep a secret around here. OK, the first thing grew out of a lot of little things that kept bothering me— but it was something you said, Maybelle, that really snapped it all into place."

"Something I said?" Maybelle looked genuinely puzzled.

"Yes. I thought it was odd right from the start that sometimes they made samples disappear and broke into our computers, and so on, yet sometimes we were able to get things past them, like Maybelle's package."

"The time lag and the inability to concentrate on everything at once," said Lester, "even if you have access to everything at once. We've already talked about this. Those things have to be there."

"Right," Pilar agreed, "so in themselves, those inconsistencies proved nothing. But there was also the fact that our images of the orbiters were always so fuzzy that we couldn't even tell how big they were or how many there were. And then, the first time Xiphar made his 'Wizard' appearance, and I realized the whole thing looked real but wasn't, I wondered if the orbiters themselves might be something like that. Obviously not *pure* illusion, since they were doing real damage to our probes and now to all their 'experiment' sites; but maybe they were *mostly* illusion, to make us think their fleets were bigger than they are. Remember, Lester, when we were flying back from Mount Taurus I asked you about active stealth? This is what I was beginning to think about."

"Well, yes," Lester said thoughtfully, "I can see that, up to a point. It does sort of fit in with the way our guys couldn't find enough remains when they shot down an orbiter. I don't buy that hooey about disappearing into subspace, but maybe if there just wasn't as much there as we thought to begin with—"

"But there can't be *too* much less," said Maybelle. "They're doing a *lot* of damage, all over the world."

"But they have a lot of cybernetic help," Pilar reminded, "if they just seeded the planet with tiny things that used local materials to make more and more of whatever remotes they needed." She drew a deep breath. This was the part she hadn't wanted to mention to Hwang, if only because it sounded crazy. But if she could say it to anybody, it was these two. They really were her friends, and it did feel good to get this off her chest. "I think there may be a *lot* less," she said. "A whole lot less."

Lester and Maybelle frowned in unison. "How much less?" Lester asked cautiously.

"One alien," said Pilar, and then paused to let it sink in.

They both just stared for at least half a minute. Then Maybelle said, "One?"

"One," Pilar repeated. "In one of the orbiters, with the other two just puppets or decoys. And maybe he's mostly been telling the truth—but probably not entirely. I know it sounds absurd, but I think it explains what we've experienced better than anything else.

"Consider this: they say they just wanted to observe for the sake of science. It was only when we refused to ignore them and be a nice well-behaved system pretending to be unperturbed that they started their 'experiments.' To us they look like attacks, mostly, but in a way it makes more sense to suppose that they *are* experiments. From a military point of view, as I understand such things—which is not very well—they don't seem to make any sense, to serve any strategic purpose. They haven't made any demands, except that we let them observe us without resisting. Maybe the simplest explanation for that is that they really *do* just want to observe us, and experiments are—from their point of view—just the next best thing if we won't let them."

"But the experiments don't make sense!" Lester objected. "They're lousy science!"

"Exactly," Pilar agreed. "We've all thought that, and that it seemed like they were more interested in tormenting us than in systematically studying anything. You, Maybelle, put it into words better than anybody else. You said it was like some dumb sadistic kid playing with an anthill. I knew at the time that something seemed really significant about that, but it wasn't until a little later that it really fell into place.

"And then I thought: what if it really *is* a big kid playing with an anthill?"

Lester and Maybelle both tried to talk at once. "How could

one kid—" "Kids don't have access to that kind of—"

Pilar held up her hand. "I know, I know! I've thought all those same things myself. But look at what's happened to *us* in the last century or so. One person with the right automated tools can do things that used to take a whole factory full of laborers. Four-year-olds have toys that incorporate computing power that no university could muster a few decades ago. If you imagine that trend continuing a few more decades, why *couldn't* a kid run off among the stars with toys that could spy and wreak havoc on whole worlds?"

Maybelle was staring at her with something that looked star-tlingly like admiration. It made Pilar feel good, but she didn't stop to ask why. "OK," she said, "maybe not literally a kid. At first even I found that too hard to swallow. At first I was thinking in terms of a group, just smaller than we'd been picturing—maybe a hundred aliens instead of ten thousand, or even ten instead of a hundred. But the more I thought about it, the more I wondered whether it had to be even more than one. And in ways, one individual seemed to make more sense. After all, we are talking about what looks to us like childish behavior, and that's harder to believe in a group of adults, no matter what the species. They'd tend to act as checks and balances on each other's follies and excesses—"

"Ever read anything about mob psychology?" Maybelle asked gently.

"Yes, and Xiphar doesn't sound like a mob. He seems too calm and dispassionate about what he's doing. And besides, he slipped up once, right before the experiments started, and said 'I' instead of 'we' when he was trying to pose as the spokesman for a great and powerful fleet."

"I believe," said Lester, "he didn't claim to be just a spokes-man, but the exalted high commander. So that slip may not mean much."

"Except that he got flustered when he did it, as if he thought he'd slipped up. You're right, no one thing proves that the alien fleet is just one warped alien—but so many things suggest it that I think it's a good working hypothesis. I still doubt that he's a kid—but he may well be a warped genius, a grown-up but emotionally immature scientist with way too big a toy budget and not nearly enough social skills."

Lester and Maybelle chewed on that silently for a while. Then Lester said, "So why didn't you want to tell the President your idea? If there really is just one alien, and we can find out how to take him out—that may be all we need to do."

"That's why I didn't want to suggest it to Hwang, at least not yet. I still don't think that will make it anything like easy—even if it is just one big brat up there, he's a brat with a tremendous amount of snooping ability and firepower at his fingertips. But it might well make it easier than if there really were ten thousand of them spread among all the orbiters. If Hwang and Edwards believed that, I think their whole emphasis would shift to figuring out the best way to kill that lone brat. But I don't like that kind of solution if something better might be possible."

"And you thought you saw one?" said Maybelle. "That way to trick them that you mentioned? Or him? Or whatever?"

"Yes," said Pilar. "It seemed to me that just as it should be easier to destroy an individual than an army, it might be easier to change an individual's mind. Or in this case, to help it grow up. If Xiphar is an intellectual genius who's never got around to developing any sense of empathy, what if we could trick him into using the same tools he's spying on us with to see how the experiments look to us?

"So I suggested that he try it. I think the idea caught him off guard; he seemed to find it as hard to believe that we have any real intelligence or feelings as most humans find it to believe that about other animals. But I planted the bug in his ear—sorry, I guess that's a poor choice of words—and I think he's intrigued by the notion, sees it as a challenge. I'm pretty sure he has the technical capability, and I think he just might try it. And if he vicariously experiences a few hundred painful, senseless deaths— well, he may become a little less enthusiastic about them."

"Well," Maybelle said thoughtfully, "it's certainly an intriguing notion."

Pilar grinned. "It's still a little hard for me to swallow, too. At best, it's a long shot—but if there's really just one person out there—can I say person?—and there's any chance we can turn him into a decent one, I'd rather do that than just blow him up. Besides, have you heard anybody suggest anything else more likely to help us?"

"I sure haven't," Maybelle drawled. "I think we should keep a close eye on the news and see if there's any sign of a letup in the experiments. In the meantime, though, do you mind if I give you one little suggestion, Pilar?"

"OK."

"I think you should go tell President Hwang what you just told us. You're probably right that he already knows it, but I think it would do both of you good for him to hear it from you. He's running at least as scared as any of us, and I think he needs some reassurance that you're on our side."

 **Hwang remained more** skeptical of Pilar's idea than Lester and Maybelle. But he did seem pleased that she had come to tell him about it, and his attitude toward her seemed to soften just a bit. "But," he added sternly, "we can't afford to do a lot of waiting in the hope that your wild idea is right. If it is, your friend up there had better get on the ball. We'll be watching for signs that support your theory, and if he shows any sign of being what you claim and wanting clemency, we'll consider any reasonable deal. In the meantime, we've made our position clear and we cannot and will not back down from it. We have quite an elaborate contingency plan in place now, and we're pretty sure much of it is still viable. As long as the alien 'experiments' continue, we will regard them as acts of war by an alien army, and do everything in our power to stop them."

Pilar made no further attempt to dissuade him, but returned to quarters and spent a lot of time in the TV room with Lester and Maybelle and occasionally Dan. But the news failed to provide what she was hoping for.

For the first few days, the experiments continued unabated. It was harder to tell about attempts to knock out orbiters. The media were not reporting any failed launches. That might mean that there weren't any—or it might simply mean that they'd been told, or decided on their own, that it would be best to keep them quiet.

On the third day after Pilar's return, Lester patted her reassuringly on the shoulder and said, "This must be very disappointing for you. There's not much sign that they're paying any attention."

They, she noted. *Does that mean even Lester has written off my idea?* "Oh, I don't know," she said. "We could hardly expect immediate results. My hope is that he'll be influenced by the results of experiments where he concentrates on the thoughts and feelings of the victims. Unfortunately, that means he still has to do some." She shuddered at the realization that, in a sense, she herself had urged him to do those experiments. But wasn't the idea that that way he might ultimately do fewer than he otherwise would have? "Besides," she went on, "have you thought about what's *missing* from the reports?"

He frowned. "Besides any reference to what we're doing to stop the mayhem? I'm not sure what you mean."

"Runaway gray goo," she said. "Most, if not all, of these plagues and disasters are being carried out by nanopuppets. Our biggest worry, especially if we get rid of the puppeteers, is that they'll continue to spread without limit and we won't know how to turn them off. But that hasn't happened. Each one has been confined to a village or a valley or some smallish, well-defined area like that. None that we know of has spread beyond the target zone. Most seem to have run their course and stopped."

"So far, anyway. There could still be an alien counterpart of a dead man's switch. Still, I suppose it's at least tentatively encouraging."

"It had better be," Pilar said grimly. "We need *something* that is."

They got another such something the next morning. President Hwang's face again broke into the newsfeed, and to Pilar's astonishment he was smiling. "This is another special for the conference group," he announced. "It's not the sort of thing we want to announce publicly until the results are final, but our luck may be turning. As you've probably guessed, we've had a number of failed missile launches—but now we've had a splendid success.

We got a biggie off the pad without a hitch, and it's rock-steady on course for one of the invading orbiters. Can't tell you which one, of course, or where it was launched from, but we'll keep you posted."

By now Pilar had grown much too cautious to rejoice at that kind of news. *Have they really licked the problem,* she wondered, *or is Xiphar just toying with us again, trying to lull us into a false sense of security before he hits us again?*

The answer was not long in coming. Two hours later Hwang was back on the screen, this time looking crushed—at least to anyone who had learned to see through his public mask. "I'm sorry to report," he said in flat tones, "that the missile for which we had such high hopes has been destroyed in flight, without providing any useful new information."

His face vanished without further comment or discussion.

Four more days, four more attempts, two more fizzles on the pad, and two more successful launches, each destroyed a little closer to its target.

Definitely toying with us, Pilar thought. *Like a cat with a mouse.*

And then, apparently, he tired of the game.

The next time Hwang broke into the public newsfeed, Pilar could see no trace of his public mask of confidence. He looked, to put it bluntly, close to tears—and at the same time furious. "This time," he said, his voice close to a growl, "they've gone way too far. They've—" his voice caught and he tried again "—they've destroyed Kennedy Spaceport! I'll see you all in the conference room, immediately."

Chapter 31

Evidently," Hwang said as soon as the whole group was assembled, "they had a whole array of nano-bugs quietly infiltrating various parts of the space-port, setting up booby traps in spacecraft, fuel reserves, and electrical systems, so that on command they could blow the whole thing. And they did."

He, too, said "they" instead of "he" or "it," Pilar noted. Evidently nobody was taking her idea very seriously, whether because they found it too improbable or too humiliating. "I don't want to tell you," he went on, "the actual numbers describing the death and destruction; so I won't. I don't think I need to put in words the magnitude of the insult to our people and everything we stand for and aspire to. The time has come for a heroic final effort. We've simply run out of other options."

Pilar didn't like the sound of that, to put it as mildly as possible, but she was hardly surprised. She listened intently as the president went on, "I've told some of you in the recent past that we have an elaborate contingency plan and a good deal of confidence in it. That confidence has been badly shaken by events of the last few days. Worse yet, the plan itself has been seriously weakened. Kennedy Spaceport and its resources were a major part of its strength. With that gone, we seem to have no hope left but to bet everything we still have on one all-out push to destroy whatever is out there—and by 'we,' I mean all the space-capable nations of the world.

"Ms. Branford, Colonel Edwards, and I have already conferred with the Joint Chiefs of Staff and agreed that this is what we must do, and very soon. Either it will work, or it will not. After it's done, we will have essentially nothing left to work with. This is, in every sense of the terms, an all-or-nothing, last-ditch effort. So if anyone has any last-minute suggestion as to how to avoid that, no matter how off-the-wall it might seem, I would very much like to hear it right now."

He looked around the assemblage, one face at a time. Did he really dwell extra long on hers, Pilar wondered? No matter, at this point she was not going to say anything. She'd already made her pitch; she'd honestly hoped it would work, but now it, too, had failed. She would not humiliate herself further by suggesting any more attempts at talking or waiting. Even she had to admit that the time for that was past, though the thought of blowing off all their remaining resources at once was both scary and depressing.

President Hwang nodded. "Then we proceed. What we have left is some additional weapon stockpiles and launch facilities scattered around the world. Some of them are ours; some are other countries'. Some of them you've heard of, some of them most of you haven't. We've already established that targeted secret commands to individual sites are too easily intercepted to be trusted. We'll instead be following the same general pattern we've been using, of sending a general preparatory notice to everybody in charge of such facilities that they're to unleash them toward a specified target when they get an 'execute' command. Both the preparatory and execute commands will be 'hidden in plain sight,' open to public view, with the hope that only the few who need to know will recognize them for what they are."

My method, Pilar observed, *though I don't expect any credit for it at this point.*

"When the second command set goes out," Hwang continued, "everybody who has any weaponry left will launch, all at once, each for a designated target. Both remaining orbiters will be attacked. As usual, we don't expect everything to get through; but we do hope there will be enough to confuse the enemy and over-whelm their defenses. If our experience with the first orbiter is any indication, one good strike on each of the others may be all we need. The superlasers we'll hold in reserve, in case the missiles don't work as well as we hope." He paused. "Any questions?"

"Just one," said Branford. "When does all this happen?"

"Soon," said the president. "But even in here, I don't think I should be too—" He cut off abruptly, frowning and sniffing. "What's that smell?" His eyes darted around the room. "And what's that dust around the edges of the room?"

Dan Felder sprang from his seat and crouched down to look and sniff. Then he stood back up. "I think," he said quietly, "our shielding is being disassembled. It can work with a lot of holes in it, but maybe not if it's converted to a different chemical form—or if their puppets just make their own 'pipelines' through it. Even one can breach security. I suggest an immediate and thorough inspection. In the meantime, I don't think we should consider this facility secure any more."

"Not another word!" Hwang barked. "From anyone." With expressive hands he urged everyone toward the exits—except Edwards and Felder, whom he beckoned to follow him.

And the question of when the strike plan would be carried out, Pilar thought, was suddenly moot. She couldn't imagine the president's waiting another minute.

Chapter 32

 **It felt to** Pilar as if they had in one stroke been exposed, thrown naked to the entire world, and shut off from it more thoroughly than ever. The feeling that the shielded hideout provided at least a modicum of protection from Xiphar and his minions (if any) was gone. But so was the public newsfeed. Hwang explained privately that since there was nothing the public could do to aid this war effort, and it would all be over so quickly, there was no point in torturing them with information about what was happening. Any information that *could* be withheld, which was precious little, *should* be withheld, he reasoned—just in case it was still possible to put something past the aliens.

So the screen in the TV room spent most of its time insolently blank, taunting the captives with the unspoken message, *I know something you don't know.* And Pilar and her friends found themselves in the odd position of knowing that this bizarre "war" had entered a decisive phase, and they had no way of watching its progress.

They pictured it as Hwang had described it: dozens, perhaps hundreds or even thousands of high-speed missiles springing forth on a single cue from launch sites all over the world. Each would follow its own path into the blackness of space, but ultimately, with luck, groups of them would converge on the two remaining alien orbiters. Some of them would be detected and blown out of the sky before they ever reached their destinations. But maybe a few would get through and put an end to this sword of Damocles, restoring peace and privacy to Earth.

Maybe. Half of Pilar wished they could watch live displays as they'd done before, looking in on each missile in turn to see that it was still on its way. The other half wondered whether she could take the repeated blows of watching missiles destroyed in flight. So on the whole, she grudgingly accepted the screen's blankness. She and her friends still spent much of their time gathered in front of it, just in case, but almost nothing happened.

Until, with no warning, the Wizard's face appeared, filling the screen and speaking in a voice filled with a frantic urgency she'd never heard from it before. Pilar leaned forward, listening intently as it said, "People of Earth, we never imagined that you would mount such a suicidal folly as this. We have detected your missiles and will destroy them, but the real danger—to you even more than us—is that we will not get them all. I see now that I have erred, too, and unwittingly exposed you all to a danger far larger than the one you thought you faced. It is possible that we can still deflect that danger from you, but that is your only hope.

"And that slim hope requires us to be alive, our equipment undamaged, and our feelings toward you favorable. It is absolutely imperative that you call back or destroy your missiles at once, and that we then talk.

"I'm transmitting this to every receiver on Earth. I implore every one of you in a position to do anything about implementing my request to do so at once—"

The Wizard was cut off abruptly, replaced by Hwang. "You want to talk?" he sneered. "The time for that is long past. It's obvious that you're scared, Xiphar, and with good reason—because you finally realize we're not as helpless, and you're not as powerful, as you thought. You had your chance, and you blew it!"

He was shaking visibly as he stopped and the cameraman belatedly faded him out. A verbal newsfeed began scrolling across the bottom of the screen, expressionlessly announcing that two missiles had just exploded. As the words kept marching across the screen, the Wizard's face, superimposed on them, started over. "No, no!" it said. "You don't understand. We *both* blew it—you and we. We never intended to endanger either you or ourselves, and now we're both in a danger that goes beyond mortal. Only together do we have any hope—"

Pilar had had enough. Numbly, she tuned out both the Wizard's pathetic cries and the ominous casualty statistics streaming across his face. She thought of seeking solace or insight from Lester or Maybelle, but they looked as dazed as she felt. She walked slowly to her room to await whatever came, thinking as she did that Xiphar really did sound scared. But there was something else, too. Was this new pitch, this transparent-sounding rant about having inadvertently exposed Earth to a greater danger, just the desperate ploy to buy time for himself that it seemed? Or was there more to it than that?

She locked herself into her room, flopped down on the bed, leaving the lights down, buried her face in the pillow, and cried.

And her phone rang.

It rang a couple of times before the reality of it even penetrated to her. She had become so used to the fact that the comcenters in their quarters were disconnected that she'd almost forgotten that it *could* ring. The only person who had ever sent a message on it was Hwang.

Why would he be calling her now?

Frowning, she turned the lights up just a little, sat up on the edge of the bed, and pressed a button to take the call on the speaker. "Yes?" she said dully.

But the voice that answered was not Hwang's. It was the bird who had visited her in the woods—or, more precisely, it was to that voice as a rich human voice heard close-up is to the same voice heard on a cheap handset. "Pilar," it said urgently, "you've got to help."

Her frown deepened before she accepted the identification. "Xiphar?"

"Yes, of course. Please listen, Pilar. I've built a pipeline into your comcenter and disabled Hwang's bugs in your room, but I'd still rather you picked up your handset."

"Why?" she demanded.

"Please, we don't have time for this. All our lives are in danger. Just do it."

She hesitated a couple of seconds, then did it. "What's this all about? Why are you calling me?"

"Because I desperately need your help, and you need mine. And nobody else will listen to me."

"I see," she said flatly. "And why should *I* believe you? What good will it do any of us if I do?"

"I understand your skepticism," he said. "But you see, I did as you suggested. I refined my emotion-monitoring equipment so I could see things as your people do. I understand now that I have ignored massive evidence right in front of me all along that your race is truly sentient and intelligent. And I have now altered my equipment so it works both ways, partly by reprogramming the spies in your bloodstream to build an interface after my 'bird' visited you. I can let you feel *my* emotions, so you'll know I'm sincere and telling the truth."

"Oh? How would I know *that* isn't just another of your illusions?" She remembered the time her own phone had shocked her and added, "Or will you use your new toy to get rid of me once and for all?"

"You're already holding the handset. If I had wanted to use it against you, I would already have done so. Give me permission to turn on the connection. The fact that I'm asking permission is the best I can do to convince you of my sincerity."

She hesitated, then said, "I'll try it. But I'll hang up at the first sign of treachery. So what is all this about?"

She waited tensely for several more seconds, then jumped at the sudden, utterly unfamiliar sensation of feeling strong emotions that were not her own: nostalgia, shame, regret—and above all, fear. And something she couldn't place, something—alien.

She struggled to keep her own feelings separate as Xiphar began his story. "I was born into a people we call the Patingar, on a world we call Tingarex and your astronomers call—I should save that as a bargaining chip for later.

"When we reached the stage of our technology most comparable to yours, our people were even less inclined than yours to take collective risks, yet more inclined to let individuals take risks affecting only themselves. We did not always have the best judgment about which was which.

"These tendencies made us more leery than you of nanotechnology, once the possibility suggested itself. On the other hand, population pressures like yours, together with the existence of a possibly habitable world only nine hundred astronomical units away, led us to develop space travel more vigorously than you did. By the time of my personal career, so much effort had been put into this that our space travel was quite advanced. Intrasystem travel was routine and we'd even learned some interstellar shortcuts. This kept us so busy, and our fear of what some of you call 'gray goo' kept us so cautious, that nobody bothered with nanotechnology.

"Until I came along. I was what you might call a 'computer geek' in a plant where several lines of work were being done, including some early nanotechnology. I was, if I may say so, a very *good* computer geek." He paused and Pilar felt echoes of pride in past glories and regret for lost opportunities—and profound loneliness. "In particular, I had an unusual knack for seeing big patterns and interrelationships. Looking at several of the things being done where I worked, and elsewhere, suggested to me the potential for combining nanotechnology with macrocomputers and telepresence to do very large-scale, very detailed surveys."

"Just like Maybelle said, right at the beginning!" Pilar blurted out.

"Yes. An astonishing intuitive leap on her part," said Xiphar, and Pilar felt an undercurrent of what felt like genuine respect. "She's a remarkable individual, especially for one who I gather is near the end of her natural lifespan.

"Anyway, I found that when I encouraged fields to cross-fertilize, with the help of massive parallel processing, they could even advance the nanotech at very high speed, to a level far beyond where you are now. Soon we had the ability to send a small expedition to another planet, seed it with replicators and instruction packets to grow information-gatherers and matter-manipulators, and do quite a thorough—"

He broke off abruptly, and Pilar felt a surge of something like panic. "Oh, damn! Those were close."

"What?" Pilar asked.

"Two of your missiles. They were headed for . . . one of my orbiters, and I didn't recognize them until it was almost too late."

"You destroyed them?"

"Of course. But there are so many things flying around out there. Just as your friend Lester guessed, I can't keep track of them all at once, and I can't afford to squander my defenses on everything that *might* be a threat." Pilar felt him consciously suppressing his panic, his feeling of being overwhelmed, but could tell he didn't get it very far below the surface.

"Back to my story," he said abruptly. "I'm sorry I must cut corners. . . . The possibility of that kind of exploration was so exciting I was eager to put it into practice. Initially I just wanted to use it for a much better survey of that nearby planet, which had received only cursory spot-checks comparable to those done by your early Mars probes. Hoping to stir up enthusiasm and funding, I arranged a demonstration by doing such a survey of an uninhabited island.

"It worked splendidly—in scientific terms. But I was naïve about my own people in those days, and I never anticipated their reaction. It scared them silly, and it gave some of them ideas that

I should have been scared by. But I wasn't. I was too blinded by my enthusiasm for what I saw as the most spectacular research tool ever invented.

"For me, it was a way for a small number of people to learn a great deal very quickly. I saw the sheer exhilaration of doing that, and the benefits to my people if we could learn quickly how to build a successful colony on Pingalix. Others saw a possibility that my methods could also be used by an oppressive government to monitor and control every detail of its people's lives. There were actually factions in our government that wanted to do that, in the name of safety and security; and others that considered that the greatest danger of all. The latter won out. Not only was my proposal for an intensive survey of Pingalix rejected, public discussion of my techniques was banned.

"I just kept pushing it harder. It was too important to pass up because of what I saw as petty politics. Eventually I was declared *persona non grata*, and denied access to public communications. But I had seen that coming, and secretly made some arrangements. I had outfitted a ship—magnificently—to do what I wanted, with so much artificial intelligence that I could operate it alone—and I stole it.

"My original intent was just to go to Pingalix and do my survey on my own, figuring that once I had the data and they saw how useful it could be they would have no choice but to welcome me back. I was followed there—which I didn't understand at all, because I didn't feel dangerous—and they tried to destroy me and my ship.

"I had energy tools on board that I could have used as weapons to destroy their ship before they could strike at mine. But strange as it may seem, Pilar, I still thought of myself as loyal to my people, as trying to do them a great service. I could not imagine killing any of them, not even those who intended to kill me. So I did the only thing I could do instead to save myself. I jumped, through one of those interstellar shortcuts I mentioned, more or less at random and in a way that would be at least difficult for my pursuers to follow.

"My jump brought me out near Earth, and for a while I thought I was, in your terms, in heaven. A huge planet that I could explore at my leisure, with an astonishing diversity of land-forms, oceanic and atmospheric phenomena, life . . . Even structures apparently built by that life, so sophisticated as to suggest intelligence, though at that point I couldn't seriously imagine that any non-Patingar had *real* intelligence. True, I would probably never see any of my people again, which was regrettable but seemed a small price to pay for what I had gained. I could live with it."

But not, Pilar noted from the turbulence and pain beneath the words, *as easily as you let on*. "So there really is only one of you?" she asked.

"Yes," he said. "I am all alone." For a moment a wave of loneliness, both wistful and painful, threatened to overwhelm the words. But then he went on, "I had a whole new world to study and unprecedented means to do it. That could easily keep me happy for the rest of my life, and I settled down to do it. But there was an unexpected catch.

"I set up shop in orbit, splitting off two other stations to space around the planet so that I would have direct or indirect contact with my probes on the whole planet at all times. Then I seeded the planet with millions of tiny nuclei that could set about build-ing many kinds of mobile probes and fixed relay stations." He paused. "Your friend Lester is pretty clever, too, and his life has had more sadness than it deserves. In ways, I can identify with him. . . .

"But I digress. At first I reveled in the flood of information coming back to me. The incredible diversity of landforms and plants and animals and all their complex interrelationships far exceeded my wildest dreams. I didn't personally understand it all, of course, but my AIs were busy sorting and correlating data and I could dip in and sample it at will. I was, in your terms, like a kid turned loose in a toy store—until the catch gradually dawned on me."

"What catch?" Pilar prompted.

"You. Humans. Intelligent natives. None of the previous probes Patingar had sent elsewhere had detected anything like you. Our philosophers had long taught that we were unique in our intelligence and sentience, and our scientists agreed that they were such unlikely things to evolve that the philosophers were almost certainly right. So I was totally unprepared for the presence of intelligence and civilization here, and it took me a while to recognize them for what they were. When it became clear that there were things on Earth that looked very much *like* intelligence and sentience, I began dedicating some probes to trying to study this startling phenomenon. Oh!"

Again he cut off, his transmitted emotions very agitated. After a moment he said, "That one was much too close. Its blast debris breached my shell in several places. My remotes can probably fix it, but I don't know how much longer I can hold out."

And she knew that he was frightened, so scared that she had to work hard to remind herself that it was his fear and not hers. "How many probes have you . . . dealt with while we've been talking? I don't understand how you've been able to spare the attention for me—"

"The AIs and remotes," he interrupted with palpable impatience. "They do things like that for me, and the latest tally is sixty-eight."

Does that mean he's doomed, Pilar wondered, *or we are? Or both? I don't even know how many we have!*

"The bug that 'stung' Lester," Xiphar continued, "was one of the first probes designed to study humans, and unfortunately a primitive and clumsy attempt. I did not intend to harm him, though I must confess that I didn't worry about the possibility because I still hadn't grasped the idea that you people might be as intelligent and sentient as us—much as many of you still dismiss that possibility for so-called lower animals like apes and dolphins. All that probe was supposed to do was send in smaller probes to chart his nervous system and try to analyze its information storage; I now deeply regret that it caused him pain.

"They couldn't report back right away—they couldn't do that until the bugs that got inside your headnets by the relay station on Mount Taurus retrieved them and returned to the transmitter. Meanwhile, when Lester went to your hospital, his large bug released several others to sample other nervous systems nearby, again in an unfortunately disturbing way. When their reports started coming back, some of the AIs began to conclude that there was a big problem here, but still at a pretty low level in the hierarchy.

"I didn't become personally aware of the problem until you and your friends began to investigate. I realized then that my agents in the hospital had called too much attention to themselves, and I began looking for a way to put the cat back in the bag. My original intention was simply to observe, for the pure joy of learning and understanding, with as little disturbance of your world as I could possibly manage. Having quasi-intelligent subjects notice and get excited and work others up into a panic would ruin that whole plan. So I needed to stop you even as I tried to make sure the same thing didn't happen elsewhere.

"I sent AI puppets to try to persuade each of you to drop your investigation so I could go back to what I came for. But as you pointed out and it took me too long to realize, humans aren't built that way, any more than the Patingar.

"You, personally, were particularly stubborn. Your visitor—I trust you've noticed I've learned quite a bit since I cobbled that one together!—decided it would be better to kill you and seriously scare the others than to let you run around stirring things up. His attempt backfired, of course, and I had to become more involved in what I still thought of as the pseudointelligence problem. You were all bugged now, with assemblers in your bodies that I could use to build things I would find useful—beginning with beacons that I could use to track you. And I decided to fill your efforts with so many little mishaps that I hoped would persuade you to give it up. Anything more aggressive would call too much attention to me, and my fondest wish was to get rid of *all* attention.

"I'd disguised my orbiters as stealthed fleets as soon as I arrived, not because I anticipated native intelligence or technology here, but just in case pursuers from home did manage to track me here. So far that hasn't happened, but it wasn't long before your military observers noticed the orbiters and started trying to figure out what they were. I hoped they would give up after their first casual looks showed nothing profoundly interesting. When they sent a probe that got too close, I hoped that making it explode mysteriously would convince them that snooping was too dangerous and they would drop it.

"Unfortunately your officials took that personally. Before I knew it I had to deal not only with you people being too curious about my observation minibots, but widespread panic about hostile aliens in orbit and military organizations planning to destroy me. I wished I could find a way to tell them to ignore me and they'd be in no danger, as I'd done with you and your friends, but I couldn't do that without admitting who I was.

"But soon we had ultimata to which I *had* to respond, so I tried to do it as intimidatingly as I could. Ultimatum and counterultimatum, bluff and counterbluff, and things had escalated to the point where the leaders of Earth believed I was an invading force waging war and they couldn't understand why." A note of pathetic pleading: "Why wouldn't they listen, Pilar? I told them what I wanted, and I told them the truth."

"Your claim was unbelievable," she said coldly, "whether it

was true or not. Especially when you were laying waste to human lives and land all over the planet. If you really understood us, you would understand that."

"Yes," he said, and she pictured a person closing her eyes in remorse. "I would have. Personal feelings and interactions have never been my main area of interest. I was like Maybelle said: a big kid playing with your planet as if it were an anthill. You were very wise to suggest that I concentrate more attention on what was going on inside your people. It was a profoundly painful experience, but I've learned from it."

"Oh? What have you learned?"

"That you *are* really people. I have felt the pain of those caught in my experiments, and I mean that literally." His emotional undercurrent swirled in a complex eddy of many remembered, shared agonies. "My desire to learn did not justify inflicting such pain. I came to regret having done it.

"The turning point was during my destruction of Kennedy Spaceport, as I tuned into the mind of a young researcher who worked there. I found that I had a great deal in common with her: curious, eager to learn, unskilled in her relationships with her fellows—but utterly dedicated to a far-seeing dream much like mine. Her pain on seeing the means of realizing that dream wiped out was almost unbearable. How could I have done such a thing to someone so much like myself—and, by extension, to so many others of her kind, each with their own dreams? I resolved to stop at once, and start undoing whatever damage I could.

"But it was too late. Your leaders, having already destroyed one of my auxiliary orbiters and thereby weakened both my surveillance capabilities and my defenses, had hatched their plan for a coordinated assault to wipe out the rest of my 'fleets.' To my horror, I realized that your missiles were already on their way and probably too numerous for me to stop.

"And to my even greater horror, I realized the danger I had put you in."

"So," said Pilar. "Are you finally going to tell me what you're talking about?"

"Of course. I left my home system as a fugitive, feared and reviled as a very dangerous individual with far too much power at my command. At first I thought that by jumping far from Tingarex, I would leave all that behind, that they would decide I was no longer a threat to them and it would be too hard to come after me.

"But then I realized that they *could* follow me if they really wanted, and some might be determined enough to try. They considered my marriage of computers and telepresence and nanotechnology such a grave danger that they could not rest as long as there was any possibility of my returning. So they may well come after me, and while they detest my methods, they will not hesitate to use them against me, if that's what it takes. 'For the duration,' as so many of your dictators have said." He paused, the pleading note now strong and urgent. "Do you see the problem?"

"Not really," said Pilar. "I believe your story, because it's clear that you do. But I still can't trust you. You've shown yourself a great danger to Earth. If others like you come to remove that danger, how would it not benefit all of us—except you?"

"Oh, my!" he said, now with a note of frustration, compounded by another spike of anxiety as he squashed another missile. "You really don't. It wouldn't benefit you at all, Pilar. If they destroy me, your troubles will have barely begun. If they find that I've seeded your planet with what they see as evil nanomachinery, they may decide to sterilize it—and they will be quite as well-equipped as I. But there will be many more of them, and they will not know you as I do. *Now* do you see the danger?"

"Oh, my God!" Pilar breathed as the picture clicked together in her mind. Her throat suddenly very dry, she croaked, "What do you want me to do?"

"Get them to call off the dogs," he pleaded. "Talk to Hwang. Get him to call back or destroy the missiles and persuade your other leaders to do the same. Then, if my pursuers do come, I can surrender myself voluntarily and cooperate with them in decontaminating Earth without harming the people and things that belong here. That's the only hope I see, unless they don't come after me—and you can't count on that. Please, Pilar—talk to Hwang, right away!"

"I don't know if it will do any good," she said.

"But you have to try. I—" Another interruption, longer than the others, as he dealt with more missiles. "Please, Pilar!"

"I'll . . . try," she said. "That's all I can promise." She paused, then said, "Xiphar, what do you look like?"

"Does it matter?" he asked.

"Not to me," she said, and she thought she believed it. "But I think I should know, anyway. And . . . I'd like to know."

"I'll tell you," he said, "because I want you to know me as I've known you. And . . . you may never have the chance to see me for yourself. My body shape is qualitatively similar to yours, but smaller. If you picture something vaguely between a human and a gibbon, in both shape and size—" He broke off abruptly, the waves of alarm rising to a new peak. "Please, Pilar, hurry!"

"I'll do my best," she promised with sudden resolve. "Hang on, Xiphar—and good luck!"

Leaving the handset dangling, she was out of her door like a shot and running through the corridors, heart pounding.

Chapter 33

There *is* only one alien!" Pilar said breathlessly, having made enough fuss outside Hwang's temporary office to get past the Secret Service guards in short order. "And he was telling the truth about wanting to study us, but we misinterpreted and he couldn't explain without giving himself away and things got out of hand and—"

"Please, slow down!" Hwang interrupted, holding up a hand and rolling his eyes. "What's this all about?"

"There isn't *time* to slow down! I'll explain it all later, and he'll do it even better. The only thing that matters now is stopping the missiles—calling them back or blowing them up or—"

The president regarded her coolly. "I don't think that's either possible or desirable."

"But it's necessary! A matter of life and death for all of us."

Hwang raised an eyebrow. "Now how could that possibly be?"

"Xiphar is a fugitive. I think he's reformed, at least a little, as a result of a suggestion I made, but the officials who were pursuing him may follow him here. If he surrenders and helps them clean up the mess he's made on Earth, we may be safe. But if we've killed him and left the mess, he says they're likely to just sterilize the Earth."

"Well, he would say that, wouldn't he? It would certainly enhance his survival chances, especially if we've squandered all our defenses and nobody comes after him after all. Then we'd be completely at his mercy, whereas now we've got him on the run.

Can you think of any reason why you should believe him about this desperate ploy?"

"Yes," Pilar said emphatically. "He's rigged my phone so I can directly sense his emotions. It's scary, but I'm sure he's telling the truth. In fact, he's been telling the truth most of the time, and our troubles came from not knowing that." An idea popped into her head. "Why don't you try talking with him on my phone yourself? Then you'll see, too."

"We've already had abundant proof," Hwang said wearily, "that we see what he wants us to see. Why should shared emotions that he claims are his be any different? No, Pilar, thanks for the offer, but I think I'll pass. I've got my hands quite full with things that look a lot more promising. Besides, I really don't think it's possible to stop the missiles now."

"Can you at least ask?"

"Ask whom? May I remind you that I am the commander-in-chief of our armed forces? Trust me; I've looked at the situation and made the best decisions I could. I stand by them. Now, if you'll excuse me . . ."

Pilar stared numbly at him for several seconds. Then she said stiffly, "Thank you for your time, sir. But please give it some thought." She stepped out into the hall, walked past the Secret Service men without looking at them, and sprinted back to her room.

The phone was still off the hook, and Xiphar was still on. Tears streaming down her cheeks, Pilar said, "I tried, Xiphar. He wouldn't budge. I don't know what else I can do. I'm sorry."

"So am I," he said. She was struck by the absence of noticeable anger, and saddened by the sense of resignation. "But I thank you for trying. I wish I could think of something else to tell you or do for you, to make up for what I've done to you. But I can't. I'm sorry for that, too."

"Are the missiles still coming?" she asked.

"Fast and furious, with lots of decoys mixed in to confuse me and tempt me to waste *my* defenses. I don't have many left, at either site. Excuse me. . . ." Another flurry of agitation, but there was something new in it, a subtly unnerving kind of calm, as if he was getting used to going through the motions and no longer held out much hope of ultimate success.

Then, without warning, a huge spike of terror, frenetic action, and despair.

Followed by several seconds of nothing.

"Xiphar?" Pilar said tentatively. "Are you there? What happened?"

Several more seconds passed before he came back on line, voice weak and shaky, the emotional background fatalistic. "They got the other auxiliary orbiter," he said. "There's nothing left out here but me now. I don't see anything else coming right now, but it's probably only a matter of time."

"How many more can you handle?"

"I don't think I should say. Do you have any idea how many more you have?"

"No. They don't tell me much, either."

"The coast still looks clear right now. Dare I hope that they've run out?" A long pause. "Listen, Pilar. I have thought of one last thing I can do for you. It may not help, but I have to try. For what it's worth, I've started the wheels in motion. You people have a saying about gifts that it's the thought that counts, but it isn't always true. I think you know the thought's sincere, but in this case I sure hope the gift is actually worth something."

Pilar remembered dying patients she'd seen in the hospital and thought, *Is he delirious?* She hoped he didn't pick that up as she asked cautiously, "I'm afraid I don't follow you, Xiphar. What are you talking about?"

"I'll explain if I have time, but I may not. I think first I'd better say good-bye."

Pilar could barely force the words out. "Good-bye, Xiphar. I wish I could—"

"Uh-oh, here comes another one." Another flurry of excitement, then, "OK, we got that one, but it was close. I can't believe that was the last, but at least I only have to protect one site now. Let's give this a try. After I'm gone—"

The last word turned into a chillingly human scream, accompanied by a surge of pure agony on the emotional channel. Both scream and surge cut off with startling abruptness, and then there was nothing.

Absolutely nothing.

It was so still that Pilar heard her heart hammering, and then she realized that while Xiphar's final shrill pain had stopped, it continued to resonate in her. "Xiphar?" she whispered finally, and when no answer came she repeated it in a frantic shout.

But still there was nothing, and over a period of a minute or so, she finally admitted to herself what had happened. *So that*, she thought, *is what it feels like to die.*

 Her eyes were still red and her anger congealed into a hard knot when Hwang called her in for a private audience a few hours later. He looked happier than Pilar had seen him in the entire time since they'd met; he fairly beamed with relief and pride. Pilar found that vaguely annoying.

"So it's over," he said after he'd shown her to a comfortable chair and offered her refreshment, which she declined. "And as we all know, you were right. I owe you an apology and gratitude, both personally and on behalf of all humankind. Please consider them delivered. I hope you can accept them."

"I don't understand," she said simply. "Gratitude for what?"

"Why, your invaluable contribution to our victory, of course. You made it possible."

Her puzzlement deepened into an overt frown. "How? You didn't use any of what I did or learned. . . ."

"Ah, but we did," he said with a smile. "While you had him distracted on the phone—and yes, I am finally convinced that there was only one—we traced the signal he was using to talk to you to know exactly where he was. We already knew pretty well, of course, since the other two orbiters were gone by then. But knowing that there was only one, and tracing the signal, let us pinpoint him so precisely that we could collimate a laser beam as tightly as possible, putting all its energy right where it could have the most effect. He never knew what hit him."

Pilar closed her eyes and shuddered. "Yes, he did," she said grimly. "I know, because I experienced it with him. I wish you

307

and everyone involved could have, too. It was a thing too terrible to put into words. I'll never forget it, and you'll never know it." She paused, then added very quietly, "And it seems I must share the guilt, too."

Now Hwang frowned. "Guilt?"

"For his murder. This isn't at all the way it was supposed to work out. It wasn't necessary, and it may be our suicide as well as his murder."

"You're putting a serious damper on my afterglow, Ms. Ramirez," Hwang said. "Would you care to elaborate on that?"

"Weren't you listening when I tried to explain before?" Her tone softened. "I'm sorry, Mr. President. Of course I realize you were under tremendous stress, and I was in a hurry and I can well imagine that what I was saying did sound crazy to you. I must make allowance for that. May I try again to do it right?"

"Please do."

"Think about what happened here. Initially we saw so much happening that we assumed we were being invaded by a fleet of nearly omniscient and omnipotent beings. Nothing less seemed even remotely possible. Yet in the end we defeated them, though just barely.

"It was, as the boxing promoters say, a fair fight—between one little alien who didn't want to fight and a planet of nine billion. The outcome was always in doubt, but *only* because there was only one of him to sort through all that data and decide what was worth his attention. What if it really had been a fleet of ten thousand with their abilities augmented like that, and they really had it in for us? They would have been unstoppable—and they may still be coming."

He listened, this time attentively, as she filled him in on Xiphar's story of how he had pushed a previously feared nanotechnology to new heights, then scared his fellows with his ambition of combining it with massively powerful computers and remote monitoring and control. She told of his wish to use it for exploration of a nearby potential colony world, and of how his small-scale demonstration had led to his criminalization and eventual flight through hyperspace, or some such thing, to Earth. "He thought," she finished, "that some so feared what he wanted to do that they would stop at nothing to squelch it. Even if it meant bringing a whole fleet across interstellar space, equipped with the very technologies they're trying to suppress, and wiping out life on an inhabited planet. That's us, Mr. President."

He looked pale, but stopped short of admitting fear in words. "It sounds extreme," he said. "Too extreme to believe easily."

"We can't assume that their priorities and values are like ours. Dare we assume that they won't come, or that they won't do what he says?"

Hwang pressed his lips tightly together. "No, we can't. We can consider it unlikely, and hope we're right. But obviously hope isn't enough. We won't ignore the threat. We've collected a lot of data from this encounter, and we'll dedicate a significant portion of our resources to squeezing every bit of knowledge out of it that we can. We'll also push to develop our own nanotechnology and remote sensing and manipulation technologies as rapidly as possible. And we won't be secretive about why we're doing it. The public has to know that once anyone can do what Xiphar did, there may be more like him, and maybe worse, sometime in the future. We *won't* mention his specific threat; that might create such panic that people could never get on with their lives. But we will do all we can to prepare for the general danger, and we'll inform the public as fully as necessary if a concrete threat ever does materialize. In the unlikely event that they come, Ms. Ramirez, we'll be as prepared as we can be. Nobody can promise any more than that."

"That's admirable, Mr. President. But will it be enough?"

"On that," he said, "we can only hope and pray. Ah . . . I don't suppose Xiphar gave you any indication of *when* this might happen, if it does?"

"No, sir. I think he may have been trying, but he was . . . rudely interrupted."

"Regrettable," said the president, and this time he looked as if he meant it more sincerely than he would have preferred. "Well, I'll see that we all do all that we can. If it happened now, there'd be nothing we could do about it. But if it takes them a few years to track him here, or to decide they're ready, maybe we can be ready, too. Meanwhile, we'll get on with our lives, just as people did during the Cold War and the Terror War.

"On a brighter note, we owe you, as I mentioned when you came in, a large debt for your help, despite your unorthodox behavior and even if it didn't work out the way you intended. What matters is that it worked, and for now, at least, we're out of the woods.

"I gather—and please correct me at any time, now or later, if I'm wrong—that you'd be . . . ah . . . embarrassed by a medal of honor. But please let me at least assure you that any charges I'd considered pressing against you will be dropped. Is there anything else you'd like?"

"Just to go home," she said wearily. "Right now I can't imagine anything I'd like more than to go home and try to get back to some semblance of a normal life." She thought a moment and added, "That means no publicity. I don't know if you had anything like that in mind, but—"

"I think," Hwang interrupted gently, "that can be arranged." For a moment he looked wistfully at the ceiling. "You know, I think I might like to try that myself in a few years." He looked back at Pilar, more pointedly. "As far as this is concerned, we don't want unnecessary publicity either. We'll get you safely home and try to keep things quiet about your role in all this. In return, you must agree to say nothing to anyone about Xiphar's claim that pursuers from his home world may come here. Is that clear?"

"Perfectly," said Pilar.

"Good. I have the power to detain you indefinitely if I thought you might violate that trust, but I don't want to exercise that power." His manner softened again. "And if you think of anything you'd like later, ever, please don't hesitate to call me." He scribbled something on a scrap of paper and passed it to her. "That's my direct personal line. Please memorize it and destroy it. There are only a handful of people in the world who know it, and I'd like to keep it that way. But if you ever feel that you have a good reason to use it, I'll trust your judgment. And I'll give you any help I reasonably can."

She stared at the number for half a minute, then looked up and managed a polite smile. "Thank you, Mr. President. That's very generous of you."

 The government gave Dan, Maybelle, Lester, and Pilar a ride home. The first leg was on the same camo-painted corporate jet that they'd used for their fruitless expedition to Mt. Taurus, but this time they were headed for White Plains. Nobody talked much. Pilar could understand why: They were probably as absorbed as she was in looking out the window and mulling what had happened and what the future might hold.

From the air, there wasn't much obvious sign of Xiphar's experiments, but occasionally she saw a marina reduced to ashes, a pond with bright orange water, a field with huge graffiti woven into the crops, or something comparable. Overall, she gathered, few places had suffered really massive damage. But a few dozen people here, a few dozen more there, in enough places around the world, added up to a lot of damage. Xiphar, despite any virtues he might have belatedly acquired at the end, had been a mass murderer and vandal on an unprecedented scale. She could never truly forgive him that.

And yet there was evidence that he *had* grown up at least a little in his last hours. Part of her still felt a little sorry for him.

And occasionally puzzled over his last words. Just what had he been trying to give her, when . . .

The approach over Long Island Sound and into White Plains went smoothly, and then it was time for a parting of ways. An unmarked government car was waiting to take Lester and Pilar upcounty, another to take Maybelle into Manhattan, and a third to take Dan home to Jersey. Standing in the parking lot in front of the neat fleet, exchanging hugs and handshakes, Pilar found herself getting surprisingly choked up. "We've been through a lot together, haven't we?" she said. "It's going to feel strange going our separate ways, not seeing each other every day, trying to learn not to feel paranoid every minute—"

"Oh, pshaw!" Maybelle interrupted. "This isn't good-bye forever, you know. I assume you folks are all going to keep coming to the museum occasionally. Maybe you can even find time to look at some of the exhibits now. And if it's not too forward of me, I hope you might even invite an old geezerette from Kansas up to the country once in a while."

"And I'd love," said Dan, "to have you all out to the lab sometime and show you what we're doing." He looked pensive. "Of course, I have a hunch a lot of what we're going to be doing will be very different now. In fact, I just might be able to find jobs in some of the new stuff for any of you who are interested. I know how frustrated you got having your hands held out of the pie while the government labs monopolized the neat stuff."

"That," said Pilar with a smile, thinking of how tedious and exasperating the hospital lab had sometimes seemed, "could be very tempting."

"My card," said Dan, extending one evidently plucked from his sleeve. "Please keep it in mind. I'm serious."

"As for not feeling paranoid," said Maybelle, "don't get *too* out of practice. There's usually at least a fair reason to be, and if you don't have one now, be patient. One will be along soon enough. In fact," she added grimly, "we know of at least one doozy that could pop out of the sky anytime. But I refuse to let that dominate my life unless and until it happens." She looked at her watch, an antique analog model. "Well, it has been fun, in a bizarre sort of way, and we could go on jawing like this all day; but I suggest we save some of it. It'll give an incentive to make sure we really get together again—and I, for one, am kind of looking forward to trying to get things back to normal again."

That reminded everyone else that they'd like to try that too, and it wasn't long before they all piled into their respective cars and were chauffed off. At the first intersection they all rolled down windows to wave before the cars headed off in three separate directions, and Pilar chuckled in surprised delight when all three drivers gave playful little toots on their horns.

It seemed so refreshingly ungovernmental.

PILAR'S APARTMENT SMELLED STALE WHEN SHE LET HERSELF IN. Despite all that had happened since, she still felt a little apprehensive when she opened the door and the lights came up, as if her bizarre visitor of—was it a few weeks ago?—might still be lurking inside. But he wasn't, and the super had even fixed the broken window in her absence so it looked as good as new.

She walked around looking at things, to see if anything was missing, damaged, or otherwise amiss. But everything seemed perfectly normal.

And surprisingly lonely—especially when her inspection tour brought her to the pictures on the walls. Her family's little house in the village, the grand and neglected old radiotelescope carved into its bowl-shaped valley, and her family itself: a group portrait in front of their cottage, and Rosa's graduation picture.

Rosa! The first thing she had to do was call Rosa.

She tried the phone, and then e-mail, but neither drew a response. Suddenly the feeling of relief, the feeling that the nightmarish days were finally over, turned sour. Had things really changed that much at all?

Stop it! Pilar told herself sternly. *Don't panic. Remember a lot of things were damaged. Even if it isn't still happening, it will take time to fix everything back to normal. Give it time.*

She actually managed to calm herself quite a bit, though she still worried and she resolved to keep trying.

And then it was time to go back to work.

* * *

THAT FELT STRANGE, TOO. THE HOSPITAL CORRIDORS AND LABS were a surprisingly welcome sight, despite the bright lights and antiseptic smells and frantic bustle. And it was a relief to see familiar faces, even though none of them were particularly close friends. Two or three gathered around as soon as they saw her, eager to know where she'd been and what she'd been doing and what had happened to her. They'd heard rumors that she'd been kidnapped by aliens and that she'd been a spy for the government and all manner of other things, but she shrugged it all off.

"What's been happening back here? I heard there were some . . . ah . . . incidents in the hospital, and threats of lawsuits. Did they happen? Are we in trouble?"

"Nah," said Arlene, the dedicated mycologist. "There were plenty, here and everywhere else. But the government said that all those things were caused by the aliens. They figure acts of aliens are pretty much like acts of God, so they categorically threw out all those suits."

A better analogy than you may realize, Pilar thought, but she didn't say anything.

One of her first stops, of course, had to be the lab supervisor, Ms. Ravine. "Welcome back, Pilar," she said, but without much warmth. "I got notes from on high that say you've been on some sort of classified government work and you can't talk about it. I guess there's not much I can do about that, but it sure did throw a monkey wrench in our scheduling. Seems to me you could have at least given me a little warning."

As if you ever gave us any advance warning about monthly rotations, Pilar thought, but again she reined in her tongue. "I would have," she said, "but it really wasn't poss—"

Ms. Ravine waved her off. "Don't bother to explain. I know I have to accept it—but I don't have to like it." She looked at the schedule chart on her desk screen. "Once again you've caught me off guard. If I'd known you were coming I would have had an assignment schedule ready for you. But I didn't, so I don't. Give me an hour. Wander around and see who needs help, and when you come back I'll have at least a week of schedule for you."

So Pilar did that and wound up putting in a little time in hematology. It actually felt surprisingly good to have her hands back on the controls, but when she picked up her schedule she groaned.

Two midnights out of seven days. She *hated* midnights.

THE WEEK PASSED LIKE OLD TIMES, EXCEPT SHE STILL COULDN'T get through to Rosa, and she still worried about some of the last things Xiphar had said. But gradually she began to feel that if she could go on like this, she'd never complain—at least, very loudly—again.

Then, when she came home from work, she saw a stranger standing by the door of her building.

Except she had the oddest feeling he wasn't entirely a stranger.

With a slight shudder of *déjà vu*, she stopped, partly hidden by a large rhododendron, to size him up. A man of medium height, with dark hair and good posture, respectably dressed in a business suit of currently fashionable style, its wavy lapels edged with brilliant peppermint-striped piping. He seemed to be waiting for someone.

She gasped out loud. Xiphar's humanoid puppet, who had all but forced his way into her apartment and tried to kill her, had struck her at the time as a walking, talking mannequin, or a rough draft of a human being. If that was the rough draft, this might well be the finish.

But that notion was probably just a construct of her imagination.

In either case, this courtyard was well provided with crime-eyes. She was through running scared, and she lived here. She was not going to be intimidated by some guy who stirred unpleasant memories.

She started moving again, striding resolutely toward the door (but with her Mace and air horn close at hand). She walked right past the stranger, noting out of the corner of her eye that seeing him close-up did not reduce the impression that he was a more refined version of that first crude puppet.

She wasn't really surprised then when, just before her hand touched the door, he said quietly, "Pilar?"

She stopped and turned coolly to face him. "Yes?"

"We need to talk."

She sighed. *Not again.* "Who are you?" she asked.

"Don't you know?"

She studied him and frowned. "Xiphar?"

"Xiphar is dead, as you well know. But he offered you a parting gift, a legacy. That's what we need to talk about." He inclined his head toward the door, his nuances of both speech and body language now right on target. "In your apartment?"

She shook her head firmly. "Not a chance. I'm interested in what you have to say, but not that interested. Tell me out here."

He smiled. "Very well, Ms. Ramirez. Perhaps we could at least move away from the door?"

"Sure," she said, gesturing toward a nearby bench, set a little off the concrete and surrounded by grass. "We can sit there." Not a question, but a statement, and she sat down first without waiting for his acquiescence.

He sat at the other end, keeping a discreet distance. "Suppose we start," Pilar suggested, "by establishing just who you are. If Xiphar is dead, how did you get here?"

"You may call me Argo," the man said, "and you may think of me as Xiphar's last and best puppet. As for how I got here . . . while Xiphar and all his orbiting equipment were destroyed, a good many of his 'seeds' remained on Earth. Some were quite dormant; others were already on their way to becoming new things, but still subject to redirection. I was one of the latter.

"At the end, when Xiphar was so busy trying to defend himself against a fate he could no longer hope to avoid, he was not only talking with you and trying to get you to help him—"

"I tried," Pilar interrupted, her throat dry.

"And he knew," said Argo. "One of the advantages of having so many remote appendages is that one can attend to a lot of things at once—though not, of course, an infinite number. When he belatedly realized, and even more belatedly came to care about, the danger he had placed your people in, he felt a desperate need to make amends. His first hope, and what would have been best for everyone, was what he asked for: to be spared to help you defuse the threat. But when it became clear that that was not going to happen, he tried even more frantically to do the next best thing. He really wanted to give you a chance."

"Even when we refused to give him one?"

"Even then. He felt strongly that he owed it to you—and in the last minutes he understood how your leaders felt."

"So what is this 'next best thing'?" Pilar asked.

"Me," said Argo. "And this." Before she could flinch, he reached into a jacket pocket, much as his 'rough draft' had done, and pulled something out. He held it out for her to see, displaying it in an open palm.

It looked like a very elongated egg, about six inches long and one in diameter, of a pearlescent pale green. "What is it?" Pilar asked finally.

"Your starship," said Argo. "Or rather, the seed from which a ship can be grown. Obviously it does not contain the materials, but it does contain instructions and nanoassemblers that can start by making all the other nanoassemblers that will be needed. Xiphar intended it as a gift for you personally, and for all the people of Earth."

Pilar frowned. "Me? Why me?"

"Because out of all the people on this planet, many of whom he did speak with, you were the only one who ever showed any interest in his viewpoint or in helping him. At considerable personal risk, I might add, and despite quite credible reasons for not doing so."

"It just seemed the decent and reasonable thing to do," she murmured.

"But beyond the call of duty nonetheless," said Argo. "My creator felt that such kindness should be rewarded. That's the personal part. The other part—the part for everyone—is that he placed your entire world in danger, and giving you a facsimile of his ship to use and learn from may be your only chance to prepare to defend yourselves, if the 'cops' from his home world come here."

"If," she repeated. "That implies that they may not. Don't you know?"

"No," he said, "I do not know. Not whether, and if so, not when. It could be soon, but more likely at least a few years. But you owe it to yourselves to prepare for the possibility as best you can, and offering you this ship is the one way he knew to help you do that."

"I don't want to seem ungrateful or suspicious," she said, "but how do we know this is really to help us and not another way to start the whole pattern of spying and spot attacks again? After all, you've killed thousands of innocent humans—"

Argo winced visibly and shut his eyes for several seconds. "You've felt Xiphar's sincerity," he said. "He told you how much he regrets those deaths. I can do no more to persuade you to trust him. I can only point out that this ship, and my help with it, may be your best hope for the future. And I know how much you've dreamed of being an astronaut."

That seemed bizarrely inappropriate. "What does that have to do with anything?" Pilar demanded. "You said this was partly a gift for me. I don't see how this benefits me, except possibly as part of humanity."

"The ship can be used in two ways," Argo explained. "As you've seen, and I know you've appreciated, it makes possible an astonishing and exhilarating sort of exploration. It's fun to use—more fun than you can imagine. And it will be at your disposal. Didn't you once dream of that with some envy? Xiphar knew you did."

"More than once," Pilar admitted, with a fleeting smile of remembrance. "But if he knew about the envy, he also knew about the fear. I don't think I could trust anybody with that power. Not even myself."

"Xiphar's last wish," Argo said quietly, "was that you make better use of it than he did. But that's up to you, and your people. Use the gift wisely. For the joy of exploration, and the necessity of self-preservation. As you use the ship, your scientists can study it, try to learn the principles on which it's based, and develop their own applications."

The last hint of a smile evaporated from Pilar's lips. "So it's no gift for me. If that happens, the government will take it over and I'll be pushed right out of the picture."

"No, no," said Argo. "Not at all. You're the key to it. The ship is yours, and he hoped—and believed—that you would share it with your fellows for the good of all. But no one will be able to make it do anything you don't want it to, and if anyone tries to seize control by . . . ah . . . eliminating you, the ship will not allow that. And you will have the last word in selecting the humans who travel or study on it."

But they won't pull any punches in trying to influence my choices, she thought. "I'm not sure I really want that responsibility," she said quietly. But then she tried to imagine who else she could trust with it, and vowed to herself that she would do no worse. "I'll do my best," she said simply, and then she allowed herself a small grin. "And I actually will be an astronaut, won't I? Though all the real work has already been done. . . ."

Argo chuckled. "Not by a long shot," he said. "It's barely beginning. True, you're inheriting a very advanced technology, ready-made. But it's an *alien* technology, not designed or labeled for human users, and it doesn't come with an owner's manual. I can help you somewhat with it, but not as much as you might think or hope. I'm just a puppet. My knowledge of the ship is about on a par with the typical human's knowledge of the cars they drive. And while the seed can grow the hardwired parts of the ship's information-gathering and storage facilities, most of the content Xiphar gathered during his visit will be lost.

"And, as I believe you've already begun to realize, you'll have the problems of working with your own people. For starters, the ship-egg can't grow a ship from nothing. It will need lots of materials, in a big place from which it can launch. I don't think you can provide that on your own."

"No," she said, momentarily daunted. "I can't." But then she remembered something and her mood brightened considerably, even unto a big smile. "But I know a certain president who thinks he owes me a favor. I think he'll agree that this is important enough to call him on his private line."

Epilogue

"Out of all the places in the world," asked Maybelle, squinting against the late afternoon sun, "how did they pick this one? I can remember when this was just a dump!" She swept a hand around her to take in the whole peninsula of Croton Point, jutting into the widest part of the Hudson. They could see it all from atop the broad, mostly grassy mound—all, that is, except where their view was blocked by the Patingar-designed starship perched on the summit. Pilar had asked her to join them aboard it; but Maybelle, to Pilar's disappointment but not surprise, had decided she was too old for that—but she wouldn't miss seeing them off.

"I can't *remember* when it was a dump," Pilar said with a smile, "but I knew about it. That's why we picked it. A dump is a great source of assorted raw materials. The nanos could pick out what they needed, and turn the leftovers back into a park when they finished.

"That, and the convenient, open location. Funny, isn't it? About to take off on the biggest trip humans have ever taken, and I pick a takeoff site so my friends won't have to drive far to get there." She surveyed the small group assembled around the ship: Lester, Marv Simonetti, Dan, and a handful of scientific observers and government representatives.

It seemed an absurdly small group for an interstellar expedition, but it had still required design modifications. The original, after all, had carried only Xiphar, more the size of a single human child than a dozen adults. That, in turn, required reprogramming the nanoassemblers in the "egg," but Argo had assured Pilar he could handle that.

The ship, in any case, looked finished enough, at least to human eyes. Like its crew, it looked to Pilar too small for space, but too large for the dry land where it sat. Perhaps the size of one of the freight ships that plied the river, it wasn't even streamlined. The general plan was vaguely ovoid, and the color predominantly a deep gray-green that gleamed like polished obsidian. But it sprouted a bewildering profusion of projections with no obvious functions, and a riot of secondary colors suggesting a box of jewels that had spilled over the hull and stuck wherever they landed.

All that was missing was its name. That would appear on the hull only at the moment of takeoff, as a parting surprise for the one it honored. Maybelle couldn't go physically, but the *Maybelle* could and would.

Maybelle was staring unsuspectingly at it—again—and shaking her head. "I thought anything that big would have to be assembled in space, and if you just *had* to fly it through atmosphere you'd have to streamline the heck out of it. This thing looks like it couldn't possibly fly, and even if it could, the rocket blast would destroy half the Hudson Valley."

Lester fielded that one. "It doesn't use rockets, and somebody's supposed to have 'proved' once that bumblebees can't fly either." He grinned a surprisingly boyish grin, as if he'd decided to quit worrying about the holes in his memory and just start filling them with new experiences. "How's that for a full circle?" he mused. "From the Bizarre Bee of Boscobel to comparing bumblebees and starships in a few easy weeks."

"I wouldn't call them easy," said Maybelle, her expression turning fleetingly somber. "But I guess this is kind of a wish fulfilled for you, isn't it, Lester? I seem to recall your saying once that you'd always dreamed of discovering something new. Looks like you're finally going to get to do it."

"Many times over," he said, "I sincerely hope. If this thing really can do what Argo claims, that proves the Patingar have a control of gravity that humans up to now could only dream about. Marv and Dan and I are going to learn how it works—and in the meantime we're going to *use* it."

"I envy you," said Maybelle. "I wish I were young enough to go with you, but at least I can look forward to hearing the stories you bring back." She frowned. "And I can live with being puzzled by how it works. I've adapted to plenty of new technologies in my time; I reckon I can stand a few more."

Feeling a gentle tap on her shoulder, Pilar turned to find Argo looking at her. "Ms. Ramirez? Everything is ready. If we could get everybody aboard . . ."

With a shiver of anticipation and nervousness, she turned back to Maybelle with a weak smile. "Well, I guess this is it. Wish me luck, Maybelle."

"I don't think you'll need it," said Maybelle. "You tend to make your own. But good luck, anyway—and don't forget to bring back those stories."

COMPARED TO THE LAUNCHES OF EARTH'S PAST—THE SATURN Vs Pilar had heard tales about, for example—it would be a remarkably undramatic liftoff. Just a big, clumsy-looking structure floating lazily skyward, without any of the sound and fury that used to reverberate for miles around. The American government hadn't really believed that, of course; they'd cleared the entire peninsula and urged a voluntary but "highly recommended" evacuation of another ten miles all around. And there were no masses of media or government people around the perimeter. It was as if Hwang's government was vaguely embarrassed by the whole thing, as if it was something they *had* to do, but would carry out as quietly as possible.

Pilar, for the first time sealed inside the alien craft with a mere handful of other humans, felt relieved, but more than a little apprehensive. What if it *was* some elaborate trap, a regression to Xiphar's worst habits and attitudes?

And even if it wasn't, what if she wasn't able to finish the one last bit of business she had left undone? Argo seemed to understand how important it was to her, and yet he still hadn't been able to make it work. He was working on it, he said, but they were already lifting off. . . .

He seemed to sense her concerns. "I still think we'll get it," he said, coming over beside her. "But you need something to occupy you while I fiddle. Would you like to watch our progress?"

He leaned past her to manipulate controls blended so smoothly into the surrounding panel that Pilar could barely tell they were there, much less what they were for. That was one of the things she found unnerving about the ship's interior. Not only did it feel alien, vaguely wrong in the size and shape and spacing of things, there just didn't seem to be much there. It was all smoothly curving surfaces, in oddly mismatched pastel colors, with little that stood out as special features. She wasn't even sure she could tell the difference between a control panel and a chair, which could be more than embarrassing.

The other thing that had been bothering her, though she couldn't put a conscious finger on it until it suddenly changed, was the feeling of utter isolation, of being walled off from the universe. In all those smooth surfaces, there was not a hint of a window or a viewscreen—no way of telling what lay beyond the wall. For all she could see, they might as well be deep underground or in intergalactic space.

Until, quite abruptly, Argo's fiddlings bore fruit and the whole interior of the room filled with an utterly realistic view toward the ground. It reminded Pilar of the holotheater displays back in the government hideouts, and she jumped back as if to avoid falling over the edge.

But there was no edge. It was a straightforward view of what lay outside, just as the eye might see it if the wall had suddenly dissolved. She saw the sparkling expanse of the river, and Croton Point jutting into it, already far below and receding with visible speed even though she felt no acceleration. "There!" Argo said with audible satisfaction. "I thought this would be a good place to start, just to put things in perspective. You see our launch site down there on the peninsula, and we can zoom in. . . ."

He did something else, and Pilar felt an exhilarating sensation of swooping down toward the ground, plummeting straight toward the former-dump-turned-park with dizzying speed. She grinned in spite of herself. *I begin to see,* she thought, *what he meant about its being more fun than I could imagine!*

"Of course," Argo was going on, "there are resolution limits to what we can do with sensors up here. For a closer look, or a look back, we need to switch to remotes down there. Fortunately there are still a good many operational. . . ." Suddenly the view changed entirely, from an aerial overview to a close-up of Maybelle's face, looking skyward with tears streaming down it, framed by a halo of sunlight streaming through her fine white hair.

"Maybelle!" Pilar cried out reflexively, and was half surprised when Maybelle showed no sign of hearing her. She glanced at Argo. "Can she see me? Or hear me?"

"No," said Argo. "This one's passive only. All she sees is a pigeon flying past her face—and, of course, us." As the unseen "bird" swooped close, Pilar was startled to see their rising ship clearly reflected in each of Maybelle's clear blue eyes. Then the view switched again, this time to a direct shot at their ship against the sky. Argo did something else, and Pilar felt as if she were the bird, flying toward the ship and simultaneously zooming in for a closer view, all the while hearing the rush of the bird's passage through the air.

"Of course," said Argo, "only a few sensors can give you real-time views like that. Lester was right about the antenna requirements; it takes a fairly big remote to carry the equipment for something like this. But we can still jump around and pick up stored views from some of the relay stations, and maybe sometimes another real-time unit. Mind you, this will be pretty haphazard. I no longer have a directory of what's down there, but I can give you a sample of what the equipment can do."

From time to time his fingers took another stab at something barely visible and the view jumped, and jumped again, often making Pilar and her companions gasp at the latest change. She saw—

—the Statue of Liberty, viewed from the crown looking down. Something was crawling on the torch. Was it a butterfly, or one of Xiphar's remotes?

—the inside of a cattle barn, apparently from the viewpoint of a Holstein watching another being hooked up to a milking machine.

—a fish's-eye view of a school of longitudinally striped fish, French grunts perhaps, darting back and forth and wheeling with bright flashes among branched coral in the dappled sunshine near the surface of a tropical sea.

". . . other limits, too," Argo was saying. "Line of sight, for instance, so we can only pick up transmissions from relatively near parts of the planet. That will improve as we go higher and accelerate into orbit, passing over different parts of the surface. And when we get to a new planet we can do the same thing Xiphar did: set up secondary satellites to get full coverage all the time. Meanwhile, try this. It gets even better when you feed the other senses."

Still raptly watching the fish, Pilar felt Argo slip some kind of wispy net over her head—and then she also *felt* the warm water and its oscillating currents, and tasted its saltiness. "Direct neural feed," Argo explained. "A primitive ancestor of the emotional interface. I still hope to have that ready soon. Meanwhile, I'll leave it on autoscan. Enjoy!"

He wandered off, leaving Pilar so immersed in the kaleido-scope of immersion-images that she almost forgot what he was trying to do. She saw—and felt and heard and smelled—

—a breathtaking panorama from a high mountain peak, with sun glinting off remnant snow patches and tiny, mirror-like flecks of mica in the foreground rocks. An eagle flew by, so close she felt the wind from its wings as it landed just behind her.

—a boardroom filled with polished old mahogany, glitzy new electronics, and stuffed old shirts somberly plotting strategy for taking over a rival company.

—a couple in a dingy hotel room, doing things Pilar had never imagined a couple could do, and would just as soon not have known. Even though they couldn't see her, she looked away in-voluntarily, feeling herself blushing.

—a hand seen over its shoulder, writing a painfully personal letter to someone Pilar didn't know.

—the Grand Canyon, as seen by something skimming along over the flat desert to the south and suddenly emerging over the rim, the ground dropping abruptly away, far below. A thunder-storm had just passed; she could still hear distant rumblings and smell ozone and feel moist breezes. The flying thing carrying her "senses" banked abruptly, turning to fly straight toward an in-tense double rainbow. . . .

An unmistakably real hand on her shoulder startled her out of the illusion. She turned to face Lester, grinning from ear to ear. "Well, Pilar," he asked softly, "how does *this* compare with the radioscope at Arecibo as a way to take big bites of the universe?"

"It's great!" she said, returning his grin but then sobering abruptly as she remembered things she had seen that were none of her business. "But it will sure have to be handled with care. You know, Lester, I think I'd better revise that metaphor. 'Taking big bites' sounds too predatory. I'm going to start thinking of it as 'taking big tastes'—and try never to forget to do it gently."

"Good idea," he said. "Well, I'll let you get back to the show now."

But before Pilar could reimmerse herself in the current image, of rolling, treeless grasslands somewhere in the Great Plains, she was interrupted again by Argo. "Pilar?" he said, just loud enough for her to hear. "I've got her, but I thought you'd like this one to be private. If you could follow me?"

HEART HAMMERING, PILAR FOLLOWED HIM THROUGH A DOOR that opened silently, then closed as he left Pilar alone in a small room. Alone, that is, except for the utterly lifelike image of her sister Rosa, seated in the tiny, comfortably cluttered living room of their family's cottage near Arecibo. A bird sat on her shoulder, looking like the other half of their mother's partridge earrings. Pilar could feel the warm Puerto Rican breeze blowing through the open louvered window.

"Rosa?" Pilar breathed, hardly daring believe it. "You're all right? I've been trying to contact you for so long. I was so worried—"

"Ditto," said Rosa. "Except I haven't had a way to contact you. You wouldn't believe the things that happened here. There were riots, and fires, and massive destruction of the infrastructure. Our house was one of the few that survived more or less intact, and most of it's not in as good shape as this room. The whole island was cut off from the world for the longest time. And after your last messages, I can't tell you how worried I was about you."

"I can guess," said Pilar, though the emotional interface made it achingly loud and clear. "And the family?"

"All well and accounted for." Rosa smiled. "We're a tough lot, Pilar, in spite of ourselves."

"I hope so," said Pilar. "Rosa, you wouldn't believe what I'm about to do."

"Yes, I would. Your friend Argo filled me in. I didn't know what to think about that at first. After what this alien did to us . . ." Her voice trailed off, the gap it left filled by a flood of pure, deeply ensconced anger.

"I can't forgive him either," Pilar said quietly. "Once damage is done, being sorry can't make it right. But in the end I was able to understand *why* he did it, and feel some sympathy. And he did try to make amends. Rosa, I *have* to do this."

"Yes, I know you do," said Rosa. "Until Argo hooked us up directly, I was partly angry at you, afraid you had sold out to the worst enemy we ever had. Now I can see that I needn't have worried." She chuckled. "And you did always want to be an astronaut."

"Yes, I did. I hope I'm up to it."

"Oh, you will be. Good luck and have fun, big sister. I envy you. Just don't forget to come back."

The interface added so much that they didn't really need many more words. Twenty minutes later Pilar emerged from the private room to rejoin the group.

The holo display was quiet now, as if the ship itself was waiting. There was still no feeling of acceleration, but Argo said the antigrav lift had gradually relinquished control to gravity and speed, and they were now beyond high Earth orbit and ready to jump to a distant star system Xiphar had thought looked interesting.

"Are you ready?" he asked quietly.

Pilar nodded. "Do we have to strap in or something?"

"No," said Argo. "Let's do it." He touched another of those barely visible controls.

There was the faintest hum from somewhere deep in the ship's innards, and the display volume in the middle of the room flared once more into vivid life. Now it outdid even its previous efforts, growing *beyond* the middle of the room to surround its occupants. Pilar felt that suddenly the room wasn't there, that she was instead floating free in space, surrounded by infinite blackness liberally sprinkled with glittery stars. The blue and white globe of Earth hung far below, and the Milky Way embraced them all.

Then it all swirled, as if stars and planets and ships and people were thrown into a cosmic blender, and for an indeterminate time it was all abstracts, blindingly bright and intriguingly intricate. Colors twisted and intertwined, challenging mind to discern patterns, till at last, very gradually, the brightness faded and the frenetic motions slowed.

Until finally they were again surrounded by stars—but Pilar saw at once that they were not the *same* stars. She looked frantically toward where she had last seen the Earth, and laughed out loud when she saw a barely perceptible pinpoint surrounded by a neat red circle with an arrow pointed toward it, accompanied by the free-floating words, YOU WERE HERE.

She gradually became aware of a voice at her side saying, "Look behind you, Pilar."

She turned and gasped. There was another planet, its colors subtly different from any Earth-from-space picture she'd ever seen, its landforms dramatically so where they showed through the clouds. Gradually, as she watched, the new planet drifted to the center of the room, the rest of the display fading and the ship reappearing around them, though dimly lit as if to avoid upstaging the planet.

As if that were possible.

"Like it?" Argo asked.

"It's beautiful," Pilar breathed.

"It's yours to get to know," said Argo. "Feel like doing some exploring? This is still a distant view, with high magnification. But all you have to do is say the word, and we'll move in and start seeding it with probes."

Pilar hesitated for a long time, straining to see any sign of artificial lights on the night side of the planet, weighing the immense opportunity and the immense responsibility she held in her hands. Finally, taking a deep breath, she said, very quietly, "Send them down."

And she thought, with a mixture of exhilaration and awe and humility beyond any she had ever known, *The adventure begins.*